T0245807

resolve

resolve

PERUMAL MURUGAN

PENGUIN

An imprint of Penguin Random House

HAMISH HAMILTON

USA | Canada | UK | Ireland | Australia
New Zealand | India | South Africa | China

Hamish Hamilton is part of the Penguin Random House group of companies
whose addresses can be found at global.penguinrandomhouse.com

Published by Penguin Random House India Pvt. Ltd
4th Floor, Capital Tower 1, MG Road,
Gurugram 122 002, Haryana, India

First published in English in Hamish Hamilton by Penguin Random House India 2021

Copyright © Perumal Murugan 2021
English Translation © Aniruddhan Vasudevan 2021

Translation from the Tamil original of *Kanganam* published by Kalachuvadu in 2014

All rights reserved

10 9 8 7 6 5 4 3 2 1

The views and opinions expressed in this book are the author's own and the
facts are as reported by him which have been verified to the extent possible,
and the publishers are not in any way liable for the same.

ISBN 9780670087792

Typeset in Adobe Caslon Pro by Manipal Technologies Limited, Manipal
Printed at Thomson Press India Ltd, New Delhi

This book is sold subject to the condition that it shall not, by way of trade
or otherwise, be lent, resold, hired out, or otherwise circulated without the
publisher's prior consent in any form of binding or cover other than that in
which it is published and without a similar condition including this condition
being imposed on the subsequent purchaser.

www.penguin.co.in

Introduction

To paint a tree from a leaf

I wrote *Kanganam* in 2007. It was my fourth novel, after *Eruveyil*, *Nizhalmutram*, and *Koolamathari*. But the core of its subject matter had formed in my mind some twenty years before I started writing the novel. In the late 1980s, the issue of female infanticide received much attention in Tamil Nadu. The practice was found to be particularly prevalent in certain districts, and there was talk of new laws and measures to put an end to it. New works of literature foregrounded the topic. New movies were made on the subject. The general idea then was that the problem of dowry was the main reason behind female infanticide. Magazines published cover stories suggesting that poor people were killing off female infants because they knew they would never be able to provide sufficient dowry to marry them off in the future. There was also much speculation about the use of the milk of the erukku shrub to kill female infants.

I was a college student then. I found a huge discrepancy between the public debates about the issue and the way things actually worked in my region, where I came to hear stories of female infanticide among landholding castes and other well-to-do families. These families could certainly afford the dowry, so it was not a question of financial hardship. They did not want to diminish their holdings by giving away property to their daughters. They also could not accept the fact that when they married off their daughters, the property they gave, especially land, effectively went to 'some stranger,' an outsider. They believed that sons would be their true heirs, that they would carry the family name forward, and that they would pass on the inheritance to future generations of the family.

Such people found the Family Planning Programme introduced by the Indira Gandhi government in the 1970s quite agreeable. Landholding castes enthusiastically observed the programme's motto, 'We Two, Ours Two.' They wanted the first child to be a son. But if it turned out to be a daughter, they consoled themselves that they had another chance for a male child. That's when the madness would start—prayers and promises of offerings to deities, consultations with astrologers, etc. All with the hope that the second child would be male. And if the second child was indeed a boy, they had a permanent sterilization surgery performed on the mother right away, before getting her home from the hospital after the delivery. If the first child was a boy, they did not care too much about the sex of the second child. If the second child was also a boy, that family gained quite a bit of prestige among the relatives. 'You don't have to worry about anything. You have two sons,' the relatives said to them with jealousy and resentment.

There were also families that stopped with one child, if that child was a boy. Such families seemed to anticipate the government's later slogan, 'We Two, Ours One.'

The trouble was when both the children turned out to be female. The second child would die within days of birth. The relatives would not have been informed of the birth; nor would they come to know of the death. Everything would be kept within the family. After that, the couple would try again, hoping for a boy this time. But if it happened to be a girl again, there'd be another death. The mother's health would deteriorate from these back-to-back pregnancies. Some families let the female infant live, choosing not to have any more children and opting for sterilization. But some men married again, hoping the second wife would bear a male child.

You don't need the milk of the erukku shrub to kill an infant. There are other, simpler ways. The Tamil movie *Karutthamma* (1994), directed by Bharatiraja, foregrounded the issue of female infanticide. There is a dramatic scene in the movie, in which a female infant is killed using the milk of the erukku plant, a sorrowful song and images of burial spots and cacti adding to the pathos of the scene. The movie even shows an old woman in the village as specializing in the task. I could not help but laugh when I watched that scene. People in my part of the world seemed to have much less cumbersome ways to ensure the death of female infants.

Within a day or two of birth, they would turn the infant on its stomach on the cot or in the cradle, and step outside the room for a little while. The baby would suffocate, unable to breathe through its nose or mouth. And being

just a few days old, the baby surely couldn't turn itself
over on its back. If they gave it half an hour or so before
they went back into the room, they'd find the infant dead.
Adding grains of paddy to the baby's milk was another
way. They would add a few grains of paddy to cow's milk
or mother's milk before feeding it to the child. The grains
would get stuck in the infant's little throat and choke it to
death. These were some of the 'natural' methods.

In 1989, new legislation guaranteed women's right
to inheritance, certainly an important step in furthering
women's rights. Around the same time, new medical
scanning technology became available, which allowed
people to learn the sex of the child in the womb. This new
technology became a veritable boon to those who were
reluctant to accept a daughter's right to family property. So
it soon became a widespread practice to learn the sex of the
fetus and, if it was female, to have an abortion within the
fourth or fifth month of pregnancy. Killing the fetus in the
womb somehow seemed more progressive than killing the
child after it was born, seen and held. Such abortions made
many doctors very rich in the 1990s.

The issue of female infanticide has seen many
dimensions since the late 1970s. The ones to truly feel the
impact of all these changes are those men who were born in
the 1980s. Those whom we condescendingly call 'the 90s
kids' are bearing the brunt of these transformations, too.
One of the main reasons these young men are subjected
to ridicule is that many of them have not been able to get
married. They have had to embrace labels such as 'single'
and 'stubbornly single' in order to face up to the fact that

they may never get married. After the year 2000, there was an increase in the number of young men of marriageable age in the population, and there was a significant decrease in the number of women. A caste-based calculation of these numbers is bound to yield shocking insights. At one point, I remember coming across a male:female ratio of 1000:900 in the population. I only expect this to get worse.

All this has led to other changes in society. We seem to talk less about the problem of dowry these days. Earlier, all wedding discussions would start with negotiations of gold and cash to be given by the bride's family. It seems that is no longer the case. These days, we hear 'magnanimous' statements like 'Let the girl's family do what they can.' My region now has a significant influx of brides from Kerala. There are marriage bureaus that announce, 'For Malayalee brides, contact . . .'. Language seems to have surpassed caste. So many such changes . . .

I have not conducted any research on female infanticide, but I have been following the issue for a long time now. A novelist's job is not to offer statistics and data sets. Nor does he work directly with such research data. All he needs is a little dot that he can then extend into a line or expand into a design. Creativity lies in being able to imagine and draw a tree from just a little leaf that falls in the wind. That was how this novel was born.

I have witnessed many young male friends of mine struggling to get married. At one point, in a nearby village with a hundred households, there were thirty young men of marriageable age, and only two women. People who brokered marriages had several such statistics to offer. It seems I did take a long time to turn all my observations into a work of fiction. Instead of offering a sociological perspective and statistical data, I decided to write *Kanganam* as the story of one young man's—the protagonist Marimuthu's—struggle to get married. The word 'Kanganam' denotes the yellow thread tied on the wrist of the bride and the bridegroom during the wedding. But it also carries a figurative meaning: the resolve one has towards an undertaking.

10 August 2021   Perumal Murugan
Namakkal   Translated by Aniruddhan Vasudevan

1

It had dawned only for the birds, but Kuppan was already on his way to the orchard, dragging his son along with him. The son was not used to waking up so early, so he lagged behind, sleepy-faced and grumbling.

In the orchard, when Kuppan turned the motor on and the water from the well gushed through the pipe, he felt a tingling, a hesitation in his body. But once he stood with his head under the flowing water, he soon felt embraced in its coolness.

Then he changed into his loincloth and went to make sure the water flowing through the channel reached the brinjal patch. That's when he noticed that his son had spread some hay on the ground and gone back to sleep curled up on it. Kuppan felt a rage to kick the boy awake. But he quickly found a different, calming perspective.

'You want to sleep? Sure! I will get you married and destroy your sleep forever. You will see.'

The boy was his youngest son. Useless fellow. He just roamed around on his bicycle all day and only came back home late at night. Then he slept through the better part of the next day and sometimes all night too. Often, when Kuppan returned home after a day's toil in the fields, he was infuriated by the sight that welcomed him: the boy sleeping, unaware even that his lungi had come undone. The boy and the clothes he wore both annoyed Kuppan. He learned from his son's friends that he undertook some odd painting jobs. But Kuppan had no idea how much he earned, how much he spent, what was left over.

Whenever Kuppan's wife asked her son for some expense money, he immediately set out on his bicycle and vanished for a few days. The parents decided to deal with him in exactly the way they had dealt with their other children. Get him married and out of the house.

As he channelled the water towards the brinjal plants, Kuppan glanced in the direction of the landholder's house nearby. It looked like it was floating in the faint, residual darkness of that early hour. The narrow path that led from the house to the field was still asleep. Usually, it was the younger boss, Marimuthu, who rustled it awake when he stepped onto the path.

Marimuthu usually arrived in the fields anytime between dawn and early morning. It depended on what needed to be done that day. If you had any favours to ask, it was best to catch him in those early hours. He was usually alone, and the coolness of dawn had a softening effect on his mind. And when he looked at the water flowing through the channels, a certain contentment always bloomed on his face. At other times, there was always somebody with him. This was the reason Kuppan had roused his son so early in the morning and dragged him along to the field.

Marimuthu's father was not exactly worldly-wise. All he knew was the work in the fields. He only ever spoke when he was drunk and belching on palm toddy. Even the few words he uttered in those moments were never of any comfort.

If Kuppan were to say to him, 'Saami, I need four coconuts,' he invariably replied, 'We'll see. Maybe next week.' That was always his reply, no matter what you asked him. He never said, 'Alright. I will give it to you.' His wife was even worse. She'd start by saying, 'Only last week we gave you four coconuts . . .' Then she would spell out how many coconuts Kuppan had taken that month, how many for the year in total, and it would go on and on until she had laid out the accounts from Kuppan's father's time. He'd regret asking.

And then there was Marimuthu's grandmother who now lived here with the family! Let's describe her generosity this way: if her own son came to her when she was eating and asked for some food from her hand, she would quickly lick her hand dry. Kuppan could ask her for the coconuts and she would give him some. She'd go back into the house and bring some rotten coconuts for him. And she'd say, 'See. People here just waste these coconuts. You take them. There is enough here for ten days of sambar.' Not a single coconut she offered would be edible.

No. It was definitely better to ask Marimuthu. He might not agree to give right away. But he usually did, in a day or two. Kuppan had a difficult time convincing his son that they had to speak to Marimuthu. The boy didn't agree readily. 'I am not going. You go and ask,' he said. Kuppan

said to him, 'You don't have to ask. I will do the asking.
You just come and stand next to me. Salute him when you
see him.' But the boy didn't budge.

No matter how much Kuppan scolded and abused him,
the son never talked back. He usually just pulled a long face
and looked away. All his protests were made in silence. But
if the plan was to ask Marimuthu for some money for the
boy's wedding, how could Kuppan go without him? What
would Kuppan say if Marimuthu were to ask, 'Why, your
son won't come here and ask for it himself?' It was not
right to ask for money for his son's wedding without ever
presenting the son in question.

The boy was interested in his paternal aunt's daughter.
But he was shy and lethargic and did not do anything about it.
The last time the aunt visited, she said, 'Well, there are many
families interested in my daughter. Shall I get her married?'
That was when he finally agreed to go see the landlord.

Young men seemed to have no idea how such things
worked. Did the boy expect the landlord to come to him
of his own accord and hand the money to him? If pride
mattered so much to him, he should have worked hard and
saved up his own money. But he was not smart enough.
He wasted away his time sleeping. On those rare occasions
when he did go to work, he spent all the money on clothes
and at the cinema. Lazy ass! But why do I care how he
lives? My duty ends with getting him married. Things
will change when his wife nags him into action, Kuppan
thought to himself.

Kuppan turned off the motor once the brinjal patch
was properly watered. By then, it had dawned bright and

the day had begun. But Marimuthu hadn't arrived yet. If he did not have any important work that day, he would take his time stepping out of the house. Kuppan looked at his son. He was sleeping curled up, his hands between his legs. How could he sleep like this?! Kuppan went closer. There was a child-like charm to that sleeping face. He gently pushed away an ant that was crawling on the boy's cheek. Let him sleep. Kuppan thought about how, at his age, he was not lucky enough to sleep so peacefully.

Kuppan did not live the sort of life where he could be whimsical about going to work or not. And whatever sleep he managed to get came to him in snatches in the middle of the night. So, for a moment, he was moved by the thought that his son at least was able to enjoy some sleep.

When he realized he had been staring at his own child so intently, he felt embarrassed. As they say, a parent's gaze can cast an evil eye far more potent than anyone else's. When he was a child, Kuppan carried the boy around on his shoulders. The kid used to speak charmingly in those days. Where did he lose all those words since?

These days, every word he spoke to his father seemed to be spat out with resentment. He was the same way with his mother too. She seemed to take it in her stride, but Kuppan had a hard time. If they got him married, things would fall in place. After that, if he struggled to feed his family, he would have to come running to his parents. As for Kuppan, he was nowhere near retirement. He would have to keep working at least until he managed to pay off all the loans he had taken from the landlord.

He glanced down the path, but he didn't see anyone coming. So, he thought he might do some work while he waited for Marimuthu.

The coconut trees had grown tall and stately, arching towards the sky like the firework display during the temple festival. Kuppan remembered when the trees were planted. Ages ago, when he was a little boy, he had worked in these orchards soon after the lands had been divided between the families. He was just a little boy, he didn't even know how to push out snot from his nose, but he was already working in these fields. His job was to fill up the pits with soil once the coconut saplings had been planted. The memories of that day now shimmered like a mirage in his mind.

The trees were now as old as his labour and toil. They continued to be immensely productive. Even now, he could see at least four clusters of coconuts on each tree. All the fronds that the trees had shed just lay strewn about in the field. He decided to pick them up and pile them up on one side. While he was at it, if he also separated the stalks from the leaves, that would be a proper job done. He knew that Marimuthu's paatti, his paternal grandmother Poovayi stripped the leaves off each frond and made brooms by bundling the sticks together.

There were several bundles of such brooms piled up inside the shed, but she still wouldn't let the new fronds go to waste. She wanted to make more brooms. These people, these landowners, they didn't let anything go to waste. That old woman even collected cow dung from the lakeside and from between hedges and bushes to use as manure for the field. She could never sit still for even a minute.

She also liked women who were exactly like her, who slogged like she did. Once, Nangoor Songan's daughter had come to assist this paatti with weeding the groundnut field. The way that young woman's hands moved down towards the earth and came back up in a swift, repetitive motion was entrancing to watch. Usually, it was the old woman's square that got cleaned faster than the others'. She had been weeding since she was a child, so she was quite skilled at it. So when she saw the younger woman working much faster than herself, paatti decided to turn it into a competition.

She did not give up till the end of the day, but the young woman was still ahead of her. This was about ten years ago. Later, remarking on that day, paatti said to him, 'Kuppa, if we get that girl into our family, this small land won't do for her. Marimuthu will have to buy at least ten more acres for her to work on.'

Paatti had sent Kuppan to find out more about the girl. Her name was Poovalayi. Paatti's name was Poovayi. She really liked that there was a resonance between the names. She said to Kuppan, 'Let Poovalayi take over Poovayi's place. That will teach that rotten widow a lesson.' By 'rotten widow' she meant her daughter-in-law, Marimuthu's mother.

Paatti's vain hope was that, even though her daughter-in-law had turned out to be a disappointment, at least her grandson's wife could be someone to her liking. The girl's family had bits and pieces of land that came to more than ten acres. Poovalayi would certainly inherit a share. In addition to that, the family must have surely saved up for some jewellery. Marimuthu did his best to resist paatti's plans. But he was too young to make these decisions for himself.

Paatti said, 'She is precious like a piece of coral, da! Just like her name. She is a little dark-skinned, but she is such a hard-worker. And she is not going to come empty-handed. She will bring some land. You must be lucky to get a girl as well as some land.'

On the pretext of buying some maize stalks, Kuppan went to the girl's family and found out what they thought of this alliance. Her father Songan spoke frankly. 'Kuppa, I don't want to beat around the bush. We are not going to find a better family to marry our daughter.' But everything got thwarted because of one small problem. Poovalayi was two years older than Marimuthu.

Paatti attempted to smooth it over. 'So what? My mother was older than my father. They married and had children. They got us all married, fulfilled their duties, didn't they?' While all of this was going on, Marimuthu's grandaunt's daughter-in-law arrived from nowhere. She was just a visiting relative. Instead of simply enjoying the hospitality, eating the food offered, and going about her way, she decided to offer her opinion on the matter.

'That girl looks so manly. Look at her face! Wide as a winnowing pan. If Marimuthu stood next her, he'd look like her son.'

Once he heard her remark, Marimuthu put his foot down and refused to marry Poovalayi. But to this day paatti felt that if Poovalayi had married into the family, she would have transformed their lands into gold fields.

Kuppan laid out the coconut fronds to one side in such a way that paatti could use them for her brooms. When he walked over to the well, he saw his son washing his face with some water from the channel. He was happy that he didn't have to wake him up. He was up and now going about his work. It gave Kuppan hope that his son would become a responsible person.

He glanced beyond the coconut trees. It occurred to him that there was nothing more miserable than waiting. Even though his hands went about the task, his mind was not in it. He was anxious about Marimuthu's arrival. What if he did not come today at all? The prospect of doing this all over again—waking up his son and dragging him along here again the next day—was unbearable to Kuppan. He prayed that Marimuthu should come and have kind words to say.

When he heard a sudden squeal, he looked beyond the trees. Two blackbirds darted by. From left to right. That was a good omen. The morning breeze felt comforting to him.

2

Marimuthu came into view at a distance. He reached up and broke a twig from the neem tree by the side of the path. He then tied a towel around this head. He'd soon head down the path to the grove. Even if he walked really slow, it wouldn't take more than ten minutes. Kuppan busied himself into action. He picked up the spade and walked towards the coconut trees. Selecting the tree that was closest to the path down which Marimuthu was walking, he started cutting the grass that had grown underneath. When he saw that his son was standing around aimlessly, he shouted, 'He is coming! Come over here and gather the grass I am cutting. Don't just stand there.' The boy took his time walking to the spot. Then, using just one hand to pick up some of the grass that Kuppan had cut, he tossed it over to a side. Kuppan gritted his teeth as he said to his son, 'Shake the soil off the grass before putting it aside. I don't know how you are going to survive! Fold up your lungi and do some work.'

Without talking back, the boy did as told. In just a short while, the entire sunken ground around one coconut tree, which was meant for standing water, had been fully cleared of grass. Kuppan checked to make sure the work was beyond reproach. He seemed satisfied. But his son had left chunks of grass lying scattered on the ground. 'Pick it all up and keep it all in one place neatly,' he said. It was only a little task, but his son's shirt and lungi were already soiled and stained. Why would he do this work wearing a shirt?

Kuppan moved to the next tree. He knew he could afford to slow down a bit now. If Marimuthu saw the one channel that had been cleared up, it'd surely make him happy. As he went about his task, Kuppan kept an eye on Marimuthu's whereabouts. He was walking around the brinjal patch, chewing at his neem twig. Kuppan could see that he was looking closely at the plants, examining them with his hands. Since they had been watered well in the summer, the harvest had been good. Every Thursday, without fail, he filled and carried baskets and sacks of brinjals to the market. There was great demand for these vegetables in the summer. So, Marimuthu inspected the brinjal plants every day. They had to be checked constantly for bugs and worms and sprayed promptly with pesticides. Worms just loved brinjals. Even if the plants were left unattended for a day, worms found their way to them. This vegetable relied entirely on pesticides for its growth.

When he saw Marimuthu walking closer towards the coconut trees, Kuppan removed the towel he had tied around his head, kept it clutched in his armpit and put his palms together in respect. Then he glanced at his son. 'Unfold your lungi, da!' he hissed. The boy did as told and brought his palms together in front of his chest. But his fingers did not touch each other properly; the gesture was not complete. He pulled his hands back down and also lowered his head. Marimuthu observed it and smiled.

'Kuppa, have you taken on a helper for the work?'

'No, saami. He is my son. The youngest.'

Marimuthu gave the boy a close, intent look.

'What's your name?'

The son mumbled something. He was not used to such interactions. It was an unfamiliar setting for him. So he didn't know how to act.

'Your son is mute? You never told me.'

'No, saami. He has never been here before. That's why he is shy. Dey! Tell him your name. He is asking you. Open your mouth and speak!'

Marimuthu liked the way Kuppan was commanding his son.

'Ramesh.'

'Oh . . . Ramesh . . . It's a good name.'

Marimuthu walked towards the well to rinse out his mouth. Kuppan knew that he would also take a bath right away, and it would be a little while before he re-emerged. So he decided to keep working and to clear the ground around another coconut tree. 'Come with me,' he said to his son anxiously and moved to the next tree. He started clearing away thick bunches of weeds.

They heard the splash of Marimuthu jumping into the well. Even when the motor was on, pumping out water, he preferred jumping into the well for his bath. He still acted like a young boy. But then they were indeed young boys until they were married. He was over thirty years old, but he looked like a bull that had not mounted a cow yet. His body was firm; it had kept its form.

Standing by the side of the well, Marimuthu dried himself with a towel. Kuppan admired the way he dried his hair, shaking his head, tossing his hair. That was the moment after a bath when the body felt cool and relaxed. Men were the most agreeable immediately after they'd had a bath. So, Kuppan took his son along and walked over to where Marimuthu was standing. Seeing them, he smiled, his skin sparkling in its wetness. 'What is it, Kuppa?'

'I need your help with something, saami.'

'Tell me.'

'He is my youngest. If I get him married, I can be at peace. After that my wife and I can fully devote ourselves to working here on this land.'

'Hmm,' Marimuthu said and scrutinized the son with a look of surprise. His lips curved in a mocking smile.

'Marriage? For him? He stands like a snake-gourd that hasn't been straightened. How old is he?'

'He turned seventeen just around the time we had the feast for our deity Municchami.'

'Have you found a girl?'

'We have, saami. She is my sister's daughter. We didn't have to look too far. They live nearby, in Mannoor.'

'How old is the girl?'

'She only came of age in the month of Thaii. She must be fourteen or fifteen.'

Marimuthu went down to the well again to wash his loincloth and towel. They heard him slapping the clothes on a rock in there. The conversation was going well so far. The rest of it should go smoothly too.

Marimuthu then hung the clothes to dry on a string that had been tied across two coconut trees. With a smile, he said, 'He is only seventeen and he is itching to get married? Can't control himself?'

Ramesh looked up quickly but cast his gaze down again. The way he had raised his head in that quick motion, it looked like he was ready to run away from the spot.

Kuppan was uncomfortable at Marimuthu's teasing.

'No, saami. It's not him. It is we who think we should get him married.'

'Why do you all ruin your lives getting married at such a young age? He is seventeen, and she is fifteen! And they want to get married!' Marimuthu said mockingly.

'It is not like that, saami. This is how we do things in our community. The moment they start growing wings, we send them away to fend for themselves.'

'That's exactly why things never seem to improve for your lot.'

'We don't have any land to give our children, saami. All we manage is a new set of clothes for the boy and girl, and a thaali with just a spot of gold for the girl. But sometimes not even that. Only a yellow thread. That is how it has been.'

'That is why I am telling you. Let your son go do some work and earn some money. Let him save up a little. Don't they need a place to live? You don't seem to worry about any of these things! All that matters to you is that the mortar and the pestle get together,' he laughed out loud.

The boy looked tormented. He felt as though he was standing on a hot bed of coal. Kuppan was worried that the plan might fail.

'Whatever it is, saami. We rely on your kindness. You have to help us with the wedding expenses.'

'Oho! There is that as well!'

'Yes, saami. I lay myself at your feet. Who else would I go to? If you give me five thousand, I will manage.'

'Five thousand?'

'That will do, saami.'

Kuppan could tell that Marimuthu was considering the request.

'How much advance have you taken on next year's wages?'

'I have taken ten thousand and five hundred, saami.'

'You have taken that much already?! And you have the gall to ask for five thousand more?'

'It's not like that, saami. I am here, I will work. I will somehow repay you.'

'Kuppa, you are getting on in age. If something happens to you, how would I get my money back? Will your son come and work here and pay off the loan? I can tell just by looking at the way he stands that he can't do any work.'

'Please don't say that. My life won't leave my body before I pay off your loans,' Kuppan said, his voice breaking. He thought he might cry. Marimuthu's words had cast all his years of toil into the dustbin.

Sensing Kuppan's anguish from his voice, Marimuthu said, 'Alright, when is the wedding?' That question gave Kuppan some hope.

'I won't set a date without consulting you. You tell us.'

'Alright. Find a date six months from now. We'll figure it out.'

With those words, hc left. Kuppan walked with him up to the path that led outside. When he returned to the field, his son was already gone.

3

Marimuthu was being hounded by dreams. Even on that night, when he lay on his cot on the rooftop terrace, seeking out the moonlight and the breeze, an unusual and unfamiliar dream laid siege on him.

He is going somewhere on an impressive motorbike. There is the sound of the wind beating against the vehicle which spews out black exhaust smoke. Marimuthu is sparkling in a silk shirt and dhoti. He is wearing a thick gold chain over his shirt. A golden watch on his left wrist. A broad curvy bracelet on his right wrist. His shiny hair is combed back in its usual wavy pattern. The rear-view mirror seems to enhance his looks, but he cannot see his face clearly in the reflection.

Since he has hitched up the dhoti to mount the motorbike, he can see his exposed, hairy legs. The new black footwear he has on makes a striking contrast against the fairness of his skin. The motorbike goes on without stopping. It rides on wide highways, moving at the speed of a forceful bird.

After a while, the bike is on bumpy tar roads. Then on small roads that go into towns. On mud tracks, potholed lanes, dusty streets on which vehicles tread very rarely, narrow footpaths that have never seen vehicular smoke. It goes everywhere. It is a long journey without a break.

On the way, he sees a lot of people. He is wonderstruck at how many people inhabit the world. But they are all wearing shirts and dhotis, just like he is. They seem to be busy, walking and running, going about their business in myriad ways. Who are they? When he tries to see them up close, he realizes that they are all him.

He seems to be multiplying into innumerable other people, other forms. These forms take over the world. But they are all men. A world occupied by men. In this crowd, he goes looking for a woman. Not any specific woman. He has no clear image of her. He doesn't know what she looks like. She is lost among this deluge of men, all of whom are none but himself. But she is the only woman in the world. Where is she hiding?

He enters a village where all the buildings look like ancient ruins. The thud-thud of his motorbike drowns out the other sounds in that space. Walls once awash with rain are now blanketed by dark creepers. The raised front porches of the houses are covered in dust. Muddy entrances blocked by dried fallen leaves. Marimuthu wonders if his bike is taking him back in time.

After that, all the villages he passes through look just like that first one. None of the houses look welcoming enough for him to stop his ride, pull over and find a refuge. A little kolam on the ground in front of a house is all the sign he needs. His journey can end right there. All he is looking for is a kolam. Just one. It could be the kind of kolam that starts with a single dot and then expands out and stakes its claim over a wide space. Or it could be a kolam that's drawn around just a single dot. It doesn't matter. He just needs to find it.

There is not even a faint sign of a kolam anywhere. But the throng of men multiplying out of his own being keeps on growing. Their sorrowful faces have now turned to rage. Maddened, they run around in a frenzy. Marimuthu's motorbike raises a din as it passes through this crowd.

At some point during this seemingly interminable dream, he awoke startled. The blanket had slipped away and was lying on the floor. A mist had spread its coolness all over the rooftop. On the sky to the west, the moon cast a wholesome yellow light. Casting their bewitching magic everywhere, the mist and the moon had taken possession of the world.

He struggled a bit as he tried to sit up. He was not even aware of the deep sighs that were emanating from him. Suddenly, he realized that he was the only living thing that seemed to show some movement in that still, silent night. He rose from the cot and walked towards the parapet wall. At a distance, coconut trees looked like propped-up shadows. Palm trees of varying heights that stood all over the fields seemed to be frozen within their own loneliness. Lands seemed to be spread in tiers, reaching far and beyond and vanishing somewhere into the mist. It suddenly occurred to him, as if it were a staggeringly new insight, that there was no other house in the vicinity.

He wondered if all his miseries were due to this lonely life in a lonely place. A cow called out from its shed.

Unusual for that hour. After that, it was all one massive, unbroken silence.

What a dream! It had been long since he had sold off that bike. But it still seemed to be in his thoughts. He was once very fond of it. He used to delight at its majestic and polished look. He felt a certain pride riding that motorbike. It cast its own unique attraction.

Every time he rode that bike, he experienced a sense of adventure akin to riding a powerful horse. Little kids called him 'Bullet Anna' after the brand name of the bike. His peers, however, turned that into a mockery. They called him 'Pulutthi Anna.' Brother Prick. He dismissed them all, believing they were simply jealous of him. But he ended up selling that motorbike even though he hadn't wanted to.

He began to lose his fascination for the bike around the time he went to Tholur to see a girl for a potential match. He barely got a glimpse of her. When she turned and walked away from him, he marvelled at the length of her braid. He wondered if she wore an extension. He had to imagine her face based on the impression her hair had made on his mind. But later he heard that she'd said, 'That motorbike looks like a buffalo bull! I am terrified even to look at him.'

He wouldn't have minded if she had said something negative about him. But she had called his motorbike a buffalo bull. After that, every time he glanced at the bike, he could not help visualizing a charging buffalo bull with impressive horns. He started hesitating to ride the bike. He had relied on that vehicle for years, but just because one woman—a stranger—had made a remark, he suddenly felt a distance from the bike. Even the woman who served as the go-between brokering the marriage alliance said to him, 'Why do you need this bike? It is so old-fashioned. No girl would want to sit on it and ride with you.'

Times were such that a girl could reject a man because she did not like his bike. Why not? She had plenty of men dying to marry her; she was spoiled for choice. No wonder she felt entitled.

That very same week, he sold the bike. He bought a new Hero Honda, the kind of bike that young women fancied—women like that long-haired one he had met. But this bike was better suited for young urban men who wore neatly ironed, fashionable clothes. Not for men like him who spent most of their time in the fields, with plants and trees and cattle. He did not like that bike at all. He likened it to a woman dressed up as a man. But this was the kind that young women seemed to prefer. And still, despite the new bike, he failed to win over that girl whose long hair brushed against her buttocks.

Even though he had only had a fleeting glimpse of her face, he had imagined it for himself on many nights. In fact, in a way it was good for his imagination that he had not seen her face clearly. Now he could change her features as he pleased. But her hair alone stayed constant. The same length. Whenever the old bike cast a shadow on his mind, she too seemed to wander in. Since she had been responsible for the loss of the bike, he took his revenge by dreaming of having sex with her. She called the bike a buffalo bull. That implied that he was Yaman, the god of death. So he had to show her what Yaman was capable of, didn't he?

Reflecting on the dream he had just had, he wondered if that was his destiny—to wander endlessly. His grandmother often consoled him. 'God has already created a woman somewhere who is meant for you. It is just that we are experiencing some delay in finding her. That's all.' If god had indeed created a woman meant just for him, why was he keeping her out of sight? What wrong did Marimuthu commit to deserve this?

The vision he saw in his dream, a world in ruins and bereft of women—was that going to come true soon? If he could get married, he would live the way people lived in the old days. He wanted to have at least ten children, and he wanted them all to be girls. The world should never again witness the sorrow of a man like him.

He sat on the parapet wall. The chill of the misty night did not affect him at all. His body and mind were seething in an inner heat. He could easily understand the body's signals. Not just now, but for over twenty years, his body had been communicating with him in this exact same language. But he was never able to give it the response it deserved.

His body's needs were fairly plain. It wanted the company of a woman's body. Especially on such a misty night. But what he had was an emptiness that would not even allow room for such a thought. He had expected that his body would give up its yearnings at some point, but that didn't happen. In fact, it seemed to have turned up the fervour of its demands. Perhaps it was his fate never to be able to quench this desire, but to simply burn and perish in it. There was nothing insignificant about the agony of a thirty-five-year-old body existing without the chance to know another body. It is a sorrow. It is a deep sorrow that cannot be redressed by any other means.

That boy—Kuppan's son, who'd come and stood by silently earlier that day, looking fragile—even he was fortunate enough to find another body, and he was only seventeen. He didn't even have a proper moustache yet. Just a faint patch of hair above his lips. Marimuthu could clearly recall the youthful magnetism of that face. The boy had been so lean, Marimuthu could have grasped him with a single hand. Getting to know another body at such a young age is a sheer blessing. That boy was indeed blessed.

Marimuthu recollected how much he struggled to accept the fact that the young lad was going to get married. In that moment, he had seen that boy as his enemy. How easily his mind turned into his enemy anyone who married young! What he had felt was an intense, jealous rage to physically destroy the boy. But since he could not do it, he had injected his words with spite: 'The little fellow is throbbing to get married?' He had felt some satisfaction in saying that. The boy had felt insulted by those words. He had reared his head like a wounded snake.

At that age, when there is both shyness and yearning, words that refer to body parts can either titillate or humiliate. Marimuthu had experienced such humiliation too. During a land dispute with one of his paternal cousins, Marimuthu had spoken a little too forcefully. And his cousin's wife, that horrible woman, had responded with spite.

'You puny little thing! You haven't even grown hair on your thighs! You dare to talk to me like that? Go! Go roll naked on this land, since it is so precious to you!'

It was perhaps her curse that tethered him to the land. Perhaps that was the reason he did not get the chance to care for a woman the way he got to care for the land and make it thrive. Today, he ended up taking that helplessness out on Kuppan's son. What did he manage to accomplish with that? Postponing that boy's access to a woman's body by six months. But what was the harm in waiting six months? Let him wait. In those months, the boy's anger and irritation would be focused on Marimuthu. So be it.

If Marimuthu had wanted, he could have given Kuppan the money right away. Poor man. He only asked for five thousand rupees. The family would have managed the wedding with that small amount. Marimuthu, on the other hand, would need ten, even twenty times more for his wedding. Was that the reason for his irritation? He was actually quite an attractive boy. He had bright eyes that looked like they were kohl-lined. Defined eyebrows. An intense face that would draw anyone in.

In the cool moonlight, Marimuthu paid attention to his own body. Strong, firm ribs with not a single wrinkle or sag on his broad hairy chest. Indrawn abdomen, like he had been fasting. He may not have the youthful form and sheen of that young man, but Marimuthu was far more attractive than men his own age. They had all grown old, their chest and abdomen blending into one. Even their faces had become swollen and deformed. Marimuthu had a slightly receding hairline. But baldness had its attraction too, didn't it? A few grey hairs here and there, but nobody could spot them when he applied some oil and combed his hair down neatly. Other than this, his body was beautiful in its own gentle way. He caressed it with his fingers. That touch only made the body cry out more. That cry he had heard a little while ago from a cow now seemed to come from his own body. An involuntary 'Ayyo!' came from his lips. Then he sat huddled in a corner.

4

A rooster stuttered in its attempt to crow from the coop in the yard below. But it didn't succeed at first. Weren't roosters supposed to rouse the world awake? This one soon went breathless and stopped crowing. Perhaps it was its very first attempt. After a few tries, it finally managed to crow. Marimuthu felt like it was the first ever time he was listening to a rooster crow.

Its ability to crow is, to a rooster, what a moustache is to a man. The sound of this particular rooster attracted him very much. Today it made its first sounds. Tomorrow it would already be running after the hen. Roosters never had a problem finding hens. Why couldn't he have been born as some such simple creature? No other beast had to lie on a rooftop in the middle of the night, with the torment of experiencing one's own body as a huge burden.

Suddenly, Marimuthu started to weep. He dropped his chin, buried his face in his chest, and cried. But he found no relief. He walked back to the cot. It had gone cold, exposed to the coolness of the mist. The chill slowly crawled over his body. But the heat within his body continued to grow. It was the kind of heat that could only be put out by heat.

He rose from the cot and walked again to the parapet wall. He considered huddling his arms and legs close to his body and jumping off the rooftop. The only sound he wanted was that of his body crashing against the ground. Let the body's own cries stay and die right within it.

Perhaps he could think of it like jumping into a well from a high point. Or the joy he felt when he climbed down a coconut tree and then jumped to the ground from a certain height. Or that childhood pleasure of riding on a buffalo and then sliding down and jumping off it. All leaps and jumps were pleasurable. What happens to the fruit that falls from a palm tree? A dew drop travels a great distance before moistening the earth in the latter part of the night in late winter months. Could one calculate the distance moonlight travelled? His mind was gathering for him an assortment of the delights of jumping and falling.

Perhaps he could take a leap and swim in the coolness of the mist, in the intoxicating spread of moonlight. All of his body's heat would then be quenched. It would also kill his arrogance which had made him humiliate Kuppan's son with that mortar-and-pestle metaphor. Everyone's troubles could be ended tonight. He wouldn't have to go from town to town, street to street, asking anyone to marry their daughter to him.

His mother wouldn't have to nurse her pride by telling people 'We keep looking for a girl. Nothing seems to work out.' And it would be a relief to his father who swore and cursed and showed his cruel streak: 'No girl is going to marry this ruffian beast. He'd just have to rely on his hand.' Then there was his ammayi—his maternal grandmother—who sighed, 'Well, things can only happen when they are destined to.' If he died today, paatti—his paternal grandmother—would mourn him for a month. But after that, if anyone needed her to weed their field, she would readily oblige and carry on with her life. His younger sister who always stole things from the house whenever she visited, and his brother-in-law who seemed to think he had a claim over all of Marimuthu's things, except perhaps his underwear—they both might rejoice that the entire inheritance was now theirs. So why shouldn't he jump? His jumping off the rooftop now would put an end to so many problems. Jump . . . jump . . .

The moment he placed one foot on the wall, the dog barked from below. He woke up and came to his senses. What was he about to do! He ran back to the cot and lay face down. Jumping to his death would have some meaning if he did it after giving Kuppan the five thousand he needed. It could be an act of contrition. He pulled the blanket over his body and lay curled up. But still something from within him continued to command him to get up, go and jump.

The cry of a screech-owl came from beyond the rooftop. And it stopped as suddenly as it had started. It terrified Marimuthu. He felt that everything was targeting him. Spending any more time on the rooftop could be dangerous for him. He suddenly straightened out his curled up body and rose from the cot. The crescent moon had begun to set on the west and darkness had begun to spread. Slowly, stars grew in number. The changing sights in the sky might bring some comfort to his mind. Once again, from the neem tree opposite the house, the cry of a screech-owl. It seemed to pierce his body and peck at his soul. From below, he heard someone opening a door and shooing away the bird. Then he heard a lone voice cursing, 'Chee! What is this wretched beast doing here?' It was his ammayi, the insomniac. She might have left the front door open. This was his chance to save himself.

He draped the blanket over his shoulder, picked up the cot with his right hand and ran down the stairs. The cot's legs thudded against the walls. The dog came running and barking. He raised his voice to shoo it away. Listening to the sound of his own voice comforted him. It made him feel things were coming back to normal.

The dog licked his feet, its wet tongue tickling the hair on his feet. The dog repeatedly looked up at him and then cast its gaze down. He set down the cot and placed the blanket on it. Then he sat down on the ground next to the dog.

The dog seemed to have channelled all its affection into its tongue. He rubbed its head. It wagged its tail in great excitement and wet his face with its tongue. He made no attempts to wipe his face or shoo away the dog. Then he spotted ammayi walking back to the house from the front gate. He gently nudged the dog away, but it didn't seem to want to leave him. It curved its body and brushed against him. Then he shouted, 'Go away!' and gave it an angry kick. It ran to the entrance and lay down looking at him. The kick had been a little too forceful.

At first he tried to take the cot indoors. Then he contemplated setting it down on the front porch and sleeping right there. It was one of his usual spots. There was still some night left. It might be pleasant to lie down there. But there was still some lingering fear in him.

Right now, the only secure place for him was a walled-in space. So, he carried the cot in through the door. One of its legs got caught in the door and made a noise. 'Who is that?' came ammayi's voice. She heard even the faintest sound, that old hag. 'Who is that?' Her voice was louder this time. He could see her walking towards the door. It was funny the way she waddled, struggling to carry her heavy body. 'It's only me,' he snapped and carried the cot to his room. The windows were shut and it was warm in the room. He shut and latched the door.

In the middle of the daily calendar hanging on the wall was the deity Manchaami in all his festive splendour. Marimuthu prayed to him, 'Manchaami, my saami, it was you who saved me tonight.' Then he took down the calendar from the wall and looked at the date. It was the twentieth day of the month of Maasi. 'Six months,' he murmured. Panguni, Chitirai, Vaigasi, Aani, Aadi, Aavani. The twentieth of Aavani should be the deadline. The twelfth of that month was an auspicious day. He could ask Kuppan to hold his son's wedding on the same date. As for himself, it would be his final deadline. He needed to get everything done by then. If he failed to, he should give the money needed for Kuppan's son's wedding and then he should bring things to an end for himself. That was the absolute deadline. Manchaami on the calendar seemed to be smiling.

'Just six months,' he sighed. Then he turned off the light and went to bed. His mind seemed to have found some calm. He felt he could now feel safe and get some sleep. Sleep had a way of making all miseries disappear.

5

'Thanavadhi' Thatha, the elderly matchmaker, had no inclination to visit Marimuthu's house. But knowing that something auspicious could occur through his involvement, how could he hesitate? What else was the point of human relationships? He had to put work over pride.

He always set out for work well before dawn. That way he could get everything done and return home before it got too hot. Otherwise, he'd have to spend the day indoors somewhere and get back home only in the evening.

He went everywhere on foot. Only once or twice had he ever travelled by a motor vehicle. All his work was within a ten-to-fifteen mile radius around where he lived. He never ventured beyond that. Twice a week, without fail, he went to the markets. The Thursday market and the Sunday market. Even though he had nothing to buy or sell, he was very fond of walking around, chatting with the men who brought sheep and cattle to the markets.

'There is nothing those men don't know. They know the affairs of the country better than any of us. What could you and I know, shuttling between home and field in our loincloth?' he often said.

Once upon a time, he was the sole go-to for all marriage alliances in that area. So much so that people forgot his name and he came to be called Thanavadhi Thatha, the Elderly Matchmaker. If anyone asked what his name actually was, he replied, 'Oh it's "Thanavadhi."' But once marriage brokering became a profession in its own right, thatha lost interest in it.

He had succeeded in securing several marriage alliances, but he never took a penny as payment ever. He said that was the way things were done in those days. 'This is tradition for me, not a job.' Whenever he managed to finalize a marriage alliance, both families gifted him a dhoti-and-towel set each. 'I have never had to spend money and purchase even a loincloth until now,' he said.

He could not compete with today's brokers. They were willing to travel even five hundred or a thousand miles to make alliances happen. And they took ten per cent of the dowry money as their payment. 'I can't do all that,' thatha said.

'My time is over and done with. Why do you think god has still kept me alive? Just to witness these changes. Witnessing is my job,' he said. But people still sought him out. Nobody knew how old he was. Looking at him, you would say he was sixty. He had a lean and taut face, not many wrinkles. His hair looked like a messy mass of coconut fibre. Even he didn't know how old he was. Whenever anyone insisted on knowing his age, he said, 'I will have to ask the thatha in the mirror.'

Marimuthu was fond of him. Whenever and wherever he happened to run into thatha, he'd stop to speak a few kind and respectful words. Many times he had asked thatha to climb on to the back of his motorbike. He even offered to show thatha how to sit on the back seat. But thatha said, 'Marimuthu, I can't sit on a motorbike. These days, people seem to need a bus even to go to their backyard to pee and shit. I walk everywhere.'

Even though he was fond of Marimuthu, thatha did not really get along with the rest of the family. There were a few incidents that had left a bitter taste in his mouth.

He had been good friends with Marimuthu's grandfather. That was the reason he addressed Marimuthu fondly as 'Mapillai,' son-in-law. Once, he had gone to Chittoor to attend a wedding. Marimuthu happened to be at the same wedding, sitting together in a group with thatha and others.

Someone teased thatha, 'You old man! Isn't it enough you pushed *me* into this bottomless pit? How many more lives do you plan to ruin?'

There were many who engaged in such friendly banter with thatha. Since he had been instrumental in bringing many of those couples together in marriage, it was quite common for someone to say, 'I don't know what I did to upset thatha. He has got me trapped' or 'Thatha, where did you find this woman for me? She is going to be the end of me!' He usually just said, 'You think so? Let me speak to your wife about it.' That shut them up.

Women teased him too. There was Porasa from Kuttoor for whom he had found a husband. She made sure she ragged him mercilessly wherever she ran into him.

Once, she said, 'Don't they say that free food can do you no good? How many wedding feasts thatha must have eaten in his lifetime! How come he seems to be hale and healthy?' Thatha had a comeback for that. 'Woman, how could I ever forget the saltless kuzhambu and the sour, watery buttermilk you served at your wedding?'

On another occasion, she asked thatha, 'How goes your nose-rope business?' comparing his matchmaking work to the practice of putting a rope through a bullock's nose to restrain it. People who heard her remark laughed uncontrollably. Thatha replied, 'Let me know if you want another nose-rope. I can arrange for it.' But it hadn't been a strong enough retort. It didn't elicit much laughter in that audience.

That incident and that weak retort bothered him for a long time. He waited for the right occasion to get back at Porasa. When they met at some function, she asked him, 'Thatha, how is the cattle business?' He pretended not to understand her and said, 'What do you mean?'

She said, 'Your work. Marriage brokering.'

'Oh, dear woman,' he said. 'I have made so many marriages happen. But what can I do? You only get the man you are destined to get. What's the problem now? He is unable to last? Perhaps you should give him some more fodder. Then he might mount and do his job right.' Everyone laughed. Both men and women. Young men laughed and recounted this exchange for days. But as for Porasa, not only did she stop teasing thatha, but she also stopped talking to him altogether. Thatha felt bad about that. She was a friendly and chatty young woman. Now he had shut her up. His sharp tongue was to blame.

Reflecting on it, thatha once said regretfully, 'We don't seem to learn anything until we mess things up. What's the use of growing older? This tongue continues to go out of control. I should burn it.'

Even though it was not as bad as the way it happened with Porasa, Marimuthu too had been hurt by thatha's words. It happened at that same wedding in Chittoor.

A man by the name of Muthusami said, 'When I was young and ignorant, I allowed myself to be led astray by thatha's advice.' He and Marimuthu were from the same clan, the 'parrot' clan.

Thatha replied, 'Perhaps. But the parrot-folks are gullible in all ways.'

At this, all the parrot clansmen took offence and glared angrily at thatha. Some were beginning to worry that idle banter might lead to some serious arguments. But thatha didn't seemed to care.

'I am not just making it up. Do you know which parrot group you are?'

Someone said, 'Green parrot.' And thatha said, 'That's right. You are green parrot. Do you know about the people on the other side of the river who are the white parrot group?'

'Long ago, there was only one parrot people. And they were idiots. One time, they finalized a marriage alliance between a bride and a groom. They set a date and bought wedding clothes. The wedding ceremony was to happen the next morning. The night before, an elder from the girl's family and an elder from the boy's family were chatting about their old glories. In the course of that conversation, one of them asked the other what group he belonged to. He said parrot. So the other man said, "Come on! Quit joking. *We* are the parrot people." That's when they found out they were both from the same group. They should have had that conversation before they even talked of an alliance. But since they were not very smart people, they had not thought of clarifying that basic point. And now it had come all the way to the day of the wedding. See! Basically, a brother and sister were about to marry each other.'

'What happened?' someone asked.

'What's there to happen? It was a done deal. All that remained was for the groom to tie the thaali around the bride's neck. How could they stop the wedding at that point? It was too late for anything. So, people from both sides sat down for a discussion and decided to divide the parrot group into two groups that can intermarry. The groom's side would be the green parrot group. The bride's side would henceforth be the white parrot group. That's the kind of people you come from—people who married a brother and a sister. I am not making this up.'

Nobody knew how to respond to this. So they pretended to busy themselves with the wedding activities. Marimuthu should have kept his mouth shut. He knew thatha belonged to the 'crow' clan. So, he decided to say something that hinted at that connection.

'A crow rolls its eyes all day, and it rolls shit all night,' he said, quoting a proverb. 'Don't we all know that a shitty-mouthed crow has no scruples about what it says?'

Thatha had already secured the entire group's admiration. Marimuthu was no challenge to him. So he gave him a good hard punch in the gut. 'Marimuthu, I don't think young women would be suited for you. We need to find you an old woman, someone toothless and loose-jawed.'

Marimuthu's face shrank in shame. He was upset that thatha had drawn attention to the fact that he could not seem to get married. He was now humiliated in front of everyone. It left an unhealed wound in his heart. But thatha felt bad about it and spoke to Marimuthu the next time they happened to meet.

'Mapillai . . . Only the bullock knows the pain in its neck, not the crow that is pecking there. I acted like that crow. Please don't take it to heart. I am certain that there is a woman somewhere who is meant for you. Good things will happen. Don't worry.'

Marimuthu was moved by thatha's words. He said, 'I don't know if that is true, thatha. If such a woman is indeed born, please find her for me.'

Thatha was silent for a few minutes. He rubbed his thick moustache with his fingers. Then he spoke with a decisive movement of his head that made his earrings tremble. 'I will come to you myself,' he said cryptically and walked away.

6

A few months later, thatha took Marimuthu one day to 'buy some maize stalk'. Marimuthu said, 'Why do I need to buy maize stalk? I have enough from last year.'

Thatha said, 'Well, on the pretext of looking for some maize stalk, why not look at a girl for you? Now, that's agreeable to you, isn't it?' The land looked so hard and intractable where they had arrived that Marimuthu felt even a lizard would not lay its eggs there. Nothing but clusters of large granite rocks. And a tiny bit of land in the middle of it all. He was amazed at the thought of the amount of labour the people who owned that land must have put in to make it arable. In summer months, when they did not plant anything, they would be busy just clearing the land of rocks and stones. And still the rocks seemed to keep piling up.

'Do you see the land in the middle of the rocks, mapillai? Do you see how neatly they have kept it? This is exactly how they'd have raised their daughter too. You will see.'

The daughter turned out to be just as thatha had said she would be. She looked like a shining black plum. The kind of dark complexion that made you wonder if it might rub off on you on touching. Their pretext for the visit was to find out about the price of maize stalk. The girl served buttermilk to the guests. When she held out the pitcher of buttermilk towards him, her arms appeared to him like the dark, slender branches of the karuvelam tree. He had to resist the urge to reach out and hold her hands. He had never seen such an attractive dark complexion before. He was quite happy with thatha's choice of bride for him.

On the way back, thatha said to him, 'One thing you need to know. Whenever you visit your father-in-law's place here, you need to bring your own pitcher of water. Here it takes a two-mile walk to the nearest well.' He was exaggerating, but there was some truth to it. But it turned out that the dark-skinned girl was not to be Marimuthu's wife. It all came down to a pitcher of buttermilk.

Just the way thatha had taken Marimuthu unannounced to see the girl, one day he brought that girl's father over to Marimuthu's. Only his mother and ammayi were in the house. Thatha said to ammayi, 'The heat is unbearable. Can you get some buttermilk to drink, Virumakka?' Ammayi vanished into the kitchen for quite a while, and when she got back, she brought a pitcher of water and said, 'My son-in-law seems to have finished what was left of the buttermilk.'

A dark cloud fell over the girl's father's face. He drank the water without saying anything. But later, he said to thatha, 'I cannot believe I trusted your words and agreed to this visit. It is my fault. We might have water scarcity at our place, but we have plenty of buttermilk to offer. These people—their cow shed is jam-packed, but they don't have a drop of buttermilk to offer? She offers just plain water. My daughter won't be able to stay in such a place for even half a minute.'

After a long time, thatha had made an attempt to secure an alliance. But it didn't work out. How could those women run a household without a little buttermilk to offer a guest? Perhaps they sold all their milk to the dairy cooperative, so have none left for buttermilk or curd? Why do they need to make so much money? Whom were they saving it for?

If they were resourceful women, they would have rushed out to the backyard, plucked a few lemons and made some juice for the guests. It does not matter how wealthy you are. If you are lacking in hospitality, people wouldn't want to have anything to do with you. After that episode, Marimuthu gave standing instructions to his household that they had to make sure there was always some buttermilk in the house. It didn't matter if no one drank it and it went sour and had to be poured into the cattle vat. But it was all too late. The damage was done.

'How were we supposed to know that this old man would bring the girl's father that day? He could have let us know in advance. This is how households are. Some things we always make sure we have. Other things we don't. Maybe he had already made up his mind to marry his daughter elsewhere. This just became a nice excuse for him to say no to us. Look at our luck. We get judged by such lowly dogs!'

All the things that Marimuthu's mother and ammayi said about that incident did reach thatha's ears. He was not new to this kind of talk. He had heard many kinds in his lifetime. But he was not going to be put off by it. 'If a dog comes up to you and pees on your dhoti, do we take off the dhoti and throw it away? No!' That's how he rationalized it to himself. But he simply could not digest the other thing that happened.

Thatha did not have a fixed vocation. He was a jack-of-all-trades. Once, a woman by the name of Muttha, who wove baskets, said to thatha, 'Saami, can you help me sell these baskets, please? I will be most grateful to you.'

Thatha was quite amused at that request, but he sold some baskets for her. His reasoning was, 'People see me as someone who gets about a bit. So, they ask me if I can do things for them. Why not? What do I have to lose?' When he went to the markets, he dealt a bit in sheep and cattle, and it brought him some income. But he never took it up as a serious profession. If someone asked him to help with the purchase, he would bargain on their behalf.

One time at Marimuthu's, they had the problem of excess fodder and wastage in their cow shed. It felt like a terrible waste to throw all of it in the garbage. His mother told him to get a weaned buffalo calf from the cattle market. It would chew some of the excess fodder. So, Marimuthu went to the Sunday market. When he ran into thatha there, he decided to take his help with this purchase.

Thatha teased him. 'What is this, mapillai? You are wandering around the cattle market? The way things have been going, it looks like this is the only place where we can meet.' Marimuthu laughed and told thatha that he was looking to buy a buffalo calf.

Thatha got excited at the idea and walked around the market with Marimuthu. They found a calf. It had sparkling white curls of hair, and it looked bony and emaciated. Thatha purchased that calf for Marimuthu. He said, 'Don't be put off by how it looks now. It has been deprived of its mother's milk. It is a good breed. Once it eats and drinks well, in just about six months, it would shed all its white hair and grow into a big and dark animal.' Marimuthu's mother was happy when he brought the calf home.

She said, 'Broker thatha must have picked just the right kind of calf for us.' But she changed her tune within the week because the calf didn't eat anything. Nor did it drink any water. It just stood still like a sacrificial beast.

Then his mother said, 'That old man! He is always looking to see who is gullible, who he can swindle. That dog! I know what he is up to. He is busy advising thieves which house to set fire to, which ones to burgle. He thinks he can fool me?'

Things said about him somehow always reached thatha's ears. One wondered if crows and sparrows were his messengers. On this occasion too, he arrived at Marimuthu's place early one morning. He did not speak to anyone. Instead he walked straight to the cowshed and took a look at the calf. He opened its mouth and inspected its tongue with his hand. He drew out the tongue and examined it carefully. Then he looked into the calf's nose. After that, he walked over to the fields and brought some greens. He squeezed some juice out of it and poured it into the calf's mouth. He gave that treatment just once. After that, the calf started eating properly.

'The calf had a fever, that's all. Doesn't it happen to us when we eat or drink something in a new and strange environment? It's the same. This is a new place, new water for the calf. So it was struggling to adjust. It had a fever,' he said to Marimuthu.

Then, looking away at a tree branch, he spoke as if he was talking to no one in particular, but clearly with a specific addressee in mind. 'People have to think before they speak. If we spill maize, we can gather it up. Even if we spill kambu, we can somehow gather it back up. But not words.'

After that, thatha did not go anywhere near Marimuthu's place even though he wanted to help the young man. He kept looking for a bride for Marimuthu, but nothing seemed to work out. If he did not have any good news to report, why go to that house? It was during his search for a bride for Marimuthu that he came to realize that times had changed. No one could be a man for all seasons. Time simply kept changing the cast of people. It never hesitated to relegate gently to a side the people who were of no use to it any longer. Nor did it hesitate to bring slowly to centre stage those who could be of service to it. Humans, sadly, are not able to recognize and accept this fact. Any man who expects his significance to outlast his time is a pitiable creature. But thatha was able to accept that truth.

Even though he could not help Marimuthu with his marriage, he was glad there was something else he could do for him. That was the reason he had walked all that distance so early that morning and arrived at Marimuthu's place.

7

Marimuthu felt as if there was a bee boring and buzzing into his ears. He felt so exhausted he couldn't even sit up. He tried changing his position. The buzz in his ears now turned into a human voice. From its force and confidence, he could tell it was the matchmaker thatha's voice. He rose with a start, as if someone had yelled 'Fire!' He could make out that thatha was actually in the house, talking to his ammayi, his maternal grandmother. When two elderly people meet, they never run out of things to talk about!

'If you settle down here at your daughter's place at this age, one day or another people are going to comment on it,' he was saying to her. 'They will say, "Virumakka spent her last days at her in-laws'."'

'Oh let them talk, maama. So what if I die here at my daughter's place? These people can take care of my last rites too!'

'It is not enough to have people who can give you a funeral. It is also important that people say good things about you.'

'Oh never mind that. My reputation does not hang on their words. Once you die, who cares who you were?'

'How can you say that? There are things like pride and honour, aren't there?'

'What's the point of pride? The truth is, if you have money, you have people. Otherwise, not even a dog would come near you.'

'Looks like you have thought this through. That's good.'

But thatha did not stop at that. He set about giving ammayi advice on various things. Marimuthu opened the door. A beam of sunlight hit him, and he staggered. He shook his head to find his bearings.

Thatha was seated on a cot in the shade of the neem tree. When he heard the door open, he said, 'Mapillai, if you sleep like this now, I wonder what you will do once you are married. You may not come out of the room.'

Marimuthu blushed. Thatha was talking about marriage. He must have come today about an alliance. Marimuthu felt some excitement. Thatha had not visited them in a long time.

'Welcome, thatha. Give me a minute. I will wash my face and be right back.'

He washed his face with some soap. If he had been up a bit earlier, he could have had a shower and presented himself better, but thatha was not the kind to bother about all that. But, for some reason, these days Marimuthu's mind seemed to be very concerned about his looks. And the very thought that thatha might have found a bride for him made him feel even more concerned about how he looked. After all, thatha wouldn't have come all the way unless there was some significant development. There must be some news. Hope this one works out. It will. The six months are going to be a breeze.

In the early days of going bride-seeing, he did not take much care about how he dressed. Nor did he know how to. All they had in the house by way of grooming products was a little box of talcum powder. Even that was of an inferior quality, purchased at some temple festival. He'd take a little bit of the powder in the palm of his hand and apply it all over his face. That was all the grooming he ever did. He didn't even need a mirror for that. But things had changed since. He had more products now. Sometimes he wondered if the time he spent grooming himself was inversely related to the confidence he felt in himself.

The first time he went to see a girl, he had been just a little over twenty years old. He only had a faint moustache, and he'd been as shy and vulnerable as Kuppan's son now was. And just like that boy, Marimuthu too had been thin as a stick at that age. When they wanted him to go bride-seeing, he put up some resistance.

Back then, he had been quite adamant that he did not want to get married. His idea was that even if he actually wanted to, it was good form to say he didn't. But now he felt he could scream hoarse that he wanted to get married and it seemed to have no effect whatsoever. That very first time, his mother had prevailed. She told him that Jupiter was in a great place according to his horoscope, so they just had to go see the girl.

He still vividly remembered that girl's face. Her flushed cheeks. Her eyes brimming with naughtiness. She had been dark as a black beetle. He had contemplated how pleasurable it would be to embrace her and to just stay holding her, with his cheek against hers. But he'd felt quite shy when he glanced at her. It was only a quick look, but she had made a lasting impression in his heart. For many days afterwards, he was chanting her name. Rosamani. Two beautiful names in one. It suited her perfectly. Only some women were lucky to have names that suited them so perfectly.

Rosamani. How would he call her? Rosa? Or Mani? Which one would she prefer? How do her parents call her? Perhaps they just called her 'pilla'. Or 'paappa'. It was also quite possible they called her 'ammini'. He found it amusing that parents never seemed to realize the value and power of their daughter's name. They never addressed her as such. It took a stranger—her future husband—to recognize her value and the power of her name.

So, he made up his mind. If he called her 'Rosa', his lips stayed parted at the end of that word. It didn't feel right; it felt like he was crying out for help. 'Mani' however, sounded both compact and endearing. It was the right name to call her by. In his mind, he could chant 'Mani, Mani, Mani . . .' endlessly. And whenever he wanted to really emphasize his love for her, he would call her 'Rosamani'.

Once, he stood on the rocks in the outfields, looked up at the sky and shouted out her name. 'Rosamani'. He even sat in front of a Manchaami shrine under a tree and, like a man possessed, kept chanting her name. Some of the shepherd boys laughed at his madness. He still felt ashamed thinking about that. Rosamani had entranced him so thoroughly.

His mother, however, constantly referred to that girl as 'that blackie.' And when she said that, her face was twisted in disgust. He could not understand how anyone could take a dislike to that sprightly and beautiful face. His mother was dark too. So was his father. Marimuthu was slightly fair-complexioned. But no one in the family was really fair-skinned. His entire family and all his relatives were dark-skinned. Then how could they expect the girl who married into their family to have a rosy complexion?

The fact that Rosamani was dark-skinned did not matter at all to Marimuthu. He once had a pleasant dream in which her darkness rubbed off on him on touch and he put off showering for a few days so that it could stay on him longer. Those were the days!

Now, Marimuthu found himself standing in front of the mirror. It seemed to magnify his face. He wiped it clean with a towel and looked again. His face had gone a bit gaunt. Sunken cheeks and dark rings around his eyes. Even he couldn't bear to look at his face. It was the face of a man who had not slept in a long while and was coming unhinged.

He washed his face once again, this time more vigorously. Then he looked out into the brightness of the day in order to get his vision used to the sunlight. Then he gave himself another look in the mirror. Now the face looked a little better. His eyes looked a little more alive now. He thought if he applied some cream on his face, it might make his eyes stand out more. So he did that and put some powder on top of that. Now his face looked fresh. Then he combed his hair down neatly. He had curly hair. He always needed to sprinkle some water to make it settle down.

He cut his hair every twenty days, but it grew back quickly. Even a little extra hair can make you look older. He spotted a few grey hairs and tried in vain to hide them. Balu, his friend from school, now had hair as white as foam. He said once, 'Oh, not only the hair on my head. My chest hair, pubic hair—everything has gone grey.'

But Balu was a father of four, so that was all right for him.

'In those days, marriages were no easy matter,' thatha was saying to ammayi. 'Not like today. I had to walk back and forth endlessly to finalize an alliance. I had to walk so much that I could wear out a new pair of sandals. And I am not talking about just any pair of sandals. I am talking about the ones that have iron soles. Strong ones.'

'I didn't know they made sandals with iron soles, maama.'

They were really enjoying their chat, and it seemed to revolve around the topic of marriage. Marimuthu felt hopeful.

'Why, Virumakka! Don't you remember that moment in the Thambiyan story? He was such an ignorant and illiterate man. Remember what his clansmen did to him? They made him a pair of sandals with iron soles and told him that he could get married only when those sandals were worn out. That naïve fellow. He tried to wear those sandals out by putting them on even when he took the cattle out grazing. He even walked over rocks, but the sandals wouldn't break. How could he ever get married, then?'

Even the story thatha chose to tell had something to do with the theme of marriage.

Marimuthu decided that the next time he got his haircut, he would also get it coloured. Now, he tried to cover the receding hairline by bringing forward some hair from the middle of his head. It occurred to him for a moment that if he had married Rosamani, he wouldn't have had to go through all of this.

As a compensation for her being dark-skinned, Rosamani's father offered fifty sovereigns of gold and fifty thousand rupees in dowry. But that was not enough for Marimuthu's mother. She acted like her son would be making a huge sacrifice in marrying a dark-skinned girl. She demanded a motor vehicle for his son. The girl's father agreed to that too. He said he would buy Marimuthu a vehicle within one year of the marriage.

There was no reason not to trust the word of a man who was offering fifty sovereigns of gold and fifty thousand rupees right away. But Marimuthu's mother wanted the vehicle right away, as if all she desired was to see her son and new daughter-in-law ride together on the bike the very next day after the wedding. Everything had been going well, but things fell apart on account of this matter of the motorbike. A lot of people tried to counsel her, but she acted as if her entire honour depended on having that motor vehicle. She did not even look at him; she did not take his wishes into consideration at all. Marimuthu had been too young and shy to voice his opinion then. He had no part to play in these discussions. Once it became clear that Rosamani was not to be his wife, his mother said, 'So what if you cannot marry that darkie? There are many other girls to pick from.'

If he had been as confident then as he was now, he would have shut her up and brought Rosamani home as his wife. But he had been too timid then. To this day, he was facing the sad consequences of not speaking up when he should have. So much has changed in the ten or twelve years since. Fifty thousand rupees and fifty sovereigns? He couldn't even imagine expecting that now. Forget that, he couldn't find a wife easily even if he offered money.

Marimuthu was quite crushed that he could not marry Rosamani. He had fallen in love with her. He had built a lot of dreams around her, and he didn't know what to do with it all. He had set aside three-fourths of the space on his bed for her. What would he fill that with now? For a long while after that, he had a hard time reckoning with his loneliness. He cried silently at nights. When he was out in the fields, he cried out loud. He let his stubble grow. And he drank one more pitcher of toddy than was usual. If he had married Rosamani at that age, his entire life would have been fragrant like toddy froth. Whenever Rosamani came to his mind, he could not help but feel hatred towards his mother. Why did she make such a big deal about a motor vehicle? Couldn't he have bought that himself? And how would a vehicle render the girl's dark skin immaterial? He still felt the sting of the helplessness that had kept him from saying to his mother, 'You and your stupid talk about the bike! Get lost!' and marrying Rosamani.

Since then, he had seen several potential brides. They were all nothing but fleeting illusions. They were like images made of smoke that vanished even before his eyes could take them in properly. Rosamani was the first woman he had seen, and she deserved the entire expanse of his heart. But it was not as if he declined the other women he saw. Somehow, nothing worked out.

He only had one guiding principle now. He had learned it from his grandfather.

'All women are the same. Don't think too much about it, no matter how she looks. Even someone so-so will do.'

But it had been hard to hear the first time.

8

While grooming his moustache, he spotted a single grey hair sticking out just below the right nostril. He tried to make it inconspicuous by combing it down with the rest of the moustache. But, like the shiver of a ram's mane, it refused to submit. He urgently looked for a pair of scissors and cut that strand of hair off at its root. Then he let out a sigh of relief. He regained a sense of contentment now that all was well. But this tactic would work only when he was dealing with one or two grey hairs. What if there were many? He had six months. Would he go totally grey by then?

'Even women don't take this long to get ready. What is mapillai doing?'

'Here I come, thatha.'

He put on a shirt and stepped outside. The early morning light made everything appear fresh. He felt that his pale yellow shirt was quite the right choice.

Thatha stood up, commenting, 'Oh wow! Look at you! I wish I had a daughter to offer in marriage to you. Shall we walk to the fields?' He was wearing his towel over his head to protect it from the heat. The wrinkled expanse of his back gave away his age. Marimuthu followed thatha quietly. All his experiences going bride-seeing had taught him one sure lesson—not to be the one to initiate the conversation. Once they had entered the coconut grove, thatha sighed in relief as he removed the towel from his head. Then he looked up at the trees.

'There must be around fifty trees, mapillai?' he asked.

'There are sixty-seven,' he replied, and pointed to a slab that was laid out under the shade nearby. Thatha went and sat down there. It was a quite convenient spot—thatha could sit stretching his legs out in front of him. As he went to sit down on a rock nearby, Marimuthu asked, 'Do you want some coconut water?'

'Let us rest for a bit first,' thatha replied.

Marimuthu liked thatha's sense of leisure.

'Have you leased out the work of harvesting the coconuts?'

'This grove is not big enough to be leased out, thatha. We do it ourselves. Kuppan works for us. He takes care of the stalks and husks, and I take the coconuts to the market.'

'And you handle all the accounts?'

'You ask like you didn't know that.'

Thatha smiled. Then he took some tobacco from his waist pouch and put some in his mouth.

'And what's your liquidity like?' he asked.

'Oh we have some, thatha. We won't starve.'

'Oh you are being discreet about it!' Thatha said admiringly. 'And you have enough water for the trees?'

'Yes, the trees are well cared for. But when it is time for the coconuts, we cannot attend to anything else.'

'These days every house has a borewell machine. Why don't you get one too?'

'But we need a water source for that, don't we? We checked four or five spots. But none of them was satisfactory. I am considering fixing an additional bore pump in the well.'

'Yes. Do something. We shouldn't keep the land wanting,' thatha said, looking intently at him. Marimuthu wondered why thatha was talking about everything else but the subject of marriage.

'A good farmer would never consider leaving his land wanting attention and care. Land is like the goddess Sridevi. Would anyone consider leaving the goddess unadorned and uncared for? In my father's days, he wouldn't let even a tiny, palm-sized portion of land unattended. "If I drop some seeds there, crows and sparrows would get something to eat." That's what he said. Who thinks that way anymore? Their pride has become more important to people than their lands.'

Marimuthu struggled to understand why thatha was talking about these things. But then elderly people never could come straight to the point.

'Thatha, I was hoping you will have some good news to talk about. But you seem to be talking about land and things.'

Thatha laughed out loud, showing his yellowed teeth.

'Why, mapillai? Didn't you notice I called the land Sridevi? I am talking about a woman, don't you see?'

'I don't understand such things, thatha. Why don't you speak directly?'

'Mapillai, I knew that's what you would expect from me. But things can happen only when it's their time. It is not in my hands, and it is not in yours. It is indeed my desire to get you married as soon as possible. But it is proving difficult. Times have changed. No matter what I do, things don't seem to work out.'

Marimuthu suddenly felt hopeless. After that, it did not matter what thatha wanted to talk about. The eagerness he had earlier felt now drained away completely.

'No one expected things to take such a turn, mapillai. Take my village, for instance. There are twenty boys ready for marriage. How many girls do you think there are?'

He just stared at thatha. Thatha shook his head sadly.

'Just four girls, and one of them has just come of age. You do the math for your village. How many?'

Marimuthu started counting in his mind. He was the oldest among the men who hadn't married yet. So, he was the first. Then there were two brothers in Selankadu. The older brother had gone completely bald. The family had decided that no one was going to marry him, so they were looking for a match only for the younger brother. Then there was another boy who was a truck driver. People said he had AIDS. That rumour seemed to precede him wherever he went bride-seeing. But he was outraged. 'Who spread this rumour? I am ready to get my blood tested anywhere you want me to,' he said. Still, nothing seemed to work out for him.

There was the soda-seller Perumal's son. He looked like a skeleton as he rode on his bicycle carrying an incredible number of soda bottles. You would marvel at his strength.

Then there was also the son of the 'car man', the first man from the village ever to drive a four-wheeler who now co-owned a trucking rig. He was often away in north India for six months at a stretch. There were people to attend to the actual work; he only had to oversee things. He was known to rent room in hotels, drink beer and eat huge quantities of meat. The first time he returned from his trip, he weighed eighty kilos. People couldn't recognize him. His cheeks had become so chubby, they made his eyes look tiny. Now he was trying to lose weight because he couldn't find a girl to marry.

Marimuthu could keep counting . . . the number kept growing. Over twenty. But the girls were far fewer in number. He could list them right away. Just three of them. There was one girl in Seethan's family, but kin rules meant Marimuthu could not marry her. Then there was Amavasayan's daughter. She had plenty of offers from rich rig truck owners. Amavasayan could easily give twenty sovereigns of gold, but he did not want to marry his daughter to anyone local. And then there was Parattaiyan's daughter. Technically, Marimuthu could marry her, but his mother and the girl's mother were both paternally related. So it couldn't happen.

Marimuthu wondered why it had not occurred to him until now to do this math himself. That dream he had had a few nights ago—was that informed by this reality? Thatha had come today to explain to him his dream. Marimuthu was overcome by exhaustion. He couldn't bear the morning sun and he felt faint. But thatha went on talking.

'We are responsible for this. If the firstborn is a boy, people are happy and stop having any more children. Just one child. Only if the first child happens to be a girl, people attempt again. If the next child is a boy, they keep it. Otherwise, no. These days people find out the sex of the unborn child and they have it aborted if it is a girl. Even five months into the pregnancy. Now tell me, how do we expect to thrive?'

Marimuthu did not care who did what. All he needed was one girl to marry him. Beyond that, it did not matter to him what happened to whom. This old man seemed to want to save the world. Marimuthu lost interest in the subject. He stood up stretching, and he looked up at a tree, thinking of finding some tender coconut. Noticing his lack of interest, thatha changed the topic.

'Don't think I have given up looking for a match for you. I am still looking. I will soon return with good news. Don't worry. Today I have come to you with some other task in mind. But before we talk about that, go bring me some tender coconut you offered earlier.'

What could thatha have to talk about other than marriage that could be of interest to him? Feeling quite sure that he wouldn't be interested in anything else thatha had to say, Marimuthu walked towards a short tree. The tree's neck was studded with tender red coconuts. He didn't even need a rope to climb the tree. He just used his hands and legs and was up the tree in just four swift moves. He twisted apart some coconuts and dropped them on the moist and soft ground in the irrigation channel. Then he climbed down swiftly. He picked up a scythe and shaved and opened the coconuts. Thatha was watching him at work. He accepted with an admiring smile the coconut water Marimuthu offered him.

'Mapillai, are you sure this coconut water is going to be sweet?'

'Thatha, do you have to ask? I guarantee it will be sweet as honey. Try it. Among these sixty-seven trees, I know which one is sweet, which one is salty, which one's tender, which one is hardened. Did you think I am just a show-off?'

'I am impressed. You are so thorough with your work, mapillai. I can't think of any other fellow your age who can climb the tree in just four strides!'

Thatha's praise made him happy, but he did not like that reference to his age. Thatha, however, was keen on making use of this opening in the conversation to bring up what he wanted to say.

'This land and the water here are the reasons these coconuts trees are doing so well. If anyone suggested to you that you should leave this land unused, would you agree with that?'

'Why would I leave this land unused, thatha?'

'Then how come you have done exactly that to that red-soil land which is far more fertile than this one?'

He understood right away thatha's motive for the visit. Thatha lived five miles away from the village. Who could have told him about the dispute? Who in his uncle's family now cared about that land?'

'In our elders' time, they let lands lie unused when there were small disputes. That was long ago. They didn't know better. But why should we be the same way? These days, things are in the hands of young people like you. Shouldn't we find a solution?'

Marimuthu was already annoyed with thatha. Now this subject of the land made him even more irritated, so his words now came with a sting.

'Let it be, thatha. The land is not going to go anywhere. That land is, in fact, the only witness we have for how badly my grandfather and grandmother were treated. If the land issue is settled, those other things will be forgotten. So let us keep our distance.'

Thatha now decided to be a bit cunning in his response.

'No one is asking you to mend the relationship with your uncle's family. Let that be the way it is. Even if you want to reach out to them and get back together, your grandmother will not agree to it. Forget about the relationships. Look at the land. You know what that land is worth today. Then why let it go to waste? These days, even lands that are rocky and uncultivable are worth quite a lot. In all my life, until now, I never saw anyone assess a land's value in terms of money. It's a new approach. Earlier, they looked at land differently. "This land has good soil. Maize will grow well here. Kambu will do well in this land. In the rainy season, we could keep standing water in it. This land is smooth and even." That was how people evaluated land. Now the yardsticks are: Is the land close to the road? Is the bus-stop nearby? Can we sell it as plots for building houses . . .?'

Marimuthu interrupted him.

'Thatha, I agree the land would possibly fetch quite a bit of money. But who is going to sell it now? Let it be. We can talk about it after grandmother's time.'

But thatha was not ready to let it go. 'You please consult your grandmother. Poovayi has toiled hard in that land. She will not like that it now lies covered in thorny bushes. It was your uncle's son—the youngest one, Selvarasu—he was the one who approached me about this. He came to our village to attend a wedding. As we were chatting about various things, he said, "We are three of us. We could use some money. Marimuthu anna might have some use for the land. He may not need it, but it will help us. He will listen to you. Please try talking to him." That was the reason I came today . . .'

Marimuthu sensed that he was hinting at something: if thatha could not accomplish this task even by coming in person, that would mean there was not much respect left for him. That insinuation bothered Marimuthu.

'I will speak to my grandmother and will come and see you myself, thatha. Also, Selvarasu is the only one in that family who still speaks to me when I run into him. So, I need to respect that as well. Maybe we can resolve at least the matter of the land,' said Marimuthu, sighing.

Thatha was pleased by his response. 'Please don't worry, mapillai. The moment that land becomes yours, your wedding too will be fixed. I keep feeling that leaving that land unused is the curse that is ruining your chances for marriage.'

Marimuthu knew that thatha was merely offering words of consolation.

9

Marimuthu was lying in the coconut grove on a rope cot that sagged in the middle. He couldn't focus on any work. He felt like just lying there aimlessly. An unusual weariness had taken hold of him. He had lost faith that broker thatha would somehow find a girl for him to marry. All of thatha's words had been cleverly crafted. Honey-tipped arrows.

Thatha was only intent on getting his way through. He was quite adept at ensuring his own survival under any conditions. He had said that the reason for the delay in marriage prospects was the fact that the red-soil land lay unused. None of the astrologers they had consulted had ever made that connection. But now thatha had! Now he would share that with everyone. He would tell everyone that that piece of land was the thing that would bring marital luck to Marimuthu. But Marimuthu had no such hopes. He was past that phase when words could offer him comfort and consolation.

That land had lain unused for over thirty years. The reason was the fiery words exchanged between two families

long ago. Marimuthu had been an infant when it happened.
But his grandmother had told him the story several times.

The land belonged to Marimuthu's paternal grandfather
and the grandfather's younger brother. About three-and-a-
half acres. It had a huge well—the largest in the vicinity.
The well had been dug deep into the earth, boring through
rocks like a passage to the netherworld. Not far from the
well, the land started sloping towards a lake. So, the water
level in the well had been excellent back in the day. In the
rainy season, you could look down into the well and see the
water. The brothers shared the water, using it on alternate
days. They had separate plots of land on the elevated side
as well as the low-lying parts. They had divvied it up
amicably, and the farming was going on well.

In his granduncle's family, there was no one capable
enough to take charge of all the farming work. His wife
had been sickly. It was a miracle that she managed to raise
her daughters. And how much land could the granduncle
oversee on his own? He owned both some flat lands and
some elevated ones. Over ten acres. But he came to regard
the raised, red-soil land as of lesser use. He sowed maize, but
he did not even have the time to irrigate the land properly.

Marimuthu's grandfather, on the other hand, had his
adult son to help him with the work. His son—Marimuthu's
father—knew nothing but hard work in the field. He didn't
even go to the markets. He didn't do bookkeeping. All he
needed was some gruel and some kambu meal with thick
milk curd. And, of course, palm toddy.

One must say he was quite a hedonist even in those
days. He always lay his cot in the sheep enclosure or in

the shed in the field. Only very rarely did he ever say he was tired and asked Marimuthu to take over the night watch at the enclosure. But it had nothing to do with tiredness; he had to attend to his body's urges. In those years when Marimuthu's father and grandfather worked together in the land, it was always lush and bountiful, like a woman at the height of pregnancy. They used the water his granduncle had not made use of, and they irrigated the entire land. Since the soil was fertile, whatever they sowed ended up thriving. Ragi grew well, its stalks sagging under the weight of their own harvest. And when they planted brinjal, they were able to sustain it for two years. The time they cultivated cucumber, there was so much fruit left that even the crows got to eat some.

Marimuthu's paatti ran herself ragged with daily trips on foot to the nearby town of Karattur. It was around the same time that she started wearing that thick gold-braided chain around her neck. Since she wore that saradu all the time, some people even called her 'sarattukaari' for a while. She only took it off when grandfather died. But before doing that, she sang a lament, weaving in the story of the chain into it, remembering how fondly her husband bought it for her from the profits from the chilli pepper harvest, how her gold chain had once been everyone's envy and how unfortunate it was that she did not die before her husband, with the saradu still around her neck . . .

The braided chain must have been about five sovereigns of gold. She gave it to Marimuthu's aunt, his father's sister. That upset his mother, and it became one of the reasons for her to dislike paatti.

The point was that their land was so fertile and the yields so plentiful that they could buy a braided gold chain from the profits. That was why Marimuthu's granduncle and grandaunt envied them. Even though they were quite affectionate on the outside, they fumed in their hearts. It was the same land, the same well. But on one side the crops were always green and lush, while the other side was largely left for sheep and cattle to graze. And some sad-looking maize it was. How could they account for this stark difference?

There was a tall neem tree on the raised boundary between their lands. One day, Marimuthu's grandfather pruned the top branches to make sure they didn't cast a shade on the crops. Seeing that, his brother came running, picking up a hoe from near the water channel.

'Why the hell did you chop down the tree that is growing in my land?'

'This tree is on my side of the border, da!' said grandfather.

'How shameless are you? You stole my water.'

'You grew up drinking the milk that I left over. Don't give me that nonsense!'

The argument got heated, and granduncle hit his brother on the head with the hoe. Since grandfather had had the quickness of mind to stagger backwards, he escaped with a minor bruise. But granduncle did not stop with that. He ran towards the well with a sense of purpose. Grandfather sat down on the border, holding his head in his hands. Hearing the noises, people came running. Granduncle broke the wooden pulley system from the well and cast it down into the depths. That was when grandfather understood his brother's feelings.

After that, no one affixed a new pulley system for the well. The well was not used for years. In the rainy months when the water level rose, young boys jumped into it for a swim. But older people felt they might fall sick if they bathed in the stagnant water. The disputes were not resolved even after they went to the revenue officer for mediation. It even became a police and court case. Paatti had told Marimuthu all about it.

'If he had hit my husband with even just a bit more force, I would have been widowed that day.'

The case languished even though both sides spent quite a lot of money in the process. And the land lay uncultivated. His grandmother cursed the other family, throwing a handful of earth in their direction. She even went to Municchami temple, had some sorcery done, brought a lemon and buried it somewhere for lasting effect. Since then, the two families had been estranged. No conversations. No visits.

Grandfather died, and both granduncle and grandaunt passed away. Paatti alone was still around but quite frail, her days numbered. Granduncle had three grandsons. Their father—Marimuthu's uncle—was very proud of the fact that he had three male heirs.

He used to say, 'My cows only yield bull calves. My wife births only male children.' When Marimuthu's sister was born, his uncle kept repeating that line to make sure it reached Marimuthu's father's ears.

Of the three sons, the first was married. The youngest, and also the friendly one, was Selvarasu. He always smiled at Marimuthu when they ran into each other, and he also always stopped to exchange a few cordial words. It was through him that the land dispute was going to find a resolution now.

What happened to all those hateful words the elders had flung at each other back in the day? Now the land might be divided again. It might see more farming than it ever did in the past. Or they might sell portions of the land as several small house plots. All that murderous rage and all those angry words that were exchanged—what did they all come to? Nothing. Just like the words that thatha now spoke. All empty words. But Marimuthu could not help but marvel—even though he was a man of an earlier time, how much thatha knew about today's mores! Besides, not only thatha, anyone would find all that talk about land's worth in monetary terms intimidating.

If Marimuthu did manage to secure that land, it was not going to be of any immediate use to him. He would have to spend a lot of money clearing it of all the thorny undergrowth. He would have to get the well desilted and a new motor fixed. Then he would have to hire help to do the farming work. It was not easy these days to find reliable farm labour. Kuppan could only toil for a few more years. Would his son take over the job and work for him for a fixed annual wage? Marimuthu remembered how quick-tempered and reactive that lanky boy was.

He felt that his grandmother was not going to say no to the land. Chilli pepper yields from that land had got her the braided gold saradu. So, she was likely to have a lot of attachment to that land. Marimuthu, on the other hand, had no special feelings associated with it. When it was abandoned, he had been an infant, still suckling at his mother's breasts. The only thing he knew about the land was that half of it belonged to his family. Other than that, he had one vivid memory of passing through that land. It was to do with Vasanthi, who had been at school with him till the fifth standard.

10

He could not recollect if he ever spoke to Vasanthi during their school years. He mostly preferred to hang out with the boys. When he was in the fifth standard, the headmaster of the school had given him the responsibility of ringing the school bell for the year. He felt a certain delight every time he struck the hanging piece of rail with the iron rod. It continued to reverberate in his ears long after he stopped striking it.

The bell-ringing routine really became a matter of pride for him. He truly believed that the entire school functioned because he rang the bell. Therefore, for that entire school year, he never took a day off. He went to school even on feast days at home when they cooked meat, and even on holidays. Younger kids at school called him the 'bell-ringer brother'. But the boys who did not get the chance to ring the bell made up a song mocking him.

Marimuthu rang the bell
tunnn . . .tunnn . . .tunnn . . .
His uncle's daughter came running to him

tinggg . . .tinggg . . .tinggg
He forgot how to ring the bell
toinggg . . .toinggg . . .toinggg . . .
He stood gaping at her
tunggg . . .tunggg . . . tungggg . . .

That song made Marimuthu very angry. He swore at the boys and ran away from that spot. On one occasion, Vasanthi had been among the crowd that taunted him. So, he had come to hate her.

But years later, when he saw Vasanthi in all her youthful splendour, he forgot those feelings. If there was any such thing as pure, flawless beauty, it was surely Vasanthi.

In those days, in the street behind the red-soil land, there used to live a healer. He had cures for cattle diseases, scorpion bites, thorn wounds, and many more ailments. So, he had a steady stream of people going to him.

Vasanthi had an infection in the nail of her right middle finger, so her grandmother took her to see the healer. Since their house was in the middle of a grove in the next village, it was a long walk to the healer's. As they walked past Marimuthu's house, Vasanthi's grandmother felt exhausted and needed to rest. She sat down on the stoop on the porch in front of Marimuthu's house.

Then she said to Marimuthu, 'Can you please take her to the healer and bring her back while I wait here? You will be blessed.' His own grandmother also said, 'Go, take the girl to the healer. Let the lady rest here for a bit.' Even though he hesitated a bit, he wanted to go with Vasanthi.

She walked a little behind him. He had to keep turning back to make sure she was following him. She was beautiful, like a neem sapling that had been allowed to grow without being pruned. This was the first time Marimuthu was walking so close to a girl his age. He had never even spoken to her or any of the other girls. Now he felt like saying something to her, but he was tongue-tied.

But as they were walking along the narrow path winding through the thorny bushes in the red-soil land, he found a bit of courage. He thought about what he could say to her. Perhaps he could say, 'Be careful. The thorny branches can snap back at you'? Or he might ask, 'Does your finger hurt a lot?' Or just simply, 'Are you well?'

He couldn't decide what to say, but he just said faintly, 'Vasanthi . . .' She heard him and said, 'Hmm?' That was music to his ears. He said, 'Do you need medicine for the infection on your finger?' She just said, 'Mm.' By the time this exchange ended, they had reached the destination.

When she stood in front of the healer to get her bandage done, Marimuthu kept looking at her intently. She closed her eyes in fear that the betel leaf bandage might hurt. Her wet lips looked like ripe aloe fruit.

On their way back, she walked a few steps in front of him. He wanted to touch her braided hair that moved against her back. When they were walking amidst the thorny bushes, he lost his sense of control. He called out to her, 'Vasanthi . . .' She said, 'Hmm?' and turned to look at him. He rushed to her in just two strides and kissed her on her lips. It lasted just a second. Then he ran away from the spot and hid himself in the little shed in the orchard.

He continued to think about the feel of her lips. But more than that he was afraid she might have complained to her grandmother or his ammayi. He only went home well after it grew dark. Ammayi did not ask him anything. It was only after he was quite sure that Vasanthi had not complained to anyone did he start thinking more about the touch of her lips.

She had not screamed when he kissed her. Nor had she mentioned it to anyone. It was he who had got scared and run away from the spot. He regretted his stupidity. That had been his first kiss. His mind was suffused with thoughts of Vasanthi in those days. Now, he felt a sudden yearning for those long-gone days.

When he contemplated the fact that the red-earthed land had played a role in getting to know Vasanthi, he now felt an extra fondness for it. He had to secure that land somehow.

In fact, at one point, Vasanthi's horoscope had been among those they considered as a match for his. But since her birth star was Moolam, she could only marry someone whose parents had already passed on. When he heard about that, Marimuthu even wished his father, who did nothing but wander as aimlessly as a quail, and his mother, who only cared about money and status, were dead. Then, when he felt terribly guilty at such thoughts, he said to himself that he was ready to lose anyone if it meant he would marry Vasanthi.

If he had married her, he might have found a way to unpack the dense meanings in the 'hmms' she had uttered three times. They had signified her fondness for him, but then they vanished into thin air. All they now accomplished was to haunt his recollections and stir feelings of self-pity. It is possible that Vasanthi, who was now happily married and had children, might find some secret meaning in that past moment. But for him it all came to nothing.

Sun's rays pierced through the gaps in the coconut fronds and fell directly in his eyes. He closed them and turned on his side. He sensed that someone was standing not far away, but he couldn't see clearly for the glare of the sun. Who was it? Was it Vasanthi? Had she come alive from his thoughts? What a ridiculous thought!

It was Kuppan. He had been waiting for Marimuthu to notice him. Now that he had, Kuppan said, 'Saami,' and saluted him. Feeling like he had just arrived from another world, Marimuthu sat up and said, 'When did you arrive, Kuppan?' He wondered if Kuppan had been standing there for a long time, even observing him as he had all those ridiculous visions.

Now he said with some anger, 'Why have you been standing still like a buffalo? Why didn't you rouse me?'

'I just arrived, saami. I was not sure if you were sleeping or not. So I just stood by the side,' he said. Marimuthu looked at Kuppan's face. He wanted to check if Kuppan was teasing him. But there was no evidence of anything of that sort on Kuppan's expressionless face. He wondered how Kuppan always managed to hold just that one expression all the time.

'Are you done with all the work?'

'Yes, saami. I need to pluck brinjals in the evening. We have the market tomorrow. Our landlady has said she would go to the market too.'

'How much brinjal do we have?'

'Three sacks, saami. Or two sacks and one basket.'

'Alright. Then we can carry everything in the TVS moped. If there is more to carry, we can rent the bullock cart from the Kadunkadu folks.'

'Okay, saami.'

But Kuppan didn't budge. Pretending not to notice it, Marimuthu asked him, 'Have you moved the cattle between sheds?'

'We can do it tomorrow, saami. There aren't too many sheep droppings to worry about in this summer heat.'

'Alright. Go, do your work.'

'Saami . . . our senior lady, your grandmother, has given a list of things to purchase in the market tomorrow. Shall I tell you now?'

Paatti's list was never long. No vegetables. Tamarind arrived from her daughter's house. They had chilli pepper right here in the field. They also had enough pulses and lentils. So, it usually turned out to be some small items she needed.

'She wants two rupees, worth of jeera seeds and black pepper. Then a lantern lamp shade. And some dried Bengal gram for five rupees.'

'Okay. Is that all?'

It looked like Kuppan had something more to say, but he was hesitating. Marimuthu raised his eyebrows as if to ask what.

'That thing . . . my son's wedding . . .'

Marimuthu felt a rush of anger. 'I told you what to do the other day. What is it now?'

'You said six months, saami. That will be the month of Aavani. Shall I go ahead and set a date for the wedding in that month? I will do it if I have your command.'

Marimuthu went silent for a few minutes. Then he said, 'Yes. Set a date for the end of Aavani.'

Kuppan saluted him happily and walked away. Now it was confirmed that Marimuthu would give him the money for his son's wedding. Things would proceed swiftly. It was also likely that at some point, Kuppan would ask for some more money and Marimuthu would give it reluctantly. Long after Kuppan had left, Marimuthu still lay on the cot. In his mind he kept hearing the words *six months . . . the end of Aavani . . .*

11

Marimuthu used the TVS 50 exclusively to carry vegetables to the market. He had fixed a plank in front for the extra load. On that plank, he now secured two baskets and set out for the market. There were two more sacks of vegetables, but they would follow in the bullock cart he had rented from the Kadunkaadu.

He loved the buzz and excitement of the market in the morning. The only people who showed up at that hour were the farmers who brought their produce, the labourers who did the lifting and carrying, and the many vendors who set up their stalls. The activities of that hour always seemed to him like a great, unchanging painting.

He used to wonder if it was the energy of those pre-dawn hours that kept the rest of the day going. He loved observing that bustle, so he was always there on Thursday mornings even if he had nothing to offer. But he usually had some coconuts to sell, and he had his regular vendors who bought them from him for a reasonable price. Marimuthu didn't like to bargain much.

The market was an endless source of wonder for him. Seeing how constant that setting had stayed for ages, he questioned his usual sense that the times had changed. On the pretext of purchasing things for the house, he often carried a sack and wandered around the market as it expanded and grew in the light of dawn. He knew the layout, what was available where and where the various traders had their shops. He was also friendly with many.

Once when he went to buy the lanterns his paatti had asked for, he became friends with the man who sold them. On Marimuthu's land, when it was the season to harvest groundnuts, workers came in large groups from Kallur, Sangoor and other places, and they all set up camp on the rocky patch nearby. Their dinner preparations were a boisterous affair, and they needed lanterns to light up the place. So, Marimuthu always kept five or six lanterns in the shed. When it was the season for groundnut harvest, he'd bring them to this man to get them serviced and the glass shade fixed.

Sometimes when the vendor needed to take a break for tea or lunch, Marimuthu took charge of the shop. Very few people used lanterns anymore. Only elderly people living in remote rural areas. He often wondered, why sell lanterns for a living? How much money could the man make from it? But what he learned from the vendor was that on every market day, he sold fifty lanterns. In addition to that, he also made money from repairs and servicing jobs.

'Marimuthu, I know you are a farmer. So please don't take offence when I say this. The truth is, as long as there are farmers, there will be a market for lanterns. The women in your families still use lanterns even though you all have electric lights now. In many houses, a lantern is the only source of light after eight in the evening. They want to save on electric use. They think electricity is a miracle, and like all miracles, it should be used sparingly.'

Marimuthu was also fond of going to the astrologer who used a parrot to draw cards. He did that every week without fail, even though it had never worked out for him. Once he got a card with Rama and Sita as a divine couple at their wedding. He even had Murugan with this two wives. Even Sivan and Parvati feeding the world, accompanied by their children Pillaiyar and Murugan. Even though none of those predictions for family life came true, visiting that astrologer every week made him feel better.

The other thing that he was fond of was the spicy koottucchaaru made by Poonkizhavi, the old woman who ran the idli stall. She had been selling idlis at this market for ages, and her koottucchaaru gravy was delectable. It just melted in the mouth. She started her business at six in the morning. She had chaaru in a large pot and idlis piled up on a plate. More idlis would be getting ready in a steaming pot nearby. By 9 o'clock, she would run out of the chaaru. But people would patiently wait with empty plates in their hands as she rustled up more of the spicy gravy. She disarmed everyone with her toothless smile. Her grandson or granddaughter helped her in the shop.

Once, when he went to this woman's shop to 'drink some gravy' (that's how people put it), he ran into one of his former schoolteachers. A man who carried a box of betel leaves with him. Marimuthu knew the teacher wouldn't

remember him. He had been his seventh standard math
teacher. Dressed in white, the teacher too had arrived at
the market early to eat koottucchaaru. Suddenly feeling
respectful, Marimuthu gestured a vanakkam, but by raising
only one hand.

The teacher acknowledged Marimuthu's gesture and
asked him when he had been in school. He tried to count
the years in his head, but it all got jumbled. Eventually, he
said, 'Seventh standard, sir.' The teacher said, 'And all you
learned from me was how to say vanakkam with just one
hand?' Marimuthu didn't know how to respond to that.
As far as he knew, except perhaps at weddings, no one was
in the habit of saying vanakkam by bringing both hands
together. The teacher just said, 'Hmm.' Marimuthu was
not upset. After all, as a teacher, it was his duty to point
out such things.

This time, as he sat eating idlis and koottuchaaru, he
remembered the teacher. He wanted to pay that man a
visit. He had been to consult him several times in the past,
but nothing had come out of it. It was only yet another
expenditure. But he would give it one last try.

He knew that he might come to the same conclusion
about the teacher as he had about matchmaker thatha.
Neither could help him. Why should he keep relying on
the same old methods that had clearly not had any effect?
Couldn't he try new ways? Not that he knew what these new
ways were, but that did not mean he had to keep returning
to the same old stone walls. He told himself he would give
them one last try. Now that he had made up his mind to
visit the teacher, he speeded up his errands at the market.

He bought all the things needed for the house. He also made sure he got all the things paatti had listed to Kuppan. In addition, he also bought a calabash. Paatti loved that vegetable, but she never bought it for herself. The other thing she liked—the only snack she enjoyed—was peanuts roasted with rice puffs. If he bought her ten rupees, worth of roasted Bengal gram and some snack blends, she would treasure them and make them last for over a week. But he had to tell her it cost him only five rupees. Otherwise, she would be upset he'd spent too much.

Paatti still seemed to think that prices in the market had stayed the same since her days. When she was younger, she used to arrive at the market early in the mornings carrying a basket in her head, because she knew that she'd get better prices at that hour. On the other hand, since she went to work in other people's lands, weeding or harvesting, she did know that the wages had gone up. She had no problems with that. But she expected the prices of things to remain the same.

He also bought some adhirasam for paatti. She rarely got to indulge her taste buds. When he happened to walk past the shop selling lemons, he remembered he needed a few for his visit to the teacher. He carefully picked two shiny lemons. The teacher always found something to criticize. The first time Marimuthu went to see the teacher, he had gone empty-handed. After his retirement from the school, the man had become a marriage broker. Why did Marimuthu have to bring gifts to a marriage broker? But the third time Marimuthu went to him, he was given some friendly advice.

'We need to look for good practices everywhere and make them part of our lives. It might be a simple thing, but it will bring a sense of order to our life. Let's say we go to visit someone. Can we go empty-handed? There might be children in the house. They'd look at the guest expectantly. It is possible that we may not have money to spend. In that case, we could take just a lemon with us and offer it to the elder in the house we visit. There is, at least, one elderly person in every family. It's a mark of respect.'

After that, Marimuthu always made sure he carried a lemon with him and offered it to the teacher, who always accepted it with a big smile. Sometimes, the same lemon would be offered back to Marimuthu in juice form. One time, one of the lemons he carried had a scar on it. The teacher gave him a lecture about that too.

'You are from a farming community. You are a farmer. How should you conduct yourself? It doesn't look like you take particular care about your own work. We pay for these fruits. Don't they have to be good, ripe fruits? If it is not the right season, then that's a different matter. Then we will just make do with what is available. But this is the season of plenty. You need to pick them with care.'

He always found something to expound on in this manner. Marimuthu did not want to give him a reason this time, so he picked the lemons with care and walked away from the market. All around him were the sounds of sheep and their traders and the voices of fruit vendors yelling things like 'Five for one rupee!'

Marimuthu walked away from all of these, thinking about how he would proceed if it turned out that the teacher did not have anything positive to offer him that day. What would be his excuse to end the visits for good? But why did he need to offer an explanation? He could just stop going. However, for all the money he had spent so far with these visits, he felt he had to say something. On the other hand, if Marimuthu's horoscope was a hopeless one, what was the point in taking it out on the teacher? The man was just trying to have a lucrative career in his retirement.

He spoke so much about good conduct, but Marimuthu wondered why there had not been much evidence of all that good conduct in his own life as a teacher. None of the boys had liked him as a teacher.

He always carried betel leaves and nuts in a box. The moment he entered the classroom, everyone had to go absolutely silent. He'd open his metal betel box. The boys would look at the engraving on the lid of the box—two deer leaping. The box always shone brightly, evidence that it had been rubbed clean with tamarind. The teacher would unroll the betel leaf carefully, smear some lime paste on it, place some pieces of areca nut, fold it all carefully and stuff it into his mouth. All this would take ten minutes. He'd start talking only after he had chewed the betel carefully and the juices had started flowing in his mouth. He was the head teacher for that section. Marimuthu was in the seventh standard then, and that was his math class. But he had no recollection of the man ever teaching any math.

It was also the year when there was some big excitement in local politics. A leader from the KMK party had defected, started his own party and was gearing up to contest the state legislative assembly elections. The betel-box teacher was a strong KMK loyalist. He would turn the classroom into a political rally. He'd imagine himself to be the speaker and turn the students into a mute public. He would hold forth, his voice rising and falling, speeding up, expressing anger, raising questions.

'Do you think a man who wields a cardboard knife is going to protect this country? Don't you have to know politics? You call yourself a great actor? Can you even cry? You turn your face away from the camera to cry! Have you even been to a protest? Have you been wounded? Do you know what action means? Do you think it means holding on to an actress' sari and running around a tree? You start your own party?! Such shit-eating . . .'

That was how the speech would go. The students had no idea what he was saying. All they knew was that the teacher was attacking the leader of the new party. But why? What had any of this got to do with math lessons? The entire year went like that. At the end of it, the only thing the boys remembered was that betel nut box.

12

It was the strong memory of that betel nut box that brought the teacher back to Marimuthu's mind. He had long contemplated the fate that made him repeatedly seek out that man and his insults. Even now, when Marimuthu was pulling up in front of the teacher's house on his motorbike with two empty baskets in the front, he was certain he would hear some lecture on good conduct. The man was very astute. He had a way of extracting information that was relevant to him. The first time he had run into the teacher somewhere, he had asked his name and village.

Then he asked, 'Are you married?'

Marimuthu said, 'No,' and lowered his head in embarrassment. Then the teacher gave him the directions to his house and asked Marimuthu to pay him a visit.

'I run a matrimonial information business now. Come and see me. We will get you married in a month. I have several horoscopes of girls. When you come, bring a copy of your horoscope and a passport-size photo.'

Marimuthu showed up at his place the very next morning. There was a huge wooden sign outside the house:

'Yogam Matrimony'. Under the name of the business, it said, 'Consultant: P. Subramaniyan, Teacher (Retired)'. That was the first time Marimuthu got to know his teacher's name.

From the faded quality of the signboard, he surmised that the man had been in the business for at least a few years. He took Marimuthu to a room on the rooftop. He was thrilled that Marimuthu had come to see him the very next day. That room had been set aside as an office space for his marriage brokering business. So far, all the other brokers Marimuthu had met did home visits. If he was busy working in the orchard, they went there to talk to him. But this 'betel-nut box' teacher worked differently. He made people go to him.

He brought down a number of files from the shelf and laid them in front of Marimuthu. They were filled with information about the people who were waiting to be married. There were forms with a photo affixed on each and containing relevant details about the person. And a copy of the horoscope was attached. He then explained to Marimuthu the terms.

'First, you need to pay five hundred rupees and register yourself. Then, when a girl's family comes to me looking for a suitable match, I will share your horoscope with them. Likewise, you will receive the horoscopes of prospective brides. You can read the information given in the applications and pick the ones that appeal to you. Once you get the horoscopes scrutinized and let me know if the match works, then I can arrange for you to meet them directly. Let's say you are from the parrot clan, then

your application will go into that file there. I have different
files for men from different groups. And likewise for the
girls. Do you know how many girls there are in this group?
There are sixty as far as I know,' he said, laughing.

Marimuthu found a reason for hope in that. If there
were sixty girls waiting to be married, at least one of them
could be a match for him? The teacher spoke further.

'I do this only for our community. I don't get a big
income out of this. In my old age, when my daughters
all got married and left the house, I decided to serve my
community in my own small way. That's how I got into
this.'

Marimuthu was quite amazed to know that vocation
and service could grow out of an attachment to the
community. He liked the teacher's sense of care. So what
if he had not been a good math teacher? He was going to
bring some true change in Marimuthu's life. That's what
Marimuthu came to believe that day.

He told Marimuthu about the various alliances he
had successfully secured. His work went far beyond
the few districts that Marimuthu had thought were the
main settlements for their peasant community. Teacher
even mentioned neighbouring states. 'Our people are
the majority there,' he said. His work had even extended
abroad. Marimuthu paid up the five hundred rupees and
registered himself right away. After seeing the photos
attached to the applications, he wanted to get a new photo
taken. Teacher read his mind.

'Bring a better photo when you come next. Just go to
Devaji's studio and say my name. He'll take an excellent

photo. Now read the applications and take the horoscopes that look good to you. For each horoscope you take, you need to pay a fifty-rupee fee. Look in all the files for girls from communities other than yours,' he said and went downstairs. Marimuthu started browsing through the files. He could tell right away that the girls in the photos were of what one might say 'our kind'. But they were all well-qualified. He was surprised to see so many girls had had such good education.

He suddenly realized that there was a whole other world he didn't know. He had failed his tenth standard. But he set 'twelfth pass' as the level desired for the girl. Even then, he found only a few. And from among those, only two seemed suited for him. He now felt discouraged. Observing him, Mr Betel Nut Box said, 'You come back next week. I will keep ten horoscopes vetted and ready for you.'

After that, he got one or two so-so horoscopes from him each time. He'd go from time to time to get those from teacher. The man would indulge in sweet talk, foist two horoscopes on him and milk him of one hundred rupees. So, whenever he went to see him, Marimuthu had to make sure his wallet was loaded.

This time when Marimuthu parked the bike outside and entered the house, the teacher was seated on a recliner and reading the newspaper. When he gave him the two lemons, Marimuthu noticed how his face softened and blossomed into a smile. Then teacher picked up his betel nut box and took Marimuthu to the room upstairs.

'I have set aside two horoscopes for you. I have a feeling one of them will work out. I feel bad that things have not gone great for you for some reason. But it is going to happen this time. You will see.'

Marimuthu felt a bit hopeful at those words. But he thought they still needed to know what exactly that 'some reason' was. So far, he did not think there was any rhyme or reason for things turning out the way they did. But if someone gave him a hundred rupees, Marimuthu too would gladly speak even finer words of hope.

The moment he read the two applications, he realized neither of those would work for him. They might be from the same peasant community, but there was a lot of difference between people who lived on either side of the river. One of the girls seemed to be from the other side of the river. Those people usually hesitated to marry into families on his side. They made an exception only if they really liked the groom and he had a very good job. These families grew sugarcane and turmeric, and they were usually ready to offer several kilograms of gold. So, they did not even consider men who were into farming or trade. On this side of the river, no man usually went past high school. By then, the families pulled him into traditional occupations.

The other girl had completed her schooling and had learned typewriting. Now she was pursuing an undergraduate degree by correspondence. She was also temporarily employed in a computer training centre. She did not look at all to Marimuthu as the kind of girl who would pick a farmer to marry. He resolved to thwart the broker's plan of foisting these two horoscopes on him and milking him of a hundred rupees.

'What is it, thambi? Why are you looking like that? Both these families expressly said they would consider farmers. That's why I picked these for you.'

Teacher's wife brought two glasses of lemon juice. Around her neck she wore a gold chain as thick as a rope. Mr Betel Nut Box smiled, his fat face expanding, and offered Marimuthu a glass. Juice with ice cubes in it. It felt cool and comforting in Marimuthu's stomach. He had been thirsty since that breakfast of idlis and koottucchaaru at the market. The juice was perfect for that. But he was not going to be fooled by any of this.

He had fifteen years of experience dealing with such brokers. This might be a new kind of place, the man might present himself differently, but the fact was that he was a broker. So, he employed all the machinations that were the tricks of the trade. It was indeed true that all that novelty of registration and organized filing system had somewhat clouded Marimuthu's judgement in the beginning. But now it was clear to him that none of that was going to help in any way. So, he spoke as soon as he set the glass down.

'Neither of these will work out for us, sir. If something else comes up, please call me on the phone.'

Then, without waiting for an answer, he rushed downstairs and out, started his bike and left. That was it. He had closed this chapter. There was no way he would come back here. If he had stayed sitting there, smiling and grinning and talking to him, teacher would have started off on some story. He would have gone into great detail about some marriage alliance he had recently secured.

Surely the bride or the groom would have been out of state. It would certainly have been a long-delayed marriage, but would have come to fruition only a month after teacher's intervention. Bragging just seemed to go with the idea of becoming a professional. He might have told Marimuthu that he would find two new horoscopes for him next week. And Marimuthu would have kept wasting two lemons every week.

As he sped away from there, he recollected one match that teacher had found him in the past. The moment he saw the girl's photo, he'd felt happy. She was beautiful in a simple way. It looked like she was not anxious at all that the photo was being taken for matrimonial purposes. She seemed natural and unaffected. Just a little bit of talcum powder on her face. Bright eyes. She wore a very thin chain necklace. The information given about her was also perfect. She had only completed tenth standard. Agrarian family. When they checked the horoscopes, they found it was an eight-count match. Marimuthu built a lot of hope around that.

The girl was from Mongoor. Marimuthu's former classmate Senthil was from that village. Even though it was years since they had been in school together, Senthil was still very friendly. Whenever they ran into each other, they always stopped for a chat and had tea together before going their separate ways. Senthil owned and drove two lorries. Marimuthu decided that he would go to Mongoor on the pretext of seeing Senthil and would find out about the girl. He was tired of other people doing that job for him.

Fortunately, Senthil was home that day. He said he had returned just the week before from some long lorry trip. He was delighted that Marimuthu had come all the way to Mongoor just to see him. He had a four-year-old son. They took the kid along and went to the temple in that village. It was quite a famous temple.

Every month, food offerings from that temple came to Marimuthu's house. Once a year, the priest came and collected the annual contribution from them. Every time he visited, he pointed out how high the postal rates had gone. And Marimuthu's mother would argue with the priest about the amount to be given. So, Marimuthu had some strong connections with that temple. Once or twice, he had even attended the festivities around the Maha Amavasai, the most important new moon night of the year.

When he went to the temple with Senthil that day, he felt a particular fondness for the place. He stood looking for a long time at the deities who seemed to radiate compassion. He even made a pact. 'If this alliance works out, I will sacrifice a pig for the Maha Amavasai.' There was no temple where he had not promised some such offering. Once he got married, it would take years to fulfil those promises.

As they sat in the shade of a tree in the outer precincts of the temple, Marimuthu hesitantly showed Senthil the photo of the girl. Senthil did not say anything about her. Instead, he said, 'Come with me. Let's just go and see her.' Marimuthu didn't know what was happening.

The house was in the middle of a secluded farmstead. A big house with a brick-tiled roof. Senthil received a warm welcome there. It seemed they were in-laws.

'Come, come, mapillai! When did you return from your road trip?'

Once these exchanges were over, Senthil said, 'Where is Amudha?'

Amudha emerged from inside the house with a child on her hip. 'Come, mama! I was inside, just feeding the boy.' Thaali around her neck, a child on her hip. Betel Nut Box had taken fifty rupees from Marimuthu in exchange for the horoscope of a married woman.

In the Thambiyan story, his clansmen give him an iron-soled shoe and tell him that he could get married when they wear out. Marimuthu wondered if god had done the same thing with him. Perhaps God had slid on an invisible pair of iron-soled shoes on Marimuthu's feet. He was not able to shake them off. He tried to wear them out by dragging them on rocks until his feet were exhausted. It made a huge racket but showed no signs of breaking. How long would it take to be rid of the ironclad shoes?

13

Taking all the purchases from the market in a bag, Marimuthu set out from his house to go see his paatti, his paternal grandmother. The day was beginning to slant towards dusk. When she saw him leaving with a bag of things, his mother mumbled something. She no more had the courage to express her grievances out loud. And he did not bother to respond to mumblings.

It had been some years since he and his mother fell out. The conflicts around matchmaking for Marimuthu had become quite severe, and they had stopped talking to each other altogether. Though ammayi usually tended to take sides with his mother, now she was the only person who served as a bridge between the two. 'Ammayi, I will be late. I will sleep in the shed,' he shouted out.

In fact, conflicts with his mother had come to a head on a market day, a Thursday just like today. It had been long since paatti stopped going to the market. Since she knew Marimuthu religiously went every week, she just gave him a list. One Thursday morning, Marimuthu was about to leave for the market with paatti's shopping list when

he heard his mother say, 'There he goes running errands
for that widowed old hag. He is her husband. He buys
her things from the market. He also buys her the rags she
wears.'

He was stung by her words. In rage, he kicked hard
a large metal pot that was nearby. It rolled and collided
with the grinding stone, reverberated for a while and went
silent. He picked up the old stone pestle that was lying
around and flung it towards his mother. It bounced against
the door frame and fell to the floor. His mother ran into
the house and locked herself in a room.

'Ayyo! He is trying to kill me!' she yelled from inside.
He kicked the door hard. Then he sat down by the
entrance, breathless. He wondered where ammayi was. He
considered both of them—his mother and her mother—as
devils who had come to ruin his life. He had come to have
an intense hatred towards them.

A possible match had come for him through his paatti,
but his mother had refused vehemently to consider it. The
girl was paatti's older brother's granddaughter. Paatti had
two older brothers and one younger brother. She maintained
cordial relationships with all of them. It seems to be in a
woman's nature to gradually push away her husband's relatives
and become closer to her own. Even Marimuthu was now
closer to the mother's side of the family than his father's. He
had an athai, a paternal aunt. But the relationship was quite
lukewarm. Marimuthu's father did not have any brothers of
his own, so no close paternal uncles. He did have one distant
paternal uncle, who was the son of his granduncle, but the
families had severed their ties with each other.

Paatti was keen on keeping her connections to her brother's family strong. She had been the only girl in the family, and the brothers had showered her with great care and affection. Even after her marriage, her brothers came to her aid whenever she was in need. Paatti always teared up when she started talking about her natal home. No matter how wonderful relationships were, if you wanted them to last, there had to be some kind of exchange. If she got her brother's granddaughter married to Marimuthu, the families would be bound together for the next generation as well. It seemed like human nature to desire immortality in the perpetuation of blood relations down generations.

That girl was two years younger than Marimuthu. They had played together as children. When he was in seventh or eighth standard, he had even swum in the well with her, holding her close as they both jumped in. They'd played in the water, she trying to get away, he trying to catch her. He was embarrassed thinking about all that.

One wouldn't call her a great beauty, but she was quite good-looking. At certain angles, he could even see touches of paatti's resemblance. If Marimuthu married her, they would have all those childhood memories to talk about. She might even accuse him of lechery, recalling his behaviour from those days. But she had loved the attention too.

Once paatti started talking about this potential match, Marimuthu started observing the girl closely during family functions. She had been a snotty-nosed kid, but now she was a beautiful young woman.

Or perhaps she just appeared to him that way. He felt a rush of affection for her. He thought she would be a good companion. By the time they came to consider the match seriously, it was the month of Aadi. People didn't take up any matrimonial matters in Aadi. So, Marimuthu waited eagerly for the month to be over.

But even before that, his mother found a reason to decline the match. The girl's mother had started developing a discolouration of skin around her lips and fingers. His mother made a big deal out of it. 'Is it my fate to marry a leper's daughter to my son? Should all my future generations be cursed with leprosy?' She was relentless about it. Paatti couldn't say anything. So that was the end of it.

In the rainy season, when the lake brimmed with water, there was plenty of fish. People came in droves carrying fishing rods and nets to catch loads of fish. Then the lake quickly ran out of fish, with only a few left deep at the bottom. Marimuthu now felt like a person who had arrived at the lake long after people had taken away baskets of fish.

More than the fact that Marimuthu was having trouble getting married, what bothered paatti was that she was losing out on strengthening ties with her brother's family. After that episode, the relationship between his mother and paatti grew strained and knotty. It showed no signs of relenting. It had been months since the two women had even looked at each other.

14

By the time Marimuthu arrived at the hut, which looked like a giant mushroom growing on that wide expanse of elevated land, the sky had turned a melancholic red. Marimuthu's paternal grandmother and grandfather had been the ones to build that house near the orchard where his family now lived. But once their son had married and had children of his own, the grandparents had quietly moved into this cottage. Grandfather had died some time ago, so now paatti lived alone here.

Paatti had a no-nonsense approach to life. 'I am not a young woman. I don't have money or jewellery to guard. All I have is a body that happens to be above the earth right now, but will one day be below it,' she once said. As Marimuthu arrived, he could tell even from a distance that there was a robust fire burning in the stove, as if paatti was competing with the sky to the west. For a moment, Marimuthu panicked, wondering if the thatched panels of the hut had caught fire. He dropped his bag and ran into the house.

Paatti was sitting in front of the stove, and there was a blackened mud pot on it. The fire rose higher than the pot,

threatening to touch the thatched roof. It only needed to
reach a little higher to swallow the entire hut in its flames.
But, oblivious to what was going on, paatti was adding more
firewood into the stove. Against the glow of the flames, she
looked like that witch who sat with her legs stretched out
into a fire, casually tearing up and eating bodies.

Marimuthu rushed to the stove, pulled out the kindling
and brought the flame down. Shaking her unkempt head
that looked like a crow's nest, she said, 'Who is that?'

'You would have burned the hut down! Why did you
have the fire so big?'

She recognized him by his voice. The pot on the stove
was hot and sizzling.

'What kuzhambu are you making, aaya?'

'Tomato. I brought some from the garden today.
I thought I'd mash them in and make a kuzhambu.'

'You go and sit outside. I will make it.'

Paatti got up and, looking like a spider on its spindly
legs, she walked out to the porch. Marimuthu lowered the
flames further and poured some oil into the pot. Since he
had not done this in a long time, he felt a bit unsure.

When he was a little boy, his mother left home early
in the morning to work in the fields. Marimuthu and his
sister made their own food and ate it before rushing off
to school. They never expected anyone to cook for them.
They'd just rustle up something quickly.

Now, he cooked the tomatoes slowly and then brought
the pot down before he mashed it into a kuzhambu. It
smelled wonderful. He poured a drop into the palm of his
hand and tasted it to check for salt. He thought that both

salt and spice levels were just right, but he didn't know what paatti might say. Now that he had brought the fire down, darkness spread over the hut. 'Why haven't you lit the lamp?' he shouted. She staggered back into the house, felt her way to the lamp and handed it over to him.

'Heat some water for me on the stove, dear. I will feel better only after a wash.'

She spoke like a child. Marimuthu found the pot for boiling water and placed it on the stove. Then he blew at the wood, and the fire started again right away. He decided to let the fire come up on its own, and he walked outside the hut and sat down on the cot laid there. Paatti had untied her hair, and she now sat running her fingers through it.

'Why can't you finish cooking when there is still daylight? Why do you have to struggle in the dark?' he asked with some anger.

'It is not like that, payya,' she said in a conciliatory tone. 'I went to Vallama's house to help shell groundnuts. It got late by the time I returned. Besides, how long does it take to cook for one person?'

She was losing her vision, but that did not stop her from going out to work. Many other elderly people in the village had been to cities like Madurai and Coimbatore, got eye surgeries done and were now even wearing glasses. But paatti adamantly resisted the idea. 'In all my life, I have never taken medicines, never had an injection. I am not going to start now.'

Even though he knew that paatti went out to work in the fields every day, it still made him angry to think about it. What was the need for her to work? Did she have daughters to marry off? He took care of all the market expenses. He also made sure she had more than enough rice. She even had four or five new saris that she had not even worn yet. She always wore some old rags. 'I wander in the dust and grime of the fields. Why do I need to wear new clothes?' she said.

It was true that paatti had endured much hardship in her life and had made sure things were alright for the family. But she did not have to continue to struggle. They were quite self-sufficient now, but she couldn't seem to bring herself to enjoy anything fully. She was always anxious about some future misery, and she rolled and tucked cash inside pots and in the gaps and crevices of the thatched panels.

If anyone needed some cash urgently, they could find it in paatti's hut in at least four or five hiding spots. She always forgot how much she kept and where. Marimuthu had long tried to find some other living arrangement for paatti, but he had not succeeded so far.

She would listen to his advice and ideas patiently, nodding her head. But then she would go right back to the way she had always been. Elderly folks were like old banyan trees. They stood firm even after losing their main root. This time, Marimuthu decided to speak to paatti in a way that might appeal to her sense of pride.

'Aaya . . . from now on, please don't go out to work for anyone. It does not matter whether they ask you to or not. You don't understand these things. You think that it speaks highly of you that you are working hard well into your old age. But do you know what others say about you?'

'What do they say, those wretched widows?'

'Now, please stop such talk. You used to be sweet and kind. What happened to that? You went to do some weeding work in Sitthaan's field, didn't you? Apparently, they said, "These oldies with no life left in them come to do wage work. Such a waste of our money."'

'Who said that? Let me tell you. Even a twenty-year-old girl cannot work as efficiently as I do. Somebody said, it seems! And you just quietly listened to it?!'

'That's not the end of it, aaya . . . It seems they also said, "This old hag can't even see properly. She can't tell the weed from the crop!"'

'Do you believe all this?'

Paatti sounded quite upset and sad. But that was exactly what Marimuthu had intended to achieve. It gave him much pleasure to tease and play with her. It was like playing with a really old child.

'How could I not? Take today, for instance. If I had not come at the right time, the hut would have caught fire. Your vision's gone bad. And you won't even go see a doctor.'

'That's only in the dark, payya. Do you think I have trouble seeing during the day as well?'

'Yes, you do. Why else would I bring this up? Why do we have to listen to people say such hurtful things? I find it humiliating.'

'Why should YOU feel humiliated?'

'Well, apparently, they talk about you even at the tea shop. They say, "Do you know Marimuthu's paatti? She still works hard to amass wealth for her grandson."'

'Why do they care?'

'You went to sort groundnuts, didn't you? You know what they said about that? That you couldn't tell good ones from bad.'

'Really! As if I wouldn't know the difference!'

'They said you mixed them all up.'

'Payya . . .'

'I am not saying these things. People in the village are. When they broke open the ones you had sorted, they found very few nuts in them. That's what they say.'

Marimuthu had mixed truths with lies. It was his wish to put an end to paatti's labouring in other people's fields. He had been trying to accomplish this for a few years now, but in vain. Now he did not want to let go of the opportunity.

He checked the water in the pot on the stove. It was warm. But paatti wanted nice hot water for her bath even in the summer. She'd say that was the best thing for body ache. 'Try taking a hot water bath before bed. You will sleep beautifully,' she'd say. Breaking and adding some sticks to the fire, Marimuthu carried on.

'From now on, you need not go anywhere out to work. Sell the buffalo calf. Do some work in and around the house. And sleep and rest well.'

'How long could I sleep and rest?'

'Alright. Take a walk by the coconut grove. See the water going down the channels. Have your bath there if you wish. Then you can take a nap there in the shade on a cot.'

'What else?'

'Then come to our house. Stay with us for a few days. My mother might keep a long face. That's true. So what?

Let her be. Chat with ammayi. If you don't want to talk to
her either, don't. Speak to the farm help. We have cows
and calves. Watch them for a while. Talk to them.'

'Mm,' she said, as if she was agreeing. But there was a
tinge of mockery in it.

'Then go visit your daughter for a few days. Ask her
daughter-in-law to make some snacks for you. Take some
fruits for them when you go. They won't let you leave.'

'Right. What is it they say about the old man in the
childless family? That he imagined himself to be the child?
Your aunt's son has been married ten years now. Why
would I go there carrying gifts of fruit now? And yes, she
will pamper me with chicken kuzhambu and sambar rice
meal! Like that's going to happen!'

'Why not? Then, from there, go to your granddaughter's
house. Spend four or five days there. Give her son hundred
rupees for the festival season. Pack and take all your new
saris with you.'

'Oh, really?!'

'Of course! If you don't wear them now, then when? If
you don't wear them when you are alive, they'd just drape
those saris over your body when you are dead. What's the
point in that? You won't be able to look at yourself wearing
them, would you?'

'That's true.'

'That's why I am telling you. You have worked and
earned and saved enough. There is no need for you to go
out to work anymore.'

'Is that so? Then maybe we should even appoint
someone to do the cooking for me?'

Paatti was merely amused by all his ideas. She had never thought about simply enjoying the fruits of her hard work. She had never considered the possibility that there could be happiness in doing nothing.

The water was steaming hot now. He brought the pot and placed it outside behind the hut.

'Sure. We can hire someone to do the cooking for you.'

'No matter how much you are ready to pay for the job, do you think any woman would agree to come and cook for me? A worker woman might come, perhaps' she laughed, referring to a woman from a lower caste.

He could hear her laughter. What more could he say? She had a way of laughing it all away and going about her life the way she wanted.

By the time she finished her bath, Marimuthu put food on a plate for her. He also served himself. Gently blowing at the rice to cool it down, she ate with relish. 'You have made this gravy really well, payya.' There was a gentle breeze. The stars in the sky looked like someone had sprinkled rice puffs. It gave him much joy sitting out in the dark and sharing a meal with his paatti.

These days, he couldn't take much pleasure in eating. He just ate because he had to. But this meal was different. He was able to enjoy every mouthful. The tomatoes had been mashed to a pulp. He could drink that kuzhambu. After making sure there was enough left for paatti, he helped himself to more. There was just enough for the two of them. There'd be nothing left for paatti for the morning. But it was always the case that only something made in small quantities tasted the best.

'Why are you struggling in the dark to cook for yourself? Starting tomorrow, I will ask them to send you every meal. If we put it in a bag, the farmhand can bring it to you.'

Paatti felt that Marimuthu was pulling hard at her very life nerve. Did he mean to stop her from functioning altogether? If she started relying on others for everything, what was the difference between being alive and dead? She only felt happy in walking to the well and fetching the water herself, no matter how hard it was. How would she feel comfortable if someone else did that for her? Paatti inhabited a different world. Marimuthu wouldn't be able to grasp even the tip of it.

'I will do these things as long as I am able to, payya. I cannot do nothing. What's the point in being alive?'

'I never asked you to do nothing.'

'What do you want me to do? You are suddenly asking me to go visit all these people. Why the hell would I go visiting anyone? I'd rather die right here in my own house. You think I will go sit in someone else's house, eating their food?'

Marimuthu was shocked at the force with which these words came from that skeletal frame of hers. She was talking about her son's, daughter's, granddaughter's families as if they were strangers. She may not be very fond of these people, but they were her relatives.

'If people don't like my work, why do they come calling? Why do they ask me to go and work for them? I have never set foot on anyone's field without being invited.'

'Maybe they ask you because they can't find enough people for the work.'

'Even then, why would they call someone who can't do the job? I need to work and save enough money at least to take care of my funeral.'

'As if that is going to be a big expense! Won't I take care of all that?'

'All my relatives will come to do their duties. Your aunt will come. Your sister will come. Will you send them all back empty-handed? Let's say you are the generous one who takes care of my funeral expenses. What do you think people will say? Won't they say, "It looks like she died without leaving a penny behind?"'

'Why should we care what anyone says?'

'Why not? Even you might say, "My paatti's funeral expenses came to twenty thousand. I spent it." That's what you will say.'

'Oh, really?'

'Of course! If you were married and had children of your own, you would understand what I am trying to say. You are an unmarried fellow scratching about the land. What would you know?'

Those words landed hard on his chest. He went silent. Everyone had their weapons ready. And they did not hesitate to use them when they found their chance.

15

The night sky lay stretched bright and clear. Stars appeared, looking like darkness' own eyes of fire. He could hear some motor vehicle at a distance. The air was absolutely still. He had been happy talking to his paatti, but it had ended with her throwing a load of burning coal on that happiness. Did she do that to get back at him for teasing her? Or was it entirely spontaneous and unpremeditated?

Marimuthu was lying on a cot outside the hut, looking up at the sky. His mind seemed empty and wanting, but he could not figure out what to fill it with. There were so many things to think about, but there was that one thing that occupied his mind, that tormented him. Only someone reaping the consequences of several lifetimes of bad deeds would have to go through this, he felt. Once you have attained something, it does not occupy your mind in this manner. It's the thing you are unable to get that magnifies itself and takes over everything.

Why did people think a single, unmarried man could not understand the world, understand other people? How did it work? The moment a woman joined a man's side, were all the mysteries of the world suddenly revealed to him? Did that mean it was women who had turned everything into an inexplicable puzzle? Then how was he to make sense of his life? Was he currently doing whatever he was doing without any understanding of it? After all, he did know a great deal about farming.

He could turn even raised pastures that others had given up on into fertile fields producing horse gram or foxgram. He was definitely adept at cultivating paddy. In the last ten years, he had been handling household accounts on his own. It had taken him just a day to take over the bookkeeping from his mother.

One year, during the time of groundnut harvest, he made up his mind. From then on, he wouldn't ask his mother even for a penny. She had funded the harvest expenses. But when he returned after having sold the sacks of peanuts, he kept the money with himself. The first day, she did not bring up the subject. She hoped he would give it to her soon. But when he did not give her the money even the next day, she panicked and asked ammayi to find out what he intended to do with it.

'Let it be with me.' That's all he said.

The moment she realized that that was the end of her control over the finances, she started her rant. 'Things have crossed a line. If he acts like this even before his marriage, imagine what he will do after! He will give me an alms bowl and send me begging.' And: 'He thinks he has become a big man now? What do I do with the money? I only spend it on this family. Does he think I have some four or five unmarried sisters and I am saving up the money to marry them off?' And: 'Who is he to keep my money? I fed him from my own breasts. Now he flings mud at me.' She said whatever came to her lips. But Marimuthu did not respond to any of it, so she took her complaints to his father.

The father said, 'Did you expect he would just take after me? Did you think he would just work the land, drink toddy and keep to himself? He is *your* son too. He'd have at least half your brain, won't he? Just let him be. If he is keeping accounts, let him keep the money too.'

Once her husband had given his opinion on the matter, there was nothing much she could do. She spent the next two days in bed, crying and refusing to eat. Ammayi consoled her. Then she was slowly back to normal. She made sure the money from the milk sales came directly to her. And Marimuthu did not interfere with that.

In this way, Marimuthu had managed to secure control over the entire household accounts. But today, paatti had asked him, 'What would an unmarried man know about the world?' In fact, when he had taken over the finances from his mother, paatti had supported him. She had said, 'He's been born just to bring her under control.'

He knew a great deal about many things. But perhaps knowing was different from understanding? Perhaps, just like paatti had said, he lacked understanding? If it was true that only marriage would bring understanding, did that also mean Marimuthu was destined never to understand how the world worked?'

He felt exhausted and discouraged. He tried to close his eyes and go to sleep. Ignorant of all that was troubling his mind, paatti was out feeding the buffalo calf. Then she called out to the dog and gave it some food. She cleaned and put back the dishes. And as she went about these tasks, she kept talking. She lashed out at all the people who called her out to work but spoke ill of her.

He could not hear her words clearly, but her rant reached him as a vague, intermittent sound in the background. He had nothing left to say to her. She had shattered all his arguments and disarmed him with just one word. 'Unmarried'. What a reputation to bear! He should have lost that epithet as soon as he had turned twenty. But clearly, he was destined to hear that at this age from paatti's lips.

Now, he could not even remember what he'd wanted to talk to her about. He chided himself for forgetting his purpose and instead getting into an argument with her about something else.

The land. That was the only way now to distance himself for a while from the question of marriage. This was his chance. It would take some time to survey the land, divide it up and make it his. It had been lying unused for a long time. So, it was not fit for cultivation right away. He would have to spend at least two years to get it ready. The well needed to be repaired, or they'd have to fix a new borewell.

If he engaged himself in rendering that land cultivable, his mind would be distracted from marriage and stuff. Now, he was already beginning to imagine what he would do with that land. It calmed his mind to think of that land turning into a coconut grove.

Paatti sat down on her cot, letting out a sigh of relief at finally being done with the day's work. She would fall asleep quickly. It was not like she had things plaguing her mind. She said, 'Payya . . . are you asleep?' He was not in a mood to talk. He just said, 'Mm.' But it looked like she was in the mood to talk to him.

'There was something I wanted to ask you. Is it true that the issues with our red-soil land are going to be resolved?'

He had not spoken about it to anyone since matchmaker thatha had brought it up. But clearly, the word had spread and even reached paatti who lived alone in a hut in a remote corner of the fields. Marimuthu guessed that his uncle's family must have been discussing it. Why were they in such a hurry to settle the inheritance among their sons? For a moment, Marimuthu considered ruining everything for them by saying he was not ready to talk about the land yet. But then he remembered that his cousin Selvarasu had been the one to intervene in the matter. That gave him pause. Alright, then. He had wanted to talk about this with paatti, and now she had brought it up herself.

'They have asked me, aaya. I told them I'd speak to them after consulting you.'

'Why do you need to consult me? I'd be dead any day. What's the point in asking me? Ask your father, ask your mother. Ask even your ammayi who has now plonked herself here. Why not speak to all of them?'

Paatti did not seem to understand that Marimuthu was really treating her as someone special by coming to her for advice. He now realized that this could be his chance to remedy some of the things he had said earlier about her old age and inability to work.

'You are the one who knows about that land. Why would I speak about it with anyone else?'

'That's true. Starting from the day I got married and moved there, I toiled so much in that land. A part of that earth is still clung to my heart, payya . . .'

Paatti was beginning to reminisce. But Marimuthu wanted to change course and bring the discussion to the present.

'Shall we agree to the plans to divide up the land?'

'Why do you have to ask? It is a wonderful piece of land! Red soil everywhere. Anything you plant will thrive on that land. In fact, none of our current lands could even come closer. I used to wonder if I would ever get a chance to set foot on that land, work in it . . . But the opportunity has come now. Accept the offer and work the land.'

'I wanted to have this conversation with you before I agreed to it. I did not want to do it if it was going to make you unhappy.'

'A good farmer should not let a land lie unused. What happened in the past was unfortunate. All because of that wretched woman. And she did not live long enough to see the land being cultivated again. At least let me be the fortunate one to see the land being used again.'

Marimuthu was amazed at her fondness for that piece of land. It also occurred to him that if paatti had passed on earlier, she'd have died with a big, unfulfilled desire in her heart. Now he had to get things moving, if only for paatti's sake.

'Alright, aaya. I will speak to them tomorrow. We can get it done.'

'Payya, another thing. As you go about the process, be very careful with your words. That whore—she is a cunning woman. Be very careful what you say.'

Paatti sat up on the cot. He was amused at her opinion of his uncle's wife.

'What could she do? They have to give us the half that is rightfully ours, don't they?'

'Not that. When they divide the land, there will be questions about how much of the low-lying land, how much of the elevated land, and all that.'

'Alright. You tell me how you think it should be done.'

Paatti untied her hair and rolled it up into a bun again.

'The red-soil land is a total of three and a half acres, isn't it? When they divide, it is not just a straightforward matter of one-and-three-quarters acres each.'

'Really?'

'Yes. In those days, in the two big plots of land closer to the lake, they dug for sand for making bricks. That brick-tiled house where your uncle lives now? It was built from bricks they made using sand from those two plots of land. My in-laws had set up an entire brick kiln for this purpose in those days. But when they divided the property later, they gave the house to the younger son. And your grandfather didn't dispute it because he was fond of his brother. But he got cheated.'

'Never mind, paatti. We should let it go.'

'That's exactly why we lost everything. Because we kept letting things go! Your grandfather let it go. Now see where I live. In an old hut in the middle of nowhere.'

'Why go into that story again, aaya? Tell me how the land should be apportioned now.'

'That's what I am trying to tell you. Because they dug sand for bricks, a portion of that land appears sunken. They would say that whoever gets that sunken piece of land should be given extra land in compensation. If they ask you which land you want, you should say, "Since my grandfather was the older of the two heirs, I will take the elevated land."'

'And if they agree to it?'

'How would they? They will want the elevated land too! Who would willingly pick a sunken piece of land?'

'Alright.'

'Then, if both parties want the elevated land, there will be a conflict. Then they'll say they will give you extra land if you take the low-lying section near the lake. Now, if they give you enough extra land in compensation, accept it and take the low-lying land.'

'What are you saying?!'

'See, the well will go to the person who owns the low-lying land. Don't agree to sharing the well. Make sure it belongs to you.'

'A well is not a big deal these days, aaya. We can set up a borewell system.'

'Don't do that. There is a source of groundwater in the well in the eastern corner between the rocks. It does not dry up even in summer. That water tastes different—it is sweet. You know that terrible famine we had in those days? There was water in our well even then. The entire village relied on that water for drinking. No borewell can get you water like that.'

'You think that source of water is still alive?'

'If we desilt the well properly and build it up with stones, we can definitely irrigate up to ten acres. In the rainy season, the water level comes up. It was during one of those times that Muniyan's mother, that old woman, weighed herself with a rock and jumped into the well. It took us two days to know she was in there. We couldn't get all the water out even after a night's work.'

Listening to paatti, Marimuthu now had clearer thoughts. He would speak to the old matchmaker tomorrow, expressing his consent to the plan to apportion the land. Then he would go take a look at the land.

'Do you think it might take about six months for all of this to be done?'

He felt a jolt at the mention of 'six months'. He remembered his deadline.

'Hmm,' he said.

'When that red-soil land comes in your possession, may something else good happen to you too.'

Paatti blessed him wholeheartedly. Matchmaker thatha had said the same thing. Maybe they were right. Maybe he was destined to find a woman to marry only when the land was settled. Paatti went on talking about the land. Marimuthu kept 'mm'-ing in response to her, but his thoughts were elsewhere. If paatti was indeed right that 'something good' was to come from that land, it should have, in fact, come long ago.

16

It happened five or six years ago in the month of Aippasi. That was when Marimuthu became friends with his uncle's son, Selvarasu. There had been some heavy rains that year, so much so that they had not had enough sun to dry the groundnuts they had harvested. Finally, he decided to sell them undried and took them to the market. The auction took place twice a week, and those who brought produce to auction needed to find a place in the market to store them.

It so happened that the sacks of produce from his uncle's land were placed not far from where Marimuthu had unloaded his, and his cousin Selvarasu was there to watch over them. They did not talk to each other right away. They had grown up internalizing the animosity between the families. If they talked and were seen being friendly with each other, it could lead to trouble. Marimuthu's mother would be so enraged, she would heat up a metal spoon and burn a mark on his skin. His aunt would feel equally intensely about it. Marriage or death, the two families never visited each other.

Once, someone who lived close to the uncle's place died. The deceased person's family didn't have water with which to cook for the guests who showed up for condolences. So, they had to use water from their neighbour's—that is, Marimuthu's uncle's—well. Marimuthu's mother refused to eat the food simply because they had used water from a family she was estranged from. Once hostilities were openly declared, the families were not supposed to talk to each other or exchange food. These things were taken quite seriously. They could resume any kind of exchange only after the families came together and made proper offerings and prayers to the deities.

As Marimuthu lay near the sacks of produce he had brought, Selvarasu approached him and addressed him affectionately. 'Hello anna, how are you?' Marimuthu was not sure if he should respond. He sat, looking confused.

'Are you surprised that I am talking to you even though our families have broken ties? All that happened in the past. Times have changed. Why should we act just like our elders, anna?'

Selvarasu was at least five years younger than him. Marimuthu was quite ashamed to hear such mature words coming from his younger cousin. He even addressed Marimuthu as 'anna', older brother. Until then, it had not even occurred to Marimuthu that he had relatives who could call him 'anna'.

After that initial exchange, he and Selvarasu hung out with each other for three days in the market. They went out for their meals together. The first time they ate out, Selvarasu paid the bill. When Marimuthu tried to resist, he said, 'Is this again about our families? Anna, money is like a whore. It's with someone today and with someone else tomorrow.' Marimuthu couldn't enforce strict boundaries with such a person. Expenses did not seem to worry Selvarasu. He ate well. When they went to movies, he bought the best tickets. He simply didn't hesitate to part with the money in his pocket.

'What else do we earn money for?' he said. 'Even if we manage to save up and build a castle, we are not going to get to take it with us when we die.'

Marimuthu felt that even though he was older, he had a lot to learn from Selvarasu. He was happy in his company. It had only been three days, but it felt like they had always been friends. During those days, the topic of Marimuthu's marriage came up. After skirting around the subject for a bit, they ended up talking about it frankly.

'Why don't you find a girl for me?' Marimuthu teased Selvarasu.

'Actually, there is a girl. They considered her for my brother, but our family couldn't agree to the conditions the girl's family laid. So, it didn't work out. But if you are interested, perhaps we could do something.'

Hearing Selvarasu speak like a marriage broker, it occurred to Marimuthu that the boy must have gained a lot of experience in the matter just by observing how things were done for his brothers. His eldest brother, Natesan was married. They were still looking for a match for his second brother, Rangasami.

The girl that Selvarasu mentioned was from near Kundhoor. The family lived close to their fields. They were three sisters. The first two were married. They did not have much by way of property—just two acres of uneven land. Even to fetch water, they had to carry pots and walk to a well some four fields away. But the girl's father was a shrewd man. He knew well how high the demand for brides was.

He had found a rig truck owner to marry his first daughter. From the bridegroom's family, he demanded two acres of land registered in his daughter's name, a thali chain made with nine sovereigns of gold, and that they split the wedding expenses equally. Also, the wedding had to happen in a temple. If the boy's family did not have land but could give more money and gold, he would still not agree.

'Money comes and goes. Land is not like that. If there is land in my daughter's name, it will be of use to her in the future. I am asking this only for a girl who is marrying into your family. Not for myself.'

He had managed to marry his two older daughters in well-to-do families and he expected the same for his youngest daughter as well. But when they considered this match for Selvarasu's brother, they could not accept these terms and conditions.

'We need to register the land in that girl's name?! Why? She is coming into our family. Why should *we* make the land over to her? We don't have to make this alliance with someone who doesn't trust us. It is insulting. And it's not as if she is so precious that she deserves a gift of land.'

This entire community relied on land for its subsistence. People won't let even a sliver of land slip away from their hands. But that was not how rig owners thought about land. Money was not a big concern for them. All they needed was a good season of sand quarrying. With that money, they could buy two, even five, acres of land and register it in the girl's name. They only cared about finding a bride.

Marimuthu agreed to check out the girl. When he and Selvarasu met the next week, they looked at the horoscopes and found that they matched. Then, one day, they went to visit the girl's family. At first, Marimuthu was not sure if it was a good idea for two young unmarried men to do this on their own without any assistance from elders.

'Oh, you don't seem to understand these things, anna. That girl's father operates very much like a broker. He does not worry about who the boy is, who comes to see the girl and all that. His primary concern is to make sure his conditions are met.' So, they set out together. The house was right next to a massive rock that looked like a mountain that some ascetic had shrunk with his magical powers. Two thatched huts. One of the huts was being used as the primary dwelling. The other they used for storing fodder, to sleep in, etc. There was no other homestead anywhere in the vicinity. Marimuthu thought that if he married the girl, he would hesitate to visit his in-laws even on festive occasions. But then, their expectation might be that if they married their daughter to a well-to-do family, the son-in-law might invite them over to *his* place.

When they arrived, only the girl and her mother were in the house. The girl was very dark-complexioned. They did not welcome the visitors. They did not offer anything to drink. All they did was to inform them that the father had gone to check in on some cattle and would be back only by ten o'clock. They didn't ask why they had come. They didn't even invite them to sit down.

Selvarasu did not react to any of this. He asked for some water and drank it. They left the bike parked outside the hut and walked to a neem tree nearby and sat down in its shade. Marimuthu could not help but recollect the pomp and respect with which he had been treated the first time he had gone to see a girl. He teared up, thinking of the fall in his fortunes. He stayed silent. Selvarasu did his best to get Marimuthu out of his funk. But he felt like banging his head against that huge rock nearby.

The girl's father returned hours later with a bullock. Selvarasu alone walked up to the man and spoke to him. Even from a distance, Marimuthu could see the nonchalance and disrespect in the man's eyes. Right at that moment, he resolved to himself that if he got married, he would have five or six girl children. Perhaps this father had already found a rig truck owner for his youngest daughter too. Some rich man with a palatial house. The girl would live there, growing fat like a piece of puffed-up dried fish.

But Marimuthu was also thinking about what he would do if he got to marry that girl. He would write his share of the red-soil land in her name. That would be a good pretext to get the land divided up among the heirs. Selvarasu could be instrumental in getting it done. But it didn't work out. Neither the girl, nor the land.

17

Marimuthu pulled over near the red-soil land. Ever since he had communicated to matchmaker thatha his willingness to get the matter of the land settled, he had been wanting to come and take a look at it himself. He wanted to explore paatti's ideas even before things progressed to the next level with his uncle's family.

The truth was that paatti was a woman of a different era. She might be right about what they could grow on the land, but she had no idea what kind of land sold for how much these days. This land was adjacent to a road, and that was a clear attraction. If they made small house plots, they would sell right away. But paatti was advising him to take the low-lying land. Who would want to buy that land to build a house? Even if Marimuthu did not intend on selling the land right away, the fact was that the village was continuously expanding, and one day the land might fetch a great price. He had to take all of that into consideration before he made a decision.

Marimuthu had not been particularly attracted to that land. As far back as he could remember, it had always lain unused. As a kid, he had been there once or twice taking sheep out to graze. He had never spent time running and playing in that land or rolling in its mud. He had never climbed the trees there. Nor had he ever planted even a small sapling. In fact, he had never thought of it as cultivable at all.

All that he had were bits and pieces of stories from his grandmother. Whenever he happened to see that land, he wondered if he had totally wrong ideas about its possibilities. But he had vivid pictures of its fecundity from paatti's narration along with stories of her youth. The land she remembered was thirty years old. Not the same land that was in front of him now. If he wanted to discover its old glory, it would take him at least five or six years of work.

The well was adjacent to the mud track. The only signs that there was a well at the spot were two pieces of stone sticking out. A narrow path led from the well deep into the land itself. A large neem tree stood on the shore of the lake closest to the road, looking like a guardian deity. Marimuthu parked his bike under the tree.

It was cool in the tree's shade. On its trunk, he could spot signs of children climbing and playing on it. The tree had shot up straight and tall from its roots and had spread into branches high on. Even on its branches, he could see scars of human activity. Under the tree there was no grass or weeds. It was a clearing that showed many signs of human use. There were small piles of stones here and there—evidence of children playing Five Stones at that spot. They were round, smooth, white stones. They must have picked them with great care. Or the stones might have acquired that shape with repeated use in the games. It was very clear to him that the tree had become a part of the commons.

The land been lying abandoned for thirty years. Between the road to the east, the residences to the west, the large fields to the north and the lake shore to the south, the land looked like an island. It was a massive island taken over by trees and bushes. The trees had grown and canopied the land completely.

It was mostly a rampant growth of thorny karuvela trees. All this plant needed was a little bit of ground to fix its roots. It then grew rapidly, spreading its thorny branches like grasping demon fingers, occupying the entire land. All other trees would lose that battle. Except for neem. Neem alone could push its foliage in and through the gaps in the thorny branches and grow tall, pushing the karuvela tree down. But neem was more picky about where it would take root. He could spot one or two neem trees on the land.

He could not make up his mind whether he wanted to walk in and explore or not. The land seemed to have shut all its entrances tight and was huddled inside quietly. But if he walked around a bit, he would get a better sense of how it could be distributed between the families. He might also be able to anticipate the questions that might come from others and prepare his responses.

He locked the bike and walked towards the well. It was completely silted up. Its encircling wall was broken in several places, looking like a mouth with just one or two teeth intact. The two main tall stones on either side of the well seemed unsteady and ready to fall any minute. Even the design of the well looked unfamiliar to him.

All wells in the region were rectangular, and they looked like a box that had been fitted deep into the ground. But this well was wide and circular. He had no difficulty peering into it. He could see a bit of water. It was almost like a small pond. Paatti had told him that the well did not dry up even in the summer. But since it had been unused for so long, the water had turned into a green slush. Even then, he could clearly see signs that children jumped and played in the well. Near the wall area, he could tell the spots from where they probably jumped and even footprints on the ground leading up to those spots. No matter in what condition a well is, the desire to jump in never goes away.

Inside the well, he could see little pieces of soap and used packets of shampoo. Little flat fish and loaches that ate dirt seemed to dart about even in that muddy water, coming up to the surface now and then with their mouths open. Somehow, the well had not been in complete disuse. It would cost him a least one lakh rupees to build the wall and desilt the well. And it wouldn't be a simple matter to get electric connection for a motor borewell. If it was going to be a difficult task, perhaps he should consider sharing the well. But he wanted the well, no matter how much it would cost to bring it back to use. He wondered if that was going to be possible.

The well had once been the main source of water for all five acres. If he rebuilt the well and had it restored, he might be able to give paatti at least a glimpse of the glories of the past that floated in her memory now. If she saw the land being cultivated and crops growing in it, she would be very pleased. Then she could die in peace.

He approached the narrow path that wound its way into the land. If he walked all the way down that path to the other end, he would reach the enclave where the toddy tappers lived. He hesitated to go into the land alone. This had been the land where his ancestors had toiled. It had also been the same land where they fought and argued and fell out with one another. He suddenly had a vision of his granduncle, clad in loincloth, walking to the well and cranking the pulley system into action to draw water from the well. Some people even said his paatti was the one responsible for the disputes. His grandaunt surely was of that opinion till the day she died.

In a small patch on their portion of the land, his grandaunt had planted some green chilli plants. She had tended to them carefully, using dirt mixed with chicken refuse as manure and watering them with great care. So, they had grown quite well and spread out into branches from which hung finger-long chilli peppers. Every week, grandaunt harvested a bagful of chillis and carried them to the market on someone or another's cart. There was much demand for the peppers in the market since it was quite rare to find chillis that looked so wholesome and fresh. Marimuthu's grandmother grew jealous of this. She ranted about this to her husband all the time.

'We work hard in the land too. But what's the use? She works only a small portion of the land, and she is able to run her entire household on that income. But we are not able to do it. That's because all you do is drink pitchers and pitchers of toddy and just lie about on that cot, holding your dick in your hand!'

Paatti always used such coarse language with thatha. Marimuthu still remembered their arguments from when his thatha was still alive. The man never opened his mouth. And when paatti did, she said rude and vulgar things. So, his grandaunt had been of the firm opinion that it was his grandmother who egged his grandfather on.

How did it happen that the buffalo wandered into the fields, its rope undone from the spot where it was tied up? It was possible for buffalos to rip apart their ropes, but how could a buffalo untie itself so neatly and wander about? A two-legged buffalo must have untied it. And then, how come the buffalo managed to avoid the maize, brinjal and so many other things growing in the fields and walk straight to the chilli patch as if someone directed it there? The buffalo destroyed grandaunt's chilli plants that night. And when it was done, it sat down right there, chewing the cud.

When grandaunt went to check on the plants early next morning, she was shocked at the sight. Her body trembled. She felt like someone had pulled the ground from under her feet, and she cried. She then flung pieces of mud at the buffalo, but it wouldn't budge. It had eaten enough for the next four days. That was the beginning of the dispute between the two families.

It did not stop with words and arguments. They even physically assaulted each other. First they threw balls of earth at each other. When one of these hit thatha on the chest, he collapsed crying, 'Ayyo!' Grandaunt picked up a spade and hit thatha on the head with it. Hearing the commotion, people came running from neighbouring fields and pulled them apart.

When she saw blood pouring down her husband's face, paatti wailed, beating herself on the stomach. In her rage, she broke the rods and threw even the pulley into the well. People struggled to wrench the crowbar away from her hand and restrain her. After that, grandaunt cursed them, flinging fistfuls of earth in their direction, severing all ties between the two families.

That was grandaunt's version of the story. Whenever anyone narrated this version to paatti, she would sigh and stay silent for a while.

Then she would say, 'That wretched whore! She tried to seduce my husband. And since I was in the way, she started saying such things about me . . .'

Marimuthu didn't know which story was true, but he knew that the two families had fought and separated from each other out of jealousy and competition. And the land fell into disuse. 'Any spot she sits on will burn to dust,' his grandaunt said about his grandmother. 'Even grass won't grow where she sets foot,' his paatti said about grandaunt.

What was the point in being siblings? The families did not even speak to one another. They had somehow managed to keep that up for all these years. He wasn't sure if they could ever reunite. It was only at this time of the third generation that they were even beginning to talk about dividing up the land. If the families did not reconcile now, then one day they would forget they were ever related.

18

The narrow footpath went winding through the land. Whenever it encountered a tree, it went around it and tried to take a straight course again. It felt like he was walking in some secret chamber concealed under a canopy of trees. Not a spot of sunlight entered through the dense foliage. Under the thorny karuvela trees lay their curved yellow fruits that had dropped to the ground. Sheep and goats were grazing in that spot, feasting on those fruits. It was an excellent spot for grazing. You could leave the animals there for the day and return in the evening to herd them back. The people who lived in the enclave nearby clearly found the land to be an excellent place to graze their cattle and sheep.

Thick-stemmed bushes had grown incredibly dense. Various kinds of creepers had climbed all over the trees. The sight of rosary peas, with their thick lower stems and green, serpentine creepers braiding their way up the trees, was terrifying. He was amazed at the jungle that this land had become. How long would it take for him to clear it and turn it back into an arable field?

It occurred to him that the last time he was on this land was with Vasanthi. He had not felt this sense of wonderment then. A shy smile crept to his lips when he remembered that he had been in no frame of mind on that occasion to notice the trees or the creepers. He tried to recollect the spot where he had kissed her, but he couldn't. All trees looked alike now.

Had the land vanished too, just like the traces of that kiss had? But the narrow mud track was intact. It was a shortcut between the main road and the enclave of houses on the other side. He thought it would be nice if the entire mud track came to be his in the settlement. But there was no way to predict how the negotiations would go.

As he walked further into the land with these thoughts in mind, he suddenly heard some rustle in the thicket and saw some movement ahead of him. It was a huge yellow rat-snake. Moving as if it was flying above the surface of the earth, it rushed away and vanished into the thicket of trees. He then heard the soft calls of a partridge. The sheep and goat stopped their grazing and lifted their heads up, listening to the sounds. Marimuthu stood fixed to the spot for a while. He had gooseflesh all over.

Why should a farmer like him be afraid of snakes? He had seen snakes up close several times. The earth and snakes were inseparable. They'd been inextricably linked for ages. Snakes turned their movements into secrets, and the earth made concealed pathways and helped keep the secret. But in those rare moments when the secret was revealed, why become fearful? Marimuthu struggled to decide whether he wished to proceed or not. The sheep went back to grazing as if nothing significant had occurred. He calmed himself, controlled the trembling in his legs and walked on with a deep sigh.

The path ended at the enclave where the toddy tappers lived. It divided the land into two clear halves. The eastern half was sunken, and it bordered the canal winding towards the lake like a black snake. Like the dip in a sari hung out to dry, that portion of the land sank in the middle, forming a gentle trough. The denseness of the trees kept that dip from view right now. The land to the west of the path looked alright. The east side might become muddy and slushy in the rainy season. He couldn't make up his mind about anything right then since everything lay covered in a tangle of undergrowth.

Underneath all that it would be good, red earth, he knew. Red soil never held stagnant water. It never became slushy. He'd have to choose between the pieces of land on either side of the path. Lands were settled between competing parties very differently in the old days. They would make an oral agreement as to which plot of land belonged to whom and go about cultivating them. After three years, they would switch. So, even if the lands were not equitably apportioned, it all got sorted out because of the periodic switching. If they introduced manure at the beginning of those three years, it would last the entire duration. Then it was just the right time to switch and start with manuring again.

But things were done differently now. They preferred to make the divisions clear and final. They did not get into the problems that came with taking turns. For instance, if someone did not do the manuring right after the switch but a year later, then when the three years were up, they might say they wanted to farm longer on the land because they still had the manure to use. Or they might plant a tree and then insist that they want chop it down for wood before they hand over the land to the other party. And the other party might dispute that. Why get into all these issues? The practice these days was to divide up the land once and for all. There was no need to deal with each other beyond that.

They might plant boundary stones along the path, clearly marking the borders. If they were willing to spend a bit more money, they could raise a fence along the path. Or even a wall, if they had the money. But if they did that, they could not plough both the pieces of land in one stretch. Along with the separation of the land, the relationships would fall apart too. But as far as this particular land was concerned, the families had drifted apart long ago. Now, it was only the question of the land. It was a mere ritual. There was no place for sentiments in this matter.

But then, if the matter was resolved amicably, perhaps there would be a chance to reconcile the relationships? Selvarasu's efforts clearly pointed towards that possibility. If Marimuthu too took some steps in that direction, it might be possible to reinstate some cordiality. At least, he and Selvarasu could become friends. If that was what he wanted, Marimuthu had to act in good faith during the settlement. They might even decide to divide the land along the path, with some extra land given to whoever took the sunken east side.

If they followed tradition, the older cousin would stake his claim first. Then the younger one. The elevated land would go to the former. The younger heir would have to contend with the sunken land.

But nobody accepted such traditions any longer. No concessions were made for age or relatedness. When they relied on the adjudication of others, why would they privilege familial relationships? If Marimuthu took the sunken land, how much extra land would he receive in compensation? If he got the elevated land, how much of it should he set aside for them? It was all very confusing. He needed to have another conversation with paatti about it. With his father too. Perhaps he should also consult a third party who was not involved in the matter.

He walked past the land and stood by the enclave of houses. There was a small garden in front of the house that was closest to the land. Even in that heat, they had managed to grow some impressive okra. There was also a flowering creeper. They must have encroached into at least a little bit of the land. In these thirty years, the boundary markers would have vanished without a trace. They would have to survey the area again. That might create disputes with the people in the enclave. Turning these possibilities in his mind, Marimuthu walked along the cart road leading towards the lake.

'Muthu, how come you are here?'

He turned around to see Vatthan walking towards him. He wore a small loincloth on his waist and a towel around his head. On his ribs, Marimuthu could see the dark scars made by harness ropes. Teeth darkened from biting at the sheath around palm fruits. Marimuthu was delighted to see him. Vatthan was a close friend who knew Marimuthu's troubles and tribulations quite well.

Back in the day, when Marimuthu was in the habit of drinking a lot of toddy, they hung out together all the time. It was usually ten or eleven at night by the time Vatthan usually finished climbing palm trees, tapping toddy. But Marimuthu would keep him company, and they would drink some toddy here and there. Then they would end the night with some toddy from the last tree Vatthan climbed for the night. Even now, Marimuthu remembered the sharpness of the toddy that Vatthan tapped.

Now they stood in the shade to chat.

'I came to see the land,' said Marimuthu. He was used to teasing Vatthan about this large family. He said, 'So, when is your next production?'

Vatthan laughed. He had five daughters. He was of the same age as Marimuthu. After he got married, he had one child every year for the first three years. When Marimuthu said to him, 'Can't you space it out a bit?' Vatthan had said, 'It is all god's grace. Not in my hands.' And when Marimuthu teased him, 'I know it is not in your hands, but it is certainly inside your loincloth,' Vatthan just smiled in response. Even after giving birth to five children, Vatthan's wife looked quite strong and healthy. Marimuthu even said to Vatthan, 'Are you giving all your strength to your wife?' Again, Vatthan just smiled.

'So, you are not going to stop until you have a boy?'

'I don't know, da. There is no guarantee a son would take care of us in our old age. He might humiliate us for not having enough money or property to give him. At least

with daughters, we can marry them off and be done with
our duties.'

'Oh! So it looks like you have decided to stop with five
children.'

'Yes, we went and checked last month and found out it
was going to be a girl. So, she had an abortion and also the
operation. That's it. Enough.'

Vatthan somehow managed to feed and clothe five
girls. And he used to long for a male child. He would say,
'If I had a son, he would help me with the work. He'd
climb ten trees, I'd climb ten, and we'd complete the job.
But now, if I fall ill, I don't have anyone to climb even
two trees in my place. What's the point in having so many
daughters? They will have to toil indoors, helping with the
tedious work of making palm jaggery.'

But that had been then. That was the logic for those
days. It changed from time to time. People always found an
argument to justify their positions at any given time.

Vatthan asked Marimuthu, 'I heard something about
the land being divided . . .'

'Yes, that's true. I didn't initiate anything. They
approached me through a third party. I have no dearth of
land. In fact, the difficulty is finding people to work on the
land. But their plight is different. They are three brothers.
So, they suggested we settle the land between us.'

Marimuthu framed the whole thing carefully, in a way
that would let him keep his pride intact.

'That's true. They let it fall into disrepair in those days.
It is good to settle matters now. Don't be fooled. Pick the
west side.'

Vatthan spoke with true concern. It looked like everyone preferred the west side of the land. Vatthan was looking at the land, and now he said, as if he was speaking to himself, 'If you chop down all those trees and sell, that money would take care of a lot of expenses.'

Marimuthu realized that Vatthan was right. All that karuvela wood would make excellent firewood. People would buy it even to use in the brick kilns. But he shouldn't chop down the neem trees. There was a beauty to them standing here and there on a piece of land.

He said, 'Not bad, Vatthan! You are smarter than I thought.'

Vatthan laughed. 'I don't need to be smart to know this much!'

Marimuthu was amazed at how easily Vatthan laughed. It was as if he did not feel burdened at all by the fact that he had five daughters. The people who thought deeply about everything and sought meaning in everything were utterly unable to relish anything. Those who had very little and carried on with their lives day by day did not seem to worry about meaning and purpose, and were happy. He felt envious of Vatthan. He wondered if he too could have been happy if he had married at that age.

'Muthu, please don't chop down the palm trees. There must be at least twenty-five of them on this land. I have heard that the juice is excellent on those fruits. My grandfather has climbed these trees. He has told me about them. Whatever trees come to you in the settlement, you should let me tap toddy from them. Only me! I live right here. I will do it!'

'Of course. Who else would I bring to tap toddy on those trees?!'

Marimuthu glanced at the palm trees. He could see only some of their heads. None of the trees had been pruned and cleared of dead leaves and dried fronds in ages. Vatthan would need a month just to get that done. There were likely to be piles of fronds. At the moment, he could not even tell how many palm trees there were on the land. Only if they cleared it of all the other growth would they figure out.

'I have someone who can chop and clear the ground. Shall I send him a word?'

Marimuthu had to give him a non-committal response.

'It is not for me to decide. Usually, they get a third party to do all that work. If I recommend someone, it might become a problem. But if they ask me, I will speak to you.'

It was midday and the sun was overhead. Even though they were standing in the shade, the heat was becoming unbearable. When he said goodbye to Vatthan, he asked Marimuthu somewhat hesitantly,

'When will you come drink with me?'

19

Marimuthu knew the true meaning behind Vatthan's question. Vatthan was only being indirect about something that many others had asked him quite bluntly. But Marimuthu did not know how exactly to respond to it. So, as he walked away, he said, 'Give me six months.' He did not know how he came to arrive at that deadline. How did it become so impressed on his mind? Was there some meaning to it? Or was it completely random? Vatthan had been very subtle with his question.

It would be seven years since that summer. He still remembered the fragrance of that toddy. Sour and slightly sweet—even the thought of it made his mouth water now. Those were wonderful years. He used to wonder if savouring toddy was the sole purpose of existence.

He used to set out in the misty chill of winter mornings, carrying a dried and hollowed bottle-gourd. All he wore was a dhoti around his waist and towel around his head. He didn't wear a shirt. He found the touch of the chillness comforting. Being exposed to it never affected his health in those days. His rib cage would expand, widening his chest like a slab of marble.

He'd drink as much toddy as he could and also take some in the gourd bottle. In those days, during the toddy season, a woman came selling idli and kuzhambu. She was careful about rationing the kuzhambu. Only two spoons of kuzhambu per idli. She had come to that decision after seeing the endless amounts of kuzhambu the men consumed when they were drunk on toddy. After that, she did not even have to bring a lot of idlis to sell.

During the day, whenever he felt hungry, Marimuthu would drink more toddy from the gourd. The same way at night. He drank all the time. For dinner, he would buy some fried meat or parotta for both of them. Vatthan would sit down to drink with him only after he was done climbing all the trees. 'If I climb a tree drunk and fall down dead, who will take care of my family?' he said.

Marimuthu and toddy were inseparable for four or five months at a stretch. In that period, no other thought bothered him. Toddy kept him in a state of pleasure. He could even differentiate the tastes of toddy tapped in different months. He had tasted toddy that came from the first spathe of palm flower and also from a more mature one. And the toddy tapped from the stages in between. As far as Marimuthu was concerned, toddy—which was basically palm-milk—was nothing but the elixir of the gods.

But he had to abandon all those pleasures one day. A family from Nettur—which was not far away—had married one of their daughters to a man in Marimuthu's village. They were a well-to-do family. Marimuthu knew that the woman had a younger sister back home even though he had never seen her in person. But based on his impressions of the older sister, he had created in his mind a fond image of the younger one.

The family was having a difficult time finding a match for their younger daughter. Then, it so happened that Marimuthu's horoscope turned out to be a good match for hers. The girl's father owned a big textile mill. He had more than a hundred looms. So, he was not keen on marrying his daughter to a farmer who worked in the fields. He had hoped to find a tradesman. But it didn't work out. He hoped that if he got his daughter married to Marimuthu, he might be able to rope him into the mill business. But before things could proceed further, someone said to the girl's father, 'He is a drunkard. All he does is drink from morning to night.'

There were some people in the village whose main vocation was to ruin other people's chances. They were even ready to incur expenses in the process. It was true that Marimuthu had become an avid drinker. But why did anyone have to take it upon themselves to mention that? Once the girl's father heard that, he had second thoughts about the match. When Marimuthu came to know about it, he kicked the calabash bottle and spilled the toddy on the ground. That was the end of his drinking spree. But despite giving up drinking, he did not get to marry that girl. Maybe her father found her a mill owner to marry. Marimuthu could not understand why families looked to make alliances only with others who were in the same line of work.

Anyway, he had resolved not to drink again until he was married. And he had kept that up. That was what Vatthan was hinting at today. How astute he was!

Marimuthu was truly amazed at Vatthan's personality. What if he too could train his mind to set all other concerns aside and just focus on the land? He made a conscious attempt to focus on his desire to secure that land as soon as possible.

20

Coconut fronds lay drooping like tangles of matted locks. Young coconuts that had begun to grow in the dried spathes had shrivelled and dropped. Even the ones that managed to survive only grew to the size of palm fruits. The coconut trees were clearly showing signs of some affliction. For all this, they had been diligently cared for. The sixty-seven coconut trees in the orchard had been divided into two groups, and each group was being watered every other day.

The heat of the month of Chithirai snipped away at all living things, entering even the well-shaded orchard and sucking away all moisture. The entire orchard presented a depressing sight. When a sudden gust of shrieking wind blew in, it terrified the trees. With their fronds ripped away, broken and hanging, the trees looked utterly disfigured. The heat had driven away the peace that used to suffuse the orchard. Even the squeals of the squirrels now sounded like cries for help. Vegetables on the plants dried up rapidly and showed their withered, drooping faces to the world.

Marimuthu lost the joy he used to feel in coming to the orchard. He felt that if they were pruned and cleared, the

trees might look presentable. But he could not get hold of
Vatthan to do that job. This was a busy season for Vatthan,
as busy as the months after the rainy season were for the
farmers.

Vatthan was familiar with some remote parts where
some palm trees still had juicy spathes sprouting even in
that season. He would quietly go to these places, climb
those trees and drink their juices to his heart's content. If
he found more than enough, he sold it to a select group of
people for a weekly rate. But that was all the toddy tapping
he had to do in that season. He was in great demand for a
different job. People who owned orchards sought his help
with clearing and pruning the trees of dried fronds and
leaves.

Farmers had very little work in those months. They
started ploughing the field soon after the first rains.
With the second rains, they did the sowing. Vaigasai,
the next month, was the perfect time for getting started
on groundnuts. And they had to attend to the palm trees
before the start of the sowing season. Since the trees usually
bordered the fields, the fronds they cut down could fall right
on the land and ruin all the preparations they had done. No
one wanted that. But it was also not an option not to prune
the palm trees. Otherwise, they cast large shadows on the
fields and ruined the crops.

So, Vatthan was quite busy in those months. His job at
each site was completed only after he pressed the fronds flat
with his feet, stacked them up and bundled them together.
His wife worked alongside him, gathering palm sheaths
and barks. The landowners kept the fronds, but Vatthan

could take the sheaths and barks. Once the fronds were all
pressed and readied, they could be used for weaving roofs
for huts and sheds. All those landowners who hired Vatthan
to tap toddy on their trees also relied on him to fetch people
who could weave thatched roofs. Since Vatthan was so
busy working with palm trees, it was not easy to turn his
attention to coconut trees. After struggling for a few days to
get hold of him, Marimuthu finally managed to meet him
and talk to him about pruning the sixty-seven coconut trees
in his orchard. The job would take two whole days. Vatthan
told him he could do it the week after.

Marimuthu said, 'I had to come in person to make
this request, and you are still acting pricey! You will need
a favour from me one day, won't you? I will remind you
of this, then!' Marimuthu was only teasing, but Vatthan
was alarmed at the remark. He began to worry that if he
did not take up Marimuthu's job right away, he might lose
out on tree-climbing prerogatives on the red-soil land once
Marimuthu took possession of it. Vatthan really hoped to
secure that work. The land was very close to where he lived.
He did not have to walk long distances. It would be terrible
to lose that job.

'Please don't say that, Marimuthu. I will be happy to
do it,' he quickly said in a placatory tone. He agreed to start
the work in two days. Marimuthu knew that Vatthan was
excellent at his job. No one could ever find any fault with his
work. In the past, he used to tap for toddy on coconut trees
too. All trees seemed to respond well to Vatthan's touch.

Despite that conversation, Marimuthu was relieved
only when Vatthan showed up for work two days later. He

had to do most of the climbing in the earlier part of the day before the heat came to full force. After that, work would inevitably slow down. So, very early in the morning, Vatthan started the pruning job with the coconut tree that was on the water channel near the well. Since the water from the well always embraced the roots of the tree on the way down the channel, that particular one was always hale and healthy. Sitting right on the tree, he twisted apart a tender coconut, sliced it open and drank the water. The coconut water tasted incredible, as if it contained all the beauty and goodness of that morning hour. He then took a coconut for Marimuthu and put it in his bag.

Marimuthu observed the neatness and precision with which Vatthan went about his task. If he was not sure about cutting down a frond on the top side, he consulted Marimuthu. And if he wanted to be sure some of the coconut clusters were mature and ready to be cut, he first cut just one fruit and dropped it down for Marimuthu to check. Other than that, he worked quietly and swiftly.

When Vatthan finished his work for the day, they sat near the well and had their meal. Ammayi had sent some paruppu kuzhambu with the farmhand. How did ammayi manage to infuse so much taste into these thuvarai lentils, Marimuthu wondered. He could eat that kuzhambu every day.

Vatthan had pruned thirty-five trees that day. The wage was ten rupees per tree. He'd finish pruning the rest of the trees the next day. After Vatthan left, Marimuthu lay down in the shade of a tree and closed his eyes. Since morning, his mind had been preoccupied with work and had no time for any other thoughts. It was good that he was going to be busy for the rest of the day and the next day as well. He could never overestimate the happiness he got from work. It had the miraculous power to push away all other thoughts and completely draw his attention in. As long as he did not wrestle with it or resist it and instead submitted himself to it, work gathered him in its embrace. On days when there was a lot of work to focus on, his mind kept its tail between its legs and stayed out of trouble. Work was the only remedy for the mind's mischief. But no matter how much work he sought out, there were always days when he had nothing much to do. Those days were the hardest, as difficult to surmount as the prospect of leaping over the seven seas.

He opened his eyes when he heard voices. It had only been a short nap, but he felt refreshed. Kuppan and the farmhand Sakthi had arrived for work. He could see that his father was ordering them around. Sakthi must have taken the sheep for grazing and brought them back to their enclosure. It was too hot for the sheep to stay out on the pasture. As for Kuppan, he only came to the orchard for specific tasks. The only daily task he had was to water the coconut trees. He didn't have to do that today.

Because Marimuthu had sent word for him the previous day, his father had arrived that day from his regular haunt—the fields in Minnakkaadu. Nobody knew what was so special about that place that Marimuthu's father never wanted to leave from there. Marimuthu's mother had not come to the orchard in a long time. She only attended to the cows and the calves. Since she had no control over the

profits from the fields anymore, perhaps she decided not
to involve herself in its day-to-day running. But his paatti
came to work in the fields on days she did not have work
anywhere. Marimuthu even offered to pay her the same
wages others paid her, but she said, 'Why? So that people
can say that I took wages from my own grandson?'

When he stood up and looked around, the orchard
was in total disarray, like a place where two giant animals
had just engaged in a fight. Palm fronds lay scattered,
stretching their arms. Coconuts lay on the ground, some
in bunches, some loose ones scattered about. Scales of
palm spathes were strewn all over the place, looking like
insects in the rainy season. There were numerous palm
sheaths as well. It would take him most of the afternoon
to clear and put away everything. It was good that he
had workers to help him. He involved himself in work
again. His father used a sickle to separate coconuts from
their bunches. Kuppan and Sakthi were arranging the
coconuts in piles.

'Sakthi, go fetch the big basket. We can get this
done only if we carry them in baskets and store them in
the house,' Marimuthu said. So, Sakthi ran towards the
house to bring the basket. Then it would be Kuppan's job
to carry the baskets of coconut to the house. There were
around a thousand coconuts. Kuppan would have to make
several trips carrying the basket. If there was good demand
for coconuts, they could sell them right there from the
orchard. But since everyone nearby had their own coconut
trees, it was not very easy to sell them here. Earlier, only
a few orchards had coconut trees. Now, they had installed

as many as four borewells on each land. Then they planted coconuts right away.

If they stored the coconuts in the house, he could take them to the market when the demand grew. There were usually a lot of weddings in Vaigasi, the next month. Coconuts would surely be in demand then. Weddings. Just when he thought he could lose himself in work, that single word managed to latch on to him with force. But he countered it with the thought that it did not really matter to him how many auspicious days for weddings came by. His job was to see if coconuts were in demand or not. That refocused his mind.

In an effort to release himself from the clutches of those thoughts about weddings, he busied himself with filling up the basket with coconuts. When the basket was full, Kuppan carried it on his head. Marimuthu stood looking for a minute at Kuppan walking away with that heavy load on his head. Unbeknownst to himself, he sighed. Then he walked to the spot where his father was separating the coconuts from their bunches. He wanted to distract himself by talking to his father for a while. He also had specific things to say to his father. Theirs was, however, not an easy relationship.

'They have approached me about settling things with the red soil land.'

'Mm.'

That was all his father seemed to have to say on the subject. 'Mm.' It had been years since Marimuthu addressed him as 'Appa'. When he was a young boy, his father carried him on his shoulders when he went to drink toddy. He was the one who introduced Marimuthu to alcohol. He said to his son, 'Drink, my dear. If your mother has a problem with it, I will handle her,' and thrust a cup of toddy in his hand. It was also from his father that Marimuthu learned how to farm.

The odd thing was that Marimuthu's father never had the courage to step out of his comfort zone. He was like a bandicoot that wouldn't venture out of its burrow. Initially, Marimuthu was just amazed that a man could be so contented and confined. But later on, the same thing became a cause for annoyance. So, whenever he felt that he had the duty to convey anything to his father, he usually said it in a perfunctory manner, not even looking him in the eye, and staring at the trees or the cattle instead.

'Let me know which side of the land I should take.'

'You pick whichever side you prefer.'

What was the meaning behind that remark? Was he expressing frustration that he had no authority on such matters? Or did he mean it was not his burden to figure such things out? Or did he want to suggest that he had no say in the matter anyway, so why consult him at all? How could Marimuthu speak to this man who only knew two things in the world—his hard work in the fields and the toddy he loved? Marimuthu looked at his father. He was wearing a cheap, old-fashioned towel on his head and a small loincloth on his waist. But his body looked like it was sculpted out of stone.

Marimuthu felt a sudden rage to pull his father by his unkempt hair and punch him in his back. But, instead, he turned his face away in disgust. He did not even want to stand next to his father. He walked away to fill another basket of coconuts for Kuppan to carry.

There was a lot more work to do that day. There were tonnes of coconut fronds to be sorted. They had to chop the lower, sturdy half of the fronds away from the leafy part above. People who ran brick kilns would come and take the hard lower part. They had no use for the leafy part. They'd have to be burned. Earlier, his paatti would come on her free days and peel the long leaves off their thin midribs. Then, she would bunch them up together and make brooms out of them.

Two fronds would yield one broom. It was backbreaking work. But she would use a small scythe and rip away the leaves in swift motions. He could not think of anyone more patient and diligent with their work. Once she had made about twenty brooms that Marimuthu took to the Thursday market to sell. Each broom sold for four or five rupees. He'd hand over the profits to paatti, and she would beam with joy for an entire day. He could not fathom how money seemed to bring the same expression to everyone's face.

The mounds of coconut kept diminishing as Kuppan carried them in batches to the house. The workers were also stacking up the fronds to a side. Sheaths and spathes also needed to be piled up neatly. He usually gave them to Kuppan, who then carried away a small load every day for domestic use. Sakti, the young fellow, was very smart about it. Every day, he would make a bundle of the sheaths and set it aside as soon as he arrived in the morning to take the sheep out for grazing. Then, when he brought the sheep back to the enclosure, no matter how late it was, he carried his bundle home with him. He clearly managed to take home more than Kuppan did. He was very enterprising that way.

It was not an easy task getting Sakthi to be consistent with the farm work. Either later that year or the next, he was sure to bound away like a calf, looking for other things to do. His biggest dream was to become a lorry driver. He was only coming to work in the fields as a means to work off his father's debt. If anyone spoke to him harshly, he wouldn't show up for work the next day. Then they'd have to cajole and placate him.

The sun was overhead by then. Since they had been working in the shade of the coconut trees, they had not felt the full force of the heat yet. But now it was beginning to creep into the shade. Sweat rolled down his body in rivulets. Now, there were only minor tasks to complete. It was always Kuppan who tied up the loose ends and wrapped things up. Sakthi ran and switched on the borewell motor. Marimuthu's father had a wash, standing with his head in the water gushing out of the pipe. Sakti jumped into the irrigation channel and thrashed about. But none of these could equal the pleasure of jumping straight into the well for a swim. Water from the pipe cannot give the joy of spreading one's arms into the water in the well. Marimuthu sat down to let the sweat cool down.

21

His father was washing himself, holding his body blissfully under the water that flowed in a cylindrical stream from the pipe into the irrigation channel. Even at this age, he had a firm and agile body that looked like a big, dark block of wood had sprouted arms and legs. Why was Marimuthu destined to have this man for his father—a man who never thought beyond the immediate needs of his body? How wonderful it would be, Marimuthu thought, if we had the option of choosing our mothers and fathers. His father never involved himself in anything beyond his ken. Somehow, such people managed to survive in this world. Marimuthu felt a surging rage towards the man.

Looking at his father, he thought—why keep even that loincloth on? Why not cast that away and wander naked like a man with no self-respect whatsoever? Even before his thought ended, his father drew the loincloth away from his body to which it had clung in its wetness. Shameless man. He then sat on his haunches in the channel, squeezed the loincloth dry, and wore it back on. The boy Sakti, on the other hand, was still enjoying his time in the water, jumping into the channel and falling and rolling in it. How could he find so much joy in playing in the water where the older man had just squeezed out his loincloth? Marimuthu shouted at Sakti.

'Hey! Go turn off the motor. Go!'

His father had walked away from the grove even before the motor fully came to a stop. Now, until evening, he'd go lie like a corpse in a little hut in a different part of the fields. Marimuthu walked to the well. Inside, at a great depth, he could see the clear surface of water. In the summer, there was no way he could jump in for a bath and swim. But then, these days, he rarely jumped in even when the water level was high.

No matter what time of day it was, he was not afraid to climb down into the well for a wash. He always felt the well to be a safe and comforting place. Besides, the water in that well was always warm. Once he started swimming in it, waking the water from its sleep by swirling it about, it would slowly bring up a chillness from its depth. It was only about six feet deep. His mind elsewhere, he now went down into the well and bathed.

He was still thinking about his father. He felt that if his father had been a better man, his life would have been more fulfilling. As a child, he had been very fond of his father. Later, at some point, the relationship had soured. What's the point in being a father if you cannot understand your son's changing needs?

It was his father who taught Marimuthu how to catch rats and rabbits. It was he who showed Marimuthu the secret treasures hidden in that elevated pasture in Minnakkadu.

But now, Marimuthu could not even bear to look at his face. Why did he have to leave so early today? It was not as if someone else needed anything done. He could have stayed on in the grove and helped complete more work for the day. He seemed to have the knack for draining away the joy, the comfort, the satisfaction Marimuthu derived in working in the grove. Marimuthu knew the way his father's mind worked—now that he had done some work, he was entitled to take some coconuts later when he needed to trade them, when toddy season was over, for some arrack. Thinking about his father seemed to make his body burn with anger. So, he plunged himself again into the water.

His father had never expressed his opinion on anything. Everyone in town called him 'Vegulan', the naïve one. He only ever went into town at the time of the festival in the temple. For all those ten days leading up to the festival, he'd take part in the festival dance with much verve and involvement. People in the town said he was the best dancer—no one could beat him at that. They made fun of him. 'If we want Vegulam to come to town, all we need to tell him is that the dance is happening.' There was one rare occasion when this man offered his opinion on something. And that opinion threatened to ruin Marimuthu's life.

A year ago, through Veeduthi, the marriage broker, a potential match had come to Marimuthu's attention. Over the years, he had given her a lot of money for this work, but she never brought anything worth considering. Except once. One girl alone seemed to be a miraculously good fit for Marimuthu. But there were some hurdles. The girl was from a village near Iruppuli. She had been married three months. The groom worked in a private company in a big city and earned thirty thousand a month. So, the girl's family gave one lakh rupees and a kilogram of gold to get her married to that man. The very next day after the wedding, the couple moved to the city. In those three months they were married, they visited the village only once or twice. One night, when the husband rode past a roundabout in his motorbike, he collided with a lorry. She was riding pillion and was thrown away to a side, and she survived with some injuries. But her husband fell right next to the vehicle, and the lorry's back wheel went over his body. He died on the spot.

The woman's family was distressed to see their daughter return to her natal home after just three months of married life, bringing back the money and gold she had taken with her. Thankfully, no one insisted that, as a widow, she needed to wear only a white sari from then on. Thankfully, the horror of inflicting the white sari on young widows was a dying custom.

The one good thing was that she did not become pregnant in those three months. Otherwise, she would have had to bear the burden of raising the child alone. When five or six months had passed since the accident, some people wanted to find out if the family would consider marrying their daughter again. So, they sent word. Initially, the woman's parents were at a loss because widow remarriage was an utterly new idea to them. But when they gave it some thought, they felt that if a man was ready to marry their daughter and if a new life was possible for her, why should they hesitate? They said yes. After that, many men expressed interest in marrying her. But they were all men without any wealth to their name. Such men had a hard time finding wives. Even men like Marimuthu, who had some property to their name, struggled to find a woman to marry.

There was much interest in that woman because people knew that she would bring all that gold and cash with her. But her parents had to think carefully about everything. What if a man married her just for the money and then spent it all in a few months and kicked her out of the house? How could they be certain that the new family would take good care of their daughter? They felt that if the man who married their daughter had some wealth of his own, then he might marry her, not for the money, but out of his genuine interest in her. Such a marriage might work, they thought. So, they asked Veeduthi to find a man who was reasonably well-off.

When Veeduthi brought this matter to Marimuthu as a potential alliance, she really built it up for him. She offered many compelling arguments in its favour.

'Saami, we have tried so many alliances for you. Nothing has worked out. And you are past thirty years of age now. How can we ever be sure that women who have not been married before have been chaste? This woman, she is guileless. She was married only three months. That is all. There are women who take to prostitution after their marriage. If such people can stay in marriages, what is the fault with this girl, tell me?'

'Veeduthi, there are all kinds of things that happen without others knowing.'

'How is that fair, saami? So it is not wrong if it happens in stealth? In my community, we marry even four or five times. What's terrible about that? We have children, we make our living, don't we? Please don't worry about these things. If you marry her, I tell you, she will be most faithful to you. More faithful than any other woman can be, because she'd be anxious that people would think less of her for marrying twice.'

'That's not the reason. People in the village . . .'

'Why do you care about the village? There are so many men who are keen on marrying her. They don't seem to worry about the village. Why should you? In the past, they used to marry young boys to older girls. Until the boy grew up, it was his father who acted as the girl's husband. Ask your grandmother about this.'

Marimuthu was quite convinced by Veeduthi's arguments. Women remarrying had become quite a common practice. He had considered several alliances and seen many potential brides by then. He had even made a family with some of them in his own imagination. So, the idea of marrying a woman who had spent three months of marital life with someone else did not seem like a big deal to him. But before discussing it with anyone, he thought about it carefully from all angles. Then he came to the conclusion that he could marry her wholeheartedly.

People would say that she was unlucky because she lost her husband in just three months. But, Marimuthu thought, rather than living a long and miserable life, he would not mind dying after living with her for three months. What's the worst his relatives could do? If he ended up living

well and long, they'd soon grin and ingratiate themselves.
If he didn't, they'd say he ruined himself because of this
marriage. Did he even have to care about their opinions?

Marimuthu had boldly made up his mind to ask
Veeduthi to proceed with the matter. But before he could
do that, she happened to mention the matter to his father.
The man came running to him in a frenzy, unmindful even
of the fact that his loincloth had come undone.

'Dey! If you think you can bring a whore as my
daughter-in-law, I will hang myself, I swear. You will have
to perform my funeral before you tie the thali around her
neck.'

What would his father have done if Marimuthu had
replied, 'Go ahead. Hang yourself and die'? He should
have said exactly that. He pictured his father hanging from
the noose, his tongue sticking out. Even though he felt it
was cruel to picture that, it gave him some satisfaction. He
plunged himself into the water three times before climbing
out of the well.

22

These days, he fell asleep at all odd hours. He felt perpetually tired and wanted to sleep all the time. It was a far cry from when he could not sleep even at night and spent the day sore-eyed and tired. Now, even when he was in the middle of a conversation, he felt like he was talking in his sleep. Getting up in the mornings had become difficult. But he did not want the people in the family to comment on it, so he woke up in the mornings and sauntered towards the fields. And he just sat there, brushing his teeth for longer than necessary.

His mind seemed to be emptied of thoughts. Even though his eyes cast their gaze around, they did not really take in anything. He could not even hear the motor pump running. He seemed to have wandered away from himself. In those rare moments when he experienced some clarity, he wondered seriously what had happened to him. But even before he could find some answers, his mind emptied itself of thoughts again. When he returned home and had his dinner after spending long days in the fields, he just wanted to lie down right away. But he was afraid of what his ammayi would say if he went to bed at that hour. So, he tried his best to busy himself with some tasks.

Until the next rains, there was not much work in the fields. So, he rode his bike into town. It appeared to him that everyone besides him was busy with things to do. He drank some tea and read the newspaper. But these were all mere actions, empty gestures. He returned home with no sense of having gone anywhere. Then he went to bed.

His room had that quality of being walled in on all sides. There were two bureaus and a cot in the room. If he shut the windows, he could feel that he was cut off from the world. He did not particularly have any special respect for his ammayi, but he feared her in a way.

It was amazing how she even managed to walk carrying that heavy body of hers. But she never sat down exhausted. She was always in the middle of some task or another. She did all the cooking in the house, but no one knew when she got it all done. Whenever there was a visitor, she sat chatting with them as if she had nothing else to do. She was always scolding that boy Sakti for coming late to work or for not cleaning up the cattle floor. It seemed like she thought of Sakti as a genie who needed to be kept busy with tasks continuously.

Sakti was terrified of her and did his best to avoid her. He was keen on completing all his work around the house as quickly as possible and to run away to work in the fields. Ammayi was in the habit of watching some television serials without fail. Those were the only times one could find her staying put in one spot.

When an elderly woman like her took on so many tasks, Marimuthu certainly felt guilty about his laziness. Ammayi disapproved of anyone sleeping during the day. She never made any pointed remarks, but she muttered her disapproval. Her constant muttering would turn into an endless buzzing and torment everyone in the house. It was hard to ignore it. She seemed to be of the opinion that everyone had to be engaged in some task or another all the time. If she saw anyone idling, she was annoyed. So, with her around, how could Marimuthu sleep whenever he wanted?

In fear of her, he'd pretend to read a book for a little while. If she thought that he was not just lying on the cot but was in fact reading a book, she'd let him be. He'd gently close the door to his room. In the past, Marimuthu had a regular habit of reading. On days when issues of '*Rani*' and '*Kumudham*' magazines came out, he went into town without fail. When his friend Siddhesh became a lorry driver, he brought certain kinds of books for Marimuthu— the kind he had never dared to openly ask for in the shops. But he was very eager to consume them.

Every time Siddhesh came back to town in his lorry, he gave Marimuthu these books that seemed to describe everything with incredible openness. The men featured in them seemed to have an endless supply of women around them. These women also seemed to be quite willing and ready. Reading these books, Marimuthu felt that the reason he was single was that he lived in the middle of nowhere. He really wanted to live in a town. It'd be even better if he lived in a city. He imagined himself indulging in various kinds of pleasures.

Once, when Siddhesh handed him some books, Marimuthu said, 'Enough, da. What's the use in reading these?' And his friend laughed: 'That's true. There is no use in reading, only in doing!' He also said, 'Come with me in the lorry once. I will show you things that are exactly like in these books.' But, for some reason, Marimuthu couldn't make himself go. Later, again he had the opportunity to take up Siddhesh on his offer, but he was too shy to act on it.

Siddhesh still had those books. He still asked Marimuthu if he wanted any. But he had lost interest in them. In those early days when he started reading these books, they used various words to refer to the male and female parts. But that was not the case any longer. They simply referred to them by their actual names. So, there was no excitement in reading them. He had even bought a cupboard just to hide these books. There might still be one or two in there, but he had no inclination to read them. He didn't know what he could do after he read them. There was no solution to that. So, the only reason he picked up anything to read these days was to fool Ammayi.

If she saw him lying down, she'd come and wake him up: 'How can a farmer sleep during the day?' Whenever her mumblings didn't have any effect, she resorted to direct action. When ammayi first moved in with them after walking out of her son's house, Marimuthu had been very happy about it. But she turned out to be different from his expectations. She seemed to have assessed everyone properly and was cautious in her dealings.

Marimuthu was also bored doing the same set of tasks every day. He felt like just dropping everything and running away. That might give him some relief. He need not care about day or night. He should just sleep; he should allow himself to give his body and mind all the rest they needed. Let ammayi get worked up about it. Let her get upset about the fact that he went back to bed at eleven in the morning. So what? What's the worst that could happen? The world does not wait for anyone. Only those deluded by self-importance would imagine that the world could not get by without them. Ammayi surely suffered from such delusions.

But she wouldn't understand such things. All that mattered to her was that the people in front of her eyes were busy with their tasks. That was enough to convince her that the world was functioning as it should. Even if a single task slowed down, it upset her immensely. The very reason ammayi fought with her son and moved to live with her daughter was that her daughter-in-law was lazy. When ammayi lived with her son, she did all she could do make her daughter-in-law busy and active. But nothing had worked. The daughter-in-law was a frail, thin woman—thin as a snake-gourd that had been straightened by tying a stone to its end. So what if she was not active? Even with her frail body and health, she had managed to give birth to children. They had grown up well. The family was well-off too. But ammayi could not tolerate it. She was worried that if she continued to live there, all her savings would be depleted. So, she decided to find a way to safeguard them.

Around that time, ammayi's son—that is, Marimuthu's maternal uncle—decided to sell a piece of land that had not been put to much agricultural use. It was teeming with avaram and white acacia trees. The only income from the land came from selling these trees for wood every four years or so. Otherwise, it was simply grazing pasture, and it lay uncultivated just like the red-soil land. At least the red-soil land would surely thrive once they cleared and cultivated it. But this land of uncle's—it was only capable of taking, not giving.

All year round, all the cattle from the village grazed in that land. Ammayi collected the dung and piled it away for manure. That was a source of income for her. In the rainy season, the land got very muddy and no one could set foot in it. It had been in their family for generations.

A cardboard manufacturing company was interested in purchasing the land. Since it had a stream flowing nearby, they could use it for the effluents. So, they offered a good price—more money than even what a fertile piece of land could yield. If uncle lent that money out for interest, he would make in one year what the other lands fetched him in four years of work.

However, that land was in Marimuthu's grandfather's name. This grandfather had died when Marimuthu was a toddler. The only things he recollected faintly about his grandfather were his topknot and ear studs. In order to be able to sell this piece of land, uncle needed ammayi's fingerprints. It shocked everyone when ammayi told her son categorically that she would affix her thumbprint to the sales document only if he gave her half the money from the sale. Marimuthu's uncle tried his best to placate his mother.

'You are a lone old woman. If I give away half the money to you, what will I do? Do I take my wife and children with me and go begging?'

But ammayi was an equal match to him.

'This land is the only thing that remains in my husband's name. If I let it go, what security do I have?' she asked.

'Do you think I am going to cast you away, leave you to die alone? How can you be so distrustful of your own son?' he shouted in rage.

'This is all yours after I die. Am I going to take it with me? You can't even trust your own mother,' she retorted. 'I need some money of my own so I can buy and eat the things I like. I can buy little gifts for my grandchildren. Do I have to go begging to you for every little thing?'

Nobody could counter that reasoning. They only advised uncle, 'Just agree to a sum and give it to her.' All this led to daily quarrels at home, mother and son constantly yelling at each other. All that the daughter-in-law felt she could do was to keep to her corner and cry about it.

This situation went on for over a month. The owner of the cardboard company lost his patience. Uncle also found out that they were looking for other lands. He knew that if he let this opportunity go, he would never get such a good offer ever again. So, he brought the company folks for a direct negotiation with ammayi. The only way to get anything done was for all the parties to relent a little. So, it came to this: It wouldn't be possible to give her half, she could only get one-third. Ammayi accepted it without any objections. Her share came to one lakh rupees. What shocked everyone was what ammayi did after that. The plan had been to take the money after the day of the sale and deposit it in the bank. But early that morning, ammayi took her money and left for her daughter's house.

23

Marimuthu was not pleased with the way ammayi had moved in with them so suddenly. After all, her daughter's marital home was not her rightful place. It was her son-in-law's home. If she had no son, then no one would mind her living with her daughter. But she had a son. The appropriate thing would have been to visit her daughter and spend a few days now and then. But to move in with them? That was disgraceful. It led to a complete severing of ties with his uncle's family.

Marimuthu's uncle came and shouted at them. He alleged that it was their ploy to make ammayi come to them with the money. Marimuthu's mother shouted back at him. And, even in her frailty, uncle's wife threw a fistful of sand at them and cursed: 'This family has stolen what is mine. May it go to ruins. Let it burn like the rage in my belly.'

Marimuthu occasionally wondered if it was his aunt's curse that lay heavily on him. Uncle's children were all much younger than him, so they did not think much about the end of these relationships. If his uncle had any daughters Marimuthu could marry, he would not have allowed ammayi to upset relationships in this way. Besides, the fact that ammayi was coming with one lakh rupees also sweetened the pot. At that time, he never wondered if his uncle's wife's curse would come true.

Marimuthu had only one maternal uncle. And now, their relationship had ended. His father had no problems with ammayi moving in with them. 'My mother-in-law has come? Oh, she is welcome. She wants to live here? Oh, she is welcome.' That was it. Ammayi was very pleased with such reception. 'My son-in-law is a generous man, spotless like white corn,' she said to everyone.

Marimuthu's mother was ecstatic that her mother had come to live with her. She had brought a lot of cash. Why wouldn't she be excited? She had her own reasons to be unhappy with her brother. 'That land was in my father's name. He sold it and made a lot of money, but did he think of me, his older sister? He is so much younger than me. I raised him. Did he think of giving me a little money from the sale of that land?'

What could anybody say to that? Ammayi was too shrewd for all this. She'd pull something right out of your throat if she suspected it was something of hers you were swallowing. So, she did not hand over all her money to her daughter. Instead, she deposited the money in her own name in the bank and nominated her daughter as the heir. She derived interest from it every three months. Whenever she had any minor disagreement with her daughter, she would say out loud as if she was talking to herself: 'I am not the kind to bear ill-will towards anyone.'

Why did she have to say that? Marimuthu's mother knew why. It was her mother's way of saying she could take the money and go back to her son's any time she wanted. For these reasons, no one crossed ammayi. Now that Marimuthu had made some money of his own, ammayi's one lakh did not matter to him much. If things went well, he could make that amount from a single year's harvest of groundnuts. But his mother continued to show her affection to ammayi because she knew that her mother's hard work and the money from the interest were both for her benefit.

However, ammayi did not hand over the entire interest amount to her daughter. She launched into elaborate antics every three months when the time came to collect interest. She kept track of the exact date and told him the previous day, 'Marimuthu, please make sure you have no other tasks tomorrow.' He had to understand from that remark that it was about the money. The next day would start with much excitement. She had a pure white polyester sari that she wore exclusively on that occasion. She would take the bank passbooks in a yellow cloth bag and sit outside the house, all ready by nine. She'd apply a lot of oil to her hair, comb it down neatly, seamlessly attach a hair extension piece and make a tight bun covering her nape.

In those moments, ammayi looked much younger and full of excitement. In the time it took Marimuthu to get ready and get the vehicle started, she would pace up and down between the porch and the gate at least ten times. She wanted to be the first customer to arrive at the bank. What if she was late and they said there was no more cash left to give and asked her come back another day? These mornings were the only special occasions when ammayi stepped out of the house.

But she also did not want Marimuthu to ride too fast. 'Go slow,' she'd command. Those were the moments he could see how attached the old woman was to her life. No matter how carefully he drove, he was not going to be able to please her. Once she got the money, she would keep it in her yellow cloth bag, secure it with a knot and step outside the bank. Then, as if she was offering him his fee for giving her a ride to the bank, she'd say, 'Here, da. Go eat something,' and hand him a hundred-rupee note. In those moments, she always had an expression of great benevolence on her face, as if he had never eaten at a restaurant before and she was the benefactor who had come to remedy that. But she herself wouldn't eat food from a restaurant. 'I have never even set foot inside a restaurant. A woman from a good family doesn't go to such places,' she'd boast. Marimuthu would take the money without making any remarks, but he would not spend it at a restaurant. And ammayi knew that. But still, every time she gave him the money, she said, 'Go eat.'

She also kept accounts for everything related to the trip. Money for petrol for the trip and down. Money for him for one meal. And some contingency money. The hundred rupees she gave included all that. Even when she gave money to her daughter, ammayi did so according to some clear accounts she kept. Money for her stay in the house, for food expenses and fee for the work she did around the house—it included both expense and income.

But his mother received whatever ammayi gave her with a grinning acceptance.

Occasionally, someone might casually remark, with a tinge of jealousy, 'How lucky you are, aaya. Your grandson takes you out on his vehicle.' She would reply, 'He is not doing it for nothing. I pay him for it, don't I?' Or, if someone said, 'Why are you living at your daughter's?' she would justify herself, saying, 'I am not freeloading. I give them this much every month.'

She loaned the rest of the money for interest among the workers. Her purse was always full. How would she secure her future if she just gave away the money without adding to it? Ammayi's attitude to work was the same as her attitude towards money. How could anyone just lie on the cot in the middle of the day? If a farmer slept like this, how would the land show its compassion and give its yield? And people who might consider giving their daughter in marriage—won't they be put off if they heard about such laziness? She'd speak as if the only reason no one offered their daughter in marriage to him was that he slept too much. But Marimuthu now slept all day until all her mutterings and objections lost their sting. Sleep had taken such a hold of him.

On that day, ammayi was watching a TV serial, sitting with some other old women from the farmsteads nearby and some women who worked in the fields. Their own comments and responses were louder than the sounds from the TV. To free himself from all that noise, he gently closed the door to his room and lay on the cot under the ceiling fan. Even though he felt guilty about sleeping so much, sleep still comforted him, freed him from his many problems. All those dreams that used to haunt him—they seemed to have vanished without a trace. In the warmth of that room, he felt safe, like he was in a womb, and he slept without any worry or concern. He was not even afraid that ammayi might come and wake him up. Even though the heat of the midday had spread a stuffiness in the room, he covered himself with the blanket.

24

Just when he had lost himself to a deep sleep, he heard a voice thundering: 'Dey, Marimuthu!' He woke up with a start. At the door that was half open, ammayi's face appeared in a haze. He felt like slamming the door on her face. Fearful that he might say something rude, she quickly said, 'Veeduthi has come,' and walked away. Marimuthu just did not want to get up. He was also quite tired of talking to Veeduthi. She must have come to show a few more photographs and horoscopes, and she'd expect some money for that. So many horoscopes so far. So much money.

Veeduthi had built a multi-storied house with all the money she made from this work. Hers was the biggest house in her neighbourhood. Every day, very early in the morning, she'd take the first bus out and get to town. Anyone could see her at six in the morning at the tea stall run by a Malayalee man on the east corner of the new bus stand. Some ten others—both men and women—would have assembled there. They were all from different villages, all from families of field labourers, and they worked as marriage brokers. Sitting there, they'd exchange the horoscopes and photographs they brought with them. They'd also give and take money among themselves. They had an arrangement. If an alliance worked out, they'd get ten percent of the dowry money. If the dowry was one lakh, the broker got ten thousand rupees each from the bride's and the bridegroom's families. The families also had to give them new clothes as gifts.

At least twice a month, Veeduthi came over to see Marimuthu. He had even set aside a certain amount for her, like a monthly salary. But now, he had no desire to see her. He didn't even bother to wash his face. Just draping a towel over his chest, he stepped out of his room. Ammayi and the other women did not even look away from the television. Veeduthi was sitting outside under the neem tree. Chewing betel leaf and swirling her tongue in her mouth, she said, 'Our little landlord now sleeps in the afternoons?'

He replied, 'Maybe people like you who make money without much hardship can do with a night's sleep. But for us who labour hard in the fields, our bodies yearn for a bit of rest in the afternoon. What to do?'

'I make money without hardship? I wake up at dawn and I go around calling at so many houses and fields like a crow. By the time I get home, it is dark. Even then, landlords like you have a hard time paying me for my work.'

'Why don't you lie down for a bit in the places you visit?'

She couldn't tell if he was insinuating something by that remark. She now spoke in an irritated tone. 'Well, we need to take a good look at our own arse before taking a dump on others.'

Marimuthu wondered if that was a dig at him. He just wanted to be rid of her soon. 'So, what brings you here today?' he asked. She pulled out some horoscopes from her yellow bag.

'One of these will work out for you, saami. Look at this one. The girl is twenty-five years old. The family let her get some higher education simply because she insisted. Now, men don't want to marry her for being overeducated. Our folks here don't make their sons complete their basic education, do they? So, the girl's family says they'd be happy with a farmer. The girl is so beautiful, she looks like a statue in our village temple . . .'

Veeduthi carried on as usual, but he had no more patience for this.

'Veeduthi . . . until the matter of the red-soil land is sorted out, let us put things on hold. We will resume later.'

But after coming all the way, she was not ready to go away without making some money.

'Let the land matter unfold as it does. We can also work on this on the side. Perhaps your wedding is destined to happen the moment the land issue gets sorted out.'

She was the only one who had not made that remark yet. He was tired of hearing it.

'No, Veeduthi . . . Someone is coming to chop down the trees this week. That is all I have time for.'

He was really keen on sending her away. His eyes were heavy with sleep. And she realized nothing was going to work out that day. She spat out the betel leaves she had been chewing and wet her lips with her ochre tongue. As she walked away towards the panchayat road, she said loudly enough for him to hear, 'Now, the only place we can find a girl for you is from our part of the village.'

She seemed to know exactly the words that would wound him and rile him up. He felt rage mounting within him, but he did not say anything. He lowered his head and looked up only when he felt calm again. In the haze of the midday heat, he could see Veeduthi walking away at a distance. He went back into the house.

It looked like the TV show was over. The old women were chatting among themselves. Without turning to look at them, we went into his room and turned on the fan. There was a power cut. He opened the window. It was very stuffy. Then, he heard ammayi's voice.

'I suffered a lot under my mother-in-law too. What they are showing now in this TV show is nothing. Do you know how my mother-in-law treated me? She followed me around all day and found fault with whatever I did. I was very young then. All I could do was cry.'

'How old were you when you got married, aaya?'

'I was eleven. They got me married even before I came of age. I moved into my husband's house only when I was twelve. That woman—my mother-in-law—she did not even let me take a good look at my husband. By the time he got to come near me, I was fourteen . . .'

The women laughed. Marimuthu was irritated by all that chatter and laughter. He stepped out of the room and yelled at them.

'Don't you all have work to do in the afternoon? You have come to hear stories about women finding their husbands when they were ten-twelve years old? Go away!'

The women felt insulted, and they went away. One of the elderly women mumbled as she left, 'He thinks he is the only one who has got a TV. Useless fellow.'

Ammayi sat leaning on the wall and said nothing. After saying his piece, Marimuthu rushed back into the room and fell on the cot. He felt somewhat pleased. He thought he might be able to sleep in peace for a while. But his mind was alert and awake. He remembered that Veeduthi was responsible for the purchase of the TV.

On that day, too, she had arrived with a horoscope to show. When they told her that it was a good match, she told them more about the girl. She was an only child and conceived after years of marriage. So, the family had pampered the girl a bit. No one woke her up in the morning. She rose whenever she wanted, and she spent most of her day watching television. The girl's father had made one thing clear to Veeduthi. 'It doesn't matter where she gets married. Just make sure it is a family with a TV in their house. Our daughter can part from us, but she cannot live without a TV.'

Veeduthi had excuses to offer for each girl whose horoscope she brought along.

'These days, no girl can be without a TV, saami. This was not the case in your mother's time or your grandmother's time. We can't expect today's women to drape a work sari and toil hard in the fields and the cattle shed. Things have become far more civilized these days. It is the girl's father who will pay a visit first. Buy a TV as soon as possible. That will make him happy.'

He bought the TV that very same week. But there was no cable connection available in the area. Their house was out in the middle of nowhere. It would take a great length of wire to secure a cable TV connection. The cable guy said he would provide the connection if Marimuthu would bear the expenses for the wire. Marimuthu had no other choice. So, he paid for it and got the cable connection from a long distance away. He placed the TV in the common area so that when the girl's family came to visit, they'd see it right away.

Initially, his mother expressed her annoyance. 'He has not bought this TV for me. He has bought this for the lucky girl who is going to marry him. If they tell him that they'd marry their daughter to him only if he wipes her ass, he'd probably do that too. I am not going to watch this TV. It is not for me.' But no one came from that girl's family. All that drama and expense—but nothing came out of it. Some other match must have worked for the girl.

In the beginning, amma did not watch TV. But once ammayi slowly got sucked into the habit, his mother too joined her. Perhaps if Marimuthu had married that girl, his mother might have stayed away from the TV for good.

He had taken Veeduthi's advice seriously and spent over twenty thousand rupees. Instead, he could have just flung fifty rupees at her and shut her up. She'd have taken it with an ingratiating grin. Now that she saw that nothing had worked out for him yet, she dared to say she would find him a wife from her part of the village. Feeling hurt that he had become such a laughing stock, he buried his face in the pillow. He had just been trying to take his mind away from everything and to get some sleep. Why did she have to come looking for him?

She would never come back again. He had hoped that she would bring a solution to his problem. But now, he had ensured that that path was closed to him—closed not with a rock but by a dense thorny tree he had felled on the path himself. But it was Veeduthi who brought the thorns. He told her to let things be for a little while. She could have accepted that.

On the other hand, what did he have to lose by marrying a girl from her part of the village? It was a wretched sense of honour that came in the way of something like that. Why? What was it the girls from that community lacked? They all had striking features and they looked fair-complexioned. In fact, Kuppan's son must be marrying just such a girl. But would people accept it if Marimuthu gave up caste allegiances just for the sake of a girl?

What would Veeduthi do if he said to her the next time he saw her, 'Alright. Go ahead and find me such a girl'? Would she say, 'It won't work out between our families, saami'? How would it look if their people came over together, as relatives, and stood in front of Marimuthu's house? What would such a scene look like? He imagined various such scenarios. In one, his mother wailed, hitting herself on the stomach. His ammayi carried her bag of money and ran back to her son. And he could not find his father anywhere—he seemed to have vanished into the fields like a rat. Then, suddenly, the house was filled with the sounds of celebration. But was it a wedding or celebration of a life after its passing? He could not say for sure. Sleep had now deserted him completely. He couldn't bear the stuffiness of the room.

He went to the backyard and poured some water over himself from the vat placed there. Then he changed his clothes. He felt an urge to get away from that place as soon as possible. As he took the motorbike out from the porch, he caught a sudden glimpse of ammayi who still sat leaning on the wall. It looked like she had been in that position for a long time. It occurred to him that his words must have wounded her.

He stood holding the bike. He wondered if he wanted to go back in and comfort her. When she had a grandson of over thirty years of age still struggling to get married, she was busy telling everyone how she enjoyed her married life with her husband when she was twelve. Wasn't it understandable that it would make him angry? She might be elderly but she lacked discernment. It was alright if a few harsh words were to make her reflect on her behaviour.

He started the bike, all the while looking at ammayi who sat still as a doll.

25

In the red-soil land, daylight finally got to caress the earth. It was a touch that had been denied for years. The earth seemed to smile through the gaps between the felled trees that lay on the ground. Marimuthu nudged up a bit of the soil with his foot and picked it up in his hand. Its luscious, ochre-red coolness spread on his palm. He examined it carefully and saw that he couldn't find even tiny gravel in it. It was all moist, smooth soil. Soil of such quality could be achieved only after years of ploughing, bringing all the gravel from underneath to the surface, and then clearing them away. It must have taken extraordinary labour to accomplish that.

The many hands of his ancestors must have toiled hard at the task of removing stones and pebbles from this soil. Thoughts about all those faceless people who had managed to leave only the most fertile land for their future generations ran through his mind. Just one generation had managed to lay to waste such a precious piece of land. May it see good times at least from now on.

Some men were at work, clearing away the thorny shrubs. They cut away the branches and blunted the main stem. Only the thick parts of the branches they piled separately to a side. The thorny twigs they had chopped away now lay criss-crossed on the ground, looking like nets had been spread out on the earth. In the midst of all that had been chopped and cleared stood two neem trees, breathing free for now. They too would be chopped down in a few days. The men had been at work for only a day, but they had already cleared away quite a bit. By the time dusk fell, they would bring some order to the parts they had chopped and cleared.

Getting rid of these thorny trees is no small task. When they first come up, they appear quite harmless. But they gradually take over the entire space. Even if it did not rain for an entire year, these bushes would remain unaffected and resilient. And if it rained a lot and water stagnated in the field for months, these thorny trees would not be affected by that either. They did not rot or wither. They stored their poison on the tip of their thorns. Even a small prick can cause much damage. If you stepped on a thorn and the tip broke and lodged itself under your skin, that's much worse. It has to be removed very carefully. The men had pruned some of the long branches of these very thorny trees and were using them for their work. They were working methodically to clear a passage into the land.

As he walked in, the workers saluted him.

'Theethan, tell me, do you think you will be done with this work in ten days?' An elderly man with a taut and trim body replied, 'We can complete the task in eight days, saami.'

'If your wedding gets fixed by then, let us know. We have enough firewood here to do all the cooking.'

Marimuthu looked at the man who made that remark. It was Veeduthi's husband. He had now turned his face away on the pretext of moving the wood to a different spot. Marimuthu knew that the man must be pleased with his remark. At the moment, all the other men showed restraint. But as soon as Marimuthu was out of earshot, they would talk about it and laugh. Realizing that his silence would make him a meek partner in their ridicule of him, he said in an irritated tone, 'Well, if the wedding gets fixed by then, we can buy gas stove for the cooking. Take all this wood away. Maybe it can be used to burn someone.'

He did not want to linger there in their midst, so he moved away from their gaze. Even casual conversations had become so difficult. People seemed to be waiting for the right opportunity to turn their words into arrows. Or it was Marimuthu's own words that flew out like fire. What's the use of words if all they were capable of doing was burn and wound? It was better if people did not speak to one another at all. He had already minimized his interactions with his family. Now, perhaps he needed do the same with others too. The trouble was that he had to use words even to say hello to someone and to ask how they were doing. But those words kept growing until they ended in silence. However that was not all that words accomplished. Words also led to relationships falling apart. Ammayi came to his mind. When he saw her last, she had been sitting, leaning against a wall and staring at the ceiling. He had almost stopped talking to his mother, and with his father he spoke only when it was necessary. It was only with ammayi that he'd had a cordial relationship. Now there was a minor crack even in that. He did not know then that it would become a much bigger rift.

He had expected that she would not talk to him for a little while. Definitely not for the rest of that day. Perhaps not the next day either. He had thought she might even choose to punish him by not talking to him for five or six days. But, in fact, she packed her bags and left the house. The farm boy Sakti told him that she carried her clothes and utensils in her big tin box and walked out of the house in the sweltering heat. Apparently, she left a message with Sakti: 'When the landlady comes, let her know I have gone home.'

They came to know more the next day. Once she reached her son's place, she did not go in. She sat under the neem tree in front of the house. It was the grandchildren who noticed her first. Since it had been five or six years since she had walked out of their home, they were apprehensive about approaching her and instead let their parents know that she had come. The moment he saw his mother, the son could understand everything. For six years, he had resolved never to look at her ever again. But now as he saw the tin trunk, he understood what must have transpired. He turned a page over in his mind and felt love towards his mother. 'Amma, why are you sitting here? Come inside.' At this, she looked up at him and then broke into uncontrollable sobs. What could communicate more emphatically than tears? Her son did not ask her to explain anything. The daughter-in-law pulled a long face, but she did not make any remarks. It is doubtful whether such scenes of affection would have occurred if the old woman had come back empty-handed. She went away with one lakh rupees, and now she had brought back all of it. What is more, she now also had the interest on it.

However, even though the people who were directly involved in the matter might prefer to keep things to themselves, they could do nothing to stop other tongues from wagging. This was the topic of conversation at the tea shop. The women who had come to watch television with ammayi must have dressed up the story a bit. It came to his ears that people were saying that he had said to ammayi, 'Are you yearning for a husband at this elderly age?' People said, 'Whatever their problems, she is an elderly woman, a close relative who has come to live with you. How could you ask her such a question?'

'If we step beyond what is ours and where we belong and instead come to rely on others, we will have to hear such insults one day.' 'Marimuthu seems nice enough when you talk to him, but he has a twisted mind.' 'No wonder he has not been able to get married.' 'Do you think he will be able to get married now? The old woman's curse is bound to have an effect.'

Underneath all these comments, Marimuthu could sense their glee at the fact that ammayi's one lakh rupees would not go to him now. But he felt relieved that at least now people would not accuse his family of depriving his uncle of his rightful inheritance. He also learned that two days after ammayi left, his uncle came to their village to meet some of the farm labourers. He had come to explain the situation to all the people who had taken loans from ammayi and to collect the dues.

Apparently, despite her son's exhortations, ammayi kept to herself and even insisted on cooking her own food. She moved into the little thatched hut that was right across the street from her son's house. In the past, she had lived there with her husband for several years. Of late, it had been used as a storage space. But she cleaned it up, had it organized and turned it into her living quarters. She could walk out of her daughter's house when her grandson insulted her. But now, if her son or daughter-in-law were to treat her poorly, where would she go? So, in order to avoid such a situation, she decided to keep to herself, have her own space and make her own food. Later, the gossip at the tea shop brought the information that one day, ammayi went with her son to town. It was not yet time to collect the interest amount from the book. So, this trip to town must have been to make changes to the nominee and heir information at the bank.

Marimuthu did feel some guilt about his harsh words to ammayi. He had lost control and given his wretched tongue a free rein. When her thirty-two-year-old grandson was lamenting his singlehood, why did his grandmother have to chat about being married when she was only twelve? She might be elderly, but she was certainly not very wise. Then there was Veeduthi. She was the one who had put him in a bad mood that day.

Many things had conspired that day to make those words come out of his mouth. What could he have done? No one had asked ammayi to come and live with them. She had done it on her own. Now, she had left on her own accord. That was all there was to it. Perhaps she would not have left if he had apologized to her right away. But no one knew she would pack up and leave. She had moved in six years ago. He had thought that she was a part of the family. Clearly, he had been wrong. It was clear now that no matter how long she had lived here, she had not thought of this place as her home.

As for him, no matter how many arguments and fights happened, there was no place else he could go. Nor did his mother. As for his father, it wouldn't even occur to the man that he could perhaps go away for a while. Clearly, ammayi had thought of their house only as a temporary arrangement for her. In her mind, *her* home, *her* wealth, *her* relations have all been at her son's. What occurred between Marimuthu and her simply became a moment when that truth could reveal itself. It could easily have come out at any other time. In that moment, Marimuthu became the reason. People become mere excuses for things to unfold themselves. That's exactly what had happened here.

But no matter what he did to console himself, his mother was not going to let it go. The moment he walked into the house, she started yelling. And there was no way to predict what she would say. 'He asked the old woman if she was looking for a husband. Who knows how many wives he is looking for?' she said once.

His mother's problem was not only that when ammayi walked away, all the money went with her too. The truth was that ammayi used to be very active and performed a lot of chores around the house. Since the day ammayi moved in with them, his mother hadn't washed dishes. She hadn't swept the floor. Even on festive occasions, his mother didn't decorate the house with chalked lime. Ammayi did everything. His mother did not pack lunch for the farm boy. No matter what you said about ammayi, you had to acknowledge this—she had shouldered a lot of responsibility with much grace.

Now that all the work fell on her, his mother couldn't manage. She used to attend to the calves, the milk sales and the sale of vegetables and coconuts. She used to spend her time out of the house, in the village, attending to these things. And now that she had to stay home and do all the things ammayi used to do, she protested.

She said, 'What sin did my mother commit? All these useless dogs could laze around because she did all the work. Now they find fault with her!'

Marimuthu always ate alone. He'd help himself to the food in the kitchen. No one really knew when he had his meals. Whenever ammayi checked the pots and saw that the food was still there, she would grow concerned and ask him why he hadn't eaten. But now, his mother seemed to be waiting for those hours when he went to have his meals. 'Who does he think has to do all the cooking so he can just show up to fill his stomach? Why can't he go find a wife to cook for him? Why burden me?' Then she'd turn away and pretend to shoo away a dog or a buffalo that had wandered into their yard: 'Hey! Hey! Go away! Cheeky buffalo! I think I should cut down your feed.' Marimuthu was reaching the limits of his patience with his mother. He had somehow managed to guard his tongue so far. If only he could also close his ears to her. But it seemed like his ears were always wide open to take in all sorts of insults.

Surely, the sense of hearing is the greatest punishment human beings have been dealt.

Tired of his mother's complaints, he even wondered if he could go and plead with ammayi to return. But something stopped him. If it was so simple, his mother would have gone there herself to bring back her mother. There was no way she would have forgotten all the things ammayi had told her about her son's behaviour when she first moved in here. So, even if it was her natal home, his mother wouldn't give up her sense of honour and pride by going there now. Her brother might behave himself, but his wife wouldn't. Even though she was frail, she wouldn't let go of a chance to fight.

If amma herself hesitated to go to her brother's to bring back ammayi, what could Marimuthu do? Perhaps he could try talking to ammayi if he happened to see her out and about somewhere. But if she had already set herself up at the new place and was making her own food, it was going to be difficult to convince her to return.

When his mother learned that ammayi went with her son to the bank, she wailed. Marimuthu happened to be eating his dinner at that time. 'He has earned my curse! A woman's curse! He will go to ruins!' she bawled. Marimuthu picked his plate of food and threw it against the wall. He washed his hands and stormed off. For the next two days, he did not come home to eat.

If he wanted to eat at a restaurant, he'd have to go to town. But he was not sure he could go there for every meal. It was six kilometres one way. So, twelve total. Besides, it would take a litre of petrol daily if he decided to go there

three times a day. He considered going to the local tea shop
to eat. But the prospect of answering everyone's prying
questions about his family matters dissuaded him. He had
not been going there precisely because he knew they'd be
curious to know about ammayi. Now, if he started having
his meals there, it was as good as announcing to the entire
village that he had fallen out with his mother too.

A couple of times, he went to eat at his other
grandmother's, in her hut in the Minnakkadu grove. But,
even though paatti was still making her own food, it was
barely the case. Her dotage seemed to be upon her. When
she was done washing her dishes, there was still quite a bit
of grime left on the plates. Ash from the stove got mixed
with the food she made. She used to make such flavourful
kuzhambu; now she couldn't manage even a simple rasam.
It occurred to Marimuthu that he'd have to make alternative
arrangements for paatti's meals, let alone his. If ammayi
was around, things would be easier. She'd do the cooking,
and he could bring food to paatti.

Even he did not want to eat his mother's food anymore.
So, there was no way he could ask to take some for paatti.
She would be beyond enraged. He somehow managed for
a couple of days. Eating at a restaurant was not quite as
satisfying as eating a home-cooked meal. He still felt a
little hungry even after a meal. He could not bring himself
to try new and exciting dishes either. That would be fine as
a rare treat, but too expensive to do on a regular basis.

It seemed amma was a bit rattled by the fact that he
had stopped eating at home. She initiated peace talks
through his father. At dinner time, he was lying on the cot

out front. His father said, without directly addressing him, 'Not eating at home these days?'

He just said, 'Mm.'

'No matter how upset you are, you should not stop coming home to eat.'

'Do you think I am a dog? To take all the abuse and still come back to lick my plate?'

He sat up in the cot. From where he sat, he could hear his father slurping up his rice and curd. Appa then licked his hand clean. Then he washed his hands right over his plate, gulped down a large glass of water and let out a loud burp. As he was about to set out, wearing his towel over his shoulder and putting his sandals on, he said, 'She won't say anything. Go eat.'

Leaving those words behind, his father vanished into the night. Even then, Marimuthu did not relent right away. He decided he would wait till the morning to start eating at home again. When he had his breakfast at home the next morning, his mother was not in the house. In fact, she was never around when he had his meals these days. It felt like the very air in the house had gone absolutely stock-still. Even the sounds of utensils seemed to echo through the house like rocks rolling. During the day now, there was no place more unsettling for him than his own house.

Amma stopped speaking to him. The dog's barks and the cows' calls were the only sounds of life around the house. He tried to occupy himself by mending the small thatched shed in the orchard. They had built it long ago to store coconuts, but it still did not have a proper wall. They had simply propped it up with poles on four corners and two neem trunks holding it up in the middle. Since they always ended up taking the coconuts home, the shed had been in disuse and in need of some repair.

He sent for Vatthan, Kuppan and Sakti, and set about making a thatched panel to affix as a wall to make a properly enclosed shed. It was a very small shed, requiring only seven stacks of coconut fronds. Once he put up the thatched wall, the shed looked neat and compact, much like the temporary enclosures they make with fresh green palm fronds for girls when they come of age.

26

Marimuthu walked over to the well and looked at the portia tree that stood nearby. It had grown like a banyan and taken up a lot of space. There was not a single scar of a cut on the tree. The ground under it was covered by leaves and flowers from the tree. From where he stood, he had a good view of the place where they had cleared some thorny shrubs. Once they cut down this tree, this space would look just as clear and free. He had hoped he could save the tree somehow. But it did not seem likely.

When she came to know that they were planning to cut down all the trees, his paatti said, 'Please don't cut down that portia tree near the well. It came with me when I got married and moved here. When my brother came here to fetch me for a visit home, he brought the stalk with him. He thought it would be good to have a tree close to the water. It grew so big so fast. They used to hang coir ropes, the rope for the well, palm leaf mats—everything on the tree. We never broke even a tiny limb from that tree to even feed the goats! Please make sure they don't cut that tree down.'

Looking at the tree now, Marimuthu really wanted to find a way to save it. Even if they chopped off the branches, the bottom trunk would soon sprout and grow out again. But when he had gone to discuss the matter, he could not bring up the portia tree in particular. Once it was agreed that the land would be cleared of everything first, matchmaker thatha got started on the next steps. They could discuss the apportioning of the land among the parties only after the trees were cleared and the land properly measured.

Thatha went to great lengths to make sure everybody involved was fully informed and in agreement with all the steps being taken. He invited representatives from both households to the land. He brought Kattayan from Kunnankaadu with him so that they could also decide and agree on the amount for the timber. Thatha had visited the land the previous day and made his estimates. But before he decided on the amount, he discussed it with Marimuthu and his cousins.

'Give us twelve thousand rupees. But clear away everything in ten to fifteen days.'

That was how thatha started the negotiations. Kattayan replied with a smirk, 'Is that the price for the land?'

'Oh! So you are ready to buy our land? Is your business doing so well?' asked Marimuthu's cousin Natesan. There was a sting in his tone.

Kattayan was offended. 'How expensive can it be? I am sure my job is good enough to afford that. Tell me. Let's talk.'

'He is just teasing you, Kattayan. Don't be angry. Let us focus on the matter at hand.'

'Teasing? Why should he tease me? Just because he has money, it doesn't mean he can say whatever he wants. I am not here to beg him for food.'

They had not even started and things were already going wrong. But thatha had a great deal of experience in playing mediator in such situations. So, he spoke with confidence.

'Look here. What's the point in my being here, mediating this? Whoever wants to speak, speak to me. You all might have any number of grievances about one another. This is not the place to address all that, let me be clear.'

Natesan mumbled something and sat himself down on a rock nearby.

'Kattayan, tell me. Tell us an amount that you think is reasonable. Then, we will see if that is agreeable to us. Otherwise, we can look for somebody else.'

After that, only thatha and Kattayan conducted the negotiations.

'The land is covered in thorny shrubs. It won't even sell for the amount I spend in wages for clearing it away. But there is the portia tree and five or six neem trees. Those are the only ones worth anything.'

'All that's right. You had a good look. We have told you our price. You tell us what's on your mind.'

Rubbing his beard with his fingers, thatha looked around at the land. They all decided to sit under the tamarind tree. Marimuthu brought a big stone for thatha to sit on. Thatha sat down, lifting up his veshti so high that everyone could see his loincloth.

'If you agree to five thousand, I will clear away and take the timber.'

Even Marimuthu thought that was atrociously low. But it was Selvarasu who spoke up.

'Well, if that's the price, then I can hire some men and get it done myself.'

Thatha intervened, 'What did I tell you all? Please don't interrupt. Why do you think we consult people who are experienced in specific tasks? So that the job will be done quickly. Clearing away the trees is not our job. Our work is to divide up the land. So, just ask him for a higher price.'

'You are asking for twelve thousand. There is no way I would get that much by selling all this wood. The most I can do is increase my offer by a thousand.'

The matter dragged on for a while, but they finally agreed on eight thousand rupees. Even though Marimuthu had earlier hoped that he could save the portia tree and a few of the neem trees from getting the chop, he could not say anything now. It was exactly those trees that Kattayan was keen on. Apparently, Marimuthu's uncle and aunt were even ready to cut down the palm trees, but their sons did not agree to it. So the palm trees were saved, and they were going to save the land from looking completely empty and desolate.

He did not know what he would tell his paatti. Perhaps he could keep a stalk from the tree and plant it in whichever section of the land came to him. It could grow there, planting paatti's memories of her home firmly in the land and turning them into a tree.

Marimuthu looked at the row of ants climbing over the tree. The trunk of the tree was broad and robust. Even the branches would be good enough for some window frames. The portia tree would definitely earn Kattayan a handsome profit. In a week, the ants would go looking for a different tree to crawl on. Everything had to come to an end at some point. When the tree would be cut down, it was not as if the ants would die too. They would immediately find somewhere else to thrive. Nothing is dependent on nothing.

It was the time of day when a yellow heat spread everywhere and pricked at the skin like needles. The men chopping down the trees seemed eager to wrap up work and head home. Marimuthu did not want to stop to chat with them. So, he walked on and found another motorbike parked near the path. Kattayan must have come to check on the workers.

'Come, mapillai!' Kattayan greeted him and walked towards him. 'How are you, uncle?' he said in reply. 'Are you here to see how the work is coming along?' Kattayan asked him. And Marimuthu nodded, 'Mm.'

'Mapillai, what was that the other day? You were quiet and respectful, but that cousin of yours was so prickly.'

Many were apprehensive that once this matter of the land was settled, the two families might let go of their enmity and become united again. Conflict among others made people happy. It was evident to Marimuthu that there were many people working hard to make sure the two families did not come together again. Kattayan seemed invested in that too. Since Marimuthu was aware of it, he did not encourage him much.

'Well, you said something, then he said something. I think you got even,' he said.

'How can that be? There is something wrong about the way he talks to people. He is not like you, he doesn't have your qualities.'

Marimuthu laughed, acknowledging the compliment.

'Don't be fooled when you finally divide up the land. They may say they are three brothers, so they deserve more. Don't agree to any of that. Consult a few people before you make decisions.'

'All right, uncle.'

He'd already received similar advice from several others. They seemed to have decided that Marimuthu was gullible and needed their help. Pretending to be ignorant, he listened and nodded to whatever they all had to say. But now he wanted to turn the tables on Kattayan.

'What do you think, you might make a net profit of five thousand from all this wood? Clearly, you are the one who has fooled us with a lower price!'

'You bastard! If I made five thousand from each site I worked in, won't I be a billionaire by now?'

'You must be a billionaire already. You think twice even about buying a cup of tea. All your money goes straight to the bank!"

'Yeah, that's what they say! But then, I can't be like you, can I? I can't keep my money hidden under my seat. But tell me this. How did you manage to lose that one lakh? That old woman—your ammayi—lived with you for all those years? You could have convinced her to transfer it to your name.'

'That's alright, uncle. Let it be. Why do I need someone else's money?'

'You are clueless. What does it matter whose money it is? Money made selling fish doesn't stink, does it?'

'All we need is to be able to enjoy our own earnings, uncle. I don't have a rightful claim over others' money, do I?'

'Perhaps, mapillai. But tell me this. What exactly did you say to the old lady that she walked away from your house without a word to anyone?'

Kattayan was clearly trying his best to get Marimuthu to divulge things which he could then share with others in the village. Marimuthu just smiled. Then he talked about things in very general terms without offering details.

'When things are stacked against you, your words can be easily misinterpreted, uncle.'

'I guess you are right, mapillai. You have enough money of your own. You don't have much use for others'. Besides, when you get married, your wife will bring a lot with her.'

As Kattayan was saying this, the workers arrived at the spot. He started asking them about the day's work. He preferred to transport the wood to a timber shop or warehouse the day it was cut. As for the thorny sticks and twigs, they went to charcoal pits or to brick kilns. The wood from the neem and portia trees would definitely go to the shops. Since he knew he was not needed for that discussion and since he was eager to get away from Kattayan, Marimuthu said, 'Alright, uncle. I will see you later,' and started his motorbike.

'Okay, mapillai. Invite us all to your wedding feast soon!'

Marimuthu drove away, pretending not to have heard those words. The bike's exhaust seemed to reflect the fact that he was fuming in his mind. He was really annoyed with Kattayan. Wedding feast indeed. People who ate nothing but gruel and balls of kambu millets day after day would certainly yearn for a wedding feast. Such people eagerly looked forward to a wedding feast so they could finally spread paddy rice and paruppu all over a banana leaf and eat to their heart's content.

Kattayan belonged to an older generation, the kind of people who made a lot of money but could never bring themselves to spend any of it. Every morning, he carried fresh milk to the tea shops. They made the first cup of tea only with the milk he sold them. But he wouldn't drink a cup. He'd say, 'I just had some at home.' He wouldn't leave either. He'd stay and keep chatting with everyone. If anyone offered a glass of tea, he'd first make a show of refusing it but finally accept. In all these days, he had never bought anyone a single cup of tea. He had made an art of getting free cups of tea. So, it was no surprise that his mind was on a wedding feast.

Kattayan only had two daughters, both of whom were married. All his money would certainly go to them in the future. Marimuthu remembered that, in fact, there had been a third child long ago. Kattayan's wife had their third child at the city hospital. They were not happy that the third child had also turned out to be a girl. They looked like they were in mourning.

They hoped people wouldn't visit to see the new baby. But a lot more people did than they had when the first two were born. And they all had various consolations to offer: 'What can you do? You are destined to have three daughters.' 'You think daughters don't take care of you and only sons do? As long as you have money, they will all fawn over you.' 'A son always takes care of us till the end.' It looked like everyone derived some satisfaction from the couple's predicament.

But all of this lasted only three days. On the fourth day, the new baby died. More people then turned up to express their condolences. The family repeated the same story to everyone: 'She wouldn't drink any milk, and she cried continuously. Then, suddenly, she stopped crying. We thought she had fallen asleep, so we let her be. Only after an hour we realized she was not breathing.' But everyone knew that Kattayan's mother-in-law was responsible for this.

Marimuthu's grandmother had been to see the dead child. Later, she smiled when she talked about it.

'That woman from Attoor is responsible for this. She turned the four-day-old infant on its stomach. It died suffocating.'

Paatti told him a lot more. 'In those days, we did not have medical procedures that stopped childbirth. But how many children could a family raise? If they turned a new infant over on its stomach, it would quietly pass away. You couldn't bear it if you stayed in the room to witness. You had to step away.'

'They did that even in those days?'

'Yes, of course. See, in our community, everyone had only two or three children. Not like some other castes where they have even ten or fifteen. But if we had that many children, each child wouldn't get even a tiny piece of land.'

'I guess.'

'Even in my case, when my last child turned out to be a girl, my mother put a few grains of paddy in the baby's milk. In just a little while, the baby died choking. If that baby had lived, who knows how hard its life would have been now?'

Who knows? If Kattayan had not killed that baby, perhaps Marimuthu would now have a girl to marry. These murderers were dreaming about wedding feasts. Marimuthu rode his bike really fast and arrived soon in front of his paatti's cottage.

27

Paatti was sitting outside on the porch, running her fingers through her hair. She rubbed some ground coconut on her head every day and washed it thoroughly, but still her scalp gave her trouble. Itchy blisters seemed to come up at night, and when she scratched at them with her blunt fingers, they burst with a burning smell and irritation, all of which ruined her sleep. For all this, her hair was not even long like it used to be.

During the years when she worked in the fields, she used to tie her hair up in a tight bun. She lost some hair from that. When she was younger, her mother used to spend a lot of time tending to her hair, combing and plaiting it.

It used to irk her father. 'These women! They seem to have forgotten they are peasant women. They are acting like whores, spending so much time combing and decorating their hair!'

'Well, your daughter has such lovely hair. What am I to do?' her mother would reply, laughing. She had come from a well-to-do family and had lost a great deal in marrying this wretched fellow. The thought occurred to her that her daughter's lush hair might serve as a reminder of all that.

Paatti decided that once she had arranged her hair to her satisfaction, she would walk over slowly to the red-soil land. She had often thought about going there, but something made it difficult. Even the prospect of travelling abroad seemed less daunting. She cursed god for keeping her family and all its land so scattered and separate.

The house and the barn were in one field. The orchard and the well were in another. The raised land on which paatti had her cottage was in a separate field. And the red-soil land was elsewhere, unattended and unused. She wondered if god had decided to make everyone in that family go their separate ways, turning their faces away from each other and tending to their own separate pieces of land. If she managed to catch hold of this god, she would ask him, 'What are these calculations of yours?' She wondered when she would get to meet her maker.

Once she was done running her fingers through her hair, she ran a comb over it. She felt the sun on her forehead. The day was moving fast. Since there were leftovers from the night before, she had not cooked anything yet. All she'd done was sweep and clean the entrance and wash her hair after massaging it with ground coconut.

If she had left by daybreak, she could have done some weeding in the red-soil land by now. After all, time didn't stop, whether you were working or sitting idly by. But she still sat combing her hair, feeling listless.

'Aaya . . . aaya . . .' she heard somebody calling. Who would come at this hour to this lonely outpost? Even if she died here, she would go stone cold before anyone found her. This place was quite a distance from everything. Only Marimuthu came to see her. But he wouldn't come at this hour. And people who wanted her to come to work in their fields always spoke to her when she was out and about. So, then, who was this? She quickly tied her hair and stepped outside. 'Who is it?' It was a young woman holding a little boy by his hand.

The woman said, 'Aaya, when all the kids were playing last evening, a fleck of dust went into his eyes. He suffered all night. I tried various things, but nothing worked. Looks like it is stuck to his eyeball.'

Paatti tilted the boy's face up and looked in his eyes. The left eye stayed shut. It was swollen, and he couldn't even open it. Poor boy couldn't have slept a wink all night. Tears kept streaming down from that eye. He stopped crying, but there were still occasional whimpers. He must be twelve or thirteen years old. Poor child! If he had a serious eye injury at this age, it might affect his vision for the rest of his life. She felt a rush of affection for the boy.

'These kids never listen to anyone. They play rough and hurt themselves and then come running to us. People say boys will do your work for you, lessen your burden. Not this one! He drives me to distraction.'

The woman carried on with her complaints. She couldn't partake of his pain, so she was ranting, trying to lessen her worries. The boy did not speak a word.

'Where are you from, darling?' Paatti asked the boy. But it was the mother who replied.

'We are coming from Nallur, aaya. We are washermen. I went to a lot of people. They all directed me to you.'

'Isn't Varadan the washerman in that village? I don't know you.'

'I am Varadan's wife. My husband died long ago. This boy is all I have. I met Varadan when I went to wash clothes. That's how we got together. But he died.'

'I don't go out much anymore. That's why I didn't know the news. I knew Varadan and his father. So, you are his second wife?'

'There was no marriage and all that. He asked me to be with him, I said yes. Sometimes he'd ask me to go away, and I would. Wherever I went, I washed clothes and earned my living.'

Paatti sighed. Then she stood facing east. The rocky hill nearby shone fiery red in the sun.

'Ayya, dear god! He is a little boy. You have to help him. Whatever it is that is trapped in his eye, however small it may be, please let it come out with the tip of my tongue.'

Praying thus in her mind, she stuck out her tongue. Its pointed tip probed the air like a snake's tongue. She could touch the tip of her nose with it. Her mother had also had a similar tongue. People came to her from all over. All she had to do was insert her tongue into the person's eye and give it a swirl. Even the tiniest piece of dust would come out sticking to the tip of her tongue. Paatti learned the trick from her mother.

Her mother's voice still rang in her ears. 'My dear, why do you think god has given us this special, long tongue? It must have a good purpose. Use it fearlessly to remove dust from people's eyes.' At first she practiced on eyes that were fine. Then, gradually, she became quite skilled at using her tongue to relieve people of the dust that went into their eyes. She had helped a lot of people over the years. This little skill made so many people from so many places come looking for her.

The boy did not open his eyes even a little. Paatti's tongue kept bumping against his eyelid. 'You have to open it a little, my dear,' she said to him gently before pulling open his eyelids with her fingers and inserting her tongue into his eye. Her tongue extended like a snail's antennae and probed his eye. The boy squirmed and trembled in pain. She could feel her tongue coming up against something, but she couldn't get it out. It was clear there was something in the eye. Why couldn't she get it out? Wasn't her tongue agile enough? Had she lost her ability to hold her tongue steady? Or had her vision gone so bad that she was not able to look into the boy's eyes clearly?

Her body became tense. She tried several times, but she could not remove the piece of dust from the eye. Her tongue came out empty each time. Paatti grew tired. She felt drained of all her energy. She was not able to relieve the boy of his suffering, but she did not want to add to it. So, she stopped and let go of him.

'I am not able to remove it, ma. Something is really firmly lodged in. Go to someone else. Or else go to the town hospital.'

'Aaya . . . aaya . . . please try again. I cannot afford to go to the hospital. I am a poor washerwoman. Please take pity on me.'

Paatti was irritated by the woman's insistence. The poor boy stood trembling like a little chick that had fallen into water. So, she spoke loudly and firmly, 'I cannot help. Please go elsewhere.' The woman walked away, crying, taking her son with her. But long after they vanished down the winding path, they lingered in Paatti's mind.

This was the first time her gift had failed her. She had started doing this when she was fifteen years old. Now, she was over eighty. The tongue that had deftly swirled around and removed specks out of people's eyes for over sixty-five years had now gone numb. The tongue that had known the cool touch of so many eyes had now stopped working. Paatti was tormented by the feeling that her life was over. Marimuthu had said to her, 'You are not able to see clearly, your hands are shaking, you are growing old.' She realized now that he was right. She couldn't even help a little boy. She couldn't remove the dust from his eye and relieve him of his pain. Of what use was she to anyone now? She lay down on the porch and stayed curled up there for hours.

28

The heat of the midday sun pierced its way into the cottage through the thatched roof. Marimuthu's paatti, who was lying on the porch, woke up when the heat was too much to bear and found herself sweating profusely. Dazed, she looked around, unable to tell how long she had been lying there. Then she walked over to the pot of water kept at the entrance and splashed some water on her face.

The water on the surface was warm. But after she had splashed a few handfuls, she found the water underneath to be cool and refreshing. Her eyes were sleep-crusted. Once she cleared it away and washed her face thoroughly, she felt she was beginning to find her bearings. She realized she had lapsed into a deep sleep for several hours. She had never slept during the day before.

If she ever felt tired or drowsy during the day, she would just lean on the wall and close her eyes. Within five minutes, she'd get up feeling refreshed. She'd feel fully alive, all the tiredness gone and all her energy back. So, the fact that she had slept during the day and for so many hours clearly meant she was seriously unwell.

She felt the stab of hunger and remembered that she had not eaten anything since morning. That little boy's face was firmly etched in her mind now. Poor child! Did anyone manage to relieve him of his pain? Or was he still suffering? And what was happening to her? Her eyes had gone fuzzy and her tongue had lost its power. Was her body falling apart? She sighed deeply at the thought. Then she went into the hut to get something to eat and opened the pot in which she had poured some water over previous day's rice.

There was a crystal-clear layer of water over the rice. She mixed it with her hand and picked up some rice from underneath. It was so soft, it felt like she was holding grated coconut in her hand. Marimuthu paid a lot of money for this rice. No wonder it was still so good even in the summer. But she did not eat the rice now. Instead, she poured some of the water into a little pot and drank a little bit of it. The water had absorbed all of the deliciousness of the rice meal. It was sweet as sugarcane juice. She drank it slowly, gently pacifying the stabs of hunger in her stomach. She did not add even a pinch of salt or bite into a piece of onion on the side.

She went back to sit on the porch. There was a hot gust blowing outside. Just past the entrance was a large acacia tree. Sunbirds had made a nest using twigs from the tree, building it to look like a pitcher in the middle. They were now busy flitting in and out of the nest. She was able to see it clearly. But everyone said her eyesight was failing. If she had managed to remove the speck from the boy's eye today, she could have proven them wrong. She had done it so many times in the past, but today she couldn't.

She had also never accepted money from anybody for that work. But people had always tried to offer her all sorts of things. Karuvayan from Kottakkadu wouldn't accept her protestations. He brought a buffalo calf as a gift and tied it up in her yard. But she couldn't bring herself to accept it. So, she took the calf right back and left it tied up in his yard. Velaan from Minnalur owned a lot of sheep. When he had poked himself in the eye with a stick of kambu millet and got a speck of it into his eye, paatti managed to take it out with just a single swirl of the tip of her tongue. He brought a healthy little lamb as a gift for her, but she refused to accept it.

She said to him, 'But if you insist on giving something, make it as an offering to our deity, Mother Kooliyaayi. Take it to her temple and leave it there. That will do.' Velaan did as she'd suggested, and it gave him some peace. From then on, if anybody insisted on offering her something in return for her services, she directed them to Kooliyaayi. If they were poor people, she gave them a simpler option: 'Tie up a single rupee coin in a yellow piece of cloth and set it aside. Then, whenever you are able to, go to Kooliyaayi's temple and drop it in the box there.'

She believed that her long tongue was a blessing from Goddess Kooliyaayi who always had her tongue sticking out. After all, very few people had such long tongues, and most of those people merely touched them to the tips of their noses to show off. They did not put their tongues to better use. But everyone in that area knew her name— Poovatha. 'You mean Poovatha who removes dust from eyes?' they said about her. Paatti had refused all the money and gifts people offered her for her work. But when it came in the form of a possible marriage alliance for her grandson, she could not refuse.

Paatti had a childhood friend from her mother's village. Her name was Poovatha too. They were inseparable and such close friends that they wouldn't even hesitate to eat food from each other's mouths. Until they came of age, they roamed around together. Then, that other Poovatha was married off to someone within their own kin in the same village. That family was incredibly wealthy. They owned so much land that they could not even cultivate all of it. Some of the fields lay unused and covered in briars.

But even though she had married into a wealthy family, the other Poovatha continued to be close and affectionate towards this Poovatha. One day, when the other Poovatha's granddaughter was eight or nine years old, she got a piece of dust caught in her eye. They had not expected such a strong gust of dusty wind to blow into their wet and well-irrigated orchard. It came out of nowhere.

It was a howling wind, the kind that suddenly formed at a particular spot and mostly swirled right on the spot. When it moved, it lost its force. It did not usually last long, but it caused a great deal of damage, lifting up leaves and dust and debris into a swirling pillar. People said it was a spirit that came in the form of a wind. If a person was caught alone in such a wind, they felt completely trapped and besieged. But if they summoned some courage and spat nonstop in its face, the wind usually relented. Somehow, the other Poovatha's granddaughter was caught in this kind of fearsome wind.

Since the girl had never seen such wind before, she was scared. And when she could not get rid of a speck of dust that had flown into her eye, causing it to redden and swell, she was terrified. They brought the girl here in a bullock cart. Her grandmother—the other Poovatha—was in tears when she came running to hug her friend.

They had planted groundnuts in the fields that year and the harvest had been an excellent one. Groundnut plants pulled by the roots lay in heaps all over the field. Workers sat in groups, separating the nuts from the plants. When they saw a small child being brought in a bullock cart, they were curious to know what had happened, so they all crowded around to see. Paatti—our Poovatha—knew what to do in such situations.

She asked the child to stop crying. Then, asking the crowd to clear some space, she stood the girl at a well-lit spot and looked into her eye. A tiny piece of maize plume had lodged itself firmly under the lower eyelid. She was just a child, but she opened her eyes properly and cooperated with Poovatha. Even elders were not this calm and patient. They squirmed and jerked their heads and made the job very difficult. The little girl's composure impressed Poovatha.

With the first swirl of her tongue, she managed to dislodge the speck from its spot. With the next swirl, she was able to remove it completely. Then she applied some palmyra extract at the spot where the piece of plume had pricked the eye.

It was Marimuthu who cut the young palmyra leaf to produce the extract. In just a few minutes, the little girl felt better and was smiling. Her grandmother, Poovatha was immensely relieved and happy. She had been close friends with this Poovatha for decades, but today she felt particularly moved and grateful. Overcome with emotion, she held her friend's hands firmly.

'Poova, listen. Is this your grandson?' she asked, pointing at Marimuthu. He had been most resourceful. He'd cut a tender leaf from a young palmyra tree and squeezed it to extract the juice. And it was he who had brought a glass of water for the girl to drink. The girl's grandmother had been observing his actions.

'I know that you never take a penny from anyone you help. So, what can I do in return? I will marry my granddaughter to your grandson,' she said.

'Poovu, such things are not in our hands to decide. We don't know what god's wishes are for these children's futures. How can we decide these things now?'

But the other Poovatha was feeling very emotional.

'No, Poovu. My granddaughter might have a lot of wealth to her name. But if she had lost an eye today, who would marry her? She was in so much pain today. You relieved her suffering in a minute. I have known you all these years, but today I really see how invaluable you are!'

'All right, Poovu. Some years from now, if both of us are alive, we will do as you wish,' she said, primarily just to appease the other Poovatha. Things said in the heat of the moment are like words written on water. So, this Poovatha soon forgot about it, but the other Poovatha did not.

One day, fifteen years after the incident, she showed up with her granddaughter's horoscope. Paatti was moved that Poovatha was making such an earnest effort to keep her promise. But she felt uncomfortable about deciding on a marriage purely based on a gesture of reciprocity. The other Poovatha, however, was firm in her resolution.

'We have to find somebody to marry my granddaughter. Why can't it be your grandson? He seems to be quite skilled at farm work. He is exactly the kind of person we need to take care of all our lands,' she said. And Poovatha found that to be sound reasoning. After all, if there was a girl with thirty acres of land to her name ready to marry her grandson, why would she object? By then, some fifteen or so potential matches for Marimuthu had fallen through. Poovatha did not want to let go of an alliance that had come seeking them out.

The horoscopes were a decent match. But there was a hurdle. A new man popped up, causing confusion like the fool in a koothu play. He was the girl's mother's older sister's son—her periyamma's son. He demanded that they marry the girl to him. It became quite a scandal. How could the children of two sisters marry each other? They were like brother and sister. No way this could happen! But the boy said, 'It is true that our mothers are sisters. But our fathers are not siblings. They are not related by blood, only by law. So why not look at the paternal relations and not the maternal ones?' No one could give a convincing response to that.

After all, it was very difficult for a man to find a girl to marry. Besides, she had a lot of wealth to her name. Why should a stranger get to enjoy all that? So, he took off with the girl in the middle of the night and married her in the Manchaami temple at the foot of the hill. The rumour was that their mothers, who were sisters, approved of this marriage. They wanted all their wealth to stay between the two families. So, they had created a drama to distract others and got the wedding done surreptitiously and with everyone's blessing in the family. After this incident, the other Poovatha never visited her friend again.

In all the nearby villages, this was all anyone could talk about. 'Can you imagine this? A brother and sister marrying each other and making a family!'

'Why not? There is some logic to that boy's argument. We usually look at the father's clan when we decide marriages. Why should we care if the mothers are sisters?'

'This particular match seems strange to us because the two women are sisters born to the same parents. Consider this. My mother and my wife's mother are paternal cousins. So, if you take our mothers into account, we are actually brother and sister. What can we do?'

'But the entire peasant world runs on such norms, doesn't it?'

Such talk lasted for a while. The couple that got married set up a home and had a child. The families combined their wealth and worked their lands to great profit. People moved on to other, newer topics. Since Marimuthu had not met that girl, he did not feel a particular sense of loss. But his paatti was heartbroken. She felt that it was god's punishment for accepting a reward for her healing work.

Paatti sat in her front porch, reminiscing about these things. Towards the evening, she set out for the red-soil land. For some reason, she was keen on seeing that land that very day. She was beginning to fear it might be her last chance. So, she walked along the mud path that cut across the fields.

After she moved to the cottage, she had been on this path only a few times. Whenever she had taken this route towards Karattur and passed by the red-soil land, she had walked past it without the least feeling that the place belonged to her. What aspect of her identity could she hope to reclaim in a place now covered with thickets and thorny bushes? But now she was eager to see it shorn of all the trees and undergrowth.

When she arrived there, she felt like she had just emerged from inside a dark cave. Five or six bullock carts stood on the land. Men were loading them with chopped trees. There were scattered piles of thorny twigs burning and smoking. She walked along a path made by the workers. The uprooting of the trees had turned the soil over, making it feel like soil on a ploughed field. Placing her bare feet on the red soil was very pleasurable.

'Saami! What are you doing here?'

She could not recognize the person who spoke to her.

'Why? Whose permission do I need to come to my own land?'

'Saami, don't get angry! It's me, Barathan's son, Subban. Don't you recognize me? I asked only because I have never seen you here before.'

'Oh, Subban, it's you! It's been months since I saw you last, isn't it? That's why I couldn't recognize you right away. Are you done with all the work here?'

'Yes, yes, we will be done in two days. We are told they will meet on Wednesday to discuss all final land matters. We've been directed to finish our work before that.'

'Oh, okay.'

Still speaking to him, paatti walked towards the well. Only when she went closer did she realize the portia tree was not there. She had been particular about not cutting down that tree. How could Marimuthu have let it happen? The trunk of the tree lay rolled over on its side. She touched it. The tree that had come from her mother's home now lay dead. Did that mean her life and link with that family was over too? Everything had been going wrong since morning. She felt dizzy and fell on the tree trunk. She could faintly hear Marimuthu calling out 'Aaya! Aaya!' and running towards her.

29

As it was the new moon day in the late summer month of Aadi, the temple was quite crowded. There would surely be an even bigger crowd in the temple on top of the hill. People who came from out of town liked to climb the hill and pray to the deity in the temple up there. As for the locals, since they saw the hill every day, they did not feel a particular urgency about going there. They always put it off for later. Going to the temple that was in the middle of town seemed to be enough for them. How did it matter which one they went to? They were both gods, weren't they? Marimuthu was very fond of going to that temple—the one in the middle of the town. Whenever he was there, he sat in a corner of its spacious outer precincts. Usually, he did not run into anyone he knew. Most of the people who came to the temple were people who lived in that town. This was very much to his liking. He could observe the crowds without anyone interrupting him. Women dressed in such an incredible variety of clothes and jewellery. Children prancing around like little lambs frolicking in a pasture. There were always fewer men. But those who did come were sincere in their piety.

Only the men marked the entire expanse of their foreheads with holy ash. And only men offered their prayers by fully prostrating at various spots in the temple. It was lovely to see the glow of bliss on the faces of some of these men. Most other men's faces were stiff and inexpressive. But women were different. As they walked around the sanctum, they laughed, shouted at their children, and engaged in gossip and chitchat. Women seemed to experience the temple as a happy place. Looking at them all, Marimuthu often felt that things were indeed as they needed to be.

Even though there were scores of people around him, Marimuthu still managed to find some solitude in that space. No one to hinder his thoughts. No one to disturb his silence. He usually went to the temple by four in the afternoon when they opened the sanctum and stayed there at least till seven. On special occasions, some devotees brought large pots of sundal or pongal offerings for distribution. There was a certain pleasure in standing in line to receive these offerings. It was an astrologer's advice that had spurred Marimuthu's very first visit to that temple.

At the time, many potential marriage alliances were falling through. So, as a remedial gesture for any unseen snag, the astrologer advised Marimuthu to go to the temple every week for seven consecutive weeks. He had recommended this particular temple because it had shrines for various deities in one place. Before that, Marimuthu had been to that temple only as a little boy going to school in town.

Back in those days, there used to be a beautiful garden within the temple complex, and there were several crepe jasmine shrubs in that garden. His paatti told him that the pristine white flowers of this plant were good medicines for the eyes, and she asked him to pluck some flowers for her from the temple garden. She used to crush those flowers and let the juice into her eyes. She said it was refreshing. Looking back, Marimuthu wondered if the temple had been as crowded then as it was now. Perhaps, as a child, he had been too anxious that someone might tell him off for plucking the flowers to really pay attention to the crowds.

As per the astrologer's advice, Marimuthu came to the temple for seven continuous weeks. He made special offerings to every deity in the temple. He dropped generous cash offerings on the plate. He had spent a lot of money in consulting astrologers. None of them ever found a serious snag in his horoscope. They only ever found minor hurdles and suggested easy remedies for them. 'Once the month of Thaii starts, things are going to take a turn for the better,' they said. And when the month of Thaii arrived, they said, 'Everything will be alright in Vaigasi.' He followed all their advice, made all the offerings they recommended.

One of those astrologers told Marimuthu that he must go to the temple for his clan deity every day for one mandalam, which meant forty-eight consecutive days. So, he rose very early in the morning and went every day to the Kooliyaayi temple that was seven or eight miles away. Another astrologer wanted him to go to the temple in Tirumanancheri, and Marimuthu did that right away.

But over time, he grew tired of everything and went to astrologers strictly only to match horoscopes.

But since then, he started coming to this temple regularly. Whenever he sat here for a little while, he felt a kind of peace come over him. It felt like all his mind's dirt and grime were dropping away and he was becoming a new man. Sometimes, he did wonder whether it was simply his mind's fanciful imagination. But then, so what if it was? We all need the kind of imagination that brings us some peace, he said to himself. Whenever he was in the main sanctum of the temple, he always lingered for a little while, standing with his eyes closed in front of his deity. When he opened his eyes, the deity appeared awe-inspiring. He had no specific appeals to make, so he always walked away in silence.

Mostly, however, he made a quick gesture of salutation at the entrance and headed straight to sit in the outer precincts of the temple. He also did not really choose particular days for his visit. He came whenever he felt like it. It just so happened that today was an auspicious day, the new moon day of the month of Aadi. At four in the afternoon, the summer sun still occupied most of the open area around the sanctum. The crowds would only get bigger towards the evening.

He saw a young lad of about seventeen or eighteen standing just inside the temple entrance, bringing his hands together and opening them in some earnest prayer. Marimuthu wondered what serious appeal the boy could have at his age. As he sat observing the boy, he realized someone was addressing him, 'Anna, how come you are sitting here?' In all these years, no one had ever disturbed his solitude here in the temple. Yet, he turned to look. It was Selvarasu.

'Are you here for the new moon day prayers? Actually, I needed to see you about something. It's good I found you here. Please stay right here. I will be back in a minute,' Selvarasu said and stepped away. Marimuthu saw him joining a woman and walking away somewhere. Did they come together? Was she a stranger? It looked like they were talking to each other, but Marimuthu could not say for sure. He could not see her face either.

He was a little annoyed with Selvarasu. He always acted as if nothing bothered him much. But, in private, he poured out his grievances. Marimuthu could not get a clear sense of the man's character. Ten days ago, when they had all gathered to discuss how the red-soil land was to be divided among them, Selvarasu had stood by, aloof, as if the matter did not concern him at all. It would not have taken much for him to stop his mother from saying the things she said. The negotiations would not have stalled.

Now, it seemed the matter of the red-soil land would not be settled anytime soon. Perhaps it all started with his paatti fainting. The issue now dragged on. Paatti took the cutting down of the portia tree to be a bad omen. Nothing would convince her otherwise. He told her that he had preserved a stalk from the tree for planting somewhere else, but she would not listen to him.

He even showed her the stalk. He told her that the stalk would not dry for even a month, and that once their portion of the land was agreed upon, his first task would be to plant that stalk. If they wrapped its base in hay, planted it and watered it twice a day, it would start showing growth in just four days. But she was not pacified. At times, she seemed to be talking to herself. He could not make out what she was muttering.

She had not seen that tree in so many years. How was he to make sense of her sudden love and affection for it? She seemed to imagine that her entire natal household was now in that tree. As she got older, it became difficult to reason with her. She was adamant about everything and she was afraid of every little thing. How to keep her from going senile? He could only help up to a point. Beyond that, things would have to take their own course.

How wonderful the land looked now, with all the trees and thickets cleared away, the soil fresh and moist like right after a rain. Once they used the money from the sale of the wood to get a proper land survey done, they could decide who got which section of the land, and he could get his work started. It would be good if the land issue was resolved soon. But women seemed to be in charge of things in the background. He had invited some important people to the discussion, but they all got snubbed.

They had invited ten neutral people to be present at the negotiations. Matchmaker thatha presided over the meeting. The village headman, trustees of the village temple and clan members were all present at the meeting. There was also a crowd that came to watch. After they took a walk around the land with the old man, they all gathered near the well. Even though the land had been in disuse for several years, they could still clearly see the slanting path taken by the bullocks as they operated the well's pulley system.

The water channel was not in a bad shape either. It was simply blocked by mud. If a few men worked on it with spades, it would be back in its original condition within an hour. The only thing was that they did not have bullocks to operate the system. In fact, the well too was not in a terrible condition. The structure had loosened in a few places and the stones had come apart here and there. But once they set them right and sealed them up with mud, it would be back in order. Marimuthu was dreaming about all the repairs he could do to the well, but he did not reveal his thoughts to anybody.

The morning sun beat down harshly. Thatha removed the towel from his shoulders and wiped sweat from his head.

'Couldn't you have left at least the portia tree? You cut down everything. Now there is not a spot of shade to stand in. This is the problem with our people. They think if there is just one tree left standing, who is going to get it? We have always been like this.'

'Well, you were born here too. Why do you speak like you are special?'

After the headman said that, the entire conversation went in that direction. It occurred to Marimuthu that the old matchmaker ended up saying exactly what was in paatti's mind. Perhaps he could have saved the tree if he had spoken up earlier. Perhaps. But then, if the tree had been left intact and it went to the other party, paatti would have been even more inconsolable. Then the entire negotiation would have hinged on the tree.

'Come, come! Let's not waste our time in idle chat. Let's get down to business,' thatha said.

'You started the idle chat!' said someone, and everyone laughed.

'Fine. Drop it. Now, how do you want to divide up the land? Ramasami, tell me. You are the eldest,' thatha said, addressing Marimuthu's father.

'What do I have to say about such things? Ask Marimuthu. He is the one who is going to toil in this land. Why ask me? I am here simply because he asked me to come. I shall quietly stand in a corner.'

Marimuthu was irritated by his father's words.

'All of you elders speak first and come up with a solution. Then we can see if that will work out or not,' he said, without addressing anyone in particular.

Thatha now consulted Marimuthu's uncle. 'Ponnucchami, what do you say?'

'You tell. Then I will consult my sons about it.'

'In the old days, when we had a piece of land, we cultivated it. We divided up the land, cultivated our portion for three years and then switched with the other party. But times have changed. One person might want to sell his share of the land to builders. But the builder might say he would purchase the land only if it had fields adjacent to it.'

'That's right. We cannot make decisions now based on how things were in the past. Times have changed. In those days, we ate our gruel and kambu and tended to the land. That was all life was. Not anymore. People dart about in motorcycles. They get to the town in no time. No young man wants to work in the land,' lamented the temple treasurer.

'Thatha, why don't you buy yourself a motorcycle? You too can get to town in no time!'

'Right! That's all I need now! Ride my motorcycle to town and find a girl to marry!'

Everyone was having a good time with all this chitchat. But thatha brought everyone back to the matter at hand.

'Hmm. All right. Then, if we are not switching fields every few years, we can agree to make a permanent allocation. Back in those days, the norm was that the older brother would take the land to the west and the younger brother would get the share to the east. Shall we abide by that norm and give Marimuthu the portion to the west, and the east side to Ponnucchami's household?'

There was no response from anyone for several minutes.

'How can we decide anything if nobody speaks? Please speak frankly.'

'Well, if we are giving up the old ways when it comes to taking turns cultivating the land, then why should we follow the old norms with this?'

'We don't have to. We can change it. Ponnucchami's family can take the west side. And Marimuthu the east side.'

Marimuthu immediately scanned the entire land in his mind. The west side was elevated land. The east side was a trough. If they divided the land east and west, it wouldn't be equitable. But he did not want to be the one to bring it up. So, instead, he followed his paatti's advice.

'There is no need for all that. I will take the west side.'

His uncle's wife immediately pushed herself forward from the crowd. 'What? Say that to some gullible idiot! He wants to take the west side!'

'That's right, di! What's wrong with that? The older cousin definitely has the first claim!' His mother had stepped forward into the fray. He had not invited her to this meeting at all. Why was she here?

'Oh! Why? Does he have something extra special that the younger cousin doesn't?' said his aunt.

'If people who only got leftover milk to drink can be so arrogant, imagine how arrogant we are entitled to be!'

'Who grew up drinking leftover milk?'

Both women were tireless in their tirade. Thatha raised his voice. 'This matter is for men to discuss and decide. All women please keep quiet.' But it had no effect. The women fiercely gesticulated and shouted abuses at each other. Their hair had come undone in all the frenzy. It looked like they might even hit each other. It was such chaos that people couldn't even clearly hear what each of them was saying. Marimuthu dragged his mother by her hair and pushed her aside. She fell face down on the ground. 'Shut up! Leave!' he shouted at her.

'Okay, then. I will shut up and leave. You two useless men stand here quietly and get fooled,' she said, standing up. She stood there, covered in dust, her hair undone, looking like a complete wreck. Then, she walked towards her husband and pulled him by the arm.

'He does not want to listen to me. You come with me. Let's go. Let's see how they decide anything without your approval. I am not like some women who have no self-

control and keep producing child after child. I don't have
to worry about how much land each one is going to get.
This land stayed uncared for all these years. Let it stay that
way forever.'

Marimuthu's father tried in vain to make his wife
loosen her hold on his arm. She dragged him away and
headed towards the mud path.

His aunt shouted back in rage, 'Who has no self-
control? Me? I slept with my husband and had three
children. Who knows whom you slept with!'

'Well, we men don't have any business where women
rule the roost. Let's go.'

After thatha said that, everybody dispersed. Marimuthu
knew that no negotiations could happen without his
father present. He was disappointed with Selvarasu for
not making the slightest effort to control his mother. He
wondered if he could have avoided the disgraceful scene if
he had invited his mother properly to the meeting. Did she
do this out of spite? She was angry at being disregarded, so
she ruined everything. Will things ever get better?

30

He could see Selvarasu talking to that woman in front of the shop that sold offerings to be made inside the temple. But since the view was partially blocked by temple pillars and the crowds, he could not see her face clearly. She must be a relative of Selvarasu's, he thought. After all, he was not familiar with the boy's relatives through his sisters-in-law. Even when Selvarasu walked with her to the temple entrance to see her off, Marimuthu could not see the woman's face clearly. This time, Selvarasu was blocking the view.

He also did not want to leave his spot to get a closer look. Selvarasu might think he was being inquisitive. The two vanished behind the temple gopuram. What did Selvarasu want to talk to him about? What excuse was he going to offer for not controlling his mother at the meeting? Perhaps he would beg Marimuthu to get the land issue resolved somehow. He was quite smart at getting things done. He looked very innocent. And he was candid in his speech. But what if it was all aimed at getting his work done?

He was lost in his thoughts when he heard Selvarasu
address him, 'Anna.' He had seen her off and was back to
sit down with Marimuthu. Selvarasu looked quite dashing
in his shirt and trousers. Marimuthu only wore veshtis.
Since he only ever worked in the fields, he never got the
chance to wear a shirt and pants. Selvarasu, on the other
hand, often travelled to other states on rig truck business.

'Anna, do you come to this temple often?'

'No, only occasionally.'

'Ah, okay. Anna, it is the new moon today. Shall we go
to the hill temple?'

Marimuthu hesitated. It was already close to dusk. If
they climbed up the hill now, it would be very late by the
time they got back down.

'If we go by bike, it will take only five minutes. We
still have some time before it gets dark,' Selvarasu said, as
if he had read Marimuthu's mind. He was about to open
the packet of food offerings in his hand, but Marimuthu
stopped him. 'Let's eat this on the hill.' Selvarasu said,
'Good idea! See, this is why I need an older brother!' He
put the packet in the plastic bag.

They walked out of the temple and got on Selvarasu's
bike to head up the hill. A crowded shuttle bus was also
getting ready to go there. The new road and the bus service
were the reasons for the influx of crowds at the hill temple.
It was sheer human ingenuity—paving a road on that hill
that was nothing but a large, smooth rock. All the little
imperfections and folds on the rock turned out to be perfect
places to lay the road. Otherwise, climbing the steps up and
down the hill was quite an ordeal. Earlier, it was nearly

impossible for the elderly to go to the hill temple. But now, it had become very easy. The bus dropped them right in front of the deity! There was only a short walk involved—the walk inside the temple.

Selvarasu drove at a leisurely pace. There was a lot of traffic, plenty of vehicles in both directions. As they kept gaining altitude, the views around them were amazing. The sky seemed to have come closer. Since he was focussed on the ride, Selvarasu did not speak much. Marimuthu now had a newfound desire to come to the hill temple as often as he could.

Even though they had made the temple as spacious as possible, the crowds were still unmanageable on special occasions. As a little boy, Marimuthu had been to this temple many times. Back in those days, the temple was crowded on new moon nights. On other days, there were only some newlyweds and a few other people. That was about it. But now, the temple was crowded every day. It was particularly so on new moon days. And on full moon days, devotees walked around the base of the entire hill.

Marimuthu and Selvarasu did not spend too much time inside the temple. They could not see the deity's face properly despite all the bright electric lamps. So, they kept moving.

Twenty or so steps up a staircase to the north of the temple was a large well. It was an incredibly deep well that had been dug right through the rock. In the past, it was filled to the brim with water in all seasons. Marimuthu eagerly peeped into the well. All he saw was plastic paper trash submerged in mucky green water. How could they keep the well in this state? They didn't seem to realize how vital the well was to that place. If they cleaned it, devotees could even take a dip in it. He tried to rotate the pulley. The screeching noise it made engulfed his deep sigh.

Selvarasu walked beyond and above the hill temple towards the peak of the hill. Marimuthu was not sure if he wanted to go there. But Selvarasu seemed to be playing the role of a guide. So, he decided to follow. Sometimes it was quite convenient to let someone else take the lead and to simply follow them rather than go through the dilemma of making decisions and choices independently. There were not too many people on this path. Since there were no paved steps on the rocks here, only the strong dared to explore it. When Marimuthu hoisted himself up over a large, sloping rock, he experienced an impressive breeze. He wanted to stand there and just enjoy it. But Selvarasu said, 'Anna, come, let us go all the way to the top,' and stepped on to the next rocky slope. He had to keep up with Selvarasu.

Selvarasu went down the slope and washed his face in the stream flowing there. Then, he quickly resumed his climb without even wiping his face. Why was he in such a hurry? The path to the peak was a dangerous one, but Selvarasu was scaling it deftly. It was clear that he had done this before. Marimuthu, on the other hand, had not been here in years. Even on occasions when he had visited the hill temple in the past, he never really wanted to climb up to the peak. His legs were beginning to shake a little now. So, he proceeded slowly.

On top, close to the peak, was a small temple. In an effort to attract devotees, the priest kept repeating, 'If you make offerings and pray to the deity here, marriages will happen without any hurdles, those who want children will conceive.'

Selvarasu produced a fifty rupee note, offered it to the priest and gave him both their names. The priest then offered prayers in both their names, blessing them separately for their marriages to happen soon, and gave them the prasadam. He was a dark, healthy-looking young man. Marimuthu wondered if the priest was married. 'Make a resolution that once you get married, you will come to this temple to offer special prayers,' said the priest.

'Saami . . . if I have entertained any sinful thoughts, please forgive me. Please make my wedding happen before the month of Aadi. I will come here and make a proper and complete offering,' he prayed most sincerely in his heart. 'Everyone who comes here has their prayers fulfilled. This deity is especially powerful to grant wishes for marriage,' the priest explained. Marimuthu was impressed that Selvarasu knew such places.

He felt that Selvarasu was overall more knowledgeable and had a wider range of experiences. He was impressed at how the boy had offered a fifty rupee note without any hesitation. Marimuthu would have had second thoughts, even though it was an offering to the deity, and he would have later felt bad about his hesitation and offered more money seeking forgiveness. But Selvarasu seemed to be of a different nature.

They had a view of the entire town from the top of the hill. The roads that radiated from the base of the hill seemed to stretch into a great distance. All the roads had

houses on both sides. As far as he could see, the view of
the land was completely covered by buildings. There were
palmyra trees all over the place and coconut palms in a few
places. Steadying himself against the powerful wind, he
took in the view around him.

'Anna, let's head back,' said Selvarasu. They put all the
coconut shells, fruits and flowers that the priest had given
them into a plastic bag. Then, with Selvarasu leading
the way as before, they started their descent. A beautiful
red sunset decorated the sky to the west. A flock of birds
flew towards the sun. Marimuthu stopped to wash his
face in the stream on the way down. He wanted to take
a moment to enjoy the coolness of the water on his face,
but Selvarasu did not stop. He seemed to be moving faster
than the wind.

Selvarasu sat down at a secluded spot behind a large
rock. It was quite evident that he was very familiar with
these places. Even before Marimuthu arrived at the spot,
he had broken the coconut pieces and split the prasadam
into two portions.

'Anna, what's bothering you? Are you worried that I
am deciding the share for my older brother?' he laughed.

Selvarasu was indeed sharp. Marimuthu sat down,
smiling. Giving Marimuthu his share of the prasadam,
Selvarasu said, 'Was I going too fast? Only because it would
have gone dark by now and we wouldn't have been able to
sit and chat like this.'

'What important matter are we going to discuss now?
You sound like someone dying to talk to the girl he is in
love with!'

Marimuthu's teasing made him blush. For a few minutes, Selvarasu sat in silence, his head bent, eating his coconut. Then he spoke without looking up.

'Anna, it is easier to talk to the girl one is in love with. But imagine having to tell that to one's parents and siblings.'

'You are right. But then, I am not your brother. So, you can speak to me freely.'

They both laughed. Selvarasu was skilled at broaching a subject. He never tried to keep things suppressed. Now, Marimuthu's remarks made it easier for him to open up. So, he came to the point right away.

'You might have noticed that girl in the temple earlier. She is the one I plan to marry.'

'Who is she? Is she related to your sister-in-law?'

'No, anna. She is not related to us.'

Selvarasu worked in the fields or travelled with rig trucks to other states where they didn't even speak the same language. How did he manage to meet a girl who was not known to his family in any way? And how did he manage to find such a girl right here in this town? But then, there were several other ways to meet women. Marimuthu did not want to probe and embarrass him. He clearly trusted Marimuthu. Otherwise, he wouldn't have brought him all the way there to open up to him. So, Marimuthu resolved not to say anything that could hurt him. He simply sat looking at Selvarasu, waiting for him to speak. After a brief silence, still keeping his eyes down, Selvarasu started speaking.

'Two years ago, for a brief period, I went to work in the mills. This girl used to work with me there. We worked the same shift. That's how I got to know her. I left that job because I felt it was more suited for wage labourers. But I still kept seeing her in the town. That's where the . . .'

'That's where the trouble started?' Marimuthu laughed. He then said in a concerned tone, 'Tell me. Where is she from?' Hesitating a little, Selvarasu replied, 'They are Mannars, anna.' Marimuthu experienced a cruel pleasure at this. His uncle and aunt wouldn't be able to keep up their preening and arrogance if their son married a girl from a lower caste.

What will happen to all their endless boasts about how they only had sons and even their cows only yielded bull calves? If Selvarasu married this girl, someone would surely ask his parents, 'How many piglets did the girl's family offer you?' At least a few people in the village would derive great pleasure in saying something like, 'If the harvest is not good in your fields, you can always go herd your in-laws' pigs.' Marimuthu was tickled by these thoughts.

'How did this pig-herder girl manage to trap you?'

He uttered those words despite himself, despite his resolve not to say anything that could hurt Selvarasu. The mockery and insult in Marimuthu's tone must have surely hurt Selvarasu. But he did not show it.

'Why does it matter, anna? We know her caste because she is from around here. So many men these days marry women from other places because they cannot find anyone to marry here. Who knows what caste they are from? If anyone asks, they always say the girl is from the same caste as them.'

'That might be so. But our ways of doing things may not be the same as theirs.'

'Why are they so important—these ways of doing things? Those people raise pigs. We buy those pigs, cook them and eat them. In fact, when I see how our folks fight for the head piece of the meat, I am almost convinced they are much better people.'

'Perhaps. But still.'

'Anna, I didn't expect this from you. I came to you because I thought you would understand. I cannot share this with anyone in my family. They will talk as if we are cast in gold and the girl's family are made of leather,' he said, feeling dejected that his trust in Marimuthu had proven to be misplaced.

Marimuthu realized that in his sadistic thrill at Selvarasu's predicament, he had wounded the boy with his remarks. Why did he do that? Was it because he was happy at the prospect of their family being disgraced in the village? Or was it because he was jealous that his younger cousin had found a girl to marry before he could? What made him so cruel? He teared up, ashamed at his own behaviour. But without revealing those feelings, he spoke calmly to Selvarasu.

'Rasu, I was not finding fault with you. I just wanted to know how you planned to deal with others when these questions would come up. Tell me, when do you plan to marry her?'

'Her father works as a watchman in a company. All her older and younger brothers have respectable jobs in various places. They have been looking for a match for her.

It seems she has a lot of relatives who are interested. In their community, they prefer to marry their daughters very young. She is twenty now, so they are in a bit of a hurry. I am friends with one of her brothers. He knows about us. He is one who has been helping us stall her family's efforts. But he cannot keep this up for too long. He also doesn't really believe that I will actually marry her and make a family with her.'

'If problems arise, can you handle them? People who live in towns somehow manage even when they marry out of caste. But we are not like that. We live in a village. Think about it carefully.'

'We can deal with all that, anna. A few dogs might bark, but I know a way to shut them up. We'll be fine. These days, there isn't much of a difference between villagers and townspeople. People cannot enforce sanctions like they did in the past.'

'That may be true, but your family has to accept the marriage. They have to give you your share of the property.'

'That's why I have come to you now. That day, the talks about the land got stalled because of the women. How could I speak up when my father and older brother were quiet? Tell me. You are an only son. You can make decisions on your own. I have to consult everyone before making a decision.'

Marimuthu agreed with that argument. After all, he could not keep his mother in control, even though he was her only son. How could he expect that of poor Selvarasu?

'All right, Rasu. It is getting late. Tell me, what would you like me to do?'

'If I marry this girl now, my family will disown me and not give me my share of the inheritance. They won't care about love and affection and all that. I am certain of this. That's why I think it will be good to get the land divided up first. Once it is in my name, I can marry her. They won't be able to do anything.'

'Did you think about that older brother of yours who is still not married?'

'What can I do about it? His situation is just like yours. They have been looking for a match for him for ages now. These days, it is so difficult to find a girl. You have to compromise. Instead, if you find fault with every girl, how can you hope to be married? I don't think he will ever get married. And if I wait for him to be married first, I am sure to die a bachelor.'

Marimuthu felt that those words had been aimed at him. He turned his face away and did not say anything in response. Who invented this thing called marriage? Did that person realize how incredibly messy and complicated it would get? Marriage was surely the brainchild of someone with a bloodthirsty desire for vengeance against the entire human race.

Dusk fell, casting a red halo. The sun seemed to have dropped all its rays. Wisps of dark clouds moved over the sky. In a little while, the darkness that lay hidden in the crevices between these rocks would envelop the entire hill. The darkness would protect him from the faces of others. He would not hear their voices. Night makes other people recede from view, and it makes one's own thoughts voice themselves. For an unmarried man, there is neither day nor night.

Selvarasu's voice brought him out of his reverie.

'Anna, you have not touched the prasadam. Eat it.'

He ate a little bit, but he couldn't taste anything.

'Anna, why don't you bring a few people on your side? I will bring a few with me. We will meet at broker thatha's house and settle the matter. If we keep dragging this, I will never be able to marry. First, we need to divide the land between our two families. Only then can I discuss with my brothers and decide which portion of our land goes to which of us. Everyone is already restless. We cannot carry on like this for long. What do you say?'

'All right, thambi. I will make sure no hurdles crop up from my side. My paatti is convinced that I will get married only if I secure my share of that land. Perhaps she is right. We can do the land survey and registration in September. But let us finish the negotiations now in August. If we are determined, no one can come in the way.'

'Okay, anna. I will consult with thatha and give you a date. But please remember this: I can get married only if this matter is resolved and my share of the land is registered to my name.'

Even in the growing dark, he could clearly sense the urgency and appeal in Selvarasu's face. Marimuthu felt affectionate towards him. 'Why could he have not been my own younger brother?' he thought.

'Thambi, I will be with you when you get married,' he said wholeheartedly. He flung the leftover prasadam towards the little monkey that sat looking at them. It deftly caught the food in its hands.

31

The road downhill was shrouded in darkness. Light from the vehicles passing each other brought moments of relief before they vanished around the curves in the road, leaving behind a darkness even denser than before. Selvarasu rode the bike very slowly, as if he just wanted to keep the engine on for the headlights. Marimuthu rode pillion, giving himself over to ruminations.

The two cousins had not spoken to each other properly since they were kids. Now, it felt like they had made up for all that in just one day. Marimuthu had still not exchanged a word with Selvarasu's older brothers. Perhaps one day soon he would get to talk to them just the way he spoke to Selvarasu today. Long ago, words had wrenched the two families apart, sowing enmity between them. Now, it was words again, but this time they showered affection.

If these relationships had not been blood ties, would this sudden intimacy have been possible today? People related by blood fought with each other one day and made up the next.

He realized he'd not had such a heart-to-heart with anybody in a long time. Before his younger sister got married and moved away, there was always laughter and chatter and playfulness. She always competed with him in everything. There had been times when he had been angry at her, even hit her. But when she got married and left from her natal home, he teared up. She hugged him and started sobbing.

Today, Selvarasu had managed to bring him to tears. He spoke calmly and with affection, in words that made a deep impression in the mind. He seemed to have assessed everybody and made astute judgments of their character. He'd somehow found the maturity to decide that he would determine the course of his own life.

Marrying a girl from another caste was no simple matter. It took a lot of gumption. But Selvarasu seemed to be taking it in his stride. It occurred to Marimuthu that if he had had a similar plan, he would have been married by now with a wife, children, a proper family.

Saroja came to his mind, with her sparkling little nose stud shining like one of these distant lights he could now see from a turn in the hill road. It was ten years ago. He had been at the height of his youth then. In those days, most of the boys in the village were busy joining the rig truck business, purchasing trucks to install borewells for various clients.

Two or three men would jointly purchase a rig truck. Each of them would invest a certain amount of money, and for the rest they took a loan from the bank. Everyone was possessed by these plans. All the young men from these parts went away for months at a stretch to far-off places in the northern states. It was as if they had resolved to bore into every inch of the earth.

Many of these men had earlier worked as drivers and cleaners for long-distance trucks and lorries. So, they took to the new job quite readily. But, while earlier the men used to be away for ten or fifteen days at the most, now they were gone for months. As usual, women took charge of running the families.

People who had some money to invest, people who could sell a portion of their land and raise the money—everybody was in demand in those days. Many of them advised Marimuthu to join too. Some showed up at his house every day, bothering and pressuring him to invest with them. What did he gain by being so attached to his land?

Even though he'd fully given himself to his land and toiled in it day and night all year round, there was not much of an income. It rained one year and didn't the next. If he purchased a rig truck, he could easily make two to three lakhs within a year. But he would have to spend months away in a place whose language he didn't speak. Language was no big deal! He could pick up a new language in four or five months. Did he plan to live his entire life working in the fields, sheltered from everything else happening in the world? There were several such reasonings and arguments. Marimuthu found these new prospects very attractive.

His family, however, did not agree. He did not control the family finances in those days. His mother objected categorically, saying she had god's word for it. Apparently, the deity once said to her in a trance, 'If you sell your land to invest in something, the new venture will go to dust.'

He staged a protest for a few days. He didn't eat properly, didn't go out to work and kept a long face.

He did not know whom his parents consulted, but they came up with a way to mollify him. They said they would buy him a tractor so that he could stay right here in town and do his work better. Happy that at least some good came out of it, Marimuthu agreed. It turned out that the new tractor had quite a demand both in the village and in the neighbouring ones. In the planting season, he used the tractor to plough the fields. At other times, he used it to move garbage, sand, gravel, bricks and more. He was busy with all this work for over a year. That was when he met Saroja.

He was working for a contractor, moving four loads of sand every day. Saroja was one of the workers who carried small loads of sand from the quarry to the tractor. She was very thin, and with her face layered in dust, she looked like a shadow that had risen from the ground. But when she washed her face after work, she appeared bright as a ray of sun shining through the coconut fronds. She had that winsome beauty that girls of sixteen or seventeen possessed.

When the workers carried loads of sand, Marimuthu did not have much work to do. So he sat watching them work and chatting with them. His gaze always followed Saroja wherever she went, moving when she walked, staying still when she stood still, looking down when she bent down. She didn't talk much. But Porasakka who worked with her was a chatterbox. It was amazing the way she never ran out of things to say. But it worked to Marimuthu's advantage.

He'd keep talking to Porasakka but keep his attention on Saroja. Whenever Porasakka said something funny, Saroja laughed. In those moments, her lips moved a little, her face shone. He set himself a goal. He would make her laugh like that at least twice a day.

The only piece of gold she wore was her nose stud. Her earrings were made of brass. She wore beads around her neck and a rubber bangle on her wrist. But she was incredibly beautiful. She could be an eternal standard for beauty. So what if she didn't have much gold to wear? He hated the people who spoke of marriage in terms of gold. He wished such people would take a good look at Saroja. If they truly had eyes, they wouldn't ask anything more of her.

It rained a lot that year. The harvests were good everywhere. He did not have much work transporting sand that season, but he somehow managed to see her at least a few times. He'd go on his tractor just to speak to her in single sentences: 'There is no work today, Saroja,' 'It will take two days. I will come back and tell you.'

Her house was four miles away on a large rock. It was a thatched hut with just a small thatched flap for a door. The small hut sat alone on a large expanse of rock. Her father, mother and younger siblings worked just a short distance away, breaking rocks for gravel. Once they were done breaking down a rock, they'd go looking for another one. On days when there was no sand quarrying work, Saroja stayed home, cooking or washing the dishes. Sometimes, she joined her family in breaking down rocks.

Whenever he went to see her, Marimuthu sat down on the rock. Even though they had a hut, their domestic life was not restricted to it. They inhabited the entire rock. It had become an inseparable part of their lives. At night, they slept on the rock, looking up at the sky. The very thought of that was appealing to Marimuthu. Even the wealthiest of people may not find such solitude and happiness.

He felt peevish thinking of his confined nights spent looking up at the ceiling of his room. He imagined how his life would be if he got to live there on the rock with Saroja. She did not reply to these musings of his, but she always smiled and hmm-ed. Very rarely, she would say, 'Sure, sir.' And he'd say, 'Sir?! I am not that old. Don't call me that!' She said, 'You may not be old, but you are still above us.' He found great pleasure in getting her to talk.

He wanted to spend a lot of time with her on the rock. But he was afraid that if her parents had a problem with it, they might keep her from coming to work. So, in an effort to show them that things were above board, he also paid them visits wherever they were breaking stones. They welcomed him, addressing him as 'Saami'. Her father's betel-stained mouth looked like a dark cave opening and closing. They'd talk about rocks and the price of gravel. Marimuthu hoped that they would never run out of rocks to break in that area.

He wanted to taste her cooking but did not have the courage to ask. She never asked him to stop for a meal. It was possible that she was afraid people might interpret that to be a new level of familiarity. But none of it mattered. All he wanted was to be able to see her as often as he could.

There was sand quarrying work one night. Marimuthu had turned his tractor's headlights on for illumination.

Later, when the work was over, he gave Saroja a ride home in his tractor. She would have been fine spending the night in the barn nearby and going home in the morning. But he wanted to take her with him.

It was a starry night. There was not a soul on the mud road. His heart beat fast with excitement. He had to lick his lips to keep them from going dry. When he said her name, she seemed to acknowledge it with a 'Mm', but he couldn't be sure. He wanted to stop somewhere and have a proper chat with her. But he did not want her to misread his gestures, so he dropped that idea. The night was still very pleasant, even though they hadn't exchanged a word. In fact, if they had spoken, the night might have ended in that moment. It was better this way. Now, he could dream about the things he could have said to her and the responses she might have given him.

The fact that he was interested in Saroja somehow became known in the village. Such bits of news had a way of spreading wings right away. One day, when he was in the tea shop, he heard someone say, 'How lucky for the rock-breaking Mannar, things are looking up for him!' On a different occasion, somebody remarked, 'After all, we are not as fortunate as rock-breakers. They don't need much money to roll around on the rock.' He also heard a man say, 'The juice from the betel leaf the Mannar women chew— oooh it tastes like honey!' Marimuthu did not respond to any of these things, but it made him anxious.

He often imagined that Saroja was with him all the time. He lost sleep thinking of her. When he did fall asleep, he was woken up by his wet dreams. He had to change his

veshti every night. Sometimes, he sighed for no reason. All
his actions seemed a bit crazed. He couldn't talk to anyone
properly. Talking to anyone other than Saroja seemed to
irritate him a great deal.

Could he get Saroja's consent and elope with her
somewhere? Could they get married in some temple?
Would she agree to these plans? He didn't know how to
broach the subject with her. One morning, determined
that he could not live without her, he rushed to her house
on the rock. But it was deserted.

Rock lizards crawled inside the hut. He saw the stove
on which Saroja used to cook and the coal stains on the
floor where she used to scrub the dishes clean. The broken
section of the rock seemed to welcome him with a grin.
The sound of someone breaking rocks came to him from
nowhere. What happened to her and her family? They still
had a lot of rocks to break. Where did they go?

He didn't know whom to ask. She had been coming
to work regularly. How could she vanish without a word?
He went to the quarry owner and the contractor. Their
replies were not satisfactory. 'A rock-breaker won't stay put
for long. He told me he'd found a boy for his daughter to
marry. So, he wanted to leave, and I agreed,' said the quarry
owner. The contractor said, 'It's not my job to follow him
around and find out where he is headed.'

No one in town seemed to know. 'Do you think those
rock-dwellers would inform me before they took off?'
'Marimuthu, you were the one who used to go to the rock
to talk to them. If you don't know where they are, how
would I?' Such responses shut him up. He went to the

neighbouring villages and spoke to the people who broke rocks there. They didn't know either. Saroja seemed to have vanished without a trail.

He wanted to die. He lay crying in his room. And he let everyone know that he wouldn't be working the tractor any longer. Saroja's absence had embittered him towards anything to do with the tractor. For years, it stood parked next to the fields. A couple of years later, he came to have a mild suspicion that his parents had been involved in the overnight disappearance of Saroja and her family. But he never made an effort to confirm it. He hoped he would run into Saroja somewhere, but it never happened.

32

Spending time with paatti had now become a painful experience. It was difficult to predict her state of mind at any given moment. There were times when she seemed perfectly fine, talking to him as usual. But sometimes, she would suddenly lose her grip on reality, and her entire demeanour would change. In those moments, she slipped into the past with an effortless ease. She lost all sense of distinction between the present and the past. And, sometimes, the future too.

Marimuthu was sitting on the porch and talking to his paatti. She was listening to him with great interest because he was telling her about the land negotiations. Suddenly, she said to him, 'I hear Marimuthu's had a baby boy. Have you seen him?' Marimuthu got angry. 'Aaya! What are you on about? Have you gone mad?' he said. Paatti stepped down from the porch. She tied up her hair in a knot and spoke to him with the fury of someone ready for a fight.

'You are such an idiot! Marimuthu married my brother's granddaughter, and now his wife has given birth to a lovely, chubby baby boy. Did it occur to you to pay them a visit? Getting drunk and licking her cunt—that's all you ever do!'

She was addressing her dead husband, Marimuthu's grandfather. 'Alright, I will go and see them,' Marimuthu said and walked away. Even from a distance, he could tell that she was still carrying on with her scolding. In her mind, her husband was alive and right next to her. While in reality, she was worried that her grandson was not married yet, her mind seemed to suggest that he had married a girl from among their relatives and they now had a son. Now, the family line will carry on. Marimuthu felt that this was good in a way. This muddled imagination was far better than her spending her last days anxious and burdened with worries.

It was evident that she had really been wishing her grandson would get married and have a child. In the midst of much bigger things to worry about, paatti had made this a priority. He felt unsettled the entire day. He wondered if his paatti would not be losing her mind if he had not been so picky and had married some girl by now.

He realized he had been wrong in thinking that his marriage was his own private problem. His paatti had clearly made it her problem too. Did his amma and appa also feel the same way? He found it incredible that even though they all kept their distance from each other, all their problems seemed to blend into one.

There was no harm in her imagining things about his future. But if she started sharing these things with others, they would laugh at her. They might even say she had lost her mind. He felt some fear thinking of the troubles paatti could cause.

A week ago, his paternal aunt's daughter-in-law Chellamma had come to visit. In the early days of her marriage, she had been very close to his family. She used to call Marimuthu her thambi, younger brother. She had even come for longer visits in the past, staying for ten to twenty days at a stretch. He did not remember when things changed. Marimuthu's sister had her baby ten months after her wedding. That could have caused troubles for Chellamma who had been married for five years and still did not have a child. So, things became difficult for her, and they grew apart a bit. After that, they only saw her during family functions and special occasions.

Occasionally, when they ran into each other in the market or on the street, they exchanged pleasantries. Even his atthai—his paternal aunt—stopped visiting them. Once or twice a year, paatti went to see her daughter. If she went in the morning, she was back by evening. If she went in the evening, she stayed there just one night and returned the next morning. That was the extent of the relationship. Relationships are all about calculations. They are all about transactions. Kinship through blood only serves as a reason to tolerate one another and to keep falling out and falling back in. What else is there in blood relations?

The day before, Chellamma had come to these parts for some condolences. But since she had heard that her mother-in-law's mother was unwell, she decided to pay paatti a visit. She brought a packet of buns as a gift and sat chatting with paatti.

Fifteen years of marriage and no child. They spent all their earnings on various medical treatments, but none of it helped her conceive. At some point, they decided to stop trying. When we are mature enough to accept something, it stops being a source of suffering. But paatti did not know about these things. In fact, it was not clear if paatti knew that the visitor was her daughter's daughter-in-law in the first place. Tearing a piece of bun and putting it in her mouth, paatti had asked, 'Where are you from?' Since Chellamma had heard that paatti experienced these mental lapses these days, she'd simply laughed and said, 'I am from Attoor, aaya. Don't you recognize me?' And paatti had replied, 'Yes, yes, I recognize you.'

Then, a little while later, paatti had said to her, 'My daughter lives in the same village. Her name is Thangaya. Do you know her?'

'Yes, of course! There is no one who doesn't know Thangaya in that village. She is a big deal, isn't she?' Chellamma had laughed, making fun of her mother-in-law. But paatti had not picked up on that.

'My grandson's wife there is childless. So, I am planning to get him married again. It will be good if I manage to find a girl for him.' The words ended up coming from within paatti's mind.

Chellamma was furious.

'You wretched old widow! You have been scheming to ruin my life! Do you hear her? She is planning to find my husband a new wife. Look at her! She is ready to die any minute, but she talks like this. Did I come to you crying that I have no child of my own? Did my husband come crying to you? It is possible your daughter has been crying about it. So, right away you started looking for a new woman for my husband? She wants him to have a second wife! Do you take me to be a complete idiot? You have children. So what? What has that got you? Here you are, living in the middle of nowhere in this lonely little hut. Even dogs have it better. People may not show up even if you are lying dead here. You got married, you had children, but look at your sad life! Don't you worry about us. As long as we are alive, we will make an honest living. If we grow frail and can't work longer, we will have our savings. If we don't have that, well, I will jump into a river or pond and end my life. When there are people to do the final rites even for you, do you think we will be abandoned? So what if that is the case? Let dogs and foxes feast on us. Once you are dead, you are a nobody.'

Her voice carried across the fields. But it looked like paatti did not understand what was going on. As Chellamma was shouting at her, paatti muttered to herself, 'Who is this insolent woman? Why is she so upset?' Chellamma swore and cursed, throwing a fistful of earth in the air. 'You are gobbling down the buns I brought for you! Why don't you go eat shit instead?' she yelled, snatching and flinging away the bun paatti had in her hand.

'I will not come here even when you die. From now on, there is nothing left between you and me, not a damn thing.'

People later said that Chellamma kept up her tirade all the way home. After that incident, paatti's mental lapses got worse. Since the day she fainted during her visit to the red-soil land, Marimuthu did not allow her to cook her own food. He took food from his house. When he was

away, Kuppan or the farm boy carried a bag of food for her
from Marimuthu's house.

The food they brought for her in the morning was
sufficient for three meals. In fact, there were still leftovers
which she fed to the dog. She ate very little food these days.
Sometimes, she even forgot to eat. If somebody put the
food on a plate and offered it to her, she ate. Otherwise, the
food carrier stayed unopened.

A week ago, one day, Marimuthu had to set out early
for some work. So, it was Kuppan who took food for
paatti. He had already taken two separate loans of two
thousand rupees each for his son's wedding. There was
not even a month left before the wedding. He now relied
on Marimuthu's kindness for the rest of the amount he
needed. Until then, he had to stay put in the orchard, doing
as much work as he could.

When Marimuthu was around, Kuppan made sure he
was continuously engaged in some task or another within
his field of vision. He also arrived in the orchard earlier
than usual in the mornings. Marimuthu's father noticed
these changes and asked him, 'Kuppan, why is the mouse
running around naked?' meaning there must be a reason for
these efforts of his. Kuppan could only laugh in the face of
that remark.

When he arrived at paatti's place with her food, he
couldn't find her. Wondering if she was sleeping in the
inner room, he called out, 'Saami . . . saami . . .' But there
was no response. He decided to go in and check, telling
himself that emergency trumped propriety. He stepped
into the porch and opened the door to the hut. A torn piece

of cloth lay spread over the cot. Didn't she have a proper sheet to spread on the cot, he wondered.

Kuppan thought about her hard life. When she got married and moved to this village, Kuppan was a little boy working in these fields. He'd witnessed paatti's capacity for hard work since then. She never tired of working. But here she was, with nothing but a torn piece of cloth to sleep on. Sighing at that thought, Kuppan walked around the hut, calling out 'Saami . . . Saami . . .' No response. She did not go out anywhere ever since her mind started failing her. Where was she now? Did someone take her away somewhere?

When he turned around by chance, he spotted paatti's white sari in the middle of the thorny undergrowth straight ahead. She was struggling like a blackbird trapped inside a thorny bush. He ran closer. Thorny seemakaruvela shrubs had grown unchecked. Kuppan could not find a way to enter the thicket. 'Saami . . . saami . . .' he shouted.

She was crawling inside the bush like a birdling that had not grown wings yet. Kuppan walked around the bush. How did she manage to get inside this? He calmed himself for a second and then ran to the hut to fetch a sickle. He hacked on the side of the bush that seemed less dense and made a way into the thicket. Paatti was gasping and frothing at the mouth. He dragged her by the arm and pulled her out through the clearing he had made.

Paatti could not stand up. He lifted her like a child, brought her to the hut and lay her down. Her eyes kept darting around in terror. He gave her some water to drink.

She drank it all up; she was very thirsty. Her wrinkled skin was bruised and bloodied by the thorns.

Kuppan sent word to Marimuthu, who brought a doctor with him. She had never had an injection ever before in her life, but now she had to take four. Broken thorn tips had lodged themselves in her skin all over her body. To remove them, they had to keep turning over her body. She screamed like a bird in danger.

They guessed that paatti might have stepped outside the hut in the night to relieve herself. Then she must have lost her way back to the hut and got trapped in the thorny thicket instead. They never found out for sure what happened. Paatti was not lucid enough to tell them. Nor could she understand them properly.

After that incident, Marimuthu took some protective measures. There was no outside gate to the porch. So, he brought a woven cot and fixed it like a door by securing it with ropes. If someone opened that door for her, paatti could step out. Otherwise, she had to stay inside the hut. He also asked Kuppan to sleep in paatti's hut every night. Kuppan could not refuse. Marimuthu also told him that on the nights Kuppan could not come, he would come over himself.

After dinner every night, Kuppan came over to paatti's cottage. The family had set aside some pots and pans just for her use. Since Kuppan and the farm boy were all touching her effects now, the family had set aside these utensils exclusively for her use. Kuppan would give her some food, after which he would lay a jute sack on the porch and lie down on it.

One night, when he was in a deep sleep, he heard pots and pans rolling around inside the hut. Right after that, he also heard the rustling of thatched panels. Kuppan was not fearful of the dark. He was used to walking around the fields at night. When he took the bullocks to the market, he often returned only in the dead of the night. He always kept a stick in his hand in case he needed to scare away snakes and critters. He was not scared even to walk down utterly deserted roads. But even he felt a little scared now, hearing the sounds coming from inside paatti's hut. Since people had been saying that it must have been a ghost that had trapped paatti inside the thorny bushes, he could not help but feel scared now.

'Saami . . . Saami . . .' he called out, but he heard no response. Things went quiet. But when he lay back down, the noises started again. Gathering some courage, he untied the cot-door Marimuthu had fastened and went inside. He made the lantern flame bigger; it had been burning low and casting a dim light until then. He pushed the door ajar and said, 'Saami.' Paatti responded in an authoritative voice, 'Who is there?' 'What are you doing?' he asked, holding the lantern up to see better. Paatti was standing in a corner of the hut. She held broken pieces of thatched roof panels in her hand. Pots and pans lay strewn around. A vessel lay on its side. 'What do you need, Saami?' he asked.

Paatti walked back to her cot and sat down, acting like nothing strange at all had occurred. 'Marimuthu, I had kept some money tucked away. That's what I was looking for. I want to give it to you,' she said. An idea occurred to Kuppan. 'Aaya, you lie down. I will find it for you,' he said.

Paatti quietly lay down. He picked up all the scattered pots and pans and put them to a side. Then he set the tipped-over vessel upright. It was an old-fashioned one, sturdy as a bronze pot. He picked up the lantern and started looking for the money by inserting his fingers into the gaps in thatched roof.

In different spots on the thatched roof, he found rupee notes folded and tucked away, and notes and coins rolled safely in plastic bags to protect from rain. He looked eagerly and thoroughly for a long time. He probed into crevices where even rats had not been. He only stopped his search when he grew absolutely exhausted. All the coins and notes he had extracted from the hiding places now lay scattered on the floor. Paatti was fast asleep. He gathered everything in his head towel and stepped outside.

In the light of the lantern, the faded old rupee notes and coins had an eerie look about them. He drank some water to calm himself. Then he shut the door and secured the latch before starting to count the money. It was difficult to unfold some of the notes. He straightened them out gently like he would rub and flatten betel leaves. In total, there were fifteen hundred rupees and some change.

He secured them with a knot in his towel and kept it close to him. He couldn't fall asleep. He thought he would take it to Marimuthu first thing in the morning and explain what had happened. But what if Marimuthu thought, 'This was all the money there was? How much did Kuppan keep for himself?' If Kuppan did not say anything to Marimuthu, he could use this money for his son's wedding. But he'd be haunted by the knowledge that this was stolen money. What could he do about that? Also, if paatti regained her memory and accused him of stealing the money, what would he do then? But she seemed to be well past getting better. After all, she stood there with pieces of dry thatch in her hands, thinking it was the money she had hidden. There was no way she was going to get better now. Kuppan's mind was filled with thoughts and ideas.

He had worked hard for this family ever since he was six or seven years old. He'd herded thousands of sheep for them. The sacks of paddy he had harvested for them over the years would easily exceed a thousand. He was always in the middle of some work for them—farming, weeding, threshing . . . Had the landlord really paid him the wages he deserved?

Even this paatti had never given him even a single measure of rice over the agreed amount. If he asked for more, she'd say, 'How many things you must have taken home from the orchard . . . Now you are asking for more!' The family lacked for nothing. This is a small amount, like water poured into a river, he reasoned. He rose at the crack of dawn when he heard the first rooster and took the shortcut home. He did not breathe a word about the money to anybody.

He felt a little troubled over the next few days. In case Marimuthu happened to find out about the money, Kuppan decided that he would fall at his feet, 'Here, Saami . . . Yes, I took it. I just wanted to conduct my son's wedding properly. Please forgive me.' That plan gave him some courage, and he was able to carry on.

Not long after, Kuppan needed to go to the Saturday market to sell a cow that belonged to his sister. It would cost one hundred and fifty rupees to take the animal in a cart. He could save some money if he walked the cow all the way to the market. If he set out right after dinner, he could arrive at the market by midnight. So, he let Marimuthu know that he wouldn't be able to sleep outside paatti's cottage. Marimuthu went instead. And the same thing happened on that night too.

Marimuthu was lying on a cot in the porch. When he heard the rustling of the roof, he thought it was a rat. In fact, it sounded like two or three rats. But when the noise carried on, ruining his sleep, he knocked on the door and looked inside. Paatti stood there laughing. 'Money, dear! Money!' she said. Bits and pieces of the thatched roof crumbled from her hands. He pulled her away and made her lie down. The room was a mess, things lying scattered all over the place.

The next morning, he brought his father along with him to paatti's hut. They brought all the pots and pans outside and looked for the money. Paatti had a lot of old saris and some new ones that she had never worn. When they unfolded these saris, rupee notes fell out of them. They looked in the roof as well and found some folded notes in a few spots. Marimuthu gathered everything in a piece of cloth. It annoyed him to think that all this hard-earned money had been going to waste. Who knew how much of the money was destroyed by the rats? Paatti was so frugal, she wouldn't even spend the two-rupee bus fare to get to the market. She'd walk instead. But what was the point?

He completely emptied the cottage, and with the farm boy's help, he washed the place thoroughly with water.

He spoke to one of paatti's neighbours four orchards away and, with their permission, drew an electric connection from there using a long wire cord. He installed two electric lamps in paatti's cottage—one inside, and the other at the entrance, positioned in such a way that the porch was well-lit.

33

It felt like a dream now—those days when he used to be happy talking to paatti, when he used to eagerly look forward to his visits to her place. But on that day, he was looking forward to something else.

He had not given paatti her food yet. She only ate if somebody put the food on a plate and offered it to her. Her world had transformed beyond recognition. He lay outside on the cot. The new electric lamp cast its light far over the space outside the hut. Insects buzzed around the lamp.

From inside, Paatti kept calling out, 'Thanga . . . Thangoyyy . . .' She stood on the other side of the cot Muthu had tied up to the entrance and called out 'Thangoyyy . . . Thangoyyyy . . .' several times, holding on to the gate with one hand and placing the other hand over her eyes as if she was attempting to look into the distance. That was how she addressed her husband—she always called him by their daughter's name. 'Aaya, stop shouting, go to bed. They will all come back, don't worry,' Marimuthu said to her. She walked back into the house, murmuring something. She had lost a lot of weight, and she did not wear her sari properly any longer. It stayed on her waist, but she did not want to cover her chest. If anybody attempted to drape anything over her chest, she immediately flung it away.

Marimuthu was expecting Raman. It had been years since they had seen each other. When they were little boys, Raman used to work in their farm for several years. In those days, they had spent time together every single day. Raman got married when he was only seventeen or eighteen years old, and he went to live at his father-in-law's village. They set up a separate home there for him and his wife, so he did not mind moving to their village.

After that, he made occasional visits here. If they happened to see each other somewhere, they would stop and chat for at least half an hour about the good old days. The day before, he had run into Raman at the Meenal movie theatre in town. After his dinner, he felt he was not going to fall asleep anytime soon. His amma had monopolized the television. So, on the spur of the moment, he decided to go to the second show.

On his earlier visit to town, he had seen the movie posters. 'Nadodi Mannan' ('The Vagabond King') was back after a long time. Even though it might be a bit like watching a koothu play which usually lasted all night, at least he'd be entertained thoroughly and he could while away some time. So, he picked the movie. But when he arrived at the theatre, there was quite a line for the tickets. It did not look like he'd be able to get one. So, he stood around wondering what else to do.

'Hey, you! What are you doing here?' shouted Raman as he walked towards him. The crowd did not seem to bother him in the least. 'There won't be such a rush for the couch tickets. You wait here. I will get them,' he said, running away. He had put on some weight and there was a maturity to his face now. But he was still short as a duck.

Marimuthu and Raman were roughly the same age, give or take six months. But Raman seemed to have arrived at his middle age with much grace, blessed with all the aspects that life was supposed to have at this stage. Marimuthu sighed at the thought. Raman returned with tickets. But he refused to accept money.

'I have money now. Do you still think of me as the same old Raman who ran around the orchards clad in a loincloth? You have spent money on me on several occasions. Let me do it for you today. Won't you accept it?'

Marimuthu couldn't refuse. He put the money back into his packet. They laughed, remembering the time they had watched the same movie as children.

'That's the last time I watched this movie,' Marimuthu said.

'Me too. It must be, what, twenty or twenty-five years ago?' Raman said. They were lost in their reminiscences. Raman told him that he had decided to leave his father-in-law's village and move back here. His in-laws had bought a little tenement flat in his name.

'How many children?' Marimuthu asked.

'Don't even get me started on that. The first two are boys. Then my wife kept lamenting that if she didn't have a girl child, nobody would cry for her when she died. I consoled her. I said to her, "We are still young. We can have another child,"' Raman laughed.

'Dey! You are quite something!' Marimuthu said with a tinge of jealousy.

'So, we had another child. Just a year ago. That turned out to be a boy too. I felt like strangling the baby to death. But we let him be. Anyway, all we need to do is to take care of them until they grow their own wings. After that, they can take care of themselves. As long as there are landowners like you around, we have nothing to worry about!' he said.

Marimuthu could not discern from his tone whether he was teasing him or he was serious.

'Then what happened to the plan to have more children?'

'Oh, we are carrying on with that. My wife won't stop until there is a daughter. She says, "What's the use of boys? All they do is eat and roam around. Only a girl will bring some charm to the house." She is right. The next one will be a girl.'

'You are worse than a pig!'

Even though Marimuthu had insulted him, Raman did not take it to heart.

'A pig might have a lot of babies, but it also takes care of all of them on its own. It does not give them away to somebody else and run away. It does what it can to protect them.'

Marimuthu could not argue with that.

Raman then told him about his various jobs. He worked for a rig company as a borewell operator. He worked in the textile mill for a while. He also did contract work for agricultural jobs.

'What do you plan to do here?' Marimuthu asked him.

'One of those things. I don't know yet. Some men have taken up painting jobs. I might join them. Or there is always the rig truck. They are really looking for people.'

'Or you can come work with me. If there is help, we can do much better farming than we are doing now. It looks like we will soon have possession of the red-soil land too,' said Marimuthu, hoping Raman would be interested and he would have someone to work with. Raman laughed.

'Who wants to work the land these days? Those days are gone. We used to think land work was the only thing to do. Not anymore. There are so many options. So, drop it,' he said, putting an end to that subject. Then he asked Marimuthu how he was doing.

'I heard you are still not married. What happened?'

'What else? Nothing has worked out yet. Everything has its right time.'

'Okay, so what do you do about it?'

'What can I do?'

'You are still the naïve little thing you used to be as a kid! I mean, what do you do when your little brother throbs for attention? How do you help him? Do you have someone on the side?'

'God, you! Don't get me worked up! I can't have anyone on the side. If I did, who would give me their daughter in marriage?'

'Not that anyone has given their daughter in marriage to you now! You have all the money and the land you can have, but you go to bed every night holding your thing in your hand. This is nonsense. Do you want someone tonight? Tell me?'

'No way,' Marimuthu said, turning his face away.

'You are still so shy even at this age! Alright, I will stop talking about it.'

They did not talk much until the movie was over. No one had ever spoken so openly and directly to Marimuthu before. Raman had not changed at all. He was the same bold and straightforward person he used be when he worked on Marimuthu's family farm. Watching the film with him this time, Marimuthu felt he really liked Bhanumathi, the female lead in the movie. Without any exaggerated theatrics, her face managed to show so many expressions. But he was not crazy about the last part of the movie. After the movie, he gave Raman a ride into the village on his bike.

'How will you get to the village at this hour? There is no bus at this time.'

'Oh, I could've walked. Back in those days, the two of us came walking all the way to watch the movie, didn't we? But you have changed. I am the same Raman!'

Raman then said, 'You use to drink toddy in those days. Do you still?'

'I stopped drinking years ago,' Marimuthu said with some yearning.

'So, shall we do some drinking tomorrow?'

'Oh, this is all so sudden.'

'Sudden? People don't look for auspicious days to go drinking! There are some things I want to talk to you about. I have a feeling it is through me that something good is going to happen to you. If I broach the matter right away, you may not like it. But if we talk about it after a few rounds of drinking, we might be able to talk freely.'

'I have not had a drink in years. Besides, it might create problems if anyone comes to know.'

'Don't be afraid. I will bring the toddy from town. Just say yes.'

Marimuthu agreed. Then they decided to do it the following night. Marimuthu gave Kuppan the night off and came to sleep outside paatti's hut. A hundred feet from the hut was a circular rock. He and Raman could sit there. There was nobody around for miles. In any case, nobody stayed awake past midnight. Raman told him that he would bring some toddy and chicken curry.

'Please make sure it is chicken curry. Don't bring any beef.'

'Why? Try eating some beef! Chicken curry can't even come close.'

'No, thank you!'

'Chicken eats shit, but you find it tasty. Cow eats grass, but you find the meat revolting? When will you all change?'

Raman always made such contentious remarks. Marimuthu didn't say anything in reply. He just smiled and gave Raman the money needed for the purchases. The plan was that Raman would buy chicken and get it cooked at his home.

34

Raman hadn't arrived yet. Marimuthu lay on the cot, worried if he had delayed paatti's dinner. Perhaps he shouldn't have relied entirely on Raman for food that night. A waxing moon slowly crept over the sky overhead, casting a golden shimmer all over the orchards. Since he was used to going to bed right after his dinner every night, he was beginning to feel sleepy. But even though he lay down on the cot soon after dinner, it always took him a long time to fall asleep. He usually just lay there, tossing and turning. But tonight, the combination of his hunger and the languor brought about by the moonlight had an enchanting effect on him.

It was not often that he got to lie under the sky like this. It made him feel like he was the lone inhabitant of the world, floating around without a care. Around him were trees standing like shadow figures. On the fields where planting was complete, he could not tell the crops apart; it looked like darkness itself was planted in those fields. From some great distance, he heard the sound of a lone heron. His eyes closed of their own accord.

He awoke when he heard a voice say, 'What is this, man? Are you asleep already?' It was Raman carrying a large woven wire basket. 'Have I come very late?' he asked. Marimuthu sat up on the cot, feeling a little ashamed for having fallen asleep. He had never enjoyed such a pleasant slumber before. Now, he could stay awake all night without feeling tired.

'Shall we move to the rock?' said Raman and started walking.

'Wait. Let us first give paatti some of the stuff.'

'That's right. I forgot. Back in those days, without any of you knowing, I used to bring toddy and arrack for paatti,' Raman said, taking the bottle out of the bag. Marimuthu mixed the drink with some water in a tumbler. Then he put two parottas and some chicken kuzhambu on her plate.

'Raman, you go give this to her yourself. She does not recognize anybody these days. But if she recognizes me by chance, she might feel weird. She might even refuse to drink.'

'Me? No! I have not seen her in years. If she recognizes me now, she might feel bad about accepting the drink from me. She is an old-fashioned woman. I go out on the rig truck these days. In those places, people who do the cooking are from various castes. And everyone eats the food, licking their fingers. But this is different.'

Raman was uncomfortable with the idea. He remembered something that had happened ages ago when he worked here on the farm. It was to do with a lead tumbler. Paatti used to drink toddy from that tumbler. It could hold quite a lot. After drinking some, she said to

Raman, 'Did you buy more than usual today? I can't drink it all. You drink a few glasses too.' Raman was already drawn to the fresh, frothy toddy.

He picked up her tumbler and filled it up with toddy from the gourd pitcher. She did not say anything until he finished drinking. But when he was about to leave to return the gourd pitcher, she said, 'Dey! Take this tumbler. You can use it to drink water.'

Raman was only relieved that paatti had not become angry or shouted at him or hit him. Besides, he found the tumbler very useful. Whenever he went to the palm grove to drink some toddy, Muniyar would ask him to bring a straw cup with him. He had to make a new one every time he went there. But now that he had the tumbler, things became easy. He now wondered what he would do if paatti reacted similarly. He was not a naïve little boy anymore. He would surely feel insulted.

'Paatti's mind is somewhere else. So, don't worry. Go!' Marimuthu urged him.

Inside the hut, paatti lay balled up like a little bird on the cot. All the clothes lay bundled up to a side. The lamp cast a dim light over the things inside the room. He wondered how to address her. But before he could make up his mind, paatti woke up, looked around and said, 'Thanga Thangoyy . . .' Raman held her hand and placed the tumbler in it, saying, 'Here, drink this.'

'You are here! I have been calling out to you for so long. Why didn't you answer?'

Raman was confused. He said, 'I just arrived.' She gulped down the drink and grunted to clear her throat.

'What have you brought for me? Have you been licking her cunt and brought her juices with you?'

Marimuthu burst into laughter from behind. The moment he placed the plate of food on her lap, she started eating with relish.

'Raman, don't mind her. She thinks she is talking to my grandfather.'

'Ah, so you sent me here to be yelled at!'

'There is no telling how she is at any given moment. She is totally unpredictable.'

Perhaps because she had not eaten chicken curry in a long time, she ate it up quickly. Clearly, Raman's wife was an excellent cook.

'Give her some more to drink. And put some more chicken on her plate. We have plenty, don't we?'

'You thought I am stingy like you? If the money you gave wasn't enough, I'd have put in my own money. I bought two kilos. I asked my wife to keep a little for them at home and brought over a kilo here.'

'Raman! I was not criticizing you. I just asked if there was enough.'

They gave paatti another round of the drink and some chicken. Everyone in the village knew that paatti was in the habit of drinking. But she still wanted to be secretive about it. When thatha was alive, he would drink some and bring her some. After thatha died, Therayan's wife brought her a bottle of arrack every week. She'd hide the bottle in her sari like a banana and bring it all the way for paatti.

Paatti never drank too much in one go. Whenever she felt like drinking, whether it was day or night, she just had one glassful. Local arrack. And that was enough to get her drunk. In those moments, it was impossible to have a conversation with her. She would talk non-stop. Even if there was no one in front of her, she would imagine someone and keep up a conversation with them. But once her mind grew addled, all of that had come to an end.

'What do you think, will paatti be able to take another round?'

'No, no! This is already too much. She is too old and frail. We don't want anything happening to her.'

'What will happen? If she dies, then that's it. At least, she'd have died eating what she liked.'

Paatti lay down on the cot again.

'She keeps yelling something every night. I don't know when she falls asleep. I go in to check in on her, thinking she is fast asleep, but she lies there, eyes wide open. At least, tonight let her sleep well.'

He pulled her sari to cover her properly and cleared things away from the cot. He reminded himself to buy two good blankets before winter. When he stepped out, the moonlight had dimmed. He looked up. A patch of white clouds was passing in front of the moon. The two of them walked over the round rock.

It was a foot-high black rock. Occasionally, they used it as a threshing floor for peanut harvest. The moment Marimuthu sat on the rock, the breeze brought in a sense of happiness from somewhere. Raman brought out the bottle.

Raman had come prepared with everything: plastic tumblers, banana leaf plates, water bottle and soda. The rock was the perfect spot to spread out the packets of parotta and the container in which he had brought the chicken curry. Raman must have got used to drinking with rig truck drivers. This was definitely not the same Raman who used to drink toddy from a palmyra shell with pickle for side dish. He mixed the drink slowly and carefully. Marimuthu was a bit apprehensive since he had not had any alcohol in a long time.

So, he ate some chicken first. It was flavourful and spicy and had a zing to it. The meat was cooked perfectly. He had eaten only two or three pieces and Raman had finished having his first drink. He pinched his nose and gulped it all down and stopped only when he was done. Then he said, 'Aah!' and shook his head and stuffed his mouth with chicken.

Everything about a person might change, but not their basic habits. Marimuthu could never drink like Raman. He'd drink a little first, let it go down slowly, burp a little and get his stomach warmed up before he drank more. But he was not able to do even that now. The pungent smell of the drink made him retch. He kept picking up the tumbler to drink and putting it back.

'God! This stinks so much. Is it safe to drink this?'

'Hey! You can't just keep looking at it. Be quick. This is excellent alcohol. See, brandy is the best liquor. And this is the best of brandies. You were generous with your money yesterday. That's why I bought this.'

Marimuthu took the tumbler close to his mouth again, but he wrinkled his nose and put it back down. Raman was beginning to feel a little intoxicated and a little angry.

'Listen, I planned this because there is something good I want to discuss. You always feel so shy about everything, like a woman who has never seen a man. So, I planned this to help you open up. Pick it up and drink. Otherwise I am leaving.'

Raman's threat worked. Marimuthu picked up the tumbler and drank half of it. Then he munched on the piece of chicken he had kept ready in his hand. He was used to drinking toddy. He'd had arrack a few times, but he'd had such western drinks only once or twice. In fact, he'd had no alcohol in the past eight years. He quickly gulped down the other half in the tumbler and chewed on more chicken. Raman started pouring the next round.

'Listen, you don't have to worry any longer about not finding a girl to marry. If you are ready to listen to my idea, you will be married in exactly fifteen days from now. What do you say?'

'I have heard a lot of people make such promises about marriage. Nothing has worked out so far. I don't think you will have anything new to say.'

'Definitely a new idea. Do you still think of me as the same old fellow who loafed around? If I promise something, I do it.'

Raman gulped his second drink down. He put some parotta on his leaf and mashed it. Marimuthu was not hesitant anymore. He now drank like an expert and finished another half a tumbler.

'Raman, dear fellow. I know you keep your promises. Remember, yesterday you said you could arrange something for me? Why don't you do that now?' Marimuthu said with a sheepish grin on his face.

'When I asked you yesterday, you acted like you don't even have a penis. Where did you find the courage today?'

'Dey Rama! Dey!'

He drank the other half and ate some more chicken. Then he lowered his head. Marimuthu was crying silently. When Raman placed his hand on his head and said, 'Please don't cry,' he broke into loud sobs.

'If you had been with me all these years, I'd have got to experience everything. But I am unlucky. Very unlucky. I am just going to die. That's my only luck.'

Raman felt sobered by Marimuthu's tears. He put some parotta and kuzhambu on the leaf and placed it close to Marimuthu. They suddenly heard the screeching of an owl. Then another owl. The sounds came from near paatti's hut and echoed all over the fields.

'It's not all lost yet. I am here. Only good things will happen for you from now on.'

'Dey, you don't know my suffering. You will know it only if you experience it. I have not shared it with anyone so far. I have been keeping it in my heart and dying on the inside. It happened five or six summers ago. We were lying on our cots outside our house, by the entrance. Me, my mother and my ammayi—three of us. It looked like the entire front area had turned into a cot.'

He stopped to take a sip of his drink. Raman had something to say, but he told himself this was not the right time. Let Marimuthu talk. Once he felt a bit lighter, he was likely to be more receptive to what Raman had to say.

'The moon on that night looked just like the one today. This moon is a treacherous thing, I tell you. It can disgrace anyone. On that night, too, I was feeling this heat in my body. I suddenly woke up and looked around. In the moonlight, right in front of me, I saw a smooth waist. I felt the desire to go and embrace that waist. I even stood up. That's when something told me—that's your mother! I ran into the house, screaming in my mind. From then on, I always sleep alone. I am such a dishonourable creature, da!'

He sobbed. His cries sounded like a dog's howl at an ungodly hour. He picked up his tumbler again. Raman felt like laughing, but he controlled himself with much effort. He realized that he had to handle Marimuthu differently. He had put up a lot of walls within his mind. No matter how high the floods grew, he'd simply built the walls higher. He never let even a crack open. And he talks about dying!

Raman slowly stood up and stretched. Moonlight seemed to roll in waves in the gentle breeze. Just as Marimuthu had remarked, the moon seemed to be observing everything from up there with a mysterious smile. Raman could not control his laughter any longer. He laughed so loud the sound carried across the fields. His veshti had come undone. He held it in one hand and laughed so hard his stomach hurt. The palmyra trees laughed. The knee-high maize crops in the fields laughed. The sky burst into laughter.

When he was finally done laughing, he looked at Marimuthu who was still crying. Raman sat down and filled the tumblers again. He seemed to have an endless supply of alcohol. Marimuthu drank with a frenzy and spoke in anger.

'So, you find my predicament funny too? Laugh. Go ahead. Everyone laughs. Why not you?'

'I will laugh whether I have your permission or not. You should laugh too! I laugh at your situation, you laugh at mine. We should all be laughing!'

'Laugh. Carry on.'

'Yes! Why should we cry? You are exactly like your father. He does not leave the fields, he never goes anywhere. You? No matter where you go, you are still in the fields. That's the only difference. What's your big mistake? Nothing! In my father-in-law's village, a man actually lives with his mother. And the mother does all she can to prevent him from getting married. The things that go on in this world! And here you are. There was a moon, you saw your mother's waist, and you think that is a big disgrace. Nonsense! If you look at it that way, then every man is definitely a scoundrel in the privacy of his mind.'

Banana leaves and pieces of paper lay scattered all over the rock. The owls that flew around the lamp outside the hut now screeched again. Then they heard paatti yelling something. She was hitting the thatched roof with some object. 'This wretched thing is falling on me. Go away!' she shouted.

Marimuthu continued to rant. 'Give her a little more to drink and put her back to bed. She is used to drinking bottles and bottles of arrack. This is nothing for her. This old hag is still alive and is running us ragged. Grandfather died. Why couldn't she? Marimuthu's marriage, his children, his children, his marriage . . . that is all she ever thinks about.

In her mind, it is all done. Only when this wretched old widow dies will something good happen here.'

Raman walked towards the hut carrying some alcohol in a tumbler and some chicken pieces on a leaf. He felt a bit unsteady and light-headed. He hadn't realized he had drunk so much. He wondered if Marimuthu would spend the night lying on the rock. Two or three owls flew in circles over the hut, screeching and eager to prey on the insects that buzzed around the lamp.

They were messengers for paatti. God has given birds and animals a capacity to know things in advance. Owls won't be so excited by a few insects. They have plenty of places to find their food. If they are now drawn to the new electric light, there must be a reason for this. It seemed that for paatti, who was lost and befuddled, the screeching of the owls sounded like the funeral drum.

She ran around inside the hut, shouting to shoo the birds away from her roof. 'Thooy! Thooy!' Raman too shouted. When they heard these human voices, the owls rose up and away from the lamp like balls thrown in the air and then flew back down towards the light again. Raman worried how he would drive the birds away and get paatti back to bed. He felt very confused and dizzy.

35

The owls went away only after Raman located the light switch and turned it off. The space in front of the hut was now awash with moonlight. He untied the cot barricade and went in. Paatti was still staggering around the room, saying 'thooy! thooy!' as if she were shooing away sparrows in the kambu fields. He pulled her by the arm and took her back to the cot. Then he stepped out to fetch the drink and meat he had left on the porch. She finished the drink quickly and put a piece of the chicken in her mouth.

'Kandha, you deserve a bracelet for your hand. With your touch, the toddy tastes like nectar.'

'Mm,' Raman said, chuckling to himself.

'Do you know how long it's been since I ate meat? The last I ate meat was at Marimuthu's wedding when they offered a goat and cooked the meat. Thanks to you, I get to eat this now.'

She smacked her lips in satisfaction. As far as she was concerned, Marimuthu was already married. If she imagined that they had made a goat offering and eaten the meat and she still remembered the taste, then that truly meant Marimuthu's wedding had already happened. Raman wanted to tease her a bit.

'I heard there was not enough mutton for all the guests at the wedding. People were saying, "What meat?! All we got was a glimpse of a tiny bit of meat. Like they were feeding the crows!"'

'Who said that? Let me tell you. People piled up the meat on their banana leaves and ate to their hearts' content. Poor people even brought containers from home and filled up as much as they wanted. You go ask anyone.'

Her words sputtered with anger. She was dragging the poor people as a measure of things now. Raman realized he wouldn't be able to win this argument. So he said, 'Alright, now lie down.'

'Kandha, come lie down here, come,' she said.

'I am going home. You sleep.'

'What are you blabbering? It's late. I'll lie here on the rock, and you will go home? Come. I won't say anything to upset you. Come, lie down.'

'Wow! Paatti is quite something!' he thought and quickly stepped outside and latched the door shut. Even if she heard the owls again, paatti wouldn't be able to step outside. He burst out laughing.

If he had lingered even for a minute, she might have pulled him by the arm and made him lie down next to her. It looked like paatti had a lot of interesting memories of her youth waiting to be dug up. And here was Marimuthu, so full of scruples and fearful of everything!

Marimuthu lay on his back on the rock. There was a little bit of liquor left in the bottle. Raman poured that into a tumbler and served himself some chicken and sat down to eat. There were still two parottas left. Thankfully, there was enough food for everybody. If they were short of anything, this was not the kind of place where you could run out and buy something quickly. That's why Raman had erred on the side of more.

As he sat eating, Raman was reminded of those days when he used to drink with Marimuthu. They used to spend the nights in the shed in the enclosure, guarding the sheep. On moonlit nights such as this one, they'd bring down the toddy pots from the palm trees and drink as much as their stomachs could hold. Those nights went by like daytime. The boys did not have too many responsibilities then, so they could stay up all night. Tonight seemed similar to those nights. The moon appeared unchanged too. From high up on a pristine sky, it poured down an enchanting light. But so much was different.

Back in those days, nobody would have believed that Marimuthu could cry. He used to be so full of play and laughter and mischief. But now, it was rare to find him smiling. He cried a lot. In the past, Raman had cried on several occasions. And Marimuthu was responsible for some of that. But now, Raman was full of laughter. Everything made him laugh. Growing older seemed to have turned everything upside down.

In the past, Marimuthu wouldn't pass out like this even if he'd drunk a lot of toddy. Even today, it was not the intoxication that had exhausted him. It was his mental anguish. How did Marimuthu become this person who could not find a way to lighten his sorrows? What exactly were the hurdles that Marimuthu and his family were facing? They had locked themselves in cages of their own making, and now they were struggling to get out. Poor Marimuthu. Raman finished eating with all these thoughts running in his mind.

He picked up all the trash and threw it away in the woods. He put the empty tumblers and the vessel in his bag. 'Hey. Hey you.' he tried to wake up Marimuthu, who just muttered something incoherent, turned over and carried on sleeping. Pieces of sand from the rock surface were stuck to Marimuthu's skin. 'Hey Marimuthu . . . Marimuthu . . .' Raman was thrilled at calling him by his name. He patted Marimuthu on his cheeks and woke him up. 'Come . . . let's go sleep in the hut.' He lifted up Marimuthu gently and made him lean over his shoulder.

'Raman, you are my god. Please stay right here with me.' Marimuthu mumbled. 'I have never had such a good time. You are here. Now all good things will come. You are my god. Show me your feet. I need to touch your feet.'

Marimuthu slid down and looked for Raman's feet. 'Hey! That's enough. Come!' Raman scolded him and dragged him towards the hut. When he was least expecting it, Marimuthu threw up noisily. Raman's hands were wet with vomit. It was also splattered all over him. 'Gently, gently,' he said and, setting his bag down to a side, made Marimuthu sit down on the ground. Marimuthu retched and threw up a few more times before sitting down exhausted.

Raman brought some water from the pot kept at the entrance. 'Here, rinse your mouth.' Raman used some of the water to wash himself. Then he moved the cot closer to the porch and asked Marimuthu to lie down.

'This has never happened before. I feel like I have more to throw up.'

'Must be because you drank today after a very long time. Don't lie down. Sit up and keep your head down. You won't throw up again.'

'It had a nice, sharp buzz. Now it's come down after vomiting.'

'That might be a good thing. I came here today because I wanted to help you. But we never got to talk about it.'

Raman sat on the porch. His body seemed to vanish into the darkness of the shadow the thatched roof cast over the porch, and only his voice emerged. Marimuthu was now in the mood to listen.

'What do you plan to tell me? You are going to say that you will look for a girl for me and that the wedding will happen soon. I am tired of hearing that, da. Drop that subject. Let's do this again, let's get together and drink. We can do it here or somewhere in town.'

Raman grew angry. He got down from the porch. His legs were unsteady. He stood in front of Marimuthu and lifted up his head.

'Look, here. What do you think of me? You think I am one of those brokers who takes your money and cheats you? I don't need even a penny from you. I am hale and healthy. I can earn money and feed my children, even if all they get to eat is gruel. I don't have to go begging anyone.'

'Alright. Alright. Tell me what you want me to do. I'll do it.'

'Good. Now you are talking! If you do as I say, you will be married in fifteen days. But you shouldn't be like—oh my mother objects, my father says no, that person says no, this person has a problem. You shouldn't listen to what anyone else has to say. Okay? If you do, I will end up being disgraced.'

Raman spoke plainly. The conviction in his voice despite the inebriation gave Marimuthu some confidence.

'No matter what happens, I will do as you say. Tell me.'

'When I travelled on rig work, I stayed in a town for two or three months. I have come to know a few people there. Even now, when I go there, I make sure I see them. There is a girl there. They will marry her to the man I suggest. But the thing is . . .'

He paused there, leaving the sentence hanging. Marimuthu lifted his head quickly. He felt like the buzz from the alcohol had completely worn off.

'What? They are farmers like us, right?'

'That's where the problem lies. Her mother is. But her father . . .'

'What is he?'

'We don't know for sure. Now it's only the mother and the daughter. The father's not around. They say he left them and went away.'

'And they have no idea what caste he is from?'

'People have different stories in the village. Some say that when she was young, the mother ran away with a man who had come to work in the fields during a groundnut harvest. He then abandoned her somewhere. When she

came back to the village with a child, her parents refused
to accept her.'

'What else do they say?'

'They also say it was a farmhand she'd run away with.
He left her and ran away because she was afraid they'd beat
him to death. The woman never clearly told anyone who
the man was. So, we know nothing about the girl's father.
But the mother always wears red saris, and she also wears
flowers and a pottu on her forehead. The only thing is they
don't have any property.'

'How can we . . . if we don't know about the father?'

'Why do we need to know about the father? You are
not going to live with him, are you? She is a good girl. Only
sixteen or seventeen years old. She is very thin and rosy in
complexion. But she has been working very hard in the
fields out in the sun, so she appears a little darkened. She is
the right girl for you.'

'All that sounds good. But what do we tell people in
the village if they ask about the girl's father?'

'Why do you keep worrying about the village? They are
now laughing at you for not being married yet. If you marry
her, they will talk for a while, they'll say you married a girl
who doesn't even know who her father is. No matter what,
the village is going to be saying something.'

'But still . . .'

'This is the problem with people like you. You might
sleep with your own mother, but you won't give up this
hollow sense of pride! Who really knows who their father
is? You know what your paatti said to me earlier? She said,
"Kandha, come, lie down with me." How are we to believe

that your grandfather is indeed your father's father? I think this girl is perfect for you. If you say yes, I can go there tomorrow and take things forward. You will be married in fifteen days. But if you still keep worrying about others, I will leave now. I will go mind my business.'

Marimuthu sat quietly for a while with his head down. Raman felt bad that he had disclosed to him what his paatti had said earlier. Never mind. He did not have a choice. Marimuthu finally said, 'Alright, da. Let's do as you say.' A rooster crowed somewhere.

36

As soon as they got down from the bus, the first thing they saw was the large rocky hillock with a small temple on top. On one of the rocks was a holy naamam mark large enough to be seen from a distance. Taking it to be a good omen, he touched his cheeks in prayer. After dropping them, the bus vanished along the tar road. 'The smell from this smoke is terrible. This is why I never travel by these things,' thatha said, clearing his throat and spitting out. On both sides, verdant fields came right up to the edge of the road and stretched out far into the distance. Light green plumes of sugarcane crops were standing up as far as eyes could see.

'What happened, mapillai? You seem speechless at the sight of this village. If we had such lush fields in our parts, men wouldn't go out looking for work in the rig business. I think we have finally found a girl for you in a nice place. You could marry a girl from here just for the beauty of the place, mapillai,' said thatha in wholehearted appreciation of the place.

'Every village looks impressive at first glance. Only when we live there do we get to know its flaws.'

Thatha laughed, appreciating Raman's remark.

'Raman, you might be young, but you are a man of experience. Otherwise, you wouldn't have found such a place for my mapillai. I tried so hard to find him a girl. Nothing worked. Looks like it was destined to happen through you.'

Raman led the way. They walked on the wide path that bordered the sugarcane fields.

'When you said the village was called Varattur, I thought it might be as dry as our village. But it looks like they draw water for irrigation from the river. I think they named the town after that rocky hill over there. I saw something like this on my way to the market in Mannoor.'

Thatha had started a story. As he walked on, Raman responded to thatha's story with frequent 'Mm's. Walking at the back, Marimuthu was happy. He'd had no hopes at all that his wedding would happen within the deadline he had set for himself in the month of Aavani. Raman's return to the village after all these years seemed perfectly timed to make it happen.

Once Marimuthu said yes to the idea when he was quite sober and clear-headed, Raman got started on the preparations. He left the very next afternoon, got to that village and even stayed there overnight. Marimuthu had no idea how many people Raman spoke to and what he said to them, but he secured their consent for the marriage. Apparently, the girl's mother was a little hesitant considering the age difference between Marimuthu and the girl. After all, she was half his age. If he had married at the right age, he'd probably now have a daughter her age. So, the mother was right to worry. But after taking all things into consideration, she agreed.

The only property the girl had to her name was a thatched hut and two cents of land around it. Her mother got that from *her* grandmother. When she ran away from the village and returned one day with a child, her father refused to let her enter the house. In fact, if she hadn't come back with a child, they might have taken no pity on her and even hacked her to bits. After that, her father wrote all his property in his son's name.

Rosamani's mother had been the first child and everyone's darling in the family. But now the family wanted to have nothing to do with her. After her father, mother and brother sent her away, refusing to accept her back in the house, she did not know where to go, so she climbed up the hill and sat in front of the temple. Her grandmother came to know only after the temple priest informed her.

At a time when no else had any love left for her, her grandmother had it in her to show her some affection. Despite her advanced age, she climbed up the hill and took her granddaughter and her child home with her. They stayed with her in her hut. When an opportunity had arisen in the past, the grandmother had got that place registered in her name, and that turned out to be quite advantageous now.

She never asked her granddaughter any questions. The girl had come back with nowhere else to go. What was the point in interrogating her? She had made a mistake, and now everybody could see it. That's all there was to it. She didn't know how to conceal her mistake from others. Paatti took good care of her granddaughter and the child. Her son—the girl's father—tried to scare her into sending the girl away. He told her he would gather the village together and have her excommunicated. But she didn't budge.

'When a thorn pricks us in the hand or on the leg, what do we do? Do we cut off the hand and the leg? We need to remove the thorn and attend to the leg. That's exactly how this is. This place is in my name. I can do whatever I want here. Don't threaten me. Remember, I am much older than you, and I can give back as good as I get,' she said to her son.

The girl was supposed to live comfortably at her parents' wealthy home. But here she was, roughing it out in her grandmother's thatched hut. But her grandmother offered her many consolations.

'What does it matter how much we earned in the past? This little hut was all I could hold on to in my old age. From now on, think of it as your home. This is the only thing that will last.'

As long as the grandmother was alive, the girl worked hard every day. But how much can you really earn and save up from toiling in the fields? They always had enough money to raise the little girl and for food for the three of them. She even managed to buy earrings worth two gold sovereigns for her daughter. And she had around five thousand in cash. That amount wouldn't be enough even to arrange her wedding in a temple with just ten guests to witness it.

Raman had explained everything to Marimuthu before bringing him over here. Since they thought it would be good to have an elder with them, they included matchmaker thatha in the plan. No one else in the village knew. They set out very early in the morning. If everything worked out, they could share the news later with the others, and he could stay firm in his decision, no matter what his mother or father or anyone had to say about it. Raman had given him much clarity.

The walkway along the sugarcane fields led to a path meant for carts. After they walked along that path for a little while, they came to a rise and dip in the road. Right past that, they saw a gentle stream flowing by. The thatched hut was on a raised land right next to the stream. The roof of the hut had been made by securing two layers of sugarcane plumes over thatched palm fronds. It must have been a few years since that roof was made. It looked darkened with wear. But it would surely last for a few more years.

Around the hut was a little garden full of vegetable plants and small trees. There was no dearth of water since the stream was nearby. They had taken good care of the place. Both Marimuthu and thatha felt contented looking at the garden. The walls of the hut were made of mud. The entrance and the floor were made of mud too. But they had washed the ground with cow dung and made it look as smooth and polished as plaster.

Two or three women and a man stepped out of the hut to welcome the visitors.

It looked like they had gathered some of the neighbours to welcome the visitors. Thatha and Marimuthu sat in chairs. Raman sat by a wall on a small stool. The girl's mother brought water in a large bronze pitcher. Thatha started his questions.

'What's your name, ma? You are the girl's mother, aren't you?'

'My name is Rangamma. My daughter's name is Rosamani,' she said and stood by the wall, looking down.

The moment he heard the name Rosamani, Marimuthu shivered all over. What's this connection, he wondered. Rosamani. Clearly, he was destined to find someone by the same name. Clearly, this meant he was destined to have a wife by the name Rosamani. But then, if that was the case, he would have married the first Rosamani he'd met. Instead, he'd had to wait for another Rosamani to be born and to grow up old enough for him to marry. Even though he was not exactly ecstatic, he definitely became very eager to see the girl. It had never occurred to him to ask Raman for the girl's name earlier. He had not cared much about the name. But now it was quite fitting that he came upon the name this way, with an element of surprise.

Thatha pointed to the man present among the hosts and said, 'Is this your brother, ma?' Taking the hint, Rangamma started introducing all the neighbours who had gathered.

'He is indeed a brother to me. After all, he doesn't have to be my brother by birth to be a brother to me. I am estranged from my family. He is our kinsman. His name is Muthurasu. This is his wife.'

'We will all stand together and marry the girl off. Please don't think they have no one. We may not be able to help financially. But what's the point in being humans if we can't offer her our support in this way?' Muthurasu said, looking alternately at thatha and Marimuthu. 'That's true, that's true,' thatha said, nodding.

'Do you have a horoscope made for your daughter?' he asked.

Marimuthu did not like the fact thatha had asked that question. So, he said immediately, 'It doesn't matter, thatha.' Thatha laughed.

'Okay, mapillai. But they may want to check the match, right? That's why I asked.'

Marimuthu felt embarrassed and lowered his eyes.

Rangamma started saying, 'We do have a horoscope. If you are interested, take a look at it. But we are not in a position to care too much about such . . .' but her voice broke and she started sobbing. Raman had not planned to get involved in these discussions, but he now felt bad and wanted to say something. He worried that thatha might ruin things with such vexatious questions. But he wondered if they would think badly of him if he intervened. Thatha, however, was good at handling such situations. Addressing a tearful Rangamma, he said, 'Amma, you are like a daughter to me. I have been to many houses in my life. But here, even though it is a thatched hut, you have kept it so clean and sparkling, and you have such a nice garden growing vegetables and fruits. It thrilled our hearts to see the place. Now, just because my mapillai has come all the way to see your girl, please don't think less of him. He is quite well-to-do. The family has more than enough fields and orchards. For some reason, we couldn't find the right girl for him so far. If I had a girl, I would certainly give her in marriage to Marimuthu. Now, I think of your daughter as my own granddaughter. Don't be anxious that you are marrying her to a family you don't know. We are all there to take good care of her. We will treasure her. Why don't you let us have a glimpse of the girl? Even I am eager to see her. Imagine how eager mapillai must be!'

Everyone laughed in delight at thatha's remarks. They all found his words very comforting and reassuring. The women went in to bring the girl. She was dressed simply and brought tumblers of coffee on a plate. She was very young, and she was so thin that it wouldn't be unreasonable to worry if she would break and fall. But thatha felt that, with some good food to eat, she would soon put on some weight and look like a proper woman.

Even though he had gone bride-seeing several times in the past, Marimuthu now felt shy looking at her. Perhaps he was anxious because they had already decided that this was the girl he was going to marry. She was quite tall. Contrary to what Raman had said, she was not rosy-complexioned. Brown. Thin, chiselled face. He thought that she was very, very thin. She offered them both coffee and rushed back inside. The girl's mother brought a tumbler of coffee for Raman. From the glow and smile on the girl's face, thatha had discerned her consent.

'What next? Why don't you all come and meet mapillai's family? Shall we have the wedding within this month?'

'We will do as you say.'

'Today is the first of the month of Aavani. The twelfth of the month is an auspicious day. It's a Monday. The twenty-eighth of the month, according to the English calendar. We can have the wedding on that day. Let us not put this off any further. This is what mapillai wants.'

'Sure. Let's do that.'

Then they decided that they would find a wedding hall in Marimuthu's village. The girl's people did not like the idea of having the wedding in a temple and then hosting a reception in a hall. Rangamma wanted her daughter's wedding to include all the appropriate rituals. They agreed to that. But when they came to discussing the wedding invitation, things hit a glitch.

'Give us the girl's father's name. We need to mention him in the invitation,' said thatha.

Nobody spoke for the next few minutes. Breaking that silence came the girl's whimpers from inside the room. Marimuthu was annoyed that thatha was repeatedly asking such awkward questions.

Raman stood up, addressing thatha, 'Ayya . . . I explained this to you earlier.'

'You did. But they can give us a name to put in the invitation. Or else, they can tell us how to word the invitation.'

Rangamma spoke calmly.

'You can say, "Varattur Chinnammal's granddaughter and Rangamma's daughter, Rosamani." Or you can simply just mention the girl's name and nothing else.'

'Thatha, there is no need for invitations. Like the old days, we can just invite people in person, with a plate of betel,' Marimuthu said with some urgency. He was scared that the alliance might fall through if this matter was blown out of proportion. All the potential alliances so far had failed precisely on account of some such small disagreement.

'Alright, ma. We can write it as you have suggested. Or we can write whatever mapillai suggests. Inviting everyone in person with a plate of betel won't work. Times have changed. If we do that, people will start making all sorts of assumptions. Please don't be hurt by what I asked. I felt that all delicate questions have to be brought up right away. It won't be good for us to bring this up later once we are back in the village.'

Thatha had a way of handling any situation. 'So, shall we take leave?' he asked, getting up.

'No, no! You haven't eaten yet. Everything is ready. We can eat in five minutes. We have agreed on the wedding date, so it is perfectly fine for you to eat here,' Muthurasu insisted.

They could not refuse. 'We will go to the stream to wash our hands,' they said, and the three of them stepped outside. The thin stream stretched like a long piece of loincloth, flanked on either side by thick undergrowth. They walked on the path that ran along the stream.

'Ayya! I was scared you might ask some awkward questions and make things complicated! But you managed somehow,' said Raman.

'Oh! I was really holding on to dear life, I tell you,' Marimuthu sighed.

'We should always bring up such questions at the right time. Instead, if we just keep it to ourselves, we will be confused, and then they will become confused. We should not let that happen. Now, see, everything is clear,' thatha laughed.

At a convenient spot, they stepped down closer to the stream. The rustling of the waters sounded to Marimuthu like the sound of Rosamani's anklets.

Thatha headed to a spot covered by shrubs for some privacy. Marimuthu huddled closer to Raman and asked him the question that had been bothering him.

'She is so thin. Will she be able to withstand . . .'

'What a question! How big is yours? Like a donkey's? Or like an elephant's? It is just as thick as a finger, isn't it? She will be able to take five or six times bigger than that. Don't worry.'

Raman laughed. Marimuthu blushed as red as the patch of red soil they saw at a distance.

37

Later that night, Marimuthu was sitting in a cot on the front porch. Kuppan had already left with dinner for paatti. Marimuthu decided to give Kuppan all the money he wanted for his son's wedding. Let them have a happy wedding. It would happen later that month, on the very last auspicious day of the month as Marimuthu had decided. The twenty-fifth of the month of Aavani. Kuppan had all the time to devote to the preparations for Marimuthu's wedding. He'd said to Kuppan, 'Be here early in the morning.' Kuppan left wondering what it was all about.

Marimuthu did not know how to inform his parents about his wedding plans and secure their acceptance. He decided that he would speak to them both together when his father was home for dinner. If they agreed, well and good. Otherwise, he could always leave at the crack of dawn and go fetch his sister. It wouldn't be much trouble for her to cook for the five people from the girl's family who were expected to visit the next day.

He could start the preparations only after their visit, and he would need someone to help him with everything.

He could ask Raman. If Selvarasu joined them, it would be a big help. But since the land negotiations between the two families were still on, it might lead to complications if Selvarasu involved himself in Marimuthu's wedding preparations.

He was confused about how to begin the conversation with his parents. His father was usually quiet, but he might bring things crashing down with just a tiny remark. Amma, on the other hand, would shout and rant. She would cry and throw a tantrum. She would dredge up and spit out all her years of anger at him.

Since there were no other houses nearby, no outsiders could hear clearly what she was shouting about. Some of them would ask the next day, 'What was all the shouting and screaming all about?' Marimuthu now anticipated all these possibilities and rehearsed the answers he could give to such questions. He should not ruin things by talking back in excessive anger. Matchmaker thatha had offered to come and speak to his parents, but Marimuthu declined it.

Mother might insult him. 'A stranger comes to inform me of my own son's wedding?' Even Raman had volunteered to speak to Marimuthu's father. That would be even worse. They might take it as a bigger insult if they came to know of the matter from someone like Raman. So, Marimuthu decided that, come what may, he would do the talking himself. But why was he hesitating now? It was not fear. What else, then? This wouldn't be so hard if he had informed them before going to see the girl.

Amma was moving things around noisily in the kitchen. The TV was on. She was able to do the chores

around the house only if the TV was on. His father had
not come home for dinner yet. Beyond the entrance to
the house, everything lay behind walls of darkness. This
was usually the hour at which his father came home to
eat before heading back to the sheep enclosure. He must
be chitchatting with somebody in the orchard, standing
under a palmyra tree. There must have been some delay in
bringing the toddy from up the tree.

These days, in order to avoid getting into trouble with
the police, they did the toddy tapping in the dark of the
night and wrapped up everything by dawn. His father
might have accompanied the toddy tapper on his rounds.
It would be hard to get Vatthan to stop talking.

When he came home in the evenings, Marimuthu's
father did not go inside the house. Instead, he washed his
hands with water from the pot kept outside and sat down
shyly on the porch. His dinner would appear on a plate.
He'd eat sitting right there, wash his hands on the plate
and go back out.

Even on those nights when he sent Marimuthu to the
cattle shed, he lay his cot on the porch. Perhaps he went
into the house at night, seeking his wife's company. But
that was the extent of his connection to this house. Things
had got even worse of late. He pretty much lived in the
sheep enclosure.

He heard the sound of sandals in the dark. He could
tell from the sound that those were sandals made by
Kuppan. The sole lasted for years without wear. He made
them sturdy like horseshoes. Marimuthu owned two pairs
of shoes—one pair made by Kuppan and the other store-

bought. When he was out in the fields, he wore Kuppan's sandals. When he went out on some errand, he wore the store-bought pair.

He could see his father splashing water on his face and washing his hands. It looked like the dog had been out with him on his rounds. It now stood nearby, wagging its tail.

He couldn't tell how his amma managed to hear these sounds. She had already appeared with a plate of food. Licking his lips, Marimuthu said, 'Serve me some food too.' She had not expected that. 'Mm?' she said, looking quizzically at him. 'Serve me some food too,' he said again and went to wash his hands. His father, sitting coyly and withdrawn as usual, had already started eating. She brought a plate and the pot of rice and set them down on the porch. She went back in again and returned with kuzhambu and rasam. Then a pitcher of water.

He sat facing his father. His hands were busy mixing and mashing the rice on his plate. Without addressing anyone in particular, he said, 'Will you be here tomorrow?' His father looked up at him. From his eyes, Marimuthu could tell that he was drunk on toddy.

'The girl's family is coming here tomorrow,' he said.

'Everything's been decided?' his father asked. It looked like he knew something. He wouldn't have missed the fact that Raman was visiting here a lot these days. He'd have guessed. Marimuthu kept mashing his rice.

'Almost,' he said.

'Then carry on,' he said, as he carried on eating.

'What? Where are they coming from?' his mother asked. She didn't have a clue.

'Ask your son.'

'It's a place called Varattur on the other side of the river. I have found a girl there. They are coming here tomorrow.'

'Oh! Things have gone that far? You go see the girl on your own and then just inform us about it? You are telling me now so that I can cook for those dogs tomorrow? Why don't you find some woman to do the cooking too? Why should I degrade myself?'

'Amma, look, don't shout. I felt that if people had known about this in advance, they would have messed it up. That's why I took Raman with me and went and saw her. Everything worked out. That's why.'

'What do mean people would ruin things if they knew in advance? Who are these people? Your father and me?'

'Who else? My father and mother have done the most messing up so far.'

The words came out. He did not manage to keep his anger in check. Since he was used to arguing with her all the time, he didn't know how to have a proper conversation.

'If any woman sets foot here, I will cut her to pieces, let me tell you. You have really gone too far. Just because we handed over all the farm work to you does not mean you can disrespect us!'

'Who else would you hand over the reins to? Do you still think I am a little baby suckling at your breast? You can't even get me married! You want respect?'

'It's all your bad luck we couldn't find a girl for you. No matter where you go, things end up not working out.'

'Sure, keep saying the same thing over and over! I am thirty-five years old now. On cold nights, I lie holding it in my hands. But you two—even though he is an old coot now and you are an old hag, you two go into your room and lock the door.'

'How can you talk like this to your parents? This is exactly how you drove away my mother. Now you are planning to send me away so that you can bring some other woman here?'

His father kept eating quietly. This was his style. He'd say a word to start things off and then sit back and watch how they played out. Marimuthu's hand went dry. He had not eaten anything yet. He panted like a hound. His face glowed with a killer rage.

'Which woman can I bring here? You find fault with every woman and ruin everything. Then which woman do I bring here, tell me?'

'Go! There must be some cheap woman for you somewhere. Go find her and bring her here and lay her down on a cot in the middle of the house! I don't care.'

'But you do care. You do have a problem! I know your plan. You want to be the only one who lies on a cot in the middle of the house here. In fact, the way things are going, you might even tell me I don't need another woman, I have you.'

'That's disgusting! Where did you learn to talk like this? This is what happens when you get too friendly with the farmhands.'

His father flung his plate away and went to wash his hands. His mother beat herself on the stomach and sobbed.

'Is this what you created me for, dear god? So I can hear such words? How can I stay alive after hearing this? All that is left for me now is a piece of rope.'

'Why should you hang yourself? I am the one who should die. You want to rule the roost here. Whereas I? I am still looking for a woman to marry when all my friends are ready to marry off their kids. Why should I stay alive? Let me put an end to this right away.'

He picked up the plate of food, of which he had not tasted even a morsel, and threw it at the ceiling. Food fell scattering all over the porch. The plate hit the ceiling, fell down and rolled on the floor. The dog kept looking cautiously at each of them in turns, wondering if it was safe to come on to the porch to eat the food that lay scattered. Marimuthu stood up and rushed towards the gate. He went to the calf that was tied up at the entrance, untied the rope and brought it back in with him. Confused at the unexpected freedom at that hour, the calf mooed to its mother.

Coming back to the porch, he threw one end of the rope over the palm trunk beam on the ceiling and tied a knot. He seemed determined and unstoppable. He fashioned a noose. Then he dragged the cot under the noose and stood up on it. His father, who had stayed silent until then, came running to him, calling out, 'Dey! Dey!' and embraced him. 'Don't die! This family will be ruined!' he cried. Stunned, his mother too came and stood by him.

His father helped him down from the cot. Crying like a child, Marimuthu rested his head on his father's chest. His mother cried, pressing the end of her sari over her mouth. 'My dear, you marry as you wish. What's left for me? I will stay here if you want me to. Otherwise, I can always move out to a hut or somewhere else,' she said. His father gently nudged him towards his mother. 'My dear, my saami, please never do such a thing ever again,' she said, caressing his face with her fingers and cracking her knuckles to ward off evil eyes. He sat down, still whimpering. Amma ran her fingers softly over his head.

Using a knife, his father cut down the rope that was hanging as a noose. He carried it beyond the gate and burned it along with a piece of thatch. The rope burned, blackened, and began to emit smoke. Marimuthu's father then walked towards the calf that was now butting its head against its mother's udders.

38

Marimuthu slept for several hours from all the exhaustion. It had been long since he had slept like that in the middle of the day. His slumber seemed to draw him deep into the coolness of the coconut grove. The scenes from the night before and early that morning appeared like a dream to him.

He didn't know where his mind and body had found all that vigour. Clearly, deep down, he had realized that it was his last chance. Now, he was not sure if he was truly capable of keeping up his earlier resolve—to end his life in the month of Aavani if his wedding did not happen by then. Was it possible to end one's life based on a resolution? He doubted it. Yesterday, his actions had had no prior planning; they were totally spontaneous. He could really have died. He went for the noose because he was distraught and overcome with emotion. But now, all that drive and determination were channelled towards the wedding preparations. No one could stop him now.

Raman went to Varattur the night before and brought the girl's family with him. There were four of them. Five, including Raman. Since Marimuthu wanted four or five people to be present on his side too, he left very early in the morning and brought his sister home. Her husband joined them as well. Thatha arrived too. And even though his mother did not seem particularly happy, she did not voice her feelings.

Marimuthu was very anxious until the guests ate and took their leave. He was worried that somebody might ask some awkward question and things might get knotty. Thatha had come ahead of time in the morning and explained the situation of the girl's family to his parents. In fact, he did something that Marimuthu had not expected at all—he lied to them about the girl's father.

'The girl's father is not with them. They had a fight and he left. Never came back. Apparently, they hear he has married someone else. They've said they will send him a word about his daughter's wedding. But it doesn't matter whether he shows up or not. It's not the father we are marrying, is it? She is a nice girl. Quite skilful at all the farm work. Just the right girl for your family. We must be fortunate to find a girl who can take charge of things, don't you think? What's the use of money and gold? Throw them in the dustbin, I say. Finding good people is the important thing.'

Even though Marimuthu's parents were not fond of thatha, the information he gave was useful to them. They basically got two things from what he told them—that the girl was not bringing any money or gold with her and that her father was not part of their lives. Nevertheless, Marimuthu was anxious until they all left. Raman went to see them off at the bus stop. Marimuthu asked Raman to meet him in the orchard after that. It had been an excellent lunch, complete with vadai and payasam. He had not enjoyed such a feast in his home in a long time. He had also not slept properly the night before, and he felt sleepy now. So, he headed to the orchard for a nap. Unlike his usual naps which were full of muddled dreams and tossing and turning, this time he lay in deep sleep, lost to the world.

Raman arrived at the orchard and sat chatting with Kuppan. He did not want to rouse Marimuthu. He decided to wait till he woke up on his own. A dry sheath from the coconut tree fell right in front of the hut. The roaring noise with which it fell woke up Marimuthu. They had pruned the trees only a few days ago, but the sheaths were already dry again. No matter how often they were watered, coconut trees still needed a proper rain—the kind of rain that would leave the curves of the new leaves holding rainwater for days.

His eyelids refused to part. Even though his mind was awake, his eyes did not cooperate. So, he lay there a bit longer. He could faintly hear Raman and Kuppan conversing in Telugu. Then, he suddenly remembered that he needed to go out with Raman and get a number of things done. He sat up in a rush, worrying it might be late. But it was still bright daylight. If light streamed into the orchard despite all the shade cast by the coconut trees, it meant there were still some hours of the day left. He stepped outside the hut, bending down at its low entrance.

'That was some nap! Try not to sleep like this after your wedding,' Raman laughed.

'Finally, there is a sparkle in our saami's face!' Kuppan joined in.

'Kuppan, how much did you need for your son's wedding?'

'I asked you for ten thousand, saami.'

'Come and take it from me in the morning.'

'I came this morning like you'd asked me to.'

'But I had to leave early and go to my sister's place. Come tomorrow. I will give it to you for sure. Raman, wait for a bit. It feels a bit stuffy. Let me have a quick wash in the well. Then we can head out.'

By the time Marimuthu finished his bath, got ready and started the motorbike, it was three in the afternoon. Raman sat behind him. Their first stop was the thevaikkarar's house—the wedding officiant. They were not sure he would be home at that hour, but he was. When they mentioned the date for the wedding, the man hesitated. He had already agreed to officiate a wedding on the same date. 'There's only ten or twelve days to the wedding. This is very short notice,' he said.

But when they promised that they would ferry him on the bike from and to the mandapam where he was officiating the other wedding, he agreed. They also told him that once the invitations were printed, they would bring him his advance. On the way back, Marimuthu complained, 'He was making too much of a fuss. How many weddings involve a thevaikkaran these days? One in a hundred. Men just go to a temple and tie the thali. Or they ask a priest to officiate. We could do the same thing, but the girl's family thinks they will find acceptance only if all the proper rituals are done. What can we do?'

He bypassed the town. There were some mandapams, both small and big ones, on the outskirts near Kallur. It would be great if one of them was available. There were only ten days to the wedding. Most people booked the wedding halls months in advance. Would he be able to find one this close to the date? But he already had a fallback in his mind: they could cover the front-yard and the rooftop with awnings and hold the wedding at home.

But a wedding hall would certainly be more convenient. There would be plenty of space for guests to sleep the night before. Moreover, all the utensils, stove, everything would already be included in the amenities. If they held the wedding at home, they would have to arrange for everything. They first went to a big wedding hall. 'Siddhayammal-Vallusami Wedding Hall', read the name board. When they mentioned the wedding date to the manager, he laughed hard, betel spit oozing from the corner of his mouth. Marimuthu sensed mockery in that laughter. He started the motorbike without even waiting for a proper reply from the man.

The next wedding hall was inside an orchard not far from the main road. There were no houses nearby. 'Vallammal–Chinrayan Wedding Hall.' Marimuthu stayed outside on the bike. Raman went in but was back out fast.

'What happened? This one's not free either?'

'No, no. It is available. They are asking for details. Come.'

Marimuthu got down from his bike and walked towards the building. A portly woman was watering some plants by the side of the building. When she saw Marimuthu, she dropped the hose and came towards him.

'Is it your wedding, saami? In that case, you should be the one to come in and talk to us. It is hard for us to answer when you send your man.'

'It's not like that. I just sent him to see if anybody was here.'

'He walks in here and talks to me like he is a big landlord. Not a bit of humility.'

'Oh, I will admonish him. I am from Nangur. My wedding is on the fifteenth of Aavani.'

'He mentioned. The thing is, we have a coming-of-age ceremony for a girl here that very afternoon. They are our relatives. That's why we have not rented out the place to anyone for that day. Most people seem to need the place for the afternoon too. But that won't be possible. You will have to vacate the place by nine in the morning. That is non-negotiable. You can hold the lunch feast at your own place. If you are fine with this, we can rent the place to you.'

Marimuthu agreed. He would make sure everybody dispersed as soon as the wedding was over. He'd manage it somehow. The woman asked him to write down his name, his mother's name, his father's name, the bride's name, her mother's name, her father's name, the names of their villages—everything in a notebook.

He was afraid the woman might change her mind if he told her that he did not know the bride's father's name. So, he just wrote the name that came to his mind: 'Sornavel'. The advance was three thousand rupees. He signed the

contract and gave her the money. At the sight of three
thousand rupees, her plump face blossomed into a smile.
He'd have to pay the remaining seven thousand on the day
of the wedding. She then showed him the place. There
were a hundred plastic chairs lying around. Pots and pans
had been kept to a side.

The place had once been a textile workshop operating
a hundred looms. Once the looms were dismantled, they
had turned it into a wedding hall. The dining area was very
small. He made note of all the conditions that she listed
with a smile on her face. Chairs, cooking utensils, electric
supply, dining tables—everything was a separate rental.
If they added up everything, the total would come up to
fifteen thousand.

He did not mind the amount, but he was not satisfied
with the place. He consoled himself that at least he was
able to find a place at such short notice. Once upon a time,
he had dreamed that his wedding would happen in a huge
hall in front of a thousand guests. Sighing at that thought,
he stepped outside.

'Hey! Did you ask for the name and address of the
place to put in the invitation?' Raman shouted to him.
Marimuthu went back in to ask her.

'Why, anyone in these parts would direct you if you ask
them where Vallamma Mandapam is. Look, there—the
bus stop is right next to that tamarind tree. They call that
spot the load-bearing stone. You can mention that in the
invitation.'

Raman was sitting near the bike, smoking a beedi. He
stood up when he saw Marimuthu walking towards him.

'So, this is done. I had thought this might be the most difficult thing. But this is settled. Everything is coming together well,' Marimuthu said, starting the bike.

Sitting behind him, Raman asked, 'Tell me, will this fat woman be here on the day of the wedding?' 'Why do ask?' said Marimuthu. 'No, I just want to know if she would let me in,' Raman laughed. Unsure how to respond to that, Marimuthu laughed, too.

39

That restaurant was tucked away in a narrow street that led to the Karattur Mariyamman Temple. Marimuthu had been to that part of town several times in the past, but he had never seen that restaurant. There was an unassuming sign outside that said 'Rajaganapati Hotel'. Next to it was a high concrete wall with a small, wicket-like door in it. Only once he entered through that door did he realize how big the place actually was. He was amazed at how quietly that business had been operating for all these years.

All the roofs inside were thatched ones reinforced with layers of sugarcane plumes. There was a big cottage with four or five tables inside. Behind that were many smaller cottages. Selvarasu walked into one of the empty ones. Marimuthu and Raman followed him. It was a circular hut with its own washbasin. It could easily hold four people, but two or three more would be a little difficult to accommodate.

Folded chairs had been stacked up to a side. The light from a wick lamp had turned all three of them into shadows. Sounds of raucous laughter and conversations came from the cottages nearby, but it was impossible to hear anything clearly. Marimuthu felt that it was a very safe space to have their conversation.

'How do you know such places, Selvarasu?' he asked.

'When you are in the rig truck business, you get used to coming to such places, anna,' said Selvarasu with a shy smile. His respect for Marimuthu as an older cousin made him a little bashful in his presence.

'Raman goes out on rig business too. But you don't seem to know such places, do you, Raman?'

'Of course not. I am the type that buys the liquor, drinks it standing right outside the liquor store, throws away the bottle and keeps walking. All this hush-hush and secret drinking won't work for me.' Raman felt a little out of place there. He sat on the edge of the chair.

Marimuthu chided himself for not knowing such places despite coming to town almost every day. What was the point in roaming around the streets, sitting down somewhere for a cup of tea, and then heading back to the village? He had clearly wasted a lot of time in pointless tasks.

Selvarasu asked them what they wanted to drink and placed the order. He was also about to pay for all the drinks, but Marimuthu stopped him and paid instead. He and Raman could not decide what they wanted to eat, so they asked Selvarasu to order for them. 'Parotta and Paliyur,' said Selvarasu.

'What's Paliyur?'

'It's a chicken dish. Apparently, they made it first in Paliyur. But since it was very tasty, it became popular, and now they make it in these parts too.'

Raman said, 'Yes, I've had this dish. They have Paliyur even in roadside restaurants these days.'

'You two know so many things. I am completely useless,' Marimuthu sighed.

'It's not like that, anna. People who partner in rig business come to these places. They make so much money, they have to spend it somewhere. This is where most of those guys have their dinner. As far as I know, there are fifteen or so such places in this town.'

Bottles arrived at the table. A boy of twelve or thirteen waited on them. As soon as Raman saw the bottles, he opened one right away and started pouring into a glass. Selvarasu said, 'Wait, I'll do it' and took over the task of pouring everybody's drinks.

They had run into Selvarasu in town by chance. Without his help, they could not have figured out wedding invitation printing. He took them to a printing press he was familiar with. The printer showed them five or six folders full of samples. There were invitations in various colours, shapes and fonts. Marimuthu could not make up his mind.

He also had a little nagging worry. The printer was sure to ask for the girl's father's name, just as the woman at the wedding hall had. How could they print an invitation without that name? Should he give the same name he'd earlier come up with at the wedding hall? 'Sornavel'.

Marimuthu cursed his fate for having to marry a girl who didn't even know her father's name. It didn't matter if people found out after the wedding. But, until then, he had to keep the secret. He could not let anyone use it to derail things. When it came to marriage alliances, there had been so many hurdles over the years. Whenever he remembered how things fizzled out in the past after almost coming together, he was filled with fear and apprehension. What might happen, and when? What will be the reason this time? But who could stop things now that that he had fixed the wedding hall and ordered wedding invitations to be printed? Even though he kept reassuring himself that things were different this time, there was a little nagging worry in a corner of his mind.

He asked Selvarasu to step outside the print shop with him. He also signalled to Raman, who was sitting near the bike, to join them. He then ordered tea for all of them at the shop next door. Marimuthu didn't know how to broach the subject with Selvarasu. His eyes teared up. He did his best to control himself, but he was afraid he might break down right there.

He tried to turn his face away, but Selvarasu was worried and wanted to know what was going on. 'What is it, anna? What is it? Tell me whatever it is. We can sort it out,' he said. Raman too kept saying, 'What happened? What is it?' Looking at Raman, Marimuthu said, his voice breaking, 'You came back to the village after all these years, and you found a girl for me to marry. But couldn't you have found a girl who knows her father's name?' As he said these words, he started crying. Raman did not know how to respond. He said, 'You are not going to sleep with her father, are you? We already decided that this was not an important thing.'

'Yes, we did. But, tell me—what name should we put in the invitation? Let's say we do as the girl's mother suggested. We put the mother's and the grandmother's name. The matter doesn't end there. People will ask questions. I will have to answer them.' There was some anger in his voice now.

Selvarasu was beginning to understand the issue. Marimuthu pleaded, 'Rasu, until now only Raman, matchmaker thatha and I knew. Now, you know too. Please don't tell anyone.'

'Anna, why would share I this with anybody? Also, that's all the matter is? This is what you are crying about? These days, they have different ways for printing invitations. This is not a problem at all. Have you seen the invitations that people print when they marry girls from far-off places? They don't even print the name of the caste!' said Selvarasu.

Marimuthu didn't understand. So, Selvarasu took him back inside the printing press and showed him some of the samples in the folders. 'Ramasami's grandson and Muthusami's son'. This was the style in which names had been printed. All the names had shed the caste names attached to them. Even the names of totemic clans—the parrot people, the crow people—were absent from these invitations.

'This is all fine, but how do we not mention even the name of the father?' Marimuthu asked impatiently.

'Anna, look at this one. Here it is the bride and the bridegroom who are inviting people to their wedding. We can make ours in this style,' Selvarasu said, showing him a different sample. Marimuthu excitedly took it from Selvarasu and looked at the invitation format.

They decided to use that model. Marimuthu felt immensely relieved. The invitation now had Marimuthu's and Rosamani's names. Then it read, 'We seek your presence and blessings at our wedding. Yours, the bride and groom. Our families and friends join us in welcoming you.' They also added the names of their villages and directions to the wedding venue.

'Rasu, we could not have got the invitations done without your help today. You came at the right time,' he said, relieved and smiling.

Now, at the restaurant bar, Selvarasu had initially felt weird about drinking alcohol in front of Marimuthu. So, he had downed his first glass keeping his face turned away. But soon, he felt quite comfortable and at ease.

'This is no big deal, anna. I know places like these because I hang around with people who run rig trucks. You don't know because you work in the fields.'

'People asked me to join the rig business too. My mother said no.'

'Good. It's all a hassle. Once the land issue is settled, I am going to give up the rig work and go back to the land.'

'That's what you say now. But you are like a man with an itch. He can't keep himself from scratching. You are used to rig work. You won't be able to live without it,' Raman said, placing his empty glass back on the table.

'No, you will see. I am tired of that job. I am going to be like my brother here. Working the land,' Selvarasu replied. Then, turning to Marimuthu, he said, 'Anna, things seem to have come to a standstill with all the land negotiations.'

Eyes growing heavy with intoxication, Marimuthu looked at him. 'Shall we get this over with in the morning? Have you brothers agreed on which section of the land you all want?'

'Yes, we have agreed and decided on all that. We are waiting for the land to be settled between the two families. Then, we will divide up our portions. Only then can I bring up my marriage plans.'

'Dey . . . thambi, my mother may not have given birth to you, but you are my true brother. You pick the section of the land you want. You pick how much of it you want.'

'Anna . . .'

'I mean it. Bring your father and your brothers with you tomorrow. I will bring my father. We will meet at matchmaker thatha's place and get the matter settled. Why drag it on? My marriage came together only after we started all the land negotiations. Now I want my share of the land before the wedding. Just when a piece of land comes into my life, so does a wife. Both the land and the woman are mine.'

'Not just that,' said Raman. 'You keep saying the girl does not know her father's name, don't you? But do you realize how lucky you are in your mother-in-law? She looks like the girl's older sister! So, from time to time, you can enjoy your mother-in-law too. You might be marrying late, but you are definitely marrying well!'

'Go away! That's all you can ever talk about!'

He started eating. The food was quite spicy, but he couldn't feel the heat. He wondered if he'd drunk too much. Since he had abstained for years, now it didn't take much to get him drunk. He was not sure if he would be able to drink like this once he was married. The girl seemed very innocent. She was also very young. How was she going to deal with his mother?

Selvarasu's conversation with the waiter boy reached his ears like the distant buzzing of a bee.

'What else do you have?'

'The parrot curry is hot and fresh, anna.'

He quickly looked up. Selvarasu's face seemed far away, behind some dark smoke. As he mashed his parotta, Marimuthu said, 'Thambi, please don't eat parrot. It's not good for us. We already violate so many rules, but not this, I beg you. When we see a parrot in the orchard, our people put our hands together and pray to it.'

'No, anna, nobody eats parrots here. This is a Japanese parrot. The dish has become quite popular here now. But I will never order it. What do you feel like eating?'

But even in the dim lighting, he could tell that Selvarasu was smiling. He seemed unfazed by such scruples. Marimuthu wondered if he was alone in this fight. He looked at Raman, who was busy eating something. The piece of meat in his hand looked unfamiliar.

'Rama, is that parrot meat you are eating?'

'Yes,' Raman said, turning to face away from him.

'Dey, please don't! For my sake, please don't eat that. It is our deity.'

'But it is so tasty,' Raman said, taking another bite.

'Dey, Rama, I asked you to join me so we can farm together. You said no. But you are the reason for my happiness today. That's why I have decided that once the matter of the red-soil land is settled, I am going to hand it over to you. Then it will be my thambi, you, me—all working side-by-side. You don't need to give me any money. You cultivate it and make your living. But please don't eat that parrot now. Please.'

'But these bones are so crunchy, it is so good!'

'Dey! I am not going to pay for this meal. If you are going to eat parrot, don't sit in front of me. Get up!'

They thought he was just rambling, but he was angry now. In his frenzy and outburst, he fell off his chair. Selvarasu and Raman picked him up and sat him back in the chair.

'I am eating chicken! I was just playing with you. Do you think your thambi would buy me parrot meat to eat?'

'Dey! I might even marry a girl who does not know her father's name. But I will never eat a parrot. It is our saami.'

Long after they dragged him out of the restaurant, he was still talking about parrot.

40

The early morning air was chilly. As they rode on the motorbike, the wind hit their faces with some force. Marimuthu did not remember the route that the bus had taken during their earlier trip. So, Raman was giving him directions from behind. If they had taken the bus, the entire day would have been spent on the journey back and forth. But on the bike, they could be back home by ten. Then, they could start distributing wedding invitations.

The day before, Marimuthu gave Raman a thousand rupees and asked him to take time off from work for ten days or so. Having Raman with him was equivalent to having four or five men for help. Marimuthu could hand over any task to him and stop worrying about it. Raman would go around on his bicycle and get things done.

Marimuthu had been to thatha's house the day before for the arbitration of the land. His father needed some persuading to go with him; he was worried he would miss out on the morning toddy. So, he spoke to the toddy tapper in advance and made sure there would be some for him to drink before he set off. He needed some cool toddy in his stomach to energize him for the day. Besides, he knew that the talks at thatha's house might last for hours. There was a chance things would be settled that day, but it was also possible that they might continue on to the next day. Either way, it would be late morning when they wound up. By that time, the taste of the toddy would have changed. It would no more have that early morning coolness to it.

He tried saying to Marimuthu, 'Let's focus on the wedding first. We can sort this out later. There's no hurry.' But he didn't agree. Why would his father understand that the matter of the land and his marriage were connected? But his father was the one who had to sign the agreement once it was drawn. Also, people who came to arbitrate the matter would not agree to proceed without his presence. 'Appa! Just come with me. Stop being a pain!' he said in anger. After that, his father went along quietly.

Marimuthu did not like how his father was dressed. Just a single layered wrap-around over his loincloth and a frayed towel over his shoulder. He was likely to be dressed the same way on the day of the wedding. Would he at least put on a shirt? The man spent all his time in the fields, like a burrowing rat. Even after they arrived at thatha's house, Marimuthu's father did not involve himself in the conversations. He simply said, 'Alright, get it done quickly,' and sat down on the porch.

Selvarasu was already there with his brothers. His father, Marimuthu's uncle, sat quietly in a corner. It occurred to Marimuthu that the man's role in this might be exactly the same as his father's. There were fewer people. No women to start yelling and screaming and derailing things. He felt hopeful that the matter would be settled that day. He exchanged a quick smile with Selvarasu without anyone noticing.

Since Marimuthu was quite drunk the night before, Selvarasu had been apprehensive if he would show up at the meeting in the morning. So, now he seemed relieved and happy. Marimuthu felt that the Mannar girl that Selvarasu was in love with would soon energize him the way Rosamani seemed to have done for him.

Selvarasu's wedding might even happen before the end of the month. Marimuthu was happy that new and exciting things were beginning to happen for both of them. Matchmaker thatha's wife offered large glasses of buttermilk to everybody. She was wearing elaborate and heavy gold ornaments on her ears. Around her neck was the thick band of her gold thali. She had no teeth. It was very funny—the incongruence between her toothless smile and all the jewellery she was decked in.

Marimuthu's paatti too had once worn such jewellery. His mother had calculated that when his thatha died, paatti would stop wearing those jewels, and so they could get them melted and turned into new pieces for herself. But paatti invoked the convention that 'a mother's jewels go to her daughter,' and gave all her jewellery to Marimuthu's athai, his paternal aunt. Looking at thatha's wife now, Marimuthu was reminded of his paatti. He had not seen her in four or five days. Would she even understand if he told her about his wedding? On the way here, he and his father had run into Kuppan.

'She is not doing too well,' Kuppan said.

'What's happening?'

'Don't even ask. Looks like she has diarrhoea. She has done it all over the house. The cot, her clothes . . . everything stinks. I can't even stand there. I find it delicate even to take food for her. She won't even wear her sari. No matter how tightly I tie it, she manages to remove her clothes. Please come and see her.'

Marimuthu quickly asked what was on his mind.

'Kuppan, do you think she will last till the wedding?'

Nobody spoke for a minute. In that silence, he realized the cruelty in his question. He turned away, trying to avoid Kuppan's gaze.

'Nothing will happen, saami,' Kuppan mumbled.

'Okay. You will find Raman in the house. Tell him I asked him to fetch a doctor for paatti. Also, ask him to go and inform my athai. If she comes over, she can help paatti with tying the saree and everything. Paatti will like that,' Marimuthu said, before starting his motorbike.

A few nights ago, when he and Raman had got drunk at paatti's place, they had perhaps given her too much to drink and eat. She couldn't digest the food. She didn't even chew properly; she just swallowed pieces of meat. In her condition, an upset stomach was a terrible ordeal.

Marimuthu regretted the question he had asked. It was clearly an expression of his fears. Everything was coming together nicely. But what if they fell apart because of her? She really wanted her grandson to get married. She also wanted to live long enough to see the red-soil land being put to use again. But just when things were coming to fruition, paatti had become a potential threat.

He prayed in his mind. 'Amma Kooli, please keep paatti alive at least for the next ten days until the wedding is over.'

'I think the old woman craves toddy. I will take some every day. These are her last days. Let her drink and be happy before she dies,' his father said. He was always thinking about toddy. As he got on the bike, Marimuthu turned his head and spat on the ground. But his father might not even have realized that it was an expression of derision aimed at him and his obsession with toddy. After today, Marimuthu would need his father again on the day of registration. The man wouldn't have to miss his morning toddy on that day either. But what was he going to do on the day of the wedding? Marimuthu was sure he would make some arrangements for that morning too.

Raman attended to paatti as per Marimuthu's instructions. The doctor came, administered an injection and prescribed some medication, which Raman stocked up on. There was also a separate medicine for sleep. All her life, paatti had resisted going to the doctor. But now, she was not even aware of receiving an injection. Raman cleaned the hut thoroughly and used disinfectants to mask the smell.

He also informed Marimuthu's athai about her mother's condition. He later told Marimuthu that her eyes teared up and she did not say anything in response. But Marimuthu knew that she would visit her mother at least once a day. He wouldn't have to worry about paatti now.

It was nice and cooling to drink buttermilk on an empty stomach. Thatha started the meeting.

'Everybody, listen. I pressured Marimuthu to come here today. He is busy with all the preparations for his wedding, and he is here only because of my insistence. So, please talk and get the thing settled today. We can't have women arbitrating such things. Their words have no bearing on such matters.'

Addressing Selvarasu, his father and his brothers, thatha said, 'You have decided whom your share of the land goes to?'

'Yes, to Selvarasu. If things get sorted out today, we can sign both agreements today,' said Marimuthu's uncle. He sounded like he was ready to be done with things that day.

'Alright. Listen to me. The thing is, one person has to take the top field and the other has to take the bottom piece of land. But both parties seem to want the top portion. I don't know why. The lower field is as fertile as the other one. But then, these days who cares about the soil and fertility and that? They just want to see if the land is good for building houses. It's just houses everywhere.'

'Thatha, but we all need houses, don't we?' said Selvarasu's older brother Natesan.

'That's right. But if we build houses everywhere, there won't be a handful of earth left to grow good,' thatha laughed.

'We are going off-topic. Which one do you want? Top or bottom? Decide that first,' said Marimuthu's father.

'Mapillai, you sound like you are talking to your wife! "On top or below?"' Everybody laughed. Thatha had a way of turning anything dirty. Marimuthu turned his face away in embarrassment.

'Marimuthu, mapillai, you can ask the same question after the fifteenth of the month!' thatha now teased him.

'This is all pointless talk,' his father mumbled.

'Not pointless! Alright. Let's come to the matter. How many acres is it in total?'

'Three acres and forty-seven cents. The well takes up seven cents,' Selvarasu replied.

'Now that he knows that land will be his, look how sharp he is with the figures! Alright. Let's talk about the well first. Do you want to share the well in common? Or do you think it should go to whoever gets that section of the land?'

Marimuthu did not respond. He was determined not to give the impression that he was very particular about these details.

'Let the well be in common,' his uncle said.

'That's what you want? Okay. Then we need to talk about the repairs it needs. Also, you need to agree on how you want to allocate its use. Do you want to go into that now? Or shall we get into those details later?'

'We can discuss that later, thatha,' said Selvarasu.

'So, does everyone agree? Can the well be common to both lands?' thatha asked, looking around. Marimuthu looked at his father. His father looked at him. From the way he nodded, Marimuthu thought he was in agreement. Was he just eager to get things done quickly? Either way, it was good to share the well. They could share the expenses for all the repairs. The total area was only three acres. If they took turns drawing water every other day, there would be plenty to irrigate the entire land. So, Marimuthu nodded in agreement.

'Alright, good. Both parties agree. We have decided on the well, which amounts to seven cents. Now we have the rest, which is three acres and forty cents. If we were to divide that equally, it comes to one acre and seventy cents per person. But since both of you want the top section, we need to come to a compromise. Whoever gets the top section will have to give up some land from their share to the person who agrees to take the lower section. You all talk amongst yourselves and decide how much land you want to concede,' thatha said, and went into the house.

Marimuthu and his father stepped outside to the shade of the neem tree so that they could discuss this between themselves. Selvarasu, his father and his brothers conferred among themselves. Thatha came back out after a few minutes.

'Alright, let's get this over with. It's time for my meal. If I leave you to it, you will keep discussing this forever.'

Thatha started the auction at five acres. Selvarasu took it up to ten acres. The offers kept moving up by five acres and finally came to thirty acres. If they agreed to this, the person claiming the upper land would get one acre and forty cents, and the person below would get two acres. Both parties found this to be reasonable.

Marimuthu understood that Selvarasu's side was keen on claiming the upper land. So, he said, 'Thirty five.' Things were quiet for a few minutes. Thatha just kept muttering, 'Thirty-five. Thirty-five.' Then, Selvarasu said softly, 'Thirty-six.' Now it became clear to Marimuthu that Selvarasu did not want to go beyond the thirties. So, he said, without turning to look at Sevarasu, 'Thirty-seven.'

It kept going up by one acre and finally came to forty. So, Marimuthu would get two acres and ten cents. Selvarasu got one acre and thirty cents. Marimuthu was delighted that he got eighty cents more of the land since he opted for the lower field. If only paatti was of sound mind, she'd be delighted at his decision. He could see that Selvarasu was a little disappointed. But he could talk to him later and tell him, 'My father was adamant that we should not accept anything less than that.'

They wrote and signed the agreement on a twenty-rupee revenue document. Selvarasu took charge of getting the papers ready for registration. Marimuthu felt it was a good omen that the land came to his possession before the wedding.

41

Marimuthu stopped his bike at a tea shop on the other side of the bridge across the river. There was a coolness to the morning sun. The shop was adjacent to some fields. A few people were sitting on the benches outside. He and Raman ordered two teas and stood waiting by their bike. People moved and made space for them on the bench, but Marimuthu didn't want to go there. He needed to chat privately with Raman.

'Raman, what do you think? Do you think paatti will last a few days? I keep having this fear that she might die before the wedding.'

'Yes, she will last. The doctor has given her an injection and some medicines. I plan to get him to see her at least three times before the wedding. We'll be fine. I will take care of it. Don't worry.'

'Did the old woman have to take such a turn for the worse just before the wedding? I had hoped that she would happily see me get married before she died. But now she is making me very anxious.'

It was clear that Raman felt bad about it. They had been very excited and happy that night, and they did not think their actions would have such dire consequences. At any other time, paatti's health would have taken the first priority. But now, Marimuthu's wedding had come to be more important than even the possibility of her dying.

The tea was hot and sweet. Not wanting to let it go cold, they started sipping it right away. Marimuthu was constantly anxious these days. Raman tried to change the subject.

'How many invitations for the girl's family?'

'We have five hundred in total. Two hundred for them, three hundred for us. If they ask for more, we can get them printed.'

'I think they will only need a hundred or hundred and fifty to invite the villagers. I don't think they will need more. This will do.'

Then they resumed their journey. The speedometer showed that they had already travelled twenty-five kilometres. They had at least another ten to go. Thirty-five kilometres was not too far away. If Rosamani, not Raman, was sitting behind him, this journey would go even more smoothly.

Lush paddy fields all the way. It was quite a pleasant ride along that road. He tried to think of Rosamani's face. It came to him with clarity at first, but soon the image grew hazy. He tried to remember her as he had seen that one time. He was able to recollect her height and her figure, but her face kept eluding him. The faces of many women he knew seemed to have blended into one now. The eyes reminded him of Vasanthi. The forehead he saw was the other Rosamani's. Even the nose, the lips and the parting in her hair that he now imagined were not this Rosamani's. He pulled over on the side of the road. 'What happened?' asked Raman. Marimuthu got off the bike and sat squatting on the ground, shaking his head.

Why was he trying to recollect Rosamani's face now? He was going to see her in person in a little while anyway. The bottom-line was that it was a woman's face and he could imagine it to his heart's content. He pitied himself for this situation, for struggling to conjure her face in his mind even after it had been decided that he would be marrying her. But he consoled himself. Soon, he would get to spend time with her and look at her properly. Her face would acquire clarity in his mind.

'What are you thinking about? Are you wondering why you brought me along when you were going to see Rosamani? I promise I won't be in the way!' Raman laughed.

'No, no, nothing like that. In a few days, they will measure the red-soil land and put border markers. Selvarasu is busy with all that work. Once that is over, the first thing we need to do is to get the well repaired. They say it never goes dry. Apparently, the water from that well is excellent. Ever since I heard paatti talk about that well, I have been itching to jump in for a swim! So, we need to take care of the well and install a motor. Then, we can start irrigating the entire field. But all this will take at least five to six months.'

'I have been thinking about this too. I need to think about my income for all those months. After that, I will need some capital to start working the land. It will take a year for the harvest to happen. How do I take care of my family until then?'

'See, I am now using up my savings for everything. I will loan you the money you need to get started. No interest. I will also give you a small salary until the well is mended. What do you say?'

'You are kind, but I worry what your father and mother will have to say about all this. Let me think about it.'

'Be with me at least until the well is repaired. I will pay you a salary. See, if Veeduthi had secured this alliance for me, she would have surely asked for at least twenty thousand for her services. I have been thinking that I will give you that money instead.'

'Don't be silly. You are always thinking in terms of money. Don't turn me into a marriage broker!'

Marimuthu understood that Raman was not keen on farming. It didn't matter. If Raman did not wish to stay on, he could always find somebody else to help him mend the well. There was also Selvarasu, keen on getting the well repaired. In any case, Raman would stay with him until the wedding was over. He was confident about that.

42

No matter how meticulously he planned things, there was always some delay. But it was hard to avoid that when the task involved coordinating with others. By the time they arrived in the town and headed to the market street, it was already past eleven thirty, and the heat stung. He had not invited too many people. Since, according to custom, there had to be an odd number of people, he had initially decided on five. His father certainly would not want to join them, so he could rule him out. He wanted it to be himself, his mother, his sister, his brother-in-law and Raman. But his father insisted that *his* sister's family—that is Marimuthu's athai's family—be included.

After all, his athai was now coming regularly to take care of his paatti. If she didn't, it would be hard to clean and attend to paatti, who soiled herself and her clothes regularly. There was no one else to do it. This situation made him realize what people meant when they said every family needed a daughter. His athai washed paatti with warm water and wrapped the sari around her so tightly that paatti couldn't remove it no matter how hard she tried.

Athai mostly came over in the afternoons. She had
a few goats which she would herd out in the mornings
and tie them up in some pasture. Then, she would set
out to attend to her mother. After finishing her tasks at
paatti's, she would head back to herd the goats back home.
Athai's daughter-in-law, however, was not happy with this
arrangement. 'Why do you have to run all the way from
here to take care of the old woman? That family's the one
enjoying her inheritance. Why can't they take care of her?'
she tried arguing. But athai was not to be persuaded. She
walked way, muttering, 'Well, would you say that if this
was your mother?'

In deference to his father's wishes, Marimuthu
invited his athai's family on the trip. But it was his
athai's daughter-in-law who showed up, and his mother
was not happy with that. 'Why is she coming? She
shows up everywhere, this dried-up woman,' she said.
Besides, the moment she realized that her husband's
sister's family was being invited, Marimuthu's mother
insisted that her brother's family be included too. She
figured that this was a great chance to mend ties with
them. There shouldn't be too much consideration for
shame and pride when it comes to relationships. There
was nothing surprising about people falling out one day
and reuniting the next.

When Marimuthu went with his mother to invite in
person, his uncle was not immediately ready to be cordial.
But his mother managed to placate him. 'We are siblings,
after all. That's a fact, and it's not going to go away. Please
don't dwell on the past.' Ammayi did not step out of her

little cottage to meet her daughter. But the daughter went in to speak to her mother.

Marimuthu, however, did not feel courageous enough to face his grandmother. So, he waited outside. He could hear his mother's voice in little whispers. The two women were always like that. They always seemed to be exchanging secrets. Then suddenly he heard ammayi raise her voice. 'Yeah, right! What's that they say? The hopeless fellow's getting hitched on the thirty-eighth of the month! Like this is really going to happen!' Then he heard his mother shushing her. He didn't want to linger there, so he walked away a little where he couldn't hear them. Ammayi was clearly still upset with him.

His uncle's wife joined them on the expedition to purchase wedding clothes. So, now it was seven people, and it was quite a task getting everyone to leave on time. He also invited matchmaker thatha, but the man declined. 'What's my business there? It's like setting up a leather store in a Brahmin street! No, no!' The truth was that thatha did not get along with Marimuthu's mother. He only ever spoke to her when it was absolutely necessary and unavoidable.

So, now there were seven of them, and it was already eleven thirty when they all arrived in the market street in the town. But that was alright. After all, they had set aside the entire day for shopping. He was anxious for a different reason. He was worried that Rosamani and her people might have arrived early and might be waiting for them.

She already looked a bit tanned and dark from her work in the fields. What would all this waiting do to her complexion? He had asked her to arrive by ten and wait for them near the park bus stop. So, she might be waiting for over an hour. That was not acceptable. What if she concluded that he was not a man of his word? If it had been just him and Raman, they'd have come on time on the bike. They might even have arrived half an hour ahead of schedule. But there were all these rules and restrictions about how these things had to be done.

As soon as they all got down from the bus at the park stop, Marimuthu and Raman looked for Rosamani and her people. The place was not crowded then, so they could not have missed them. But still, the two men walked around the entire park to make sure they were not waiting somewhere else. They had not arrived yet. Marimuthu was happy.

His mother was saying to the women in the group, 'He rushed us all so much, but those women are not here yet. Gone are those days when the girl's family would come early and wait to welcome the groom's family. Everything is upside down these days.' Well, it was characteristic of her to say something like that. He just turned away from her, giving her no response. Raman smiled, pursing his lips.

He bought tea for everyone from the shop nearby. That could help while away the time. But before they could finish their tea, a town bus arrived, and people poured out of it. Recognizing one of the people who got off the bus, Raman rushed and welcomed them and brought them to the tea shop. Marimuthu had eyes only for Rosamani.

Looking at her now, he could not imagine she ever wore old, faded saris and toiled with domestic chores. She was now clad in a bright sari in a silk-like fabric in a combination of yellow and blue. He felt that the chain and the bangles she wore really suited her. It gave him a great deal of pride looking at her grace, her gait and her shy smile. Raman introduced everyone and ordered tea for the new arrivals. There were nine of them in her group. Marimuthu had expected only five. Rosamani's mother was very keen to make sure her side did not look weak.

They walked away from the tea shop, discussing whether they would head to Barani Silks or Chennai Silks first. Eager to get a sense of what his mother and sister thought of the bride, Marimuthu looked in their direction. But their faces were hardened and expressionless. In fact, they seemed angry, which made him apprehensive that the families might be rude to each other.

He spotted his brother-in-law staring at Rosamani. The man must be jealous that Marimuthu had found such a lovely girl for himself. Marimuthu felt like egging him on a bit. So, he walked closer to Rosamani and said, 'This sari looks great on you.' She grew shy and walked ahead to be in step with the others. Marimuthu was happy to see envy in his brother-in-law's face at that moment. They all agreed on Barani Silks as their first halt.

His athai's daughter-in-law tugged at his arm to slow him down, and she said, 'Marimuthu, is this your way of insulting us all? We are only seven of us, but there are nine of them. What kind of calculation is that? We are not short on people on our side, are we? We could have brought more of them. We have enough lands, enough money, don't we?'

'Akka, why are you making a big deal out of this?'

'How am I making a big deal? People bring thirty, forty people on these shopping trips. I didn't mind that we were fewer people, because I knew you were putting it all together at the last minute. But this is unacceptable. Nine of them and just seven of us? Make a phone call right away and get ten more of our people to show up. If not, we can do this another day. Let's go back home.'

Marimuthu felt a murderous rage. He felt like strangling her and throwing her in the middle of the traffic on the road. But he clenched his fist, ground his teeth and controlled himself. He could tell her, 'Well, if you want to leave, go ahead, leave.' She had already ruined a potential alliance in the past. Nobody invited her personally to join them today. They didn't mind that she showed up, but why can't she keep her trap shut? Raman noticed the stress on Marimuthu's face, and he immediately came closer to help him handle the situation.

He said casually, 'Oh, it is actually only five people of their side. They'd met the other four on the bus. They are here to shop for clothes too. So, Rosamani's folks invited them to join us. This way, we can all shop together.'

Even then, the woman was not entirely appeased. She walked away towards the other women in the group, still muttering discontentedly. Marimuthu was really annoyed. It wouldn't be difficult for him to get more people to show up. All he needed to do was call Selvarasu; he'd send ten, even twenty people. But what was the point? There was nothing for them to do. Even Selvarasu had not joined them. He'd said, 'Not now, anna. I have a few more days of work on the land. Let me attend to that first. Then, once we get the registration done, I will go wherever you invite me.'

Marimuthu was determined to have Selvarasu's presence at his wedding. He had to make sure that happened. Selvarasu really wished him well; he wanted Marimuthu to have a happy married life. This wretched woman, on the other hand—she'd be happy if things were ruined for him. He tried to forget about her and focus instead on Rosamani. She had worn her hair in a long plait and decorated it beautifully. She was really in proper bridal spirits. Nobody could find any fault with her. That thought gave him much comfort.

Barani Stores was a four-storey building. Their first task was to purchase a koorai sari for the bride to wear during the main ceremony. So, they headed to the silk sari section first. But there had not been a clear discussion of the price range, so they all seemed to be looking randomly at a wide variety of saris. He gently called his mother aside and said to her, 'Let them buy the koorai sari. We can go get other things.' She bit her lip in disapproval. 'We buy the koorai sari. That's the custom. They have to accept whatever we pick.'

Then, she rushed back to the group, quickly looked through a few saris, picked one and said, 'Let's get this one.' The girl's family were quite taken aback. Rosamani had been exploring her choice, placing a sari over herself and looking in the mirror to see if it suited her. She now dropped the sari back on the counter. Marimuthu was at a loss for how to handle the situation. He pulled his mother aside, the sari she picked still in her hand. Thankfully, she did not hear when someone remarked, 'Rosamani's mother-in-law seems to be a scary woman.' He said to them, 'You keep looking.' His mother asked him, 'What is it?'

'Why did we get the girl here? Just so she could pick the sari she liked, isn't it? Let them pick what they like.

You and sister go choose a silk sari each for yourselves. This way, we will be done quickly,' he said. His mother was quite stunned at the idea of a silk sari for herself. He expected her to ask, 'Silk? For me? Why?' But she didn't.

It didn't matter how much everything cost. He wanted everybody to be satisfied with their purchases. Let his mother get a silk sari for herself. And if his father wanted a silk dhoti, so be it. His wedding should have happened long ago. It was the question of clothes that had created a problem.

It was not long after he had taken over the work and the household accounts. He had been quite thrilled at the profits and was eager to make more. So, he worked hard. He'd arrive in the fields before dawn and would leave for home well after dusk, when the birds had already fallen silent. Whether it was preparing the ground for sowing seeds or weeding, he never left a task entirely to others. He always took the lead. Some tasks he performed entirely on his own. In fact, the daily wage labourers were saying, 'What's there to do in Marimuthu's land? He tightens up his loincloth and does eight men's work himself. If all landowners start working like him, what will happen to people like us? We will have to beg for our food.'

It happened during the weeding work on the groundnut beds. Marimuthu was working as hard as the women who had come to do the work. His athai, Virumakka teased him, 'Marimuthu, can't you wear a better loincloth? The one you are wearing is so ragged, it looks like your grandfather's!' He replied, 'Why wear a new one for weeding work? It's going to get dirty anyway.' But another woman, Vichi asked, chuckling to herself, 'What would you do if I pulled at it and removed it?' And he said, 'Well, try! You will be the one running away in terror!' The chatter on that first day of weeding work revolved entirely around Marimuthu's loincloth.

When he heard his father call out to him from the other side of the fields, he walked over there reluctantly, annoyed at the unscheduled break in the task. There were two visitors seated in the shade of the coconut trees. They gave him one look to size him up. He was covered in dust from head to foot. And he wore a little towel around his head and just a loincloth down there, like he was a mere farmhand. Marimuthu's father said to them, 'Please stay a bit longer. Drink some coconut water.' But when they saw Marimuthu climb up a tree in his loincloth, looking like a bat, they walked away. His father said, 'They wanted to see you. That's why I called you. But they are gone.'

The next day, Veeduthi came over and yelled at him.

'How could you show up in front of the girl's people in just a loincloth, your cock on display?! What were you thinking? Why do you walk around naked? Even goats and hens seem to feel some shame in their nakedness these days. You are a young man ready for marriage. If you walk around in a loincloth, who'd want to marry their daughter to you?'

Even if Marimuthu had presented himself in a shirt and dhoti and smelling all wonderful, there was no guarantee that they would have married their daughter to him. But it turned out that his loincloth had earned him a bad name.

43

They selected a bridal sari for Rosamani and showed it to Marimuthu for his approval. It was the colour of betel nut and had yellow dots all over. The free end of the sari was beautifully decorated in a stunning design woven with golden silk. When they draped it over Rosamani to see if it suited her, she was overcome with shyness and lowered her eyes.

She looked like she was born to wear fine clothes. Nobody would guess that she was raised in a little cottage by the side of a stream or that she grew up doing hard work in the fields. He kept looking at her without blinking his eyes and then smiled in approval. The other sari was stunning too. He asked them to go ahead and print the receipt. The saris they had bought for his mother and sister were lovely too. All colours seemed to look good in silk.

When they were purchasing a silk shirt and veshti for Marimuthu, his amma said to him, 'They have chosen a ten thousand rupee sari for her. Did they run it by you? Make sure your shirt and veshti come to at least five thousand. Let them spend some money too.'

That's when he realized how expensive Rosamani's bridal sari was. Ten thousand! Didn't it occur to Rosamani or her mother that it was a little too expensive? He wondered if it was a mistake to have given her the chain and bangles earlier. Perhaps that's what encouraged them. They now seemed to have assumed he would buy her anything, no matter how expensive.

He didn't want to look at her now. Why did she need such a costly sari to cover that body? He fumed. You wait. You will see how I treat that body day and night for a month after the wedding. I am going to run it ragged and satisfy all my desires and then leave you to herd sheep out in the sun. You just wait! Your body is used to the coolness of the fields, but by the time I am done, it is going to be like dried fish. He felt that everyone was taking advantage of him.

His mother picked the most expensive silk shirt and veshti for him. It came to over four thousand rupees. She did not know that Marimuthu was paying for everything. She thought she was incurring an expense for his in-laws.

Then they bought daily-use saris for Rosamani. These were very plain, but they still cost at least five hundred rupees each. Then one more sari for her. That's all the girl's family usually spent. Then they also bought casual wear for Marimuthu. Once purchases for the bride and the groom and their immediate families were done, they moved on to others.

'Raman, buy a veshti and shirt for yourself. Also buy something for Kuppan and the farm boy,' said Marimuthu. He wanted to speak to his brother-in-law, but couldn't find him. 'Where's machan?' he asked his sister. 'He has a lot of work. Must be attending to something. He'll be back soon,' she said. When Raman was selecting a shirt for himself, Marimuthu alone stayed with him. His mother pulled a long face and walked away from there. Raman really liked a particular fabric for his shirt. Soft material. Checkered pattern with five or six colours interspersed. Marimuthu approved that choice.

Just as the shop boy was measuring and cutting the fabric for Raman's shirt, Marimuthu's brother-in-law arrived. He selected a fabric for himself, and Marimuthu then asked for a piece of that to be cut. His brother-in-law then pointed to the cloth Raman had selected and asked the shop boy, 'What does that cost per metre?' The man checked the price, and said, 'Two hundred and ninety nine.' The brother-in-law then looked at the price of the cloth he had selected. Two hundred and fourteen. Raman's cost nearly a hundred rupees more than his. The brother-in-law's face fell.

Noticing that, Marimuthu said, 'Buy one more for yourself.' His brother-in-law seemed pleased that he was getting two shirts. Marimuthu was glad he had observed that exchange and remedied the situation. Otherwise, his brother-in-law would have gone around telling everyone, 'He buys his worker a shirt worth three hundred rupees. But I get only two hundred. Goes to show how much he respects me.'

It all amounted to a massive purchase. They ended up with a large bundle of clothes. There were seven different saris for Rosamani. One to wear during the wedding ceremony, one to change into, a spare one for travels, and four for daily wear. The purchases for Rosamani alone surpassed twenty thousand rupees. Marimuthu was not happy about that. But then it occurred to him that if he had managed to get married sooner, and the girl had brought twenty or thirty sovereigns of gold, then he'd have had to buy them whatever they wanted. He would not have objected then, he realized.

Rosamani might be a girl from a poor family now. But soon she will be Marimuthu's wife. So she needed to have good clothes and jewellery that reflected that status. It was natural for women to uphold their husbands' pride and honour. Rosamani must be thinking along those lines too. Marimuthu was coming up with reasons to feel better about these expenses. If he had found this match through a wedding broker, the fee alone would have been twenty thousand. He could think of any number of wasteful expenses for that amount of money.

Why was he so calculating about spending money on a girl who was coming to live with him? Well, they could at least have checked with him. That would have put everyone at ease, including his mother. But then, what was the fun in everyone behaving appropriately?

In addition to the silk shirt and veshti they had bought for Marimuthu, they also bought two sets in polyester. And, without telling him, they also bought a pants-and-shirt set for him. Marimuthu had never worn a pair of pants in his life. But his wife-to-be wanted to see him in these new clothes. It made Marimuthu very happy when Raman let him know of these plans. He was thrilled that Rosamani wanted to see him in trousers.

However, he was not sure if he would be able to adapt to a new fashion so readily. If he suddenly started wearing pants at thirty-five, people in the village would make fun of him. But how could he say no to his wife? They did not consult him when they bought him undergarments. They just needed to know the size. He was used to wearing boxers and half-sleeved undershirts. But they had bought briefs and sleeveless undershirts. Apparently, when Raman told them about Marimuthu's preferences, Rosamani said, 'No, let's buy these instead.'

Marimuthu wondered if she was trying to mould him into a certain image she had in her mind. He considered intervening and objecting to these changes. But he restrained himself. He did not want any unpleasantness. At least he found some release in being able to share his thoughts with Raman and Selvarasu. If they weren't around to talk to, he might explode.

Silk saris for his mother and sister. Also, one daily-wear sari each. Clothes for all three people in his athai's family. As for his maternal uncle's family, new clothes for four people, including the children. White saris for his paatti and ammayi. A dhoti and a towel for his father. The same for matchmaker thatha. Kuppan too would get a dhoti and a towel. Veshti and a shirt for Raman. A pair of shorts and a shirt for the farm boy. Then they bought two extra sets of shirts and dhotis just in case they had missed someone.

In the girl's family, saris for Rosamani's mother and clothes for Muthurasu and his family, since he was like a brother to Rosamani's mother. They also bought shirts and trousers for a boy who had to play the role of Rosamani's brother in one of the wedding rituals. But even after all these purchases, they were still not done. Marimuthu had to see them all off at the bus stand and then go buy new clothes for Selvarasu and also for Raman's family. He did not want his mother to know about these purchases. She might say something like, 'Oh wow, it looks like you are marrying into their family.' So, he could complete these purchases only after she had left. All the expenses came to over forty thousand. When amma complained that it was a lot of money to spend, his uncle's wife boasted, 'Well, ten years ago, for our wedding, we spent thirty thousand rupees.' Rosamani's family gave him some money as their share of expenses. It was the same ten thousand rupees Marimuthu had given Rosamani the other day.

When he was verifying the purchases against the bill, Marimuthu noticed a sign placed inside the store. 'A humble request to our customers. Wedding parties please bring fewer guests.' He read out the sign to Raman.

His brother-in-law, who happened to be standing nearby, said, 'That's the reason this shop doesn't seem to have too many customers. It is different at Chennai Silks. We can take everybody, there is plenty of space. I suggested that earlier, but you wanted to come here.'

'That's alright, machan. In fact, it becomes very difficult when there are too many people. If some thirty or forty of our folks come and mill around, it's going to affect the business, isn't it?' said Marimuthu.

'So what? When people come for wedding purchases, they cannot come alone. They always come in groups,' his

brother-in-law said. Marimuthu didn't say anything more
on the subject.

The families sorted out the fabrics that needed to be
taken to the tailor. Then, as per custom, the bride's clothes
stayed with the groom's family and vice versa. After that,
they all headed to a large restaurant nearby. Marimuthu's
brother-in-law and Raman decided to go somewhere
else to eat. So, they took two hundred rupees from him
and went their separate ways. Everybody else would eat
vegetarian food. Since they had come to make purchases
for an auspicious occasion, custom forbade them from
eating meat. There were fourteen of them in the group. It
took a while to find tables for the entire party. The textile
store, the street, the bus, the restaurant—it was crowded
and congested everywhere. Marimuthu had to go to the
jeweller the next day to get the thali done, and he wondered
how crowded that place was going to be.

'Who can go with me tomorrow to place an order for
the thali with the jeweller?' he asked, sitting down casually
on the chair next to Rosamani's. The custom in the old
days was for elders from both sides of the family to find
an auspicious day and hour to go to the goldsmith's with a
gift plate of fruits, betel and an advance amount. But these
days, a few people from both of sides of the family simply
went to a jeweller and placed the order. Marimuthu wanted
to make sure he included them in his plans.

'You go ahead. We can't do everything the way they
used to do in the old days. There is no need for everyone
to be running around for everything. Also, Rangamma
does not have anybody to assist her. We still have people to

invite in person and arrange for at least one wedding feast.
We don't have enough people, mapillai.'

Muthurasu was right. It didn't matter. Marimuthu
could take Selvarasu with him and place the order for the
thali. But he remembered that he still had invitations to
distribute. He'd only managed to cover half. For the rest,
he'd have to take his mother with him. He dreaded to
think of the drama his mother might subject him to. She
had already asked Marimuthu's sister to spend the week
at their place. What was his brother-in-law going to say
about that?

'How many meals? Have you bought tokens?' the server
asked.

They all looked at each other, unable to decide. 'Order
whatever you want,' he said looking at Rosamani. 'I want
parotta,' she said in a whisper. As soon as she said that,
everyone in her family also ordered parottas. He did not
want to leave her side, but he needed to speak to his mother.
'Amma, what shall we eat? Shall I order meals for the rest
of us? They've all ordered parottas.'

'Oh, parottas for them and meals for us? You are already
putting us in our place. I wonder if you will even deign to
look at us once you are married!' said his sister.

'You all eat whatever you want. I am not asking you
to order meals. I just wanted to know what you'd like to
eat,' he said, not revealing even a tinge of annoyance in his
voice.

'Then why did you ask if you should order meals for all
of us? We eat rice every day at home. Why did you bring
us here if you wanted us to eat the same thing?' his mother

shouted. But thankfully, people couldn't hear it in all the commotion of the place.

'All right, ma! I will order parottas for everyone.'

He ordered parottas for all fourteen of them. When he glanced over towards Rosamani, he saw that she was signalling with her eyes for him to come and sit next to her. She had held the spot for him. Without looking towards his mother and sister, he went and sat next to Rosamani.

44

It was four days of non-stop running around. He took his mother with him and went from village to village, inviting people to his wedding. Wherever they went, they were served large tumblers of tea. Now, drinking that much tea was as filling as drinking the same amount of toddy. But while a few burps would help ease off in the case of toddy, with tea it was a relentless heaviness.

Besides, most of the tea they got to drink was not even tasty. It was decoction diluted with tepid water and the tiniest amount of milk added. So, a great deal of time was wasted in making stops on the way to relieve themselves. Moreover, drinking so much tea meant they couldn't fall asleep quickly at night, even though their eyes burned from all the sun and dust endured during the daytime travel. If they were to tell their hosts that they were not in the habit of drinking tea, they would surely be served some watered-down milk. The tea was far better than that. But all that bad tea had numbed their tongues to the taste of good tea. If such were the ordeals to be endured in inviting three-hundred people to the wedding,

Marimuthu dreaded even to think about weddings that involved a thousand guests.

Amidst all this work, Selvarasu informed him that the land surveyor would come to assess the red-soil land one of those days. So, Marimuthu had to spend an entire day attending to that. He had thought it would take only a little time to figure out the land boundaries, but it was already eleven by the time the surveyor and the registrar arrived. Then, when they went from corner to corner trying to determine the perimeter, other issues started cropping up.

The land bordered an enclave of houses, and a section of the front yards of some of these houses belonged, in fact, to the land. And there were also portions of the land that were, strictly speaking, part of the enclave. So, this led to a dispute, and it took a long time to resolve it and agree on the boundaries. Then, they had to bring lunch from outside for the survey team. After that, they got down to measure the area—one hundred and thirty square feet on the elevated side and two hundred and ten square feet on the lower portion of the land. By the time all that work was completed, it was already evening. They also had to measure and mark the well. Then, when they looked at the boundaries, they realized that the water channel that went from the well to Marimuthu's land passed through Selvarasu's portion of the land. They remedied this imbalance by carving out a small section of Marimuthu's land for Selvarasu.

Marimuthu knew that once the settlement was complete, they would have to get the well repaired and rebuilt. They could get started on that as soon as the

registration papers were finalized. Selvarasu was attending
to that work quite diligently.

Marimuthu parked his bike outside the registration
office. He stood by his bike while his father went and sat
down on the porch. The document writer in the office had
told them that if all their papers were in order, they could
sign and submit right away.

Thatha arrived shortly. 'Mapillai, you have achieved
what you wanted. The land is yours now, and you are
going to have a wife soon too. This is how things work out
sometimes. All good things happen at once. You see, when
the time is right, nobody can stand in your way. If things
carry on this way, I think you will have a son next year! And
he will call me "thatha"!'

'Thatha, I want the first one to be a girl child. In fact, I
don't care if I have four or five daughters.'

'Sure. You say that now because you had such a difficult
time finding a woman to marry. But give it a month. You
will start saying you want only a boy.'

'No, no. I am not like that at all. Truly. I want a daughter.'

'Alright! Good. We'll see. When people go to the
doctor in the fifth or sixth month of pregnancy and find
out it is going to be a girl, they just get an abortion. Killing
an infant by laying it on its tummy or choking it by putting
paddy grains in its mouth—those were the old ways. Now,
the doctors themselves do it. How, then, are we to have girl
children? When are we going to change?'

'All that will end with my generation. When my sons
and daughters grow up to be adults, things will be different,
you will see.'

'That's impressive. Sure. Have as many daughters as you want. May people line up in front of your house wanting to marry your daughters,' Thatha laughed.

Marimuthu imagined a scene where little girls ran around and played in front of his house. He could see Rosamani keeping an eye on them from the porch, scolding them, keeping them in order. How many children were there? One, two, three . . .

'Mapillai, how is your grandmother doing?'

Thatha's question broke his reverie. It took him a few seconds to grasp what thatha was asking him.

'I don't think her condition's going to improve, thatha. I just want her to be fine until the wedding is over.'

'That's just two days from now. You don't think she will last until then?'

'I think she will be fine for a week to ten days. Beyond that, it is not in our hands.'

Marimuthu was quite anxious about paatti's health. No matter how late it was, he made it a point to visit her every night. Ever since his athai arrived to take care of her, the cottage was kept spick and span. Earlier, paatti used to walk around the cottage, but now she was totally bedridden.

Every day, with the help of Kuppan or the farm boy, Marimuthu's athai managed to lift paatti from the cot, clean her and lay her back down. She looked so frail and her stomach so drawn in, and she ate so little, Marimuthu could not understand how she could soil herself so much. Fluids were all she could consume and only in tiny portions. They couldn't even administer any medication. She simply lay on the cot and kept muttering to herself. And she fell asleep when she got tired of talking. All her conversations seemed to be with her dead husband.

If he called out, 'Aaya,' she would reply loudly, 'What?' Then if he asked her, 'Do you need anything?' she'd say, 'Are you going to the market?' No matter who addressed her, she always took them to be her husband. When he was alive, all they did was fight. They never seemed to have a loving word to say to each other. However, they never spent even a day apart. Marimuthu wondered how paatti endured the loneliness after thatha passed away.

Arguing with each other had been their way of expressing love. When there is love, such conflicts stayed within bounds. That was the reason paatti was now thinking of her husband, and him alone, in these last days. Marimuthu hoped that she could carry on this way for another week at least. He oscillated between the fear that something untoward would happen before that and the faith that things would turn out well.

Selvarasu arrived when Marimuthu was chatting with thatha. His father and brother had come along with him. The man who typed out the registration forms had his little office across the road from the registrar's. Selvarasu headed there. Thatha started chatting with Selvarasu's father.

Marimuthu looked at Selvarasu's second brother Muthusami. He seemed to have lost most of the hair on his head and looked like a family man exhausted from taking care of four or five children. The head is the first thing that reveals one's age to the world. You either lose your hair or it greys. Through its ravages on the body, time constantly expresses its lack of mercy. Marimuthu wondered if Muthusami still entertained hopes of getting married.

Perhaps he had intimately known a woman's body and had grown weary of it all. After all, men in these parts were known to have sex in the maize or kambu fields with any women ready to oblige. Perhaps Muthusami had had such experiences. His face seemed to convey a maturity beyond his years. Selvarasu had told Marimuthu about his brother once.

Apparently, once when Muthusami went to a wedding, his relatives made fun of him. 'Mapillai, you come and eat at everybody's wedding. When are you going to feed us your wedding feast and settle the debt? Or do you plan to eat free meals forever?' After that, he refused to attend any weddings or other functions. If the family put some effort into it and were willing to spend some money, they might be able to find him a girl from the Thattur area. But who knew what hurdles they faced.

Selvarasu came back with the writer. It took them half an hour to sign all the papers and submit them inside. 'Not too many registrations today. They will call you soon,' the writer said. So they waited.

If thatha had not been with them, they would have all fallen silent. He kept the conversation going with both families, keeping things cordial. For all this, Marimuthu's family had no direct conflict with Selvarasu's parents. They were simply continuing the long-standing estrangement from the previous generation.

Marimuthu wanted to end all animosities and invite his uncle's family to his wedding. But Selvarasu told him

it was not going to be easy. Apparently, when Selvarasu
casually brought up the subject with his family, they asked,
'What's the need to reunite with them now?' Marimuthu's
mother expressed the same sentiment. 'That relationship
is broken for good. There is no point in trying to mend
it.' Both men were afraid that if they pressed the matter
too much, the families might pull back even from the land
settlement. But Marimuthu was keen on making sure at
least Selvarasu would be at his wedding.

In fact, it was Selvarasu who attended to a number
of important tasks for Marimuthu's wedding. Fixing the
cooking team, deciding the menu, making grocery lists,
finalizing the decorations for the wedding ceremony dais,
arranging for sufficient drinking water—everything. He
took care of all the land matters during the day, and in the
evenings he attended to the wedding tasks.

Selvarasu also arranged a bus to fetch the bride's family
from their village the evening before the wedding. The bus
would pick them up at five in the evening, drop them at the
wedding hall and set out again for a second trip at seven.
Anybody else who needed to be picked up could come in
that second trip. There would also be a return trip at nine
for all those who wanted to go home for the night. They
expected at least half the guests to spend the night in the
wedding hall. The wedding ceremony was supposed to
happen between six thirty and seven thirty in the morning.
The bus could make another trip early in the morning to
bring the guests.

Raman went to Varattur to convey all these plans to the
girl's family. Marimuthu wanted to go there himself, but

he had invitations to distribute. So, he sent Raman. Upon his return, Raman said, 'Hey! They are all very cheerful and excited. They have installed a thatched canopy in front of their house, and they are getting ready to host a feast the day before the wedding.'

45

Once all the final land deeds were signed and registered, Marimuthu invited matchmaker thatha to join him and Selvarasu to celebrate at a restaurant. This was a tradition with him whenever he finalized any registration or sale deeds. But thatha declined the invitation.

'There is nothing nutritious about restaurant food. I will go home to eat. You all go and have a good time,' he said.

Marimuthu's father was not interested in joining them either. He preferred to eat meat, but with the wedding coming up in just a few days, they were prohibited from consuming meat. They could not violate the rule in public without people commenting on it. But if he went back to his shed in the fields, he could catch and fry a rat or a mouse. No one would know. No wedding or death could stop him from doing that.

Since Marimuthu could not take his father back on his bike, he looked for someone to give him a ride. One of Selvarasu's brothers was leaving on his bike, but Marimuthu's father would definitely not be willing to hitch a ride with him. Marimuthu stood looking down the road. There was always someone driving towards their village. That's when he saw Kattayan walking towards them, grunting and clearing his throat. Marimuthu stopped to chat with him.

Kattayan said, 'Dey, Mapillai! I always knew that you 'parrot' men are quite shrewd, but this is too much even for you. I helped clear that land of all the thorns and bushes, but you didn't even invite me for the registration. You couldn't think of treating me to a meal?'

It was quite crowded in front of the registrar's office, but Kattayan did not bother to lower his voice. Marimuthu was embarrassed.

'Why not, come with us, uncle. Let's go and eat,' he said. What he really wanted to say was, 'You are walking around town, looking for a way to get a free meal.' But he controlled himself; he knew that would lead to an argument. As Marimuthu got ready to leave on his bike, his father looked at him. He handed two hundred-rupee notes to his father, which the man took happily and secured in the folds of his veshti. He would surely buy some brandy on the way. At least two or three quarter bottles. He'd take a break from toddy for the next few nights.

After seeing his father off, he headed to Sumesh Bhavan restaurant. Selvarasu was already waiting for him there. They went in to eat.

'How are things, anna? Are you done distributing invitations?'

'Yes. There are a few families I had forgotten. But I can take care of that tomorrow.'

'Yes, please get that done tomorrow. Don't keep anything for the day after. Otherwise, we'd be very rushed.'

'Mm . . . Let's do everything differently when you get married. None of this nonsense . . . all this constant running around . . . satisfying this person . . . placating that one . . . such a lot of nuisance, da. The best way would be to take the girl with you and get married in a temple. But my mother-in-law insists on doing everything properly. She feels this is the only way people would accept their family.'

'That's alright. Why wreck her desires? All this trouble is just for two more days. That's it.'

'I need to go to the tailor in the evening to see if my shirts are ready. Did you get yours yet?'

'No, not yet. I will get it tomorrow.'

'Why don't you bring that girl to the wedding? Shall we buy her a sari, too?'

'No, let's not do that. They'll find out. I don't know what trouble my presence is going to cause.'

'But we are going to get our estrangement dissolved today.'

Marimuthu had already spoken to Selvarasu about this. Right after the registration, he wanted to get their families' estrangement ritually annulled. He'd already given the priest five hundred rupees to purchase everything needed for the ritual. They just had to head there right after their meal. Since their stomachs were full, they found it a bit difficult to climb the rock towards the hill. So, they halted at the mandapam on the way. Things would be so much easier if the day was a little cooler.

There were mounds of garbage on the steps. On the rocks beyond the steps were piles of shit. Houses were clustered around the base of the hill. In fact, some of the houses had been built right on the lower end of the rocky hill. Human presence always seemed to mean filth and stench. If they climbed a little further, they could find some temporary respite from all this.

On one of the mandapam pillars, he saw a beautiful sculpture of a man embracing a woman. Both desire and modesty came alive in stone. He walked closer and placed his hand on the woman's large, sculpted breasts. 'What a talented bastard! Look how wonderfully he has sculpted this,' he remarked. The rest of the sculpture had changed colour with gathering dirt. But the breasts alone shone black and clear. He enjoyed his touch. It felt like he was touching actual human flesh.

Selvarasu lowered his head and smiled. 'Anna, come on, come away from there. Somebody might be looking at you,' he said. Marimuthu came to his senses and felt acutely embarrassed that he had been standing there, touching that sculpture. Trying not to look Selvarasu in the eye, he said, 'Let's go.' But that touch still seemed to linger in his fingers.

In an attempt to change the subject, he said, 'Rasu, how do you suggest we go about mending the well?'

'All the stones have fallen. We need to build it up back again. We also need to drain it of all the water and take out all the mud. We will need a motor for that. Let's see if we can get a used oil engine from somewhere.'

'We can do nothing without the well. Once that's done, we need to irrigate only every four or five days.'

'Shall we just buy a new engine? What do you say, anna?'

'Yes, I agree. That's a good idea. If we buy a used one, we will end up spending a lot on servicing and repairs. Look for a new one. Let's also plant neem saplings around the well. And let's build a vat next to it. I think we should attend to the well first. Everything else can wait.'

'Yes, we will get to it as soon as your wedding is over.'

'Once we level the bottom of the well, I will then be able to jump into it for my bath. I am told there is always a good amount of standing water in that well. But we need to make sure no one else gets to go down into the well. Otherwise, people will ruin it.'

'Anna, once we repair and secure the well and start work in the fields, there will be no trespassers.'

They stopped to offer their prayers at the Maduvan temple. After that, there was a dip in their path, followed by a steep climb. As they went down into the dip, they came across a marvellous carved image of a five-hooded serpent. Devotees had covered its hood with vermillion. The way the serpent had lifted its head and was arrested in mid-movement gave him gooseflesh.

'This settlement has worked out well for you, anna. But I got a little less than I expected. Never mind, though. I have two acres of elevated pasture. I can always attend to that.'

Even though Marimuthu had had this conversation with him, it looked like Selvarasu was still unhappy about the settlement.

'Look, Selvarasu, don't worry about that. Why don't you cultivate my land too?'

'Anna, what are you saying? Didn't you offer it to Raman?'

'I did, but he is being too fussy and says he doesn't want to do any farming. What more can I do? I can't just make the land over to his name, can I? I give him money for expenses, and I have bought new clothes for everyone in his family for the wedding. Even for his little ones. There's no point handing over the land to someone who can't even raise some capital to start working the land. It's as good as leaving the land unused.'

'Do you really mean it? Will you let me farm your portion of the land too?'

'Of course I mean it! Consider it done. I can't take care of all my fields myself. It's not like the old days anymore. It's very difficult to find help these days. Kuppan's too old. But let's not speak to Raman about this yet. You first attend to the well. We will bring this up later.'

Now, Selvarasu climbed the hill with gusto. It was all about the land. Marimuthu was not able to come to a firm decision about it. There were times he thought he should leave it in Raman's charge; after all he had worked for the family since he was a kid. But why can't Raman just come straight out and ask him, 'Let me work this land?' He always said there was more money to be made in the rig business. But it was not as easy as he imagined. It involved days and nights of very hard work out in the sun, enduring even blisters on the skin. However, Marimuthu was not sure Raman would be amenable to the sedentary life of a farmer.

Selvarasu, on the other hand, would take excellent care of the land. But Marimuthu's parents may not easily agree to that arrangement. There would definitely be an argument about this. He couldn't be a married man and still be fighting with his parents. Besides, there were also times when Marimuthu considered working the land himself. After all, all the delays in his marriage were due to the fact that the land had been in disuse all these years. The entire marriage thing came together only after he initiated talks about settling that land between the families. He had lost all hope of getting married. But everything came together in just fifteen days, and the credit for all that goes to that land. So, there was a part of him that wanted to cultivate it himself. But let the wedding be over. Let them get the well repaired. He would think about it later.

Selvarasu had climbed ahead of Marimuthu. The temple was not crowded. Just a few people. Once the bus service started, fewer people climbed the hill on foot. Usually, people walked up the hill only if they had some offerings to make to the deities on the way.

The deity they had come to worship was in one of the smaller shrines. The steps that led down from his feet were called 'the steps of truth'. When people had anything stolen from them, this is where they came to appeal. And families that had flung fistfuls of earth at each other and severed their ties had to come here to make peace again. The priest had brought everything needed for the ritual. He got started on the ritual the moment they arrived. Marimuthu and Selvarasu followed his instructions.

Selvarasu placed earthen lamps on every step. The priest had already placed a wick in each of them. Using an iron ladle, Marimuthu then poured oil into them from a bowl.

'Offer your prayers with full faith in this deity. This is the god of truth. You will come to no harm,' said the priest.

They lit the lamps, and they glowed bright despite the daylight. The priest carried on with the ritual. The deity had been decorated all over with sandalwood paste. The idol was a relief carved into a large stone, and its contours now stood out thanks to the sandal paste. Immersed in the sound of the bell, both men offered their prayers.

'Please forgive us for whatever happened in our grandparents' time, whether they did it knowingly or unknowingly. We want to reunite. Please permit us to do so. We want both families to visit each other, exchange food, take part in each other's celebrations and sorrows. Saami, please accept our offering and give us your command,' Marimuthu said his prayer out loud.

The priest asked Selvarasu to do the same. He said his prayers quietly in his heart. As he stood, hands together and eyes closed, he felt all his confusions and worries withering away.

Marimuthu added, 'I need your help for this wedding to happen as I wish. I will offer you special prayers when I come here with my wife. Please protect paatti. I rely on you to take care of her until the wedding is over.'

His bare chest glistening with sweat, the priest now addressed the deity. 'Please fill our cattle sheds, fill our pots with abundant food, make the evil recede and the good gather to us. Please end this estrangement and make these relatives reunite. They have come to you for help, please protect them.'

The priest then gave them portions of the offerings in separate packets. 'Don't forget to leave some gifts for me,' he said to them. 'Haven't we already paid you for everything?' asked Selvarasu. 'That was just enough to buy all the things for the ritual. Do you know how expensive the oil was? I bought three litres of it. I will have to fill up the lamps again. They will still be burning when you have climbed down the hill,' the priest went on and on. Marimuthu took a fifty-rupee note from his packet and placed it on the priest's plate.

46

Even as he stood outside the wedding hall welcoming guests, Marimuthu was quite anxious. His mother stood next to him, smiling and happily chatting with the guests. But when the girl's family had still not arrived, she grew anxious too, and kept asking him, 'Where are they? Why is it taking so long?'

They had sent the bus as early as five, and it was seven now, but the bus was still not back with the girl and her family. Guests had started arriving at six thirty. When these guests walked into the wedding hall, there was nothing to suggest that there was going to be a wedding ceremony. The nadaswaram troupe was sitting in a corner and playing its music. That sound was the only indication to the guests that they had indeed come to a wedding. The bride had still not arrived. No sign of any ritual about to happen.

The barber had arrived. The washerwoman was standing outside the temple, holding a flame torch. But that flame was no match to the glow of the row of tube lights decorating the entrance to the hall. The wedding officiant stepped out every few minutes to see if the bridal party had arrived. Then he said to Marimuthu, 'Mapillai, where is the girl? I have a lot of work today. After finishing up here, I have another wedding to go to. They will expect me at nine. But if it gets really delayed here, I will be able to get there only at midnight. It won't do!'

'They are on their way, uncle. They will be here shortly,' Marimuthu said, trying to placate him. But he was worried if Rosamani had changed her mind about marrying him and run away somewhere. Was ammayi's curse going to come true? Will he never get married? He had to consciously drive these thoughts away.

He could breathe properly again only when he heard the bus arriving. A group of his relatives stepped outside carrying plates of fruits and accompanied by the musicians to welcome the bride's family. It was not the custom for the bridegroom to join them, so he stayed put. But he was quite excited and started chatting happily with everyone.

The wedding hall was nearly full. Since the building had originally been a loom workshop, it was quite a small space. The dining hall was even more cramped. Only thirty guests could eat at a time. The officiant had told them that they could start serving food only after the girl's family arrived. God knows why. But they couldn't contradict him.

If they did not have an officiant, they could do things the way they wanted. But now that they had one, they could not incur his displeasure. If he got upset and walked away, it was too late to find another. Rosamani sparkled as she came walking in the middle of the crowd, the nadaswaram and melam music accompanying her entrance. She was not even wearing much make-up or jewellery. Soon, she would have to go through some ritual bath and anointing. So, for now, she was dressed simply. But a certain glow in her face and the distinctness of her gait made her stand out from the crowd. Marimuthu looked at everyone with an expression of pride.

The moment the bride entered the wedding hall, the officiant and the barber got started with the rites. The first set of rituals involved the bride; the ones for the bridegroom came later. Marimuthu sent Selvarasu to attend to the food service. Now finally the place had acquired the cheery wedding ambience. It is a woman who gives meaning to a place, makes it beautiful, he thought. Things had been at a complete standstill just a moment ago. But Rosamani's arrival had set everything in motion. 'Why all this delay?' Marimuthu asked Raman in a tone of mock anger.

'You think getting a wedding party together is a small matter? They wanted to start at the most auspicious hour. Then, they had to wait for everyone to arrive. The guests were from adjacent fields, and they kept shouting out, "I will be there! I am on my way!" But they took a long time to gather. So many of them! There was not enough room in the bus for everyone to sit. Your mother-in-law was delighted. I think she'd been anxious that not many people would join them. But when she saw everyone, her face lit up. All these people who had kept their distance, the moment they heard Rosamani was marrying into a well-to-do family, they all came rushing back.'

Raman went back to the bus. He had another trip to make. This time, it would be nine by the time they returned. Since the wedding hall was located far away from everything, they had initially been worried if enough people would turn up. But people seemed to have made their own travel arrangements and were showing up in great numbers. Marimuthu was busy welcoming them and making sure the food service was going fine.

As a batch of people sat eating in the dining hall, a crowd was gathering right outside for the next batch. It was not like the old days when people would patiently watch all the wedding rituals and ceremonies and only then head to the dining hall. These days, as soon as they marked their presence and spoke a few words to the families, guests tended to head straight to the dining area. And once they had eaten, they were ready to leave. In fact, if the handwash area was located outside, they often did not even bother to come back into the wedding hall.

Only a few people were needed at the ceremonies. The rest of the action was in the dining area. So, they had to make sure everything went smoothly over there. If the food was not up to the mark or if there was not enough food for everyone, people talked about it until the next wedding. 'Mapillai, I am still full from your wedding feast,' they would tease. But thankfully, there was enough food for everyone.

The cooks had made a great variety of dishes: sweets, vadai, poriyal, koottu, appalam, pickle, rice, kuzhambu, a spicier kuzhambu, rasam, curd, payasam and more. Marimuthu had chosen an excellent team of cooks. But what was the point of all that when there was not enough space in the dining hall for the guests to sit and eat comfortably? Only two rows could be seated at a time.

Even then, it was difficult for the servers to find the space to walk between the rows and serve the food. No wonder this wedding hall was available when Marimuthu came to rent it. Clearly, it was not in huge demand.

The next time Marimuthu went to the dining hall, he could tell that Selvarasu was struggling to keep the crowd in control. Even as a batch of people was eating, others stood right behind them, holding on to the chairs, claiming their place in the next batch! How could anyone eat in peace with people standing over them, watching them eat, waiting for them to finish eating? So, people were getting up and leaving their seats even before they finished eating, leaving nearly half the food still on their banana leaves. Marimuthu didn't know what to do. But there was no use standing around, worrying about it. So, he walked over to the entrance.

As he stood there, guests on their way out stopped to say a few words, taking leave properly. As was the custom, Marimuthu asked everyone, 'Did you eat?' Kattayan showed up and said, 'Look, most of these people didn't eat. They couldn't find a place in the dining hall. But if you ask them like this, of course they will say they have eaten. Couldn't you have found a slightly bigger hall?' Marimuthu was mortified when he realized all these guests were leaving without having had the wedding feast. So, he pleaded with them. 'Please, just wait for five minutes. I will make sure you get to eat.'

Some guests pretended to wait as Marimuthu had requested, but when he was looking elsewhere, they started their vehicles and drove away. Some others were frank.

'We have another wedding to go to. We will eat there, Marimuthu. Anyway, we will be back here in the morning for the wedding. We will eat here then.' Marimuthu was beside himself. But there was not much he could do. Selvarasu was already doing his best. He speeded up the service so people could eat faster. But everyone needs a certain amount of time to enjoy the food they are served. They cannot be rushed. Besides, a lot of wedding guests really look forward to relishing the wedding feast.

Thatha approached Marimuthu, tapped him gently on the shoulder and took him aside.

'Mapillai, we need to do something. Otherwise, most guests will leave without eating. Then all the food will go to waste. It will be most upsetting. Listen to me. Let's ask them to lay a few rows in the main hall itself. The rituals can keep happening on one side, and the food service can happen on another.'

'But thatha, that will mean people will have to sit on the floor. Will they object?'

'No, no. These people are used to being served food outdoors, where they sit on the ground. All these comforts are new. What? The food won't go down unless they sit at a table? No one will have a problem. Both kids and oldies will be fine sitting on the floor. Women will join them too. This is the only way we can ease up the crowd in the dining hall.

'If I'd known, I'd have rented some extra tables and chairs.'

'It's too late for all that. Let's do what we can.'

When they laid out a few rows on the floor, at first nobody sat down. These days, when people went to weddings, they expected to eat at a table. Why would anybody want to go back to old ways? Marimuthu thought the plan was not going to work. But Selvarasu got a few kids to sit down on the floor and had the servers lay banana leaves in front of them. Then, Kattayan joined them and said, 'Bring me a leaf too.'

After that, many others sat down on the rows laid out on the floor. If a few batches of guests were served in this way, they could easily manage the crowd. It seemed to Marimuthu that there was always a solution, and the one who figured that out freed himself from his problems. He now felt calmer. Now, he could send off people cheerfully. 'The main ceremony is between six and seven thirty in the morning. Please make sure you are here by then!' he said to everyone.

By the time the current batch of guests finished eating, the bus would arrive with more guests from the girl's side of the family. Just in time. Things were now going smoothly. There were more people than Marimuthu had expected. But there would probably be fewer people in the morning. Many of the guests were amazed to see Selvarasu here at Marimuthu's wedding. His family would surely have come to know about it by now. He'd have to face them the next day.

Marimuthu sat down on a chair to catch his breath for a moment. But his amma stepped out to talk to him just then. 'Your sister is making a scene. Just go find out what's wrong.' He was tired from all the running back and forth, figuring out how the food service was getting along. He had not eaten properly since the previous night. All day, as was the custom, he had not had any proper, solid food. He could have eaten something without anyone knowing, but he was so busy it simply didn't occur to him. 'Amma, why don't you ask her yourself?' he said. 'I did, but she won't tell me. You go and find out,' his mother replied and sat down right there.

Listlessly, he walked into the hall to see what was going on. He found his sister sitting outside his room, whimpering. 'What happened?' he asked. She sensed the irritation in his tone. She turned her face away and whimpered even more. 'Did anyone say anything hurtful to you? Why are you crying? How would I know if you don't tell me.' When he sat down next to her and turned her face towards him, he could see that the poor thing was very upset and her eyes were red from all the crying.

'I knew that this girl is not right for our family. They are taking so many photos of her. She only invites people from her family to join her in these photos. I don't care if she does not invite me. But my two kids—they keep standing near her, but she does not even notice them! Me, my husband, and my kids—what are we? Just like all other guests who come, eat and leave? Fine, then; that's what we will do. And we will do the same in the morning. We will be here for a little while, then we will leave,' she said.

Marimuthu had to control the urge to bang her head against the wall. He also remembered that soon the rituals involving the bridegroom would start, and his sister had a key role to play in them. He now wondered if this was his sister's way of demanding attention. He'd have to take a conciliatory approach at least till the wedding was over. So, he spoke to her patiently.

'Look here. Our rituals are about to start now. You and your children are going to be in all the photos. Why are you upset about such a small thing? Let her do what she wants now. Once she moves into our family, we can sort her out!'

'Yeah, yeah, that's what you say now. But once you marry her, you are going to toe her line. I am not naïve. The other day, when you sat next to her, you didn't even look at the rest of us. That's how infatuated you are now. Who knows how you will behave hereafter? You all still owe me three sovereigns of gold. I had hoped I would get them when you got married. But you have told me you will give it to me later. I now have no hopes you will ever fulfil that promise once you are married to this girl.'

It was a long rant. Thanks to the sound of the melam, none of the guests would have heard her litany of complaints. Marimuthu understood that what she needed at the moment was some assurance that she would get the three sovereigns of gold owed her. He could certainly offer her that assurance.

'Listen, dear, your daughter will come of age in the next two or three years. Amma has told me that we could give you the gold then. That's why I am not giving it to you now. Do you think we will really deprive you of anything?'

There was great affection in his voice. He was surprised that he was able to say such things. How clever and opportunistic was the tongue! His sister now looked a bit mollified. 'Go, go be cheerful,' he nudged her. She went away to wash her face puffed and swollen with all the crying.

Just as Marimuthu was headed towards the entrance, the officiant called out to him. He was ready for the bridegroom's rituals. 'I will be back in just a second,' he said and rushed to the entrance. There were some guests waiting to take leave of him. He spoke to them cheerfully and then asked his mother to take over his post and see off the guests.

A few men had taken some chairs outside and were seated at the entrance, chatting. His father was amongst them. He could tell that the man was inebriated. Let him be happy, Marimuthu thought, as he walked back into the hall. The bridegroom needed a male friend for the sake of the rituals. Marimuthu's brother-in-law filled that role. Then, the officiant led them in a prayer, after which they took him outside for a ritual wash.

Back in the old days, they would pour four or five pots of water on the bridegroom. Usually, women from the girl's family would pour the water, not giving the man even time to catch his breath. But not anymore. The barber brought a bowl of water mixed with some turmeric and some vermillion and a betel leaf added. The officiant took some of that water in the palm of his hand and ran it over Marimuthu's forehead three times. All Marimuthu felt was a little wet on his face. The officiant then poured the rest of the water in front of him in a straight line on the ground. That was it. The ritual wash was over. Marimuthu then went to his room and changed into a new set of clothes.

The officiant then put a small garland around his neck and made him sit on a chair. In front of him were placed a pile of grains and a pot of sanctified water. There was also a brass plate with rice spread out on it and some chunks of jaggery placed over the rice. 'Stay right here. I will be back in a second,' the officiant said and walked away to fetch something. Marimuthu sat looking around at the guests. The food service was nearly over. Only a few people were still eating.

A woman came and stood next to him. She was not familiar to him. She must be a relative of Rosamani's, he thought. She took one look at the brass plate and frowned.

'What is this? They have just placed blunt pieces of jaggery on the plate. It should be shaped like a cone, the edge should be sharp as a knife. This is not how you present things for a ritual. If this happened in our village, our local officiant would just fling it away. It is not auspicious, is it, to start with defective things?'

Marimuthu looked at her. He knew such women. They decked themselves in silk saris and lots of jewellery just to come and stir up some trouble. He wondered if he could send her away, giving her the task of bringing sharpened pieces of jaggery. But, by then, the officiant returned, and he had heard the woman's remarks.

'Mapillai, what do we do?'

'Don't worry about it, uncle. Some tall tale,' laughed Marimuthu.

The woman made a face and walked away. Marimuthu could hear the bus arriving, and then he saw the woman running outside.

The officiant held the kanganam in his hand, the
yellow thread to be tied on the bridegroom's wrist, ritually
marking his status as the bridegroom and imposing
restrictions on his movements. He placed a piece of jaggery
in the middle of the plate of rice and asked Marimuthu
to place his hands on either side of it. Marimuthu placed
his hands in a gesture of cupping some rice in the palms
of his hands. The officiant then tied the yellow thread on
Marimuthu's right wrist.

'Mapillai, the kanganam has been tied on your wrist
now. So, from this moment on and until the wedding is
over, you are not supposed to leave these premises. If you
need something done, please delegate it. You shouldn't go
anywhere. Okay? This is the custom, so I am telling you.'

The officiant then called Marimuthu's sister for the
next ritual. The barber had kept the necessary things
ready. 'Where is the sari? Please bring that,' he called
out to someone. Marimuthu's sister still wore a look of
displeasure.

Since the officiant was in a hurry to get to another
wedding ceremony, he was now rushing through the
rituals. Wherever the rituals happened, the washerwoman
followed, carrying the flame torch. Once they were
done, Selvarasu took the officiant on his bike to his next
engagement. He would go again later to bring the officiant
back for the morning rituals. Then he would have to take
the man again to his next wedding assignment. All of this
was Selvarasu's responsibility.

A little girl approached Marimuthu. 'Akka wants to
talk to you,' she said. 'Who?' he asked. 'The bride,' replied

the girl. He had not seen Rosamani since he saw her arrive at the wedding hall. He now walked over to where she was staying. At this point, there were not too many people in the hall. They all sat around, chewing betel leaves and gossiping. Some were already lying down. Many of these were guests from the girl's side. All those who came by the second bus had decided to spend the night in the hall.

There was a card game in progress in one corner of the hall. Sounds of laughter and cheer kept erupting from there. When he entered the bride's room, some of the women who were hanging out there quickly left the room. 'Do you see this? Mapillai has already entered the bride's room!' he heard them laughing. 'He is in such a hurry, he can't wait!' someone else said, and they all burst into laughter again.

He found Rosamani in tears. 'What happened?' he asked the woman standing by her. Rosamani's mother was lying curled up in a corner of the room. Was she pretending to be asleep? He wondered. He found it difficult to talk to Rosamani with all these women in the room. Moreover, the door was open, and since the wedding hall had gone much quieter, what they spoke here could probably be heard outside.

He summoned his courage. After all, the night after, he would get to touch her, know her intimately. So, he decided not to worry what anyone thought. He walked up to her and lifted up her face. Her face was swollen and reddened with distress. He could see the hurt in her eyes. 'What happened, dear?' he asked, with the utmost affection in his voice. He didn't want to take his hand away from her face. 'Tell me.' He had to resist the urge to kiss her on the lips and to embrace her. She couldn't stop crying.

At that moment, another woman's voice sounded, shrill and sharp like the sudden blare of the municipality bell. 'We don't get any respect here. One of their women keeps coming here to ask when the girl's father will arrive. Another woman touches and examines all the jewellery and wonders if it is real or fake. You knew our limitations when you approached us. How can you insult us like this now?' she said, directing her words at the wall. Marimuthu was annoyed. He'd have liked to hear directly from Rosamani.

'Well, if anyone asks, just respond boldly,' he now said. Everyone was silent for a minute. 'If they ask when her father will come, just tell them he will be here soon. If they ask if the jewellery is fake, say yes. Or tell them it is all worth fifty sovereigns. What's the big deal?'

He had spoken harshly. Rosamani's whimpering grew more intense. He looked at her face. If she was a child, he could scold her or even smack her on the back. But she was an adult, she should be able to face such things. Was this an attempt to earn his pity? He did not want to look at her crying face any longer. He walked away, feeling that the pungency of her tears was now stuck to his body.

47

Finally, all sounds died down and a hush fell over the hall. Now and then, a laugh or a loud remark could be heard, but it quickly faded away. Marimuthu, Selvarasu, matchmaker thatha and others were sitting in the chairs placed outside the hall. Raman sat on a large stone just a little away from them. Sounds of pots and pans from the kitchen indicated that preparations were already underway for breakfast. The wedding dais was being decorated with much pomp. It looked like an impressive chariot.

'In the morning, let's make sure things don't happen the way they did last night. Food should be served even while the wedding ceremony is going on in the main hall. That's the only way to manage the crowd,' said Selvarasu. His tone betrayed the fact that he had had a terrible time handling the food service a few hours earlier and was exhausted.

'You are right, Rasu. Back in the old days, people would eat only once the wedding ceremony was over. But no such scruples these days.'

'Let's start serving breakfast at six thirty. That's the only way to keep it rolling.'

Marimuthu too was anxious about a repeat of the chaos of the evening. He wanted everything to go smoothly. So, they now planned everything— buying garlands, fetching the wedding officiant from his other engagement, sending the bus to Varattur at five in the morning . . .

Marimuthu could not ignore the urge he felt to make a trip home. He was feeling guilty that he had not been able to arrange to bring his paatti to the wedding. She had really longed to see her grandson getting married. The new white sari he had purchased for her was still in the store bag he had left in the house. The day before, when his mother happened to see that sari, she had remarked, 'I don't think this old woman is going to wear this new sari. We can give it to your athai.' But he had resolved to himself that he would drape that sari around paatti, and touch her feet and take her blessings before he got married. If he set out now, he could be back within half an hour.

'Rasu, you and thatha please go lie down. If you don't get some sleep, you will find it difficult to get through the day tomorrow. I will take Raman with me and make a trip home. I left the thali in the house. I remembered only when I got here,' said Marimuthu. In truth, the thali chain worth seven sovereigns of gold was safely tucked in the inside pocket of his shirt.

'Why at this hour, mapillai?! Once they tie the kanganam, you are not supposed to go anywhere. Send somebody else.'

Marimuthu knew that thatha would object to his plan. That was the reason he had used the thali as an excuse.

'No, thatha. Only I know where I have kept it. We will be back in no time.'

'Alright. Drive safe,' thatha said half-heartedly.

Marimuthu went into the hall to get the house keys from his mother. She was sleeping, curled up in a corner of the room reserved for the bridegroom. When he woke her up gently and asked for the key, she did not even ask why. She simply pulled out the key from where she had secured it in her waist, handed it to him and went back to sleep. As he stepped out of the room, he glanced towards the bride's room.

He could see Rosamani seated in a chair inside the room. He walked quite casually in that direction. There were several women fast asleep in that room. He found it odd that she alone was awake and sitting up. He went up to her and touched her gently on the shoulder. Shocked, she turned her face towards him, and he could tell that she had been crying. He was agitated.

'Did anyone else say anything hurtful?' he asked her in anxious whisper.

She slapped his hand away and started weeping noisily. One of the women stirred a little. Marimuthu took out the thali chain from his pocket and placed it in Rosamani's hand. 'Please keep this safe for me,' he said to her. She held up the heavy chain to have a good look at it. He was afraid that the other women might wake up. So, this was not the time to find out from Rosamani what had happened or to comfort her properly.

'Don't worry about anything. I am here for you. Please don't cry. Wipe your tears and go to bed.' He spoke to her like he was speaking to a child.

He didn't know what came over him, but he suddenly lifted up her face and kissed her on the lips. She had not expected that at all. Then he rushed out of the room in a flash, wondering what could have upset her so.

He knew that the mind was often able to cope with big challenges but found it difficult to bear a few cruel words. How did the human tongue master the art of twisting words to its will? Was she still upset about that thoughtless remark Marimuthu had made earlier? But his quick kiss would set everything right, he felt.

He could still feel her lips on his. It reminded him of the touch of Vasanthi's lips he had experienced years ago. That one kiss had been the source of a great deal of fantasies over the years. But this kiss was different. This would continue. This one would last. He held his lips still.

When he stepped outside and started the bike, he looked over towards the bride's room. He was comforted seeing that the lights were now off.

'You have been talking about your marriage for years now, and on the day of your marriage you still forgot something as important as the thali chain! What kind of . . .'

Raman spoke non-stop all the way. All Marimuthu said in response was, 'Mm'. There was not a soul on the road that was flanked on both sides by tamarind trees. It felt like he was riding the bike on air, so he speeded up without even realizing it. But when Raman said, 'Hey, hey! Slow down,' he realized how fast he'd been going, and slowed down. By the time he turned into the path that led towards his village and was passing by the red-soil land, he really slowed down by force of habit. He looked over at the land with much hope and affection. It lay enveloped in darkness. He couldn't even see the well. But he felt he could sense everything clearly.

Hearing the sound of the bike, the dog came running. Kuppan was sleeping on the front porch. They had asked him to guard the house that night. He was fast asleep and didn't seem to have heard the bike. Usually, even the faintest sound roused him.

Raman tried to wake him up. Meanwhile, Marimuthu unlocked the door and went into the house. When he found paatti's sari and stepped outside, he was shocked to find that it was not Kuppan but his son Ramesh. He was now awake and sitting up.

'Hey! Where is your father? Did he leave you here? Where did he go?'

The boy stood up and adjusted the lungi around his waist. 'Appa is sleeping in paatti's cottage.' Marimuthu yelled at him, 'You were fast asleep! Is this any way to guard the house?' The boy did not say anything in response. He'd be married next week. But nothing seemed to bother him. Here he was, sleeping like a baby.

As they rode away on the bike, the dog followed them. He stopped and shouted at it, 'Go back home!' And it stood on the spot, wagging its tail. When he pulled over in front of the cottage, Kuppan woke up.

'Kuppan, why are you sleeping here? I asked you to sleep in the house, didn't I? Your son is such a heavy sleeper, even thunder won't wake him up. How can we rely on him to guard the house?'

'Saami, why did you come here at this hour?' Kuppan asked. There was an unusual strain in his voice.

'Why, Kuppan, I am here to take paatti's blessings.'

'Did no one tell you that once they have tied the kanganam on you, you are not supposed to wander away? Please go back. You can take her blessings once you are married.'

Never before had Kuppan spoken to him like that.

Marimuthu was annoyed. Even thatha was fine with his coming away in the night. Who the hell was Kuppan to disapprove? Look at his audacity!

'Yes, yes, I know all that. You shut up and go back to sleep.'

When Marimuthu tried to enter the cottage, Kuppan stood in his way, holding out his arms outstretched to stop him.

'Kuppan, what is going on?'

Kuppan broke down in sobs.

'Saami, paatti has left us all.'

'Ayyo! Kuppan, what are you saying?'

'Yes, saami. It happened earlier in the night. I heard her wheeze. It only lasted a few minutes. Then, everything quieted down. I didn't have the heart to leave her alone. That's why I asked my son to be there outside the house, and I came over here. I was here when she took her last breath.'

'Aaya! How could you leave us like this?' yelled Marimuthu and tried to run into the cottage. But Kuppan would not let him.

'You should not go in there now. She is fast asleep. Only the three of us know that she is dead. Please pull yourself together and go back to the wedding hall. Come here after the wedding. We will figure out things then,' Kuppan spoke firmly.

'I wanted to drape this new sari around her and to touch her feet and take her blessing. But now this sari has become a shroud! Kuppan, please let me see her. I want to look at her face.'

'Raman, take him with you. Go,' said Kuppan. Then, he addressed Marimuthu. 'I know how hard you have worked for this wedding to happen. I have carried you as a child in these shoulders. Think of me as a father speaking to you. Your paatti's spirit has gone to the wedding hall to see you getting married. Go see her there. Not here.'

When Raman held his hands, Marimuthu leaned on him and sobbed.

'I am such a wretched fellow. So unlucky . . .'

'Raman, please take him away. No one should hear him cry.'

In the tears that streamed down his face and reached his lips, Marimuthu felt the touch of Rosamani's lips.